City Lights and Crossed Lines

Amara Lennox

Published by Amara Lennox, 2024.

This is a work of fiction. Similarities to real people, places, or events are entirely coincidental.

CITY LIGHTS AND CROSSED LINES

First edition. October 7, 2024.

Copyright © 2024 Amara Lennox.

ISBN: 979-8224581528

Written by Amara Lennox.

Chapter 1: The First Encounter

I slide onto the barstool next to him, my elbows resting on the counter as I try to gather my thoughts. The bar is dimly lit, the kind of place that could only be enhanced by the soft glow of string lights and the sticky charm of old wood. The scent of fried food mingles with the notes of whiskey, and it reminds me of simpler times—before deadlines and drafts and the never-ending hustle of my career. "You're not from around here, are you?" I ask, attempting a casual air, even as my pulse quickens.

He chuckles, the sound rich and low, almost drowning out the twangy country music playing in the background. "Can you tell?" His voice has an easy confidence that pulls me in like a moth to a flame. I can't help but admire how the crisp lines of his suit clash with the peeling paint on the walls, making him seem like a misplaced treasure amid the faded barstools and the locals in worn denim.

"Maybe it's the suit," I reply, the corner of my mouth lifting in a teasing grin. "Or perhaps it's the fact that you're not sweating bullets in this heat like the rest of us." I gesture at the bar's patrons—some nursing pints, others laughing raucously. He's an anomaly here, a diamond among stones.

His smile widens, revealing a flash of white teeth, and I can't help but feel like he's letting me in on some private joke. "I suppose my taste in places could use a little work. I'm typically more of a rooftop bar kind of guy." He leans in slightly, lowering his voice, as if sharing a secret. "But I figured I could do with some authenticity. You know, the real Nashville."

I arch an eyebrow, intrigued. "And what does 'authenticity' look like to you? A honky-tonk filled with the scent of spilled beer and dreams?"

He laughs, the sound deep and inviting, and it makes my heart dance just a little. "You'd be surprised. Sometimes the best stories are found where you least expect them. I'm Noah, by the way." He extends his hand, and I grasp it, feeling a jolt that travels through my fingertips and up my arm. His skin is warm, and there's something firm and steady about his grip.

"I'm Mia," I reply, my voice steady despite the fluttering in my chest. "And I happen to be on a mission to find those hidden gems. Care to assist?"

"Is that what you do? Search for hidden gems?" He leans back slightly, studying me with a glimmer of mischief in his eyes. "And here I thought you were just another tourist looking for the best photo ops."

"I'll have you know," I say, feigning indignation, "that I'm a serious journalist. I'm here to uncover the soul of the city, not just the Instagrammable spots." I take a sip of my drink, a sweet concoction that doesn't quite mask the burn of the whiskey, and give him a pointed look. "But I could use a local's perspective."

"Lucky for you," he replies, "I happen to know a thing or two about the hidden treasures in this town." He waves to the bartender, ordering another round. "How about a little adventure, then? I promise to show you some places that might just steal your heart."

Adventure. The word hangs between us, thick with promise. I can feel my heart quicken at the thought, but a small voice in the back of my mind warns me against it. This is a city filled with opportunities and temptations, and who knows what trouble I'm inviting by accepting his offer. But then again, isn't that the point of coming here? To break away from the routine, to embrace the unexpected?

"Okay, I'm in," I say, surprising even myself with my enthusiasm. "Lead the way."

Noah stands, a playful glint in his eye as he gestures for me to follow. "Trust me; I won't lead you astray." He steps outside, and the warmth of the evening wraps around me like a cozy blanket. The sun has dipped below the horizon, painting the sky in shades of purple and gold, and the streets pulse with life.

As we stroll through the thrumming heart of downtown Nashville, the sounds of laughter and music envelop us. It feels as if the city is alive, breathing with every step we take. We pass by street performers showcasing their talents—an acoustic guitarist strumming an upbeat tune, a duo singing harmonies that weave effortlessly together. I can't help but smile, the energy infectious.

"See that?" Noah nods toward a nearby alley, where a mural bursts to life with vibrant colors and intricate designs. "That's one of my favorite pieces. It changes with the seasons. Sometimes it's a tribute to the local music scene; other times, it reflects the struggles of the community."

"Art with a heartbeat," I muse, my journalist instincts kicking in. "I love that. It's like a living story." I take a photo, the colors popping in the dim light, but as I lower my phone, I catch him watching me, a thoughtful expression on his face.

"What about you, Mia? What's your story?"

I open my mouth, about to reply with something witty about being a hopeless romantic chasing after tales of love and loss, but the question catches me off guard. My story isn't just about the articles I write; it's tangled up in family expectations and dreams I've been too afraid to chase. Instead, I offer a simple smile. "Just a girl with a dream of uncovering the extraordinary in the ordinary."

He nods slowly, his gaze piercing but kind, as if he can see through my words to the fears lurking beneath. "Everyone has their own treasures to uncover, even if they don't realize it yet."

As we wander further into the heart of Nashville, I can't shake the feeling that my ordinary life is beginning to fracture, that I'm on the verge of discovering something unexpected—something that could change everything. The question is, am I ready for it?

As we meander through the vibrant streets, Noah seems to embody Nashville itself—energetic yet grounded, charming yet elusive. The city hums around us, a soundtrack of laughter and music flowing from every corner. He gestures animatedly as he speaks, his hands cutting through the warm evening air, painting pictures with his words. "You see that bar over there?" He points to a lively spot across the street where a band is setting up for the night. "They've got a killer happy hour and some of the best live music in town. It's where the locals come to unwind after a long week. You can feel the stories in that place."

"Stories are what I'm here for," I reply, allowing the excitement to show in my voice. "It's what makes this city tick, right?"

"Absolutely," he says, glancing at me sideways, a glimmer of approval in his gaze. "But you should also know that stories are often found in the most unexpected places."

Just then, a pair of street performers catches my eye. They're lost in a frenzy of music and movement, a guitarist and a fiddler weaving a tapestry of sound that pulls everyone nearby into their spell. I stop, captivated by their energy, my heart syncing to the rhythm as I sway to the beat. Noah watches me with a smile, his expression a mix of admiration and amusement.

"Care to dance?" he asks, his voice teasing.

"Dance?" I laugh, raising an eyebrow. "Isn't that a bit cliché?"

"Cliché is overrated. Life is too short to worry about being original all the time. Plus," he adds with a wink, "this could make for some great material for your article. 'Nashville: A City Where Even Tourists Dance with Strangers.'"

With an exaggerated sigh, I relent. "Fine, but don't blame me if I step on your toes."

He steps forward, taking my hand, and suddenly, the world melts away. I can't recall the last time I was swept up in a moment like this—spontaneous, carefree, and utterly delightful. We sway to the music, laughter spilling from my lips as we mimic the performers' movements. I steal glances at Noah, his eyes sparkling, completely in the moment. It feels like a breath of fresh air in a city that had seemed so foreign just hours before.

As the song reaches its crescendo, I feel the weight of the world lift from my shoulders. For a few fleeting moments, I am not Mia, the journalist burdened with deadlines and expectations; I am just a girl dancing in the heart of Nashville. The music fades, and we step back, breathless, the crowd around us erupting into applause.

"Not bad for a cliché, huh?" Noah grins, brushing a hand through his hair, a gesture that somehow makes him look even more charmingly disheveled.

"Maybe you're onto something," I admit, laughing, though my heart races for reasons I can't quite decipher.

He leans in closer, his expression shifting to something more serious. "You know, it's not just the stories that matter. It's the connections we make along the way."

His words hang in the air, charged with unspoken meaning. I can feel the vulnerability creeping in, a sensation that always leaves me feeling exposed. I've built walls over the years, brick by brick, protecting myself from disappointment and heartache. Yet here I am, sharing this moment with a stranger, and it feels oddly exhilarating.

"What about you?" I ask, my curiosity piqued. "What brings you to Nashville?"

He hesitates, a flicker of something shadowing his features before he brushes it away. "Just some work stuff. But I try to find moments like this whenever I can. Life's too short to be all business, you know?"

"Wise words," I reply, but the corner of my mind stirs with intrigue. There's something beneath his carefree exterior, a hint of depth that invites me to dig deeper. But before I can probe further, a loud crash shatters the moment. A group of rowdy patrons stumble out of the bar, their laughter ringing sharp against the warm night air. One of them trips and nearly collides with us, sending Noah stepping protectively in front of me.

"Whoa there!" he exclaims, steadying the man before he can fall. "Watch yourself!"

The man waves him off, clearly too far gone to comprehend the warning, and I catch a glimpse of Noah's protective nature—a spark of something deeper igniting my interest. It's a small gesture, but it resonates with me. He's not just charming; he's grounded and attentive.

"See? Stories everywhere," I say, nudging him playfully. "You're right about that."

We continue walking, and soon we find ourselves in a quieter part of town, where the lights are softer, and the sounds of the city fade to a gentle murmur. "This is one of my favorite spots," Noah says, stopping in front of a tiny café with a warm glow spilling out onto the sidewalk. "Best coffee in town. And if you're lucky, they might have some homemade pastries."

"Now you're speaking my language," I reply, my stomach rumbling in agreement.

Inside, the café feels like a cozy hug. The walls are lined with shelves crammed with books, and a few locals sit hunched over their laptops, sipping their drinks. The barista greets Noah like an old friend, her smile warm and welcoming, and I can't help but feel a swell of affection for this little place, for the community it represents.

"What's your poison?" Noah asks, leaning over the counter to scan the menu.

"Coffee with a splash of adventure, if you have it," I quip, earning a laugh from him.

As we order, he watches me closely, an amused smirk playing on his lips. "You really are on a quest, aren't you? Seeking out the best of everything?"

"Only the best," I reply, tossing my hair over my shoulder. "I have high standards, you know."

"I've noticed," he says, his tone teasing. "But I think you'll find this place exceeds expectations. And if it doesn't, I'll personally take you on a tour of the worst spots in Nashville."

"I'd like to see you try," I challenge, unable to hide my grin.

After we grab our drinks, we find a small table tucked into a cozy nook, the kind of spot that feels like it was designed for late-night conversations and stolen moments. The steam from my coffee swirls into the air, carrying with it the rich scent of roasted beans, and I take a moment to simply enjoy the ambiance, soaking in the warmth and comfort that envelops us.

"What's your take on the city so far?" Noah asks, his eyes searching mine, keenly interested.

"It's a paradox," I reply, taking a sip of my drink, letting the warmth spread through me. "It's both fast-paced and laid-back. Full of ambition but rich with history. I came here to write about the hidden gems, but I'm realizing that I'm drawn to the people just as much."

He leans forward, intrigued. "So it's not just about the places you visit. It's the connections you make, too?"

"Exactly," I say, feeling a sense of camaraderie in our shared understanding. "The best stories are woven through our interactions, the moments that catch us off guard. Like tonight."

Noah nods slowly, a smile creeping across his face. "You're more insightful than I thought. Maybe there's a reason I stumbled into that dive bar tonight."

"Or maybe you just had too much wine at your last rooftop soirée," I retort, unable to resist the opportunity for a playful jab.

His laughter fills the space between us, a sound that makes me feel oddly buoyant, as if we're floating on a current of possibility. "Touché, Mia. Touché."

As the evening unfolds, I can't help but notice how comfortable I feel with him, how easily our conversation flows. Each laugh, each shared glance draws us closer, unearthing layers of connection that feel both exhilarating and terrifying. I wonder if he senses it too, this electric charge that crackles in the air between us, pulling me closer like a magnet.

But just as the moment deepens, a shadow flits across his face, and I catch a glimpse of the wall he'd momentarily let down. It's subtle, a fleeting expression, but it makes my heart stutter. I want to reach out, to pry open that door and see what lies beneath, but something holds me back. Maybe it's the fear of what I might find—or what I might reveal about myself in return.

"Tell me," I say, my voice softer now, "what's one thing you've learned in this city that you wish everyone knew?"

He hesitates, his gaze flicking away for a moment as if weighing the gravity of the question. "That every moment counts, even the small ones," he finally says, his voice low. "Sometimes, it's in the quietest spaces where you find the loudest truths."

His words resonate deep within me, a gentle reminder of everything I've tucked away in my heart. As I sip my coffee, I feel a small shift, a burgeoning curiosity igniting anew. I'm not just here for the stories of Nashville; I'm here to uncover my own. And somehow, this charming stranger has become part of that unfolding narrative, a chapter I never saw coming.

Noah leans back, observing me with an intensity that sends a delightful shiver down my spine. The warmth of the café wraps around us like a soft blanket, and for a moment, I lose myself in the comfort of our shared space. The aroma of coffee mingles with the sweetness of pastries, creating an atmosphere that feels both intimate and exhilarating.

"Okay, Miss Journalist," he says, stirring his coffee thoughtfully. "Let's talk hidden gems. What's the most surprising thing you've discovered so far?"

I lean in, enjoying the challenge. "Honestly? It's been less about the places and more about the people I've met. Like you, for instance." I punctuate my statement with a playful smile, and his cheeks flush a shade deeper than before.

"Flattery will get you everywhere," he replies, feigning seriousness. "But I'm curious, what do you think of me? Just another charming suit in a city full of grit?"

"Maybe you're both," I tease. "The suit tells one story while the grit whispers another. There's a duality that's intriguing."

"Duality, huh? That's a fancy way to say I'm a walking contradiction." He takes a sip of his coffee, then leans back, a smirk playing at his lips. "What if I told you I'm in town for some soul-searching? That under this suit beats a heart full of questions?"

"Questions are the best part," I say, feeling emboldened. "What's your biggest one?"

He narrows his eyes, the playful banter shifting to something more profound. "Am I living my life for me, or for everyone else? It's easy to get lost in expectations, you know?"

His honesty hangs in the air, making the café feel smaller, more intimate. I want to tell him that I, too, have battled that same question, though the words catch in my throat. Instead, I take a deep breath, hoping to redirect the conversation to lighter shores.

"So, if we're talking about hidden gems, what's the best-kept secret you know about this city? The kind that would make my article shine?"

Noah grins, a flicker of mischief igniting in his eyes. "I could tell you, but then you'd have to promise me something."

"Sounds ominous. What's the catch?"

"Meet me at midnight by the river," he says, his tone low and conspiratorial. "There's a spot I know where the stars align perfectly with the water, and the city's heartbeat echoes beneath the surface. But you have to promise to keep it a secret."

"Secrets and midnight rendezvous? You really are leaning into the dramatic, aren't you?" I quip, but inside, a rush of excitement floods my veins. "What's the twist?"

He leans closer, a glimmer of sincerity in his gaze. "Just trust me. Some moments are worth the mystery."

I hesitate for a heartbeat, contemplating the thrill of a midnight adventure against the rational voice in my head that warns me to tread carefully. But the spark of curiosity and connection with Noah overrides my hesitation. "Okay, I'm in," I declare, feeling the words slip from my lips before I can second-guess them. "But if you're leading me into a haunted story, I'll hold you responsible."

"No ghosts, I promise," he assures me, his laughter filling the space between us. "Just the magic of Nashville."

After our impromptu rendezvous is set, we linger over our coffees, sharing stories that dance between playful banter and heartfelt revelations. As the evening deepens, it feels as though we've carved out our own little world in this bustling city. He talks about his love for music—how it shapes his dreams and shadows his disappointments—while I reveal snippets of my own life, the relentless pursuit of the next story echoing my own fears of being lost in a sea of expectations.

But just as I begin to feel like I truly know him, the door swings open, and a gust of cool air sweeps through the café, bringing with it a familiar face. A woman steps inside, her laughter ringing out like a bell. She's stunning, with an effortless grace that draws every eye in the room, including Noah's.

"Hey, stranger!" she calls out, her voice honeyed with warmth and confidence. "Fancy running into you here!"

I watch as Noah's smile falters for just a moment, a flicker of surprise crossing his features. He straightens up, a shadow passing over his expression. "Lily," he says, as if her name is a secret he's been keeping.

She strides over, and I suddenly feel like an intruder in the moment, as if I'm a third wheel on a bike built for two. "I didn't know you were back in town! What's this?" She eyes me curiously, her gaze shifting between us with an almost scrutinizing intensity.

"Oh, this is Mia," Noah introduces me, his voice steady yet tinged with a hint of defensiveness. "She's new in town, doing some writing."

"Nice to meet you, Mia," she says, extending a hand, her demeanor friendly but her eyes sharp. "Hope Noah's treating you right. He can be a handful."

"I bet he is," I reply, trying to keep the atmosphere light, but the undercurrent of tension makes my words feel heavier. "He has a knack for adventures."

Lily smirks, her expression playful yet challenging. "Oh, I can only imagine. Nashville does have a way of bringing out the best—and worst—in people."

There's an unspoken history between them, a thread of familiarity that ties them together in ways I don't yet understand. I feel the heat rise in my cheeks, a mix of jealousy and intrigue swirling in my chest. I'm not sure why it bothers me so much, but it does.

"Just showing Mia some of the city's hidden gems," Noah says, a touch of defensiveness creeping into his tone, but he doesn't quite meet my eyes.

"Is that so?" Lily's voice drips with an undertone that hints at something deeper, an implication I can't quite grasp. "Well, you know where to find me if you need any more recommendations."

As she says this, a flicker of something—longing, regret, maybe even anger—passes through Noah's eyes, but just as quickly, it's gone, replaced by that charming smile that had first drawn me in.

"Definitely," he replies, though his gaze drifts toward me, searching for reassurance.

"Anyway, I should get going. Big plans tonight," Lily says, her eyes lingering on Noah just a beat too long before she turns to leave. "Don't keep this one out too late, okay?"

Her laughter dances behind her as she steps back into the warm night, leaving a palpable silence in her wake. I shift uncomfortably, suddenly aware of the fragile thread connecting us.

"What was that about?" I ask, trying to keep my tone light, but the weight of my curiosity presses against me.

Noah clears his throat, the smile fading from his face. "Just an old friend."

"Old friends can sometimes mean old feelings," I murmur, my voice softer than intended.

"I don't think it's like that," he says, though I sense an uncertainty in his tone. "We've moved on."

"Moved on, huh?" I tease lightly, but the playful banter feels forced now. The air around us is charged with unsaid words and questions I'm not sure I want to voice.

"Let's just focus on the adventure tonight," he replies, but I can see the conflict dancing in his eyes, an echo of something unresolved.

"Right, the adventure," I echo, my heart racing. "Midnight rendezvous by the river, remember?"

He nods, the tension lingering between us like an unfinished song. "Absolutely. It'll be worth it, I promise."

As we finish our drinks, the weight of the evening hangs heavily around us. I can't shake the feeling that something is brewing beneath the surface, a storm of emotions waiting to unleash itself.

With every passing minute, my anticipation grows, but so does my uncertainty. I want to trust him, to believe in this moment we've crafted together, yet a nagging voice whispers that the deeper I dive into this unexpected connection, the more I might discover—and some discoveries might hurt.

"See you at midnight," Noah says, standing up and smoothing the front of his suit. There's a determination in his gaze, a flicker of that adventurous spirit I'd come to admire, but it's laced with an unease that leaves me wanting to reach out and tether him to me.

"Yeah, see you," I reply, but even as the words leave my mouth, I can't shake the sensation that this night holds secrets I'm not yet prepared to face.

As he steps out of the café, the cool night air washes over me, mingling with the warmth of our earlier conversation. I sit for a moment, staring at the remnants of my coffee, contemplating the shadows now creeping into the edges of my heart.

And just as I gather my thoughts, my phone buzzes to life, shattering the fragile peace I'd managed to hold. The message lights up my screen, and my stomach drops at the name I see flashing before me.

"Hey, it's Lily. We need to talk."

The words hang heavy in the air, each syllable echoing like a warning bell, sending a chill down my spine. What does she want to talk about? I can feel the night shifting around me, the anticipation of the adventure soon to unfold mixing with the uncertainty of what lies ahead

Chapter 2: Underneath the Surface

The sun dipped low in the sky, casting a golden hue over the city, making even the most mundane buildings seem to shimmer with possibility. I stood by the window of my cramped apartment, a place I called home, but only because the rent was low and the pizza delivery was quick. Outside, the streets buzzed with life—street performers twirled like dervishes, couples strolled hand in hand, and the air was thick with the intoxicating aroma of roasted chestnuts and sizzling street tacos. In the midst of it all, Ryan Cole appeared like a mirage, handsome and confident, with an air of mystery that drew me in like a moth to a flame.

"Ready for another adventure?" he called up to me, his voice warm and inviting, echoing off the brick walls of the buildings nearby. He was leaning against his sleek black SUV, one hand casually tucked in his pocket, the other waving up to me as if I were some kind of queen about to descend from my tower. The corners of his mouth lifted in that disarming smile, the one that could make anyone forget their own name. I sighed, a mixture of anticipation and hesitation swirling in my chest.

"Adventure?" I called back, feigning nonchalance. "Or just another tour of your favorite abandoned buildings?"

His laughter was deep, resonating in my bones as I descended the staircase, feeling the pulse of the city quicken with each step I took. "Both," he replied, eyes sparkling. "You'll love this one. I promise it's worth the risk."

I paused for a moment, my heart racing. I was drawn to him like a moth, but there was an undercurrent of danger I couldn't shake. Yet, the thought of missing out on whatever secret he held was unbearable. So, I bit back my doubts and joined him, ready to dive deeper into this adventure he promised.

Ryan led me through winding alleyways, away from the tourist traps and towards a part of the city that felt alive with whispers of its past. The buildings here had stories etched into their crumbling facades, their faded colors a testament to a time when they stood proudly against the skyline. Each step felt like a step into a living painting, layers of history wrapped in the bittersweet scent of nostalgia.

We arrived at an abandoned amusement park, its rusting rides silhouetted against the twilight sky, the remnants of joy fading into shadows. "This is it," he said, voice tinged with a mix of reverence and mischief. "Welcome to Paradise Falls."

"Paradise, huh?" I quipped, raising an eyebrow. "It looks more like a graveyard for childhood dreams."

He chuckled, the sound rumbling like distant thunder. "True. But it's beautiful in its decay, don't you think?"

As we wandered through the ghostly remnants, I marveled at the intricate graffiti covering the walls, vibrant colors clashing with the desolation. Each tag seemed to tell a story of rebellion, of joy snatched from the jaws of despair. I could feel Ryan's presence next to me, an electric current that made my skin prickle with awareness.

We stopped in front of a rusted Ferris wheel, towering like a sentinel over the park. "They say this was the most popular ride," he said, eyes glinting in the fading light. "It offered a view of the entire city."

"Guess that view is a bit different now," I remarked, feeling an unexpected pang of sadness.

"Not all views are meant to be pretty," he replied, the flicker of something darker flitting across his features. "Sometimes, it's the imperfections that make them worthwhile."

The weight of his words hung in the air, and I felt an undeniable pull toward the man beside me. But just as quickly as it came, he shut down, retreating behind that charming smile as if he had let something slip he hadn't intended. The flicker of darkness in his gaze sparked a fire of curiosity within me.

"Ryan," I said softly, my voice barely a whisper above the sigh of the evening breeze. "What's the real story behind all of this? Why do you bring me here?"

He turned to me, his expression inscrutable, as if I had struck a chord he wasn't ready to play. "I like the way you see the world, Ella. You notice things others don't. It's refreshing."

"Is that all?" I pressed, pushing through the walls he was building between us. "You could have brought anyone here, but you chose me."

For a fleeting moment, vulnerability flickered in his eyes, and I felt a rush of triumph. It was as if I had finally unearthed a buried treasure, something precious hidden beneath layers of charm and bravado. But then he stepped back, as if retreating from the conversation and the connection we were building.

"I see potential in you," he said finally, his tone carefully neutral. "You're not afraid to explore the forgotten places, to confront the darkness."

"And what about you?" I countered, crossing my arms, refusing to let him escape this dance. "What are you hiding beneath that polished surface?"

Ryan's gaze darkened for a heartbeat, a storm brewing behind those stormy blue eyes. "Some things are better left in the shadows, Ella."

His words hung between us, thickening the air, and I sensed the chasm opening wider, a tension pulsing with unspoken secrets. In that moment, I realized that while I was drawn to him, he was equally drawn to the depths of his own complexities, and it terrified him.

As we stood in the echoing silence of the amusement park, surrounded by shadows of forgotten joy, I knew that whatever lay beneath his charming exterior was a labyrinth I was both desperate and fearful to explore. The city around us seemed to fade, leaving only the two of us, suspended in a moment that felt both electric and suffocating. I could feel the weight of the secrets he carried pressing down on both of us, a gravity that threatened to pull us under if we didn't find a way to navigate the depths together.

The night air wrapped around us like a cool blanket, a stark contrast to the smoldering tension that crackled in the space between Ryan and me. He was a riddle wrapped in a mystery, and I was determined to peel back the layers, even if it meant losing a piece of myself in the process. As we stood beneath the looming silhouette of the Ferris wheel, I couldn't shake the feeling that I was on the brink of something monumental—or perhaps catastrophic.

"I wonder if this place was ever filled with laughter," I mused, running my fingers along the rusted metal of a nearby ride. The sharp edges were cold, unyielding, just like the questions dancing on the tip of my tongue. "Or if it was always just a place for dreams to die."

Ryan's gaze shifted to the ground, his posture tense as he contemplated my words. "It was both, I think. A stage for joy and sorrow. Just like life, really."

I felt the weight of his gaze on me, a probing look that made me feel exposed. "You sound like you have a personal stake in that philosophy," I said, arching an eyebrow playfully. "Care to share your tragic backstory?"

He chuckled, a low sound that reverberated through the stillness of the park. "And risk ruining my carefully curated image? Not a chance."

"Ah, the elusive real estate developer with a tragic past," I teased, my heart racing at the thought of prying deeper. "What a cliché."

"Clichés exist for a reason," he countered, a hint of mischief in his voice. "They resonate. Besides, who doesn't love a little drama in their lives?"

His smile was infectious, but I could see it didn't quite reach his eyes. There was something else lurking beneath, a hidden current that begged for exploration. I took a step closer, intrigued. "I'll take the drama, but only if it comes with a side of honesty. How about a trade? You share a secret, and I'll share mine."

"Deal," he said, a challenge flickering in his eyes. "Ladies first."

I inhaled deeply, summoning the courage to share something I'd kept buried for years. "Okay, here goes. I used to believe in fairy tales. You know, the kind where everything works out perfectly in the end. But life has a funny way of skewing those tales, doesn't it?"

Ryan nodded, the corners of his mouth quirking up slightly. "Go on."

"I had this dream of being a writer," I confessed, the words spilling out before I could stop them. "But after a few rejections, I started to doubt myself. I ended up taking a job in a coffee shop instead—serving lattes to people who seem to have it all figured out while I'm stuck pouring my heart into forgotten notebooks."

"That sounds tough," he said softly, his tone shifting, genuine concern threading through it. "But what if those notebooks are your real treasure? Just because they're not published doesn't mean they lack value."

I shrugged, a mix of vulnerability and defiance coursing through me. "I guess, but it's hard to see the treasure when everyone else is flaunting their shiny success."

"Ah, comparison—the thief of joy," he replied, smirking as if he had just uncovered a profound truth. "It's almost as if people forget that not everyone gets to ride the Ferris wheel."

I couldn't help but laugh, a genuine sound that felt like a release. "So what about you, Mr. Perfect? What's your tragic tale? Was it heartbreak that turned you into a real estate mogul?"

He hesitated, his gaze shifting to the empty park rides, lost in thought. "Not heartbreak, exactly," he said finally, his voice low. "More like a fire that burned everything down."

My curiosity piqued, I leaned closer, eager to dig deeper. "You can't just drop a line like that and walk away."

Ryan sighed, running a hand through his tousled hair. "Fine. When I was younger, my family lost everything—home, stability, all of it—because my father made some terrible choices. It was either rise from the ashes or drown in them, so I chose to rise. But the truth is, I'm not sure if I did it for me or for them."

I could see the shadows flit across his face, darkness creeping into the corners of his smile. "That sounds incredibly tough," I said, my voice softening. "But that doesn't explain why you hide behind this perfect facade."

"Because sometimes the façade is easier to maintain than facing the chaos beneath," he said, his words heavy with unspoken weight. "It's a shield. And if I let it down, I might lose everything I've built."

The honesty in his voice sent a shiver down my spine, and I felt a surge of empathy washing over me. "You're more than just a real estate developer, Ryan. You're a person with a past—one that shaped you. Why not let someone in for once?"

He hesitated, the flicker of vulnerability in his eyes battling against the walls he had built so meticulously. "Maybe I'm afraid of what that would mean," he finally admitted. "What if the chaos becomes too much? What if I can't keep up the act?"

"Then we face it together," I said, my voice steady and resolute. "You don't have to carry it alone."

Ryan's eyes softened, a moment of connection passing between us that felt like a fragile truce. But before I could bask in the warmth of our shared honesty, he took a step back, slipping once more into his familiar persona. "You're braver than I am, Ella. But bravery doesn't come without its price."

"And what's that price?" I asked, suddenly aware of the stark distance he had put between us.

"The truth can sometimes burn," he replied, a shadow of regret flitting across his features. "And I'm not sure if I'm ready for the heat."

I felt my heart sink, the connection we had just built threatened by the very walls he insisted on keeping up. But there was a determination brewing inside me, a desire to not let him retreat into the shadows again. "Then let's stand in the heat together, Ryan. I promise, it won't burn as much if we do."

For a fleeting moment, I thought I saw something shift in his expression—a flicker of hope mingled with fear. But just as quickly as it came, it vanished, leaving behind only the echoes of our conversation and the haunting reminder that some truths were still buried deep beneath the surface.

The stillness of the amusement park seemed to envelop us as Ryan stepped back, the air thickening with an unspoken tension. The shadows of the Ferris wheel loomed over us, the rusted metal almost a silent witness to the confessions we'd exchanged. I could feel the remnants of our conversation clinging to me, yet there was an unmistakable distance that had re-emerged, an invisible wall that felt more daunting than ever.

"Why do you keep pushing me away?" I asked, my voice steadier than I felt. "You've opened up, and I want to return the favor. Let me in."

He crossed his arms, a defensive posture that only deepened the divide. "Ella, you don't understand what you're asking. Some things are too heavy to carry, even in the company of someone else."

"That's not true," I shot back, my frustration bubbling to the surface. "If you want to talk about heavy things, I've got a whole encyclopedia's worth of baggage myself."

"Then maybe it's better we keep it that way," he replied, his tone sharp enough to cut through the thick air.

I felt the sting of his words, the sudden chill dampening my spirit. "So you want to keep dancing around the edges? I'm not a tourist in your life, Ryan. I'm here, right now, in this moment with you. Don't shut me out just when I'm trying to reach you."

He ran a hand through his hair, exhaling sharply as if the weight of the moment was suffocating him. "You think it's that easy? That I can just peel back the layers and lay everything bare? That I can trust you just like that?"

"Trust is earned, not given," I replied, trying to inject some warmth into my words, even as my heart began to fracture. "But you have to let me show you who I am. This is how it works."

His eyes darkened for a brief moment, a flicker of something more than frustration—fear? Regret? I couldn't quite decipher it, but I felt a powerful urge to bridge the chasm between us. "What are you so afraid of, Ryan? That I'll leave if I see the real you?"

He took a step back, the distance between us feeling like miles. "No," he said slowly, his voice tight. "I'm afraid you'll want to stay. That you'll see the mess I carry and decide it's not worth the trouble."

"Then I guess you don't know me at all," I replied, a wry smile creeping onto my face despite the heaviness of the moment. "I thrive on trouble. It's basically my middle name."

Ryan's gaze softened for a fraction of a second, a flicker of the man I was beginning to unravel beneath the surface. But just as quickly, he blinked, retreating behind that polished exterior that felt all too familiar. "We should get going," he said, breaking the spell. "I've got an early meeting tomorrow."

"Really? You're going to run away from this?" I couldn't keep the disappointment from seeping into my voice. "You came all this way to show me your dark little secret, and now you want to bolt?"

"It's not that simple."

"Then make it simple!" I shouted, the frustration spilling over. "You brought me here for a reason, didn't you? Or was I just a distraction?"

His expression tightened, and for a moment, I thought I saw a glimpse of the turmoil churning within him. "You're not a distraction. But this place—it has a history, and it's not just the rides and the graffiti. It's personal for me, and I'm not ready to share that yet."

"What happened here?" I pressed, not willing to let him off the hook. "Why does it matter so much?"

He turned away, staring into the darkness that surrounded us, the shadows stretching long and foreboding. "This park was once a place of escape for my family. Before everything went wrong. We used to come here every summer, laughing and pretending the world didn't exist. But..." He trailed off, his voice breaking slightly, as if he were grappling with the weight of a memory that threatened to consume him.

"Let me help you carry that weight," I urged, stepping closer, feeling the magnetic pull toward him intensify. "You don't have to shoulder it alone."

"Maybe that's the problem," he replied, his voice barely above a whisper. "I don't know how to let anyone in. Not after everything."

I could feel the raw pain lacing his words, and it tugged at my heartstrings. "What if I'm willing to teach you?" I said softly, reaching out as if to bridge that ever-widening gap.

He looked at me then, really looked, and in that moment, I saw a flicker of hope battling against despair. "Ella, I wish I could believe that."

Before I could respond, a low rumble broke the silence—a distant sound that echoed through the deserted park. It sent a jolt of adrenaline coursing through me. "What was that?" I asked, scanning the surroundings, my instincts kicking in.

Ryan's expression shifted instantly, alert and tense. "I don't know. It could be nothing, but we should probably move. It's late."

I felt a shiver run down my spine, but my curiosity overrode my caution. "We can't just leave now! What if it's something important? What if someone needs help?"

"Ella, please," he said, his voice low and urgent. "We don't know what we're dealing with here. Let's just—"

But before he could finish, another sound cut through the air, this one much closer, echoing off the crumbling walls of the park. A sharp clang followed by the sound of footsteps—heavy and deliberate.

I turned to Ryan, my heart racing. "What is going on?"

"Stay behind me," he said, a fierce protectiveness igniting in his eyes as he positioned himself between me and the noise.

I felt a mix of fear and exhilaration as the footsteps drew closer, the tension crackling like electricity. Whatever was coming our way, it was not just a random occurrence; it was a disruption to the fragile moment we had built between us.

"Ryan, I—"

But before I could finish, the shadows shifted, and a figure emerged from the darkness, silhouetted against the flickering lights of the abandoned park. My heart raced as I squinted, trying to make out the details.

"Who's there?" Ryan called out, his voice steady yet laced with an underlying urgency that sent a wave of dread through me.

The figure stepped closer, revealing a face that was both familiar and foreign. My breath caught in my throat as recognition washed over me—a face I thought I'd never see again. A ghost from my past that threatened to unravel everything I thought I understood about this moment.

"Hello, Ella," the figure said, a wicked smile spreading across their face. "Long time no see."

The world around me spun, and as the reality of the moment sank in, I realized with a chilling certainty that this encounter would change everything.

Chapter 3: A Brush with Desire

The hallway of the hotel stretches before me like a dark tunnel, the muted lighting casting long shadows that flicker and dance as I stand frozen at my door. My mind is a jumbled mess of thoughts, the remnants of the evening swirling like the last notes of a jazz solo, rich and elusive. Ryan's words echo in my ears, a haunting melody that stirs a mixture of excitement and trepidation. I want to understand what he meant, to unravel the mystery that seems to hang around him like a finely tailored coat. Instead, I'm left with a spark of something dangerous—a thrill that pulses just beneath the surface.

I fumble with my keycard, my fingers trembling slightly as I swipe it against the reader. The lock clicks open with an almost mocking finality. I step inside and let the door fall shut behind me, the thud reverberating in the stillness of the room. The air is thick with the scent of sandalwood from the diffuser I'd bought at a quirky little shop earlier that week, grounding me in the present moment even as my thoughts drift back to Ryan and that tantalizing whisper.

The room feels impossibly small now, the walls closing in as my heart races. I kick off my shoes, feeling the plush carpet beneath my feet, a soothing contrast to the sharp edges of my emotions. I drop onto the bed, its comfort engulfing me as I stare up at the ceiling, tracing the intricate patterns with my eyes. How could a single night spin my world so completely? The lingering taste of bourbon and laughter clings to my lips, a reminder of the carefree spirit I'd embraced for just a few hours.

Ryan had an easy charm that wrapped around me like a warm blanket, and I can still hear his laughter, low and rich, filling the corners of the speakeasy with life. The way he moved—each gesture deliberate and fluid, like he belonged to the world of shadows and music we'd wandered into. I'd watched him, utterly captivated, as he tossed back a whiskey neat, a confidence radiating from him that made me feel both anchored and adrift.

And then there were those moments between us, electric and palpable, igniting the air with an unspoken promise. Each brush of our hands felt like a secret, a connection simmering just beneath the surface, waiting for the right moment to ignite. The tension had wrapped around us, thickening the air until I felt as if I might suffocate from the weight of it.

My phone buzzes on the nightstand, startling me from my reverie. I reach for it, a flicker of hope that it might be Ryan, an eager wish that he'd somehow sensed my thoughts and was rushing back to reclaim the moment that slipped through our fingers. Instead, it's a notification from my best friend, Nora, a cheerful reminder of the brunch plans we've set for tomorrow. I can almost hear her voice, light and teasing, asking if I've met someone special yet.

What would I even say? "Oh, you know, just a guy I met at a speakeasy who whispered ominous warnings in my ear?" I chuckle to myself, but it's a fleeting moment of levity. My mind drifts back to Ryan, to that dangerous allure he carried with him like an irresistible perfume. I wonder if he had any idea how intoxicating he was, how easily he slid under my skin and settled into my thoughts.

In the midst of my musings, I rise and walk to the window, peering out at the city that twinkled like a sea of stars. The streets were alive, filled with laughter and the soft hum of conversation, yet I felt as though I stood at the edge of a precipice, staring into the abyss of possibilities that lay before me. I felt simultaneously drawn to the chaos below and anchored to this small sanctuary I'd created for myself.

As I lean against the cool glass, I catch a glimpse of my reflection, the woman staring back at me with wild curls framing a face flushed with emotion. I look like someone who's been swept off her feet, and I'm not sure if I should be embarrassed or exhilarated.

And just then, my phone buzzes again, a gentle vibration against the wooden surface that demands my attention. I glance down, expecting another update from Nora, but this time it's a text from an unknown number. My heart skips a beat as I click it open, half-expecting it to be Ryan, his name lighting up my screen like a beacon.

"Can we talk?"

My fingers hover over the screen, an involuntary thrill racing through me. Is this a random message or something more? A chill races down my spine as I stare at the message, trying to decipher the weight of those four words.

I type back, my heart thumping like the bass from the jazz band earlier. "Who is this?"

The response comes quickly, a stark contrast to my slow, deliberate heartbeat. "Someone who knows more than you think."

A shiver runs through me, an unexpected thrill mingling with a healthy dose of anxiety. What does that mean? And what does this person know? The air feels charged, alive with possibility and danger.

As I pace the room, my mind races. Could it be someone connected to Ryan? Or perhaps a lingering remnant of my past? There are so many questions swirling in my head, each one a thread pulling at the fabric of my carefully constructed evening. The urge to retreat into the familiar comforts of my routine gnaws at me, but the intrigue of this message keeps me anchored in place, breathless and waiting.

I can almost hear Ryan's voice in my mind, low and dangerous again. "You don't know what you're getting yourself into." His warning hangs heavy, and I realize with a jolt that I am standing at the threshold of something I can't fully comprehend. Something that might shatter the world I know.

The screen flickers to life in the dim light of my hotel room, casting an eerie glow against the walls. My heart races as I try to wrap my mind around the mysterious message. "Someone who knows more than you think." It feels like a plot twist I didn't sign up for, the kind that sends chills down your spine while simultaneously beckoning you closer. I hesitate for a moment, debating whether to respond or ignore the message entirely, my fingers poised over the keyboard like a tightrope walker straddling two worlds.

I decide to dive in. "What do you know?"

The seconds drag on like hours, each tick of the clock amplified in the silence, heightening my anticipation. Just as I begin to doubt my choice, my phone vibrates again. "Meet me at The Lantern at midnight. Bring your curiosity."

I blink at the screen, my thoughts swirling like autumn leaves caught in a gust of wind. The Lantern. It's a cozy little bar on the corner, known for its moody lighting and intimate booths, a place where whispers seem to hang in the air like smoke. My stomach twists at the thought of venturing out alone at this hour, especially when every logical part of me screams that this is a terrible idea. Yet there's a siren call to it, a sweet melody woven into the uncertainty.

After a moment of deliberation, curiosity wins out. I throw on a light jacket, the fabric brushing against my skin like a comforting reminder of the evening I just had. I can still feel the echoes of Ryan's laughter, his magnetic presence weaving through my thoughts like a favorite song. The anticipation of something unexpected, something thrilling, lures me into the night.

Stepping out into the cool air, the city greets me with its usual cacophony of sounds—the distant hum of traffic, the laughter spilling from nearby restaurants, and the faint pulse of music that seems to guide my steps. I make my way toward The Lantern, the streetlights flickering overhead like stars trapped in a concrete jungle. Each footfall is a reminder of the choices I'm making, leading me deeper into the night and the unknown.

When I arrive, the bar is alive with energy, but it still feels like a secret hideaway. The warm glow from the lanterns hanging overhead creates a cozy atmosphere that wraps around me, drawing me in. I scan the room, searching for any sign of my mysterious correspondent. My heart races with anticipation and nerves as I navigate through clusters of patrons enjoying their drinks, laughter blending seamlessly with the soft jazz wafting through the air.

Then I see him—a figure leaning against the bar, his back to me, with dark hair that catches the dim light. It's not Ryan, but the moment I spot him, I feel a jolt of recognition. This is Lucas, a man I'd crossed paths with a few times during my brief stint at the local art gallery. He had always carried an air of intrigue, his casual demeanor contrasting sharply with the intensity of his gaze. He glances over his shoulder, catching my eye, and an inscrutable smile spreads across his lips.

"Fancy seeing you here," he says, his voice smooth like the bourbon he's cradling in his hand. "I didn't think you'd take the bait."

I raise an eyebrow, a smile tugging at the corners of my mouth despite the uncertainty swirling inside me. "Is that what this is? Bait?"

He gestures toward an empty booth tucked away in a quiet corner, the kind of spot where secrets can be shared without prying ears. "Come on, let's talk. I promise I won't bite... much."

Settling into the booth, I feel the weight of his gaze, sharp and probing, as if he's assessing every part of me. I can't help but wonder what he really knows. "So, what is it that you think I don't know?"

Lucas leans in, his expression shifting from playful to serious, an intensity flickering in his eyes. "It's about Ryan."

The name hangs in the air, and my breath catches in my throat. "Ryan? What about him?"

"You're not the first person he's captivated, you know," Lucas continues, his voice low but steady. "There's a history there, and it's not just what you see on the surface."

I lean back, crossing my arms, defensively weighing his words. "What do you mean? Ryan seems... interesting, sure, but everyone has a past."

"True, but not everyone has a past that follows them like a shadow." His eyes narrow slightly, a flicker of something akin to concern dancing across his features. "He's not the kind of man who comes without complications. You need to be careful."

The warning prickles at my skin, igniting a cocktail of emotions—anger, intrigue, and something deeper, an unshakable need to understand the man who's captured my attention. "And you do know him? How?"

He takes a sip of his drink, a sly smile curling his lips. "Let's just say our circles overlap. Ryan's a lot more involved in the art world than he lets on, and it's not always for the right reasons."

I feel a spark of irritation rise within me, a reflexive defense of Ryan igniting in my chest. "So he's just a charming con artist, then?"

"Not quite. More like a reluctant player in a game he didn't ask to join." Lucas leans closer, lowering his voice conspiratorially. "He's mixed up with some people who don't play nice, and I don't want to see you get hurt in the process."

The air around us thickens, charged with tension as my thoughts race. Is this Lucas genuinely trying to protect me, or is there something more insidious at play? I want to shake off the unease creeping up my spine, to brush it aside like a pesky fly, but the truth is I'm drawn to Ryan. The way he makes me feel—a dizzying blend of exhilaration and fear—is intoxicating.

As if reading my mind, Lucas raises his glass, his gaze steady. "Just remember, curiosity can be a double-edged sword. You might uncover something you're not ready to face."

The weight of his words settles heavily between us. I can feel the pressure of the choices I have ahead of me, the lure of Ryan's mysterious charm pulling me in one direction while caution pushes me back.

"Thanks for the warning, but I think I'll take my chances," I reply, trying to sound lighthearted, but the tremor in my voice betrays me.

Lucas tilts his head, an amused glint in his eyes. "Good luck, then. Just remember that shadows often hide the truth."

As I leave the bar, the cool night air washes over me, the adrenaline from our conversation still surging through my veins. The city buzzes with life, yet I feel oddly isolated, adrift in a sea of uncertainty. I can't shake the feeling that I'm standing on the precipice of something monumental, caught between the magnetic pull of Ryan and the ominous warnings that linger like a shadow on my heart.

The night air clings to my skin as I make my way back to my hotel, each step echoing like a heartbeat against the pavement. The lingering warmth of the speakeasy feels like a distant memory, replaced by the chill of uncertainty that tugs at my insides. I replay the moments with Ryan in my mind, a dizzying mix of thrill and anxiety. What did he mean? What kind of trouble was he hinting at?

The streetlights cast flickering shadows that dance along the sidewalk, and with every passing car, my heart races, half-expecting Ryan to come striding back into view. The world feels charged with possibility, yet heavy with foreboding, like a storm poised on the horizon. I can't help but feel as if I'm walking the fine line between adventure and danger, and I'm not sure which side I want to land on.

As I reach my hotel, I glance at my phone again, the screen glowing in the darkness. No new messages, just the reflection of my wide eyes staring back at me—part excitement, part fear. I step inside, the familiar warmth of the lobby wrapping around me like a soft blanket, a contrast to the whirlwind of emotions battling within. The receptionist gives me a nod, a welcoming gesture that I return with a weak smile, feeling the weight of the night pressing down on me.

Once back in my room, I toss my jacket onto the chair and pace. The walls feel like they're closing in, and the silence is deafening. I need clarity, a moment of grounding in this chaos. I pour myself a glass of water, the cool liquid soothing as I take a sip, but it does nothing to quench the fire ignited by Ryan's parting words.

"Curiosity can be a double-edged sword," Lucas had warned, and it resounds in my mind like an ominous chime. But who could resist the allure of the unknown? As the night stretches on, I find myself contemplating what it would mean to really know Ryan, to peel back the layers and uncover the man hidden behind that devil-may-care facade.

Suddenly, the temptation is too strong. I grab my phone, fingers itching to reach out to Ryan. My heart races with the thought of his voice, that rich, low timbre echoing in my mind. "What the hell," I mutter under my breath, typing a message. "Hey, can we talk? I think I might have some questions."

I hit send and then immediately second-guess myself. What if he thinks I'm too forward? What if he doesn't respond at all? Just as I start to berate myself for being impulsive, my phone vibrates in response.

"Meet me at The Archive in fifteen. Bring that curiosity of yours."

The Archive? I've heard of it—another hidden gem in the city, a place renowned for its underground art shows and eclectic crowd. It feels both thrilling and terrifying, the idea of stepping back into the unknown. As I glance at the clock, I realize I barely have time to freshen up before I need to leave.

I toss on a pair of ankle boots and a jacket, hoping the sleekness will make me feel more confident. The truth is, I can't shake the sensation that I'm stepping into a plot I didn't write. Each moment feels charged, filled with unspoken words and possibilities that flutter like moths in the dark corners of my mind.

As I navigate the streets, the familiar buzz of the city surrounds me, but I feel like I'm in a bubble, separate from everything else. My heart pounds with every step, anticipation mingling with a hint of dread. The Archive looms ahead, its sign glowing softly in the dim light, and I pause for a moment, collecting myself.

Inside, the atmosphere shifts dramatically. The air is alive with a different kind of energy—artworks line the walls, their colors vibrant and bold, conversations hum like a live wire, and the music is more eclectic, a fusion of beats that wraps around me like a second skin. I scan the crowd, looking for Ryan, but he's nowhere in sight.

My heart sinks momentarily, then skips a beat when I spot a familiar figure moving through the crowd. Ryan's presence is magnetic, drawing the eyes of those around him as he interacts with a few acquaintances, his laughter ringing out like a familiar tune. He seems at ease, his body language open and inviting.

Taking a deep breath, I weave my way through the throng, determined to reach him. As I approach, I catch snippets of conversation—a few words here and there that pique my interest, hinting at something larger brewing just beneath the surface.

"—heard about the deal they're trying to push through..."

"—some serious connections involved..."

"—not what he seems, I tell you."

I finally reach Ryan, and he turns, his eyes locking onto mine, that easy smile breaking across his face like the dawn. "You came."

"Of course," I reply, trying to sound casual despite the flutter in my chest. "You did say you had something to discuss."

He gestures to a quieter corner, away from the thrumming crowd, and I follow, the anticipation building with each step. "You're not just curious, are you? You want to know what I'm mixed up in."

"Maybe," I admit, crossing my arms defensively as we find a secluded spot. "But more importantly, you dropped a rather cryptic line the other night."

Ryan leans against the wall, a shadow of seriousness passing over his features. "I meant it. There's a lot I haven't told you, a lot I can't explain right now."

I feel a rush of frustration. "Then why invite me here? Why get my hopes up if you can't give me answers?"

His gaze intensifies, a flicker of something darker in his eyes. "Because I think you should know the truth before you get in too deep. There are things happening that could affect you—things I want to protect you from."

"Protect me from what?" I challenge, feeling the walls of my own bravado begin to shake.

He hesitates, and for a moment, it seems like the weight of his secrets is pressing down on him. "From the people I'm involved with, the choices I've made. I don't want you to be collateral damage."

Before I can respond, a loud crash echoes through the gallery, the sound slicing through the ambiance like a knife. My heart drops as the crowd gasps, and I turn, searching for the source of the disturbance. A man has fallen, his drink spilling across the floor, and the chaos unfolds rapidly.

Suddenly, Ryan tenses beside me, his expression shifting from concern to alarm. "We need to go. Now."

"What? Why?" My pulse quickens, confusion twisting my gut.

"Just trust me," he says, grabbing my hand and pulling me through the throng of bodies, our path illuminated only by the flashes of excitement and fear around us. The crowd stirs, murmurs spreading like wildfire, and I can sense the shift in the air—something darker lurking just beneath the surface.

As we reach the exit, I glance back, my instincts screaming that we're stepping into something far beyond mere curiosity. I barely register Ryan's grip tightening around my wrist as we slip out into the cool night, the chaos behind us fading into a tense silence.

But as we step into the shadows, a figure emerges from the alleyway ahead, his face obscured by darkness, and I feel my heart drop.

"Ryan," I breathe, my voice barely above a whisper, sensing that this confrontation might change everything.

In that moment, I realize the tangled web we're caught in has no clear escape, and I brace myself for whatever comes next, a foreboding feeling settling like a stone in my stomach.

Chapter 4: Unveiling the Past

I woke up one morning with the sunlight spilling through my curtains like melted butter over toast, but instead of the usual mundane thoughts that accompanied the first rays of day, my mind was occupied by Ryan. His smile, the way his laughter danced through the air, and the subtle tension that simmered beneath his charming exterior lingered like a stubborn perfume. It was intoxicating and terrifying in equal measure. I had tried to focus on my day-to-day—work at the café, my endless book collection gathering dust, the banal small talk with my neighbors—but every attempt crumbled under the weight of my curiosity about him.

It wasn't long before I was poring over articles, tracing back through the tangled web of Ryan's family history like a detective with a magnifying glass. My laptop screen flickered with a cascade of headlines: "The Fall of the Kings: A Family Legacy in Ruins," "Nashville's Elite: The Scandal That Shook a Dynasty," and "The Kings of Country: A Fortune Built on Betrayal." I could practically hear the echoes of old-money snobbery and whispered accusations surrounding their names. Each article painted a picture of grandeur tainted by the muck of greed and deception, leaving me with the unsettling realization that Ryan was an unwilling heir to this chaotic empire.

I let out a frustrated sigh, running my fingers through my hair. "What have you gotten yourself into?" I muttered to the screen, as if Ryan could hear me. There was a part of me that wanted to turn away, to slam my laptop shut and forget this dangerous rabbit hole I was tumbling down. But another part, a more reckless part, urged me onward, lured by the magnetic pull of his dark past.

As I sifted through the layers of family drama, I stumbled upon a particular detail that sent a shiver down my spine: a family member, a distant cousin named Clara, had vanished years ago. The circumstances were murky, the theories swirling like leaves in a tempest. Some claimed she had run away, others whispered of something far more sinister. I was struck by an odd sensation, as though Clara's ghost was weaving through the air, intertwining her fate with Ryan's.

"What's the connection here?" I mumbled to myself, shoving my laptop aside. I stood, pacing the cramped confines of my tiny apartment, which felt all the smaller with the weight of the revelations hanging in the air. Each step reverberated through my mind, a rhythm that matched my growing anxiety.

Just then, my phone buzzed, pulling me from my reverie. It was a text from Ryan: "Want to meet up later? I found a new place downtown that's supposed to have the best coffee." My heart stuttered in my chest, a curious mix of excitement and dread.

Should I go? Could I face him without the shadow of his family's past looming over us? I hesitated, my thumb hovering over the screen. But then again, maybe this was my chance to confront the reality behind the man who had captured my thoughts so completely. I texted back, a simple "Sure, what time?"

Hours later, I found myself seated in a dimly lit café, the air fragrant with the rich aroma of freshly ground coffee beans. It was a far cry from the bustling corner shop where I worked. This place exuded an air of exclusivity, the kind of atmosphere that made you feel important just by being there. I fiddled with the strap of my bag, my heart racing in anticipation.

When Ryan walked in, the world around me faded into a blur. He had this effortless way of moving through life, like a moth dancing dangerously close to the flame. He caught sight of me and flashed that smile—so disarming, so genuine—that it momentarily drowned out all my doubts. He slid into the seat across from me, his eyes sparkling with mischief. "What's a girl like you doing in a place like this?"

"Trying to find out if your taste in coffee is as good as your taste in..." I paused, my breath hitching slightly, "friends."

"Careful," he grinned, leaning forward, "you might find I have a taste for trouble."

"Oh, I've already gathered that," I quipped back, the tension crackling between us like electricity. "Trouble seems to follow you around."

His expression shifted, just for a moment, and I sensed an underlying tension in the room. "You could say I have a complicated relationship with my family," he admitted, his voice dropping a notch. The vulnerability in his tone made my heart ache. "It's not as glamorous as it looks from the outside."

"Tell me about it," I said softly, forcing myself to meet his gaze. "I've been reading up on the Kings. It seems like the past is hard to shake off."

He took a sip of his coffee, the rich liquid swirling with steam and secrets. "You found out about Clara, didn't you?"

I nodded slowly, my stomach knotting. "What happened to her, Ryan?"

He leaned back, running a hand through his hair, the weight of his family's history pressing down on him like a physical burden. "The truth is, no one really knows. She disappeared, and we were all left to pick up the pieces. It's been a ghost that haunts us, and I can't shake the feeling it's tied to my life now."

The tension in the air was palpable, a silent agreement that we were delving into dangerous territory. My heart raced at the thought of the darkness that lingered beneath his charm, and I found myself drawn deeper into the enigma of his life. The coffee cooled between us, forgotten, as we exchanged our own fragile truths, each word building a bridge across the chasm of secrets that separated us.

Just as I was beginning to feel the warmth of connection, a shadow passed over his features, a fleeting moment where I saw the man beneath the mask. "You shouldn't get involved with someone like me," he said quietly, almost pleading. "There are things about my family that could put you in danger."

I stared at him, feeling the gravity of his words settle around us. "You can't make decisions for me, Ryan," I replied, my voice steady despite the storm brewing inside. "I'm not afraid of your past. But I need to understand it."

His eyes locked onto mine, a silent battle playing out behind them. I sensed he was weighing his options, caught between the desire to protect me and the undeniable pull of the connection we were forging. As he reached across the table, brushing his fingers against mine, the warmth sent a spark through me, igniting a fire that I was both eager and terrified to explore.

In that moment, we were no longer just two people sitting in a café; we were explorers, stepping into a world teetering on the edge of chaos, unraveling the threads of our intertwined destinies. The air crackled with possibility, and I knew we were about to plunge into a story far deeper and more dangerous than either of us had anticipated.

The following days unfolded like a series of vivid, chaotic dreams, each one more perplexing than the last. My life had shifted, the fabric of my routine unraveling as I became entangled in Ryan's intricate world. I found myself moving through my days like a ghost, floating between work shifts at the café and late-night readings on my laptop. Each click of the keys felt like a descent into a labyrinth, where every article pulled me deeper into the mystery of the Kings.

I noticed subtle changes in myself too. My heart raced at the sound of my phone pinging, every notification transforming my mundane world into a treasure hunt for messages from him. I began curating a playlist on my phone, filled with songs that echoed the emotions swirling between us—notes of longing, confusion, and an undercurrent of danger. It was as if music had become my ally in navigating the emotional labyrinth that was Ryan.

One evening, while I was ensconced in a corner of the café, I spotted him at the entrance, his silhouette framed by the dim glow of the streetlights. My breath caught at the sight of him; he looked effortlessly handsome, his dark hair tousled in that way that made me want to reach out and run my fingers through it. He caught my eye, and a smile broke across his face, lighting up the space around him. It sent a jolt of warmth through me, a reminder that despite the shadows of his past, he was right here, present and real.

As he joined me at the table, he looked slightly out of breath, as though he had rushed here just to see me. "Sorry I'm late," he said, slipping into his seat with a boyish grin. "I had to dodge a few reporters on the way. Apparently, the Kings are newsworthy again."

"Must be exhausting," I replied, my tone light despite the heaviness of the topic. "Are they circling like vultures, waiting for a story to drop?"

He chuckled, a sound that made my stomach flutter. "More like persistent flies. You swat them away, but they just keep buzzing around."

"Maybe you should try an insect repellent," I teased, leaning in closer. "Or do you have a family heirloom you can use? Something vintage to scare them off?"

His laughter faded, replaced by a contemplative look. "I wish it were that easy. This is not just a family nuisance; it's a full-blown circus."

"Sounds like a party," I said, though I felt a twinge of empathy. "So, what's the latest scandal? A new love child? A hidden fortune in the Bahamas?"

"More like a lawsuit." His eyes darkened. "A former employee claims they were wrongfully terminated and is digging into the family's business practices. If he finds something, it could blow the lid off everything."

"Charming family you've got there," I said, biting my lip to suppress a smile. "Have you considered running away? I hear a beach somewhere with no cell service is a great getaway."

Ryan smirked, leaning back in his chair. "Tempting. But then who would deal with the vultures? Someone has to protect the family name. Besides," he added, his gaze piercing, "it's hard to run from shadows you don't even see."

I shifted in my seat, feeling the weight of his words settle over me like a thick fog. "What if I help you? I could be your shadow, you know, the one who actually sees everything."

"You'd be putting yourself in danger," he replied, the seriousness of his tone cutting through the playful banter. "I don't want you involved in this mess."

"I think I've already stepped into the mess, Ryan," I countered, holding his gaze. "You might not want me here, but I'm already intrigued. And it seems like you need someone in your corner."

A moment of silence stretched between us, charged with the kind of tension that can only arise from unspoken truths. He was caught off guard, and for the first time, I saw uncertainty flicker in his eyes. "You're too stubborn for your own good, you know that?"

"Stubbornness is a virtue," I replied with a wink, a playful challenge hanging in the air. "What's the worst that could happen? A little adventure? Maybe some life lessons? Who knows, we might even solve the family mystery together."

"I'll need a lot of coffee if we're going to solve any mysteries," he shot back, his smirk returning.

"Good thing I know all the best places," I said, warmth blooming in my chest as the atmosphere shifted back to its lightheartedness. "Let's make a deal. For every dangerous turn we take, we reward ourselves with the best coffee in Nashville."

"Deal." He extended his hand, and I took it, the connection sending an electric jolt through me.

Our laughter intertwined with the ambient sounds of the café, a melody of two souls daring to breach the boundaries of their worlds. But as the evening wore on, the shadows of Ryan's family loomed closer, lurking at the edges of our conversation. I could feel the weight of his history pushing against the fragile barrier we had constructed, and the knowledge that I was stepping into a realm fraught with peril began to settle uncomfortably in my stomach.

Days passed, and as our clandestine meetings became a regular occurrence, each encounter felt like a dance—a waltz of half-formed confessions and shared secrets, tempered by an unspoken acknowledgment of the risks. We would sit across from each other in cafés and bars, our conversations swirling around the mundane—favorite books, ridiculous movies, and childhood memories—but always circling back to the heart of the matter: the Kings and their legacy.

One afternoon, while we sat at a park, the late afternoon sun drenching everything in a golden hue, Ryan dropped the weight of another revelation on me. "I've been thinking," he said, a shadow passing over his features. "What if I dig deeper into Clara's disappearance? Maybe it's time to unearth some old family skeletons."

My stomach twisted at the idea, and a flicker of concern washed over me. "You think that's wise? What if you find something you're not prepared for?"

"I don't know if I can keep running from it," he replied, his voice barely above a whisper. "It's been lurking in the background for too long."

"Sometimes it's better to leave the past buried," I cautioned, an instinctual fear rising in me. "You could unleash something you can't control."

"But isn't that what life is? A series of risks?" He leaned closer, his eyes intense. "You're the one who said you wanted an adventure. Don't you want to be part of my story?"

The question hung in the air, heavy and electric. My heart raced, torn between the thrill of discovery and the undeniable fear of what lay ahead. It was exhilarating to think I could be part of something larger than myself, but at what cost? The stakes felt impossibly high, a tightrope stretched between desire and danger, and with every word exchanged, I sensed the delicate balance shifting, pulling us closer to an edge I wasn't sure we could navigate safely.

As we sat there, the shadows lengthening in the fading light, I realized that the adventure was already upon us. Whatever path we chose, one thing was certain: the journey would irrevocably change us both, pushing the boundaries of who we were and who we could become. And deep down, beneath the layers of fear and uncertainty, there was an undeniable thrill in the chase—a pulse of excitement that matched the rhythm of my racing heart.

The sun dipped below the horizon, casting long shadows that danced like specters through the park. Ryan and I sat on a bench, the faint rustling of leaves punctuating the tension that had been brewing between us. Our latest conversations felt like stirring a pot of secrets, each word adding an ingredient to a recipe neither of us fully understood.

"Let's dig into Clara's disappearance," Ryan suggested, his gaze intense, pulling me into a gravity I couldn't resist. "I think it's time we uncover what really happened. Maybe it's the key to understanding my family's mess."

"Ryan," I began, hesitating as the weight of his words sank in. "What if we find something that puts you in danger? Something you can't handle?"

He turned to me, his expression earnest. "You've been brave enough to dive into this world with me. Don't you want to see it through? To understand why I'm so... tangled?"

I could feel the flutter of my heart as the thrill of the adventure battled against my instincts to protect him. "I do, but I also don't want to be the reason you end up in more trouble. You're already carrying so much."

He reached for my hand, his fingers interlacing with mine, warmth spreading through me like a lifeline. "We're already in it, and I can't turn back. Not now."

A rush of adrenaline coursed through me, a mix of excitement and trepidation. "Fine, but if we're doing this, we're doing it right. We need a plan."

Ryan chuckled, a lightness breaking through the tension. "A plan? You mean I can't just charge in like a knight in shining armor?"

"Not unless you want to add 'overzealous idiot' to your resume," I shot back, feigning sternness. "We're not just dealing with family drama here. This could get complicated—and messy."

"I thrive in chaos," he said with a playful grin. "But okay, let's strategize. What's our first move?"

"First, we need more information on Clara—who she was, who she knew, and where she might have gone. Let's hit up some public records, maybe even dig through old newspapers." I felt a rush of determination, ignited by the thought of peeling back layers of secrets. "And we need to find someone who knew her, someone who might still be around."

"Sounds like we're gearing up for a treasure hunt," he replied, his eyes sparkling with mischief. "But instead of gold coins, we might find a family scandal or two."

"Or a ghost," I said, my voice low, trying to keep the mood light despite the seriousness of our mission.

"Perfect," he said, squeezing my hand gently. "I've always wanted a ghost to haunt my family. Maybe we'll find Clara and she can finally set the record straight."

With laughter lingering in the air, we began our search. Over the next few days, our routine transformed into a whirlwind of research sessions at the library and late-night brainstorming marathons at my apartment, fueled by copious amounts of coffee and our shared determination to unearth the truth. I delved into public records, combing through old newspaper articles, while Ryan scoured online forums, searching for any mention of Clara's name.

One evening, as we hunched over my kitchen table, surrounded by stacks of papers and empty coffee cups, I found a particularly intriguing article from nearly a decade ago. It detailed the mysterious circumstances surrounding Clara's disappearance, highlighting the family's insistence that she had run away. But hidden within the text was a small note, a whisper of a sighting at a downtown bar just weeks after she had vanished.

"Ryan," I said, excitement bubbling up within me. "Look at this! There was a sighting of Clara at a bar not too far from here, just a few weeks after she disappeared. This could be the lead we need."

He leaned in closer, his breath hitching slightly. "Where?"

"The Blue Moon Tavern. It's an old place—probably hasn't changed much in years."

"Let's go," he said, his voice sharp with purpose.

The tavern, nestled in a quieter part of Nashville, looked as though it had been plucked from a different era. Dimly lit, with faded photographs lining the walls and a jukebox in the corner playing soft country tunes, it carried an air of faded glory. As we entered, the scent of aged wood and spilled beer enveloped us, evoking memories of old stories waiting to be told.

I scanned the room, my heart racing. "Now what?" I asked, nervous energy crackling between us. "Do we just start asking random people if they've seen a ghost?"

"Why not?" Ryan quipped, his eyes twinkling. "I'm sure it'll go over well."

We made our way to the bar, taking seats and ordering drinks. The bartender, a grizzled man with a face weathered by time, wiped down the counter with a rag that looked like it had seen better days. "What can I get for you?" he asked, eyeing us suspiciously.

"Just some beers, please," I said, flashing a smile. "We're looking for someone who used to come here. A woman named Clara."

The bartender's expression shifted, and I could almost see the gears turning in his mind. "Clara, huh? Can't say I remember anyone by that name."

Ryan leaned in, his voice casual but probing. "We've heard she might've been here around the time she disappeared. Any chance you could tell us about the clientele back then?"

The bartender hesitated, his gaze flickering toward the far end of the bar, where a group of rough-looking patrons sat. "People come and go, but it's a small town. Everyone knows everyone's business... or at least they think they do."

Ryan followed his gaze, and I sensed a shift in the atmosphere, a thickening of tension. "Maybe someone over there knows more," he murmured, nodding toward the group.

"Should we?" I asked, a mix of apprehension and excitement churning in my stomach.

"Absolutely," he said, his determination infectious.

As we approached the group, a palpable tension filled the air, the kind that signals secrets lurking just beneath the surface. I could feel my heart pounding, each beat echoing the gravity of what we were about to uncover.

"Excuse me," I said, summoning my best bravado, "we're looking for information about someone named Clara. We heard she might have come here a while back."

One of the men turned to us, a skeptical look on his face. "What's it to you?" he grunted, sizing us up as if we were intruders in a realm we didn't belong.

Ryan stepped forward, a glint of defiance in his eyes. "We're just trying to piece together what happened. She's family."

The man's demeanor shifted, and a flicker of recognition crossed his features. "Family, huh? That's a dangerous word around here."

"What do you mean?" I pressed, my heart racing as I sensed we were on the brink of something big.

Before the man could respond, a sudden commotion erupted from the back of the tavern, causing us all to turn. A door swung open, and a figure stepped through, cloaked in shadows. For a moment, I thought it was just a trick of the light, but as the figure approached, my breath caught in my throat.

It was Clara.

Or at least, the woman who could have been Clara. Her striking features were unmistakable, framed by a cascade of dark hair, but the storm brewing in her eyes told a different story. She moved with an air of confidence that belied her disappearance, and the room fell silent as she surveyed us, her gaze landing squarely on Ryan.

"Why are you looking for me?" she asked, her voice low and steady, each word laced with an undercurrent of danger.

A chill ran down my spine, a cocktail of fear and exhilaration coursing through my veins. The puzzle pieces were falling into place, but they weren't fitting together as I had imagined. Just as Ryan opened his mouth to respond, the tavern door swung wide once more, and another figure stepped inside—a man in a dark suit, his presence commanding and intimidating.

"Clara," he said, his voice smooth but edged with authority. "It's time we had a conversation."

The air grew heavy, and my heart raced as the realization hit me: we had stumbled into a confrontation that could change everything. The stakes had just escalated dramatically, and as I stood there, caught between two worlds, I knew this was only the beginning of a battle that would unravel secrets far darker than I had anticipated.

Chapter 5: The Confession

The air in the hotel room was thick with tension, so palpable it felt as if the walls themselves might start to tremble under the weight of Ryan's words. I could see the turmoil etched in his features, each line of worry etched deeper than the last. His usually charming smile was nowhere in sight, replaced by a grimace that pulled at the corners of his mouth. I had expected the usual banter, the witty quips that flowed like a stream of sweet tea in summer. But instead, I was faced with a tempest of emotions swirling around us.

"Everything's a lie, you know," he began, his voice a low murmur, barely cutting through the silence that enveloped us. "My family... it's all smoke and mirrors." He ran a hand through his hair, a habit I had grown to recognize as a sign of his unease. "You think you know someone, and then you find out they're just a stranger in disguise."

I leaned forward, my heart racing with a mixture of concern and curiosity. "What do you mean? What's going on?" My voice was steady, but inside, I was reeling. There was an urgency in his eyes that suggested this was no casual revelation. He was ready to lay bare the skeletons of his past, and I could either brace myself or be swept away.

"My father... he didn't just leave," Ryan confessed, his voice cracking under the strain. "He disappeared. Vanished without a trace. They said it was an accident, but my mother never spoke of him again. Not once." He paused, swallowing hard, as if the weight of those memories were lodged in his throat. "I always thought it was just the way things were. A family's dirty laundry kept hidden, you know? But as I grew older, I learned more. The whispers in the dark, the conversations hushed when I entered the room. My father was involved in things... things I didn't want to believe."

My stomach knotted as I absorbed his words. There was something dark lurking beneath the surface of his family, something that threatened to pull him under, and I found myself wishing I could somehow pull him back to safety. "What things?" I asked, my voice barely above a whisper.

"Money laundering. Smuggling. All of it washed in a tide of betrayal and greed," he said, the bitterness in his tone palpable. "When I was younger, I thought it was just an exaggeration. But then, I started connecting the dots. The shady characters who came to our house, the hushed conversations that would abruptly stop when I walked in. I was too naïve to see it."

"What happened to your father?" I probed gently, knowing I was treading on fragile ground. Ryan's gaze dropped to the floor, and I could see the pain etched in his brow.

"I think he got in too deep," he finally admitted, his voice a barely audible whisper. "He was never one for the family business. He wanted out, and they wouldn't let him go." He looked up, meeting my gaze with eyes that held a storm of grief and anger. "He was trying to protect us, but... well, I guess you can't escape a family like mine."

The weight of his confession settled heavily in the room, pushing out any remnants of lightness. I wanted to comfort him, to reach out and reassure him that he wasn't defined by his father's mistakes, that he could be his own man. But words felt inadequate, and I could only sit in silence, letting the gravity of his situation hang between us.

"I thought I could escape," he continued, his voice now a fierce whisper, filled with determination. "I moved to the city, changed my name, and tried to create a new life. But every time I thought I had outrun it, something would drag me back. Like a noose tightening around my neck." He chuckled, but it was devoid of humor, more a bitter acknowledgment of his reality. "I started to wonder if the family I had tried so hard to distance myself from would ever let me go. And then I met you."

I felt my heart flutter at the weight of his words, though the heaviness still lingered. "Me?" I echoed, my voice tinged with disbelief. "What do I have to do with any of this?"

"You were my escape," he said, a fierce light igniting in his eyes. "For the first time, I felt... free. But now that I've let you in on the truth, I'm terrified of dragging you down with me."

"Ryan," I said, my voice stronger now, "you're not dragging me anywhere. You're facing this head-on, and I want to help you. Whatever it is, we'll figure it out together." I could feel my pulse quickening, adrenaline flooding through me. I had no idea what we were up against, but there was no way I could turn away from him now.

He stared at me, as if searching for something in my expression. "You don't understand what I'm asking of you. This isn't just about me anymore; it's about everything I've tried to escape." His eyes softened, revealing the vulnerability lurking beneath his bravado. "If you're going to be in this with me, you need to know how deep this runs. My family... they don't let go easily. They will come after you. And I can't stand the thought of that."

A chill crept down my spine, and yet I felt a spark of something else—a determination, perhaps? "Then let's confront them," I said, an uncharacteristic boldness spilling from my lips. "Let's face them together."

His expression shifted, caught between surprise and admiration. "You really mean that?"

"I do," I replied, the conviction in my voice surprising even me. "I'm not going anywhere. I've come too far to turn back now."

In that moment, I knew I had made my choice. Whatever storms lay ahead, I would stand by his side. As we stood there, suspended in the gravity of our confessions, I felt an unshakeable bond form between us—woven from shared fears and a fierce resolve to rewrite the narrative we had inherited. The truth hung heavy in the air, but so did the promise of a path forward, one I was determined to walk with him, no matter how treacherous it might be.

The city outside hummed with life, oblivious to the tempest brewing within the confines of our hotel room. My thoughts raced, a chaotic blend of fear and adrenaline fueling my determination. Ryan's confession hung in the air like a thick fog, obscuring everything else, and I couldn't help but wonder what sort of monster lurked in the shadows of his past. He was a man torn between the remnants of a family legacy and the desire to carve out a new identity for himself, one that didn't involve a constant game of deceit.

"Are you sure you want to do this?" he asked, uncertainty flickering across his face. It struck me as oddly endearing, that he could still look at me with such vulnerability after laying bare the skeletons in his closet. "I mean, it's not like I come with a sparkling track record."

"Oh please, you're hardly a walking crime spree," I replied, the corner of my mouth twitching in a half-smile. "I've had my fair share of questionable decisions—like the time I thought I could cook a three-course meal with only a microwave and a bag of frozen peas."

Ryan chuckled, the tension in his shoulders easing slightly. "Is that so? I can see why you're not the poster child for domestic bliss."

"Hey, I still have all my fingers," I countered, gesturing dramatically to emphasize my point. "Besides, if anyone's going to be adventurous in the kitchen, it's going to be me. You should see my rendition of instant ramen; it's a masterpiece of culinary innovation."

His laughter echoed in the small space, breaking through the heaviness of the moment. For a brief instant, it felt like we were simply two people sharing an inside joke, not participants in a drama thick with danger. But as quickly as it arrived, the laughter faded, replaced once more by the weight of the reality we faced.

"So, what's the plan?" Ryan asked, his voice now serious, eyes narrowed as he considered our next move. "We can't just storm into my family's world without a strategy. They're not going to roll out the welcome mat."

"Agreed," I replied, running a hand through my hair as I tried to think clearly. "Maybe we start by gathering some information. You mentioned whispers and rumors—do you have any contacts? Anyone who can help us understand what we're dealing with?"

"Contacts," he echoed, the skepticism evident in his tone. "That's rich. Most of my old acquaintances are either too terrified to speak to me or too deeply entrenched in the family business to offer anything but hollow platitudes. But I do know someone—an old friend of my father's who might have insights."

"Then let's find him," I said, my heart racing at the prospect of diving headfirst into this whirlwind. "We need to know what we're up against."

"Are you really ready for this?" Ryan looked at me, a mix of admiration and concern painted across his face. "It could get messy."

"Messes don't scare me," I replied, my voice firm. "I've faced my own share of chaos, and if I can navigate a disastrous Thanksgiving with my family, I can handle whatever comes next."

He smiled, and for a moment, we both felt a flicker of hope against the encroaching darkness. The connection between us had deepened, transformed from mere flirtation into something undeniably more serious. The reality of our situation loomed large, but so did the fierce bond we were forging.

After a brief discussion, Ryan pulled out his phone, the light illuminating his determined expression as he searched for the number. "His name is Victor. He was my father's confidant—if anyone knows what's really going on, it's him."

The name sent a shiver down my spine. "Victor. Sounds like he should be wearing a monocle and plotting world domination."

"Believe me, he's not far off," Ryan replied, a smirk tugging at his lips. "If he's still as eccentric as I remember, we'll need to be prepared for a long and winding conversation. He has a penchant for storytelling, and half the time, it's impossible to discern fact from fiction."

"Perfect. I love a good story," I said, feeling a tingle of excitement at the thought of untangling the mystery. "Just make sure he doesn't try to rope us into any of his wild schemes. Last thing I need is to accidentally become part of an underground poker ring."

"Noted," Ryan laughed, a lightness returning to his tone. "But be prepared—he can be a bit... unpredictable."

"Unpredictable? My middle name. I'm practically a professional at embracing the unexpected."

As Ryan dialed the number, I felt a thrill of anticipation rush through me. This was it. We were stepping off the cliff together, ready to explore the abyss. The phone rang, each tone echoing in the silence of the room, wrapping around us like a string of fate drawing us closer to the truth.

"Victor, it's Ryan," he said as the call connected, his voice steady despite the nerves prickling at the back of his mind. "I need your help."

I watched him intently, taking in the subtle nuances of his expressions as he spoke. The way his brow furrowed, the slight tightening of his jaw—each movement told a story, revealing the layers of fear and resolve hidden just beneath the surface.

"Yeah, it's about my father," he continued, the gravity of his words hanging heavily in the air. "There's something I need to know... something that could change everything."

As the conversation unfolded, I felt the weight of the moment settle around us like a protective cocoon. With every word exchanged, we were inching closer to a revelation that could unravel the tangled web of secrets binding Ryan's family. I could sense the change in his posture, a flicker of hope igniting within him as Victor began to share information—pieces of the puzzle that could finally bring clarity to the chaos.

My heart pounded in rhythm with his words, a steady beat underscoring the gravity of our mission. Together, we were on the precipice of something monumental, a thrilling plunge into the unknown, each word drawing us deeper into a world fraught with danger and intrigue. I felt alive in ways I hadn't imagined possible, fueled by the adrenaline of what lay ahead.

As Ryan hung up the phone, a spark of determination ignited in his eyes. "He's willing to meet. Tonight," he said, a mixture of excitement and apprehension lacing his tone. "This is it, isn't it?"

I nodded, the thrill of the unknown surging through me. "Let's find out what Victor knows. I'm ready."

And as we prepared to step into the night, hand in hand, I knew we were entering a world that would challenge everything we believed about ourselves—and each other. With each passing moment, we were no longer just two individuals caught in a tangled web of lies; we were partners in a dangerous dance, ready to confront whatever awaited us on the other side.

The city glimmered like a sea of stars beneath us as we stepped into the night, the air charged with an electric anticipation. I felt a rush of adrenaline coursing through my veins, the thrill of what was to come battling against the trepidation gnawing at the edges of my mind. Side by side, we moved through the bustling streets, the lights casting playful shadows that danced along the pavement. Ryan's hand brushed against mine, and I was acutely aware of how the warmth of his touch sent ripples of courage through me.

"Do you think Victor will be on his best behavior?" I asked, glancing at Ryan with a wry smile. "Or should I bring a referee's whistle?"

"Considering his track record, I'd say it's wise to be prepared for anything," Ryan replied, his eyes sparkling with a mixture of humor and apprehension. "He has this habit of spilling secrets like they're confetti at a birthday party—only it's never the fun kind."

I chuckled, my laughter blending with the symphony of city sounds—horns honking, people chatting, the faint strains of music from a nearby bar. "Well, if he starts tossing out bombshells, I hope you've got some popcorn ready. I'm not missing this show."

As we approached a small, nondescript café tucked between two towering buildings, the atmosphere shifted. The café's sign, a faded green, creaked as it swung gently in the breeze, and the windows glowed with a warm, inviting light. It was an unassuming place, the kind where secrets could easily slip through the cracks and vanish into the night.

"Here we are," Ryan said, pausing at the door. He took a deep breath, the kind that spoke of unspoken fears and lingering doubts. "Ready?"

"More than ever," I replied, my heart racing as I pushed the door open, the bell above it chiming softly. Inside, the smell of freshly brewed coffee mingled with the sweet scent of pastries, wrapping around us like a comforting blanket.

Victor was already seated at a corner table, his figure shrouded in shadow. As we approached, he looked up, revealing a face lined with age and wisdom, eyes sharp and calculating. His hair, a wild tangle of gray, framed a face that seemed both inviting and intimidating.

"Ryan," he greeted, his voice low and gravelly. "You've grown. I barely recognized you."

"Victor, this is—" Ryan began, but I interrupted, feeling a rush of confidence.

"Hello, I'm [Your Name], Ryan's unofficial sidekick for this adventure." I extended my hand, and he took it with a firm grip, a hint of a smile curling at the corners of his lips.

"Sidekick, you say? Interesting choice of words. You must be quite brave," he said, studying me with a keen gaze that felt as if it could see straight into my soul.

"Or foolish," I countered, shrugging lightly. "It's a fine line, really."

Ryan chuckled, the tension in his shoulders easing just a notch. "We're here to talk about my father and the past," he said, his tone shifting back to seriousness.

Victor leaned back in his chair, fingers steepled beneath his chin. "Ah, the past. It has a way of creeping back in, doesn't it? Like an unwelcome guest who refuses to leave."

Ryan's jaw tightened as he locked eyes with Victor. "I need answers. About his disappearance. The family business. Everything."

"Not everything is meant to be uncovered, you know," Victor warned, his tone somber. "There are layers to this, many of which may best remain hidden."

"But I can't live in the shadows anymore," Ryan replied, his voice tinged with frustration. "I deserve to know the truth."

Victor studied him for a long moment, and I could feel the weight of their shared history hanging in the air. "Very well," he finally said, leaning forward. "But understand that the truth can be a double-edged sword. It can cut deep."

"Tell me," Ryan pressed, his voice unwavering.

Victor inhaled deeply, as if summoning the courage to reveal long-buried secrets. "Your father was involved in matters far darker than you can imagine. He wanted to extricate himself from that life, but it wasn't that simple. There are families who don't take kindly to traitors."

"What do you mean?" I interjected, sensing the shift in the atmosphere. "What families?"

"The kind that don't forgive and certainly don't forget," Victor replied cryptically. "The kind that see betrayal as a stain that must be washed clean, by any means necessary."

The weight of his words hung heavily in the air. I glanced at Ryan, who seemed to wrestle with a whirlwind of emotions—anger, confusion, and a determination that sparked like wildfire in his eyes. "So my father's disappearance was—"

"Deliberate," Victor interrupted, his gaze piercing. "He wanted to protect you, Ryan. But he also knew that to break free, he would need to make sacrifices. It's a dangerous game, and the stakes are higher than you realize."

A chill ran down my spine as the implications of Victor's words sunk in. "And now you're saying this danger is coming for him?" I asked, my heart racing.

Victor nodded slowly. "They know you're back, Ryan. They will come for what they see as theirs—one way or another."

Panic fluttered in my chest, and I felt the room close in around us. "What do we do?" I blurted out, looking between the two men. "How do we stop this?"

"We don't," Ryan said, his voice grim. "We face it."

"Face it?" I echoed incredulously. "That's your big plan? Just stand there and wait for trouble to knock down the door?"

"I'm not running anymore," Ryan declared, his eyes fierce with resolve. "I won't let them dictate my life."

Victor leaned back, a faint smile breaking through his serious demeanor. "You've inherited more than just a legacy of chaos, Ryan. You've inherited strength, and it appears that strength has found a new ally." He glanced at me, an acknowledgment of my role in this tangled mess.

"Just to be clear," I said, crossing my arms, "I didn't sign up for a duel with a criminal empire. I thought we were having coffee and pastries."

"Life is full of surprises," Ryan replied, a glimmer of mischief flashing in his eyes, a hint of the banter we had shared earlier. "Consider this a caffeinated adventure."

Before I could respond, a loud crash echoed through the café, the door slamming open as a group of men stormed in. They moved with the confidence of wolves, their eyes scanning the room until they landed on our table. My heart raced, and I instinctively took a step closer to Ryan, feeling the tension in the air thicken like fog.

"Speak of the devil," Victor muttered, his expression shifting to one of grim acknowledgment. "It seems the past has finally come knocking."

The lead man, tall and imposing, locked eyes with Ryan, a smirk twisting his lips. "Well, well, look who decided to play house. Didn't think you'd have the guts to show your face again."

"Do you know these people?" I whispered to Ryan, my pulse quickening as they advanced toward us.

He shook his head, his jaw clenched tight. "No. But they know me."

As they closed in, I could feel the air crackling with danger, the atmosphere teetering on the edge of chaos. "What do we do?" I hissed, panic rising in my chest.

"Stay behind me," Ryan ordered, but before I could even process his words, the leader leaned over the table, his gaze icy and menacing.

"It's time to come home, Ryan. You've been missed."

And with that, the world around us faded into the background as the storm of Ryan's past collided with the present, leaving no escape route in sight.

Chapter 6: A Leap of Faith

The cabin nestled in the mountains wrapped around us like a comforting quilt, its wooden beams warm with the glow of a crackling fire. Outside, the autumn leaves swirled in a dance of vibrant golds and fiery reds, each gust of wind creating a symphony of rustling whispers. Inside, the air was thick with the scent of pine and woodsmoke, mingling with the lingering aroma of the chili we'd cooked together earlier. I leaned back against the worn leather couch, its creaking under my weight somehow grounding, while Ryan sprawled next to me, his presence a comforting heat radiating into the cool evening.

"Did you ever think about running away?" I asked, stirring the pot of conversation, my curiosity piqued by the shadows that flickered across his face. The question floated between us, a tentative bridge to the deeper waters I longed to explore.

He turned to me, his hazel eyes catching the firelight, illuminating secrets I could almost reach out and touch. "Every day," he replied, a grin tugging at the corners of his mouth. "But then I'd have to leave behind all this." He gestured dramatically, his arms wide, encompassing the cabin, the mountains, and the undeniable tension crackling in the air between us.

"Oh, yes, all this," I chuckled, gesturing back to the rustic charm of our surroundings. "A life of solitude and questionable internet access." I raised an eyebrow, feigning seriousness. "What more could one want?"

Ryan laughed, a sound that sent a ripple of warmth through me. "True. But it's not just the lack of Wi-Fi. It's..." He hesitated, as if weighing the gravity of his thoughts. "It's the freedom, the simplicity. Sometimes it feels like everything back home is just... too much."

His words resonated within me, reverberating through the hollows of my own chaotic life. "I get that," I said softly, my fingers absently tracing the fraying edge of the couch. "But it's scary to think about running away. What if you never come back?"

"Then it's a risk worth taking," he said, his voice dropping to a husky murmur, sending shivers down my spine. "You know, if you never leap, you'll never know how far you can fly." The air hung heavy with the implication of his words, thick with unspoken promises and lingering doubts.

In that moment, I saw a glimpse of the man he could be. Beneath the layers of pain and the shadows of his past, there was an earnestness that shone through. It made me want to peel back those layers, to discover the beauty hidden beneath the scars. But the idea of leaping, of letting go of my own carefully constructed boundaries, sent a rush of fear coursing through me.

"What if we leap together?" I suggested, my voice barely above a whisper, barely believing the words that tumbled from my lips. My heart raced as I spoke, uncertainty gnawing at the edges of my resolve. It was the kind of spontaneity that could lead to disaster or the kind of connection I had only ever dreamed of.

His eyes widened, the surprise evident on his face. "Together?" he repeated, his brow furrowing in thought. "What does that even mean?"

I shrugged, feigning nonchalance, though my heart pounded like a drum in my chest. "I don't know. Maybe we could just... let go of our pasts for a night. No expectations. Just... us." The words hung between us, a fragile thread that could snap under the weight of reality.

He studied me, the flickering firelight illuminating his features, deepening the shadows beneath his cheekbones. "You really think we can just forget?" His tone was skeptical, yet there was a hint of something more—hope, perhaps?

"Maybe not forget," I replied, my voice stronger now, "but we can choose not to let it define us, at least for tonight." The thought of escaping into this moment was intoxicating, a siren's call luring me deeper into the labyrinth of his gaze.

Ryan was quiet for a moment, the crackling of the fire filling the silence. Then he leaned closer, his warmth enveloping me, and for a heartbeat, I could see the walls around him beginning to crack. "Alright," he said finally, a playful grin breaking across his face. "But if we're leaping, we have to do it properly."

"Define properly," I challenged, my heart fluttering with anticipation.

He glanced around, as if the cabin held the secrets to our escape. "Let's make a pact," he said, his expression suddenly serious. "No past, no future—just tonight. We laugh, we dance, we—" He paused, mischief lighting his eyes. "We throw caution to the wind and embrace every ridiculous moment. Deal?"

"Deal," I echoed, matching his grin with one of my own, excitement bubbling in my chest like the first sip of hot cocoa on a snowy day. The thought of letting go felt like standing at the edge of a cliff, the vast expanse below calling to me with promises of freedom and exhilaration.

As the fire crackled and the shadows danced along the walls, I knew we were about to cross an invisible line, leaving behind the weight of our pasts for a fleeting moment of connection. I could feel the air thickening with possibilities, the night stretching before us like an uncharted territory filled with potential.

In that moment, I was ready to leap.

The pact hung in the air, electric and thrilling, as we leaned into the unknown. Ryan stood up, his tall frame casting a long shadow against the flickering firelight. "Alright, let's begin," he declared, an exaggerated flourish accompanying his words as if he were a game show host unveiling the grand prize. "First, we need music. No cabin experience is complete without a proper soundtrack."

I laughed, shaking my head at his enthusiasm. "And what kind of music do you think fits this rustic retreat? Bluegrass? Heavy metal?"

He shot me a playful glare, feigning offense. "Please. This is a moment of recklessness, not a barn dance. I was thinking more along the lines of '90s pop. It has a certain... nostalgic energy, don't you think?"

With that, he grabbed my phone, scrolled through my playlist, and soon the room was filled with the upbeat strains of a familiar tune. The song was catchy, instantly transporting me back to my teenage years, a time when every moment felt larger than life. Ryan started swaying, his movements uncoordinated yet endearing, as if he was both fully aware of his lack of rhythm and blissfully unbothered by it.

"What are you doing?" I asked, stifling a giggle.

"Dancing, obviously. You don't get to set the stage and then sit there like a wallflower," he said, gesturing for me to join him. "Come on! The more ridiculous, the better."

I hesitated for just a moment, my instincts screaming about how foolish I would look, but then I caught a glimpse of his beaming smile. It was infectious. With a deep breath, I rose from the couch and moved toward him, letting the music take over. Our bodies collided in a chaotic whirl of laughter and flailing limbs, both of us losing ourselves in the absurdity of it all.

As we twirled and stumbled, I caught Ryan's eye, and for a split second, everything else faded away. The weight of his past, the challenges I faced at work, the uncertainty that had been my constant companion—none of it mattered. It was just him and me, two imperfect beings trying to dance our way through the chaos of life.

"Who knew you had such a terrible sense of rhythm?" I teased, dodging his outstretched hand as he attempted to spin me.

He shrugged, pretending to be deeply offended. "Just means I'm passionate. It's not about how you move; it's about how you feel." He struck a dramatic pose, hand on his chest, eyes closed as if he were channeling the spirit of a true artist.

"Ah, yes. The art of flailing," I said, rolling my eyes playfully. "Truly, a gift you have."

"Enough banter! I'll show you my true moves!" he proclaimed, launching into a series of ridiculous dance moves that would have made any self-respecting dancer cringe. I doubled over in laughter, clutching my stomach, and that was when I realized just how good it felt to let go of my inhibitions.

With a final flourish, Ryan landed in a low, exaggerated bow, and I clapped for him, my laughter echoing off the cabin walls. "Bravo! A standing ovation for the maestro!" I called, and he laughed, the sound bright and genuine, a balm to the tension that usually clung to him.

Breathless and grinning, I sank back onto the couch, the fire casting a golden glow around us, illuminating the warmth that blossomed in my chest. Ryan joined me, flopping down with a theatrical sigh. "I may not have conquered the dance floor, but I'm pretty sure I just conquered your heart."

"Bold claim, Mr. McAllister," I replied, nudging him with my shoulder. "But I think I'm still in the process of evaluating your dance prowess."

"Evaluating, huh?" he mused, turning to face me, his expression suddenly serious, though the mischief never quite left his eyes. "Well, if I'm going to win your heart, I'd better step up my game."

I raised an eyebrow. "And how do you plan to do that? More dance moves? Because that could get dangerous."

"No, I have a better idea," he said, his voice dropping to a conspiratorial whisper. "How about a midnight adventure?"

My heart raced at the thought. "What kind of adventure?"

He leaned closer, his breath warm against my ear, sending tingles down my spine. "A scavenger hunt. I've heard tales of an old lookout point that's supposed to have the best view of the stars. We can make it our mission to find it. Just think about it: the stars, the quiet, maybe a little hot chocolate... and no cell reception."

"Now that sounds tempting," I admitted, the idea sparking excitement in my chest. "But do we even know where to look?"

Ryan smirked. "A true adventurer never needs a map. We'll just follow the moon."

I laughed, feeling the thrill of spontaneity wash over me. "Alright, let's do this. But if we get lost and end up in the woods with bears, I'm holding you responsible."

"Deal!" he said, springing to his feet. "But if we run into bears, it's your job to distract them with your superior dancing skills."

We grabbed flashlights, bundled up in our jackets, and stepped outside into the crisp night air, the stars twinkling above like a million scattered diamonds. The path was rugged and uneven, but each step felt lighter, each breath filled with the crispness of the mountain air.

As we trekked deeper into the woods, the sounds of the cabin faded away, replaced by the rustling leaves and the distant calls of nocturnal creatures. I felt alive, exhilarated by the chill of the night and the warmth of Ryan's presence beside me.

"Look!" he said suddenly, pointing to a clearing ahead. "There's the lookout!"

We hurried toward it, my heart racing with anticipation. As we emerged into the clearing, I gasped. The view was breathtaking. The valley stretched out before us, the moon casting a silvery glow over the landscape, illuminating the trees and the rolling hills like a magical tapestry.

Ryan stepped closer, his shoulder brushing against mine. "It's incredible," he said, his voice barely above a whisper. "Like a scene from a dream."

I nodded, awash in the beauty of the moment. "It really is. Thank you for bringing me here."

He turned to me, his eyes serious now, a contrast to the lightness we'd just shared. "I'm glad you're here. You make the world feel a little less heavy."

The sincerity of his words hung in the air, and for a brief moment, I felt the weight of unspoken truths pressing down on us. The night was still, the stars twinkling overhead, and I knew that beneath the laughter and adventure lay a deeper connection waiting to be unraveled.

The moon hung low in the sky, a luminous sentinel watching over us as we stood in the clearing, enveloped in the beauty of the moment. I could feel the electricity between us crackling in the stillness, a tangible reminder of the connection that had grown between laughter and shared vulnerabilities. Ryan's gaze searched mine, as if he were trying to decipher the tangled web of thoughts swirling in my mind.

"Do you think it's really possible to escape our pasts?" he asked suddenly, his voice breaking the silence like a pebble dropped in a pond, sending ripples through the air.

I paused, contemplating the weight of his question. "Maybe not entirely. But we can choose how much power it holds over us." My words felt brave, but uncertainty lingered just beneath the surface.

Ryan nodded slowly, processing my response. "That's a comforting thought, isn't it?" He shifted closer, the warmth radiating from him a soothing balm against the cool night. "You know, I've spent so long feeling like I'm trapped in a cage of my own making. But tonight..." He took a deep breath, as if to draw in the essence of freedom around us. "Tonight feels different."

A rush of something unnameable surged through me, a mixture of hope and fear, as I searched his eyes. "We can make it different," I said, more to convince myself than him. The gravity of our conversation anchored us, a stark contrast to the lightness we had shared earlier.

"Let's make a pact," he suggested, his eyes sparkling with mischief again, a welcome change from the heaviness of our previous exchange. "From this moment on, we leave the past behind us. We focus on now."

"Now?" I echoed, a smile creeping onto my face. "That's a pretty tall order, don't you think?"

"Maybe. But we've already made it this far. We can handle anything else that comes our way," he replied, a confidence in his tone that was impossible to resist.

"Alright, let's do it. No past, no future—just us." My words felt like a bridge, a promise of shared adventure and uncharted territory.

As we stood side by side, our breath mingling in the chilly night air, the stars above twinkled with a kind of magic that seemed to affirm our commitment. I wanted to believe in the power of that promise, to shed the shadows of what had been, but just as I was caught up in the warmth of our newfound resolve, a faint rustling noise broke the tranquility of the moment.

"What was that?" I asked, my heart skipping a beat as I turned toward the sound.

Ryan tensed beside me, the playful glint in his eyes replaced by an alertness that sent a chill down my spine. "I don't know," he murmured, scanning the darkness. "Maybe it's just an animal. We're in the woods, after all."

"Right, just a bear looking to join our little midnight adventure," I said, attempting to inject humor into the tension, though my voice wavered slightly. "I mean, I'm sure they love pop music too."

Ryan chuckled softly, but the laugh was edged with apprehension. "Okay, how about we take a step back? Just in case it's not a bear. Or if it is, you know, for my safety."

"Always the gentleman," I teased lightly, but the unease gripped me tighter as we cautiously backed away from the clearing, our gazes fixed on the shadows that danced just beyond the treeline.

As we retreated, the rustling grew louder, an unsettling sound that resonated with the pounding of my heart. "This is definitely not what I had in mind for an adventure," I whispered, half to myself.

Ryan grabbed my hand, his grip firm and reassuring. "Whatever it is, we'll face it together." The conviction in his voice sent a flicker of courage through me, and I took a deep breath, trying to focus on him rather than the unknown lurking in the dark.

Suddenly, a figure emerged from the shadows—a silhouette against the silvery light of the moon. My breath hitched in my throat as I strained to see who—or what—it was. The shape stepped forward, and a familiar chill of recognition washed over me.

"Jack?" I gasped, disbelief washing over me in waves. It was my ex, the very last person I expected to see in this remote place. He looked different—more rugged, perhaps, with a wildness in his eyes that seemed at odds with the boy I once knew.

"Fancy running into you here," Jack said, his voice laced with sarcasm as he glanced between Ryan and me. "I thought you were done with this place."

"What are you doing here?" I asked, my heart racing. The question came out sharper than intended, but I couldn't help it. His presence felt like a storm cloud rolling in on a clear day, threatening to shatter the fragile peace we had built.

"Just passing through," he replied, his gaze flickering to Ryan, a knowing smirk creeping across his lips. "And I see you've made some interesting friends."

I could feel Ryan's body tense beside me, the air thickening with unspoken tension. "We don't want any trouble, Jack," Ryan said, his voice steady but his eyes narrowed, protective instinct flaring to life.

"Trouble?" Jack laughed, a sound that sent a shiver down my spine. "I'm not here to cause trouble. I just came to see how my favorite girl is doing."

I rolled my eyes, irritation coursing through me. "I'm not your favorite anything anymore."

"Oh, really?" he shot back, crossing his arms as he leaned casually against a tree. "You used to love this place, and you used to love hanging out with me. Funny how things change."

"You don't know anything about me now," I retorted, my heart racing as I glanced at Ryan, who stood resolute beside me, a silent strength radiating from him.

"Maybe I know more than you think," Jack replied, his tone shifting, darkness creeping into his words. "Maybe you're not as far away from your past as you'd like to believe."

Ryan's grip on my hand tightened, and I could feel the tension simmering, like a tightrope pulled taut between us and Jack. I needed to defuse this situation, to reclaim the lightness we had just begun to explore. "You should leave, Jack. This isn't the time or place for your games," I urged, my voice steady despite the chaos swirling inside me.

His smirk faltered for a moment, but it quickly returned, colder, more dangerous. "Games? You think this is a game? You really don't know me at all, do you? You're the one who walked away, and now you want to pretend everything's fine? That you've moved on?"

The words stung, a knife twisting in an old wound, and I felt my resolve begin to crumble. But before I could respond, Ryan stepped forward, his presence a solid wall between Jack and me. "You need to leave her alone, Jack. She's not interested in your past games anymore."

Jack's laughter rang out, harsh and discordant. "Oh, really? You think you can protect her? Just because you're here for a weekend doesn't mean you understand her. She'll always be tangled up in the past, whether you like it or not."

The air crackled with tension, and I could feel the walls closing in, the shadows around us stretching like fingers ready to pull me back into a darkness I had fought so hard to escape.

I stood frozen between them, caught in the whirlwind of conflicting emotions, uncertainty gnawing at my insides. In that moment, I realized the battle was not just about Ryan and Jack—it was about me, my choices, and the life I wanted to claim for myself.

As I opened my mouth to respond, the ground shifted beneath us, and a deafening crack split the night air. The ground trembled, and the trees swayed ominously, a reminder that sometimes the past doesn't just linger—it threatens to consume you whole.

Chapter 7: Haunted by the Truth

The moment we stepped off the plane, Nashville wrapped itself around me like a heavy fog. The humidity clung to my skin, a sticky reminder that summer refused to let go. I could feel the pulse of the city thumping in my chest, and it wasn't just the sound of distant honky-tonk music mingling with the chatter of travelers. It was something darker lurking beneath the surface, a sinister undertow that made my heart race. Ryan walked beside me, his hand brushing against mine, grounding me as we emerged from the airport and into the chaos of downtown.

The sun dipped low on the horizon, casting a warm glow over Broadway, where neon lights blinked invitingly, and the smell of fried food and spilled beer wafted through the air. It should have felt like home—a familiar refuge where we shared laughter and late-night secrets. But now, every smile felt brittle, every sound edged with tension. I glanced at Ryan, who had grown more silent since our return, his brow furrowed as we passed by the familiar honky-tonks, a vibrant world suddenly dimmed by shadows.

As we strolled past Tootsie's Orchid Lounge, its iconic purple exterior gleaming, I felt the weight of Ryan's worries pressing down on us like the approaching storm clouds. The chatter of tourists faded into a low hum, and for a brief moment, it was just us, standing at the intersection of who we were and who we could be. But the moment didn't last. The looming figure of Ryan's brother, Josh, appeared at the edge of the street, his expression taut. The sight of him sent a chill rippling through me.

"Hey, you two!" Josh called out, his voice carrying a sharp edge, slicing through the air. I braced myself for the impending confrontation. Ryan stiffened beside me, his jaw tightening as he forced a smile that didn't reach his eyes.

"Josh," he said, the name slipping out like an apology.

"What are you doing with her?" Josh's gaze flicked to me, his disdain evident. I felt the heat rise in my cheeks, a cocktail of embarrassment and indignation. "You know how Mom and Dad feel about this."

"Can we talk about this later?" Ryan replied, his tone calm but firm, as if trying to defuse a ticking bomb. I held my breath, waiting for the inevitable explosion.

"No, we can't," Josh insisted, stepping closer. "You're making a mistake. You know how they think. This isn't just about you. It's about family." His voice dropped, a low growl that sent shivers down my spine.

I watched as Ryan's frustration bubbled to the surface. "You don't get to decide that for me, Josh." The defiance in his voice was a fragile shield against the onslaught of his brother's expectations. I wanted to reach out, to place my hand on his arm and remind him that he didn't have to shoulder this burden alone. But the storm was brewing, and I was merely a bystander in this family drama.

"You think you can just waltz in here and turn your back on everything? On us?" Josh's voice rose, drawing the attention of passersby. Their curious glances felt like daggers, the weight of judgment heavy on my shoulders.

"Enough," Ryan snapped, his voice cutting through the tension like a knife. The air crackled between them, thick with unspoken words and lingering resentment. "I'm not asking for your approval, and I'm done feeling guilty about who I choose to spend my time with."

With that, Josh's expression hardened, the façade of brotherly concern cracking under the weight of his anger. "You'll regret this," he spat before turning sharply and stalking away, his footsteps echoing down the sidewalk, a haunting reminder of the familial loyalty that had suddenly become a threat.

I let out a shaky breath, the adrenaline coursing through my veins as I turned to Ryan. "You didn't have to say that," I whispered, my heart aching for him.

Ryan ran a hand through his hair, the frustration melting into exhaustion. "But I had to. I can't let them dictate my life. Not anymore." He looked at me, and in his gaze, I found both vulnerability and strength. "I want you to know how much this means to me."

Just then, my phone buzzed in my pocket, pulling me from the moment. I fished it out, and my stomach dropped as I read the anonymous message on the screen. Stay away from him. This is your only warning. The words hit me like a slap, cold and jarring, shattering the fragile peace we had managed to create.

I blinked, unsure how to respond, and looked back at Ryan. "I—" But the words lodged in my throat. How could I explain this new fear that coiled around my heart like a serpent? Instead, I shoved the phone back into my pocket, willing myself to be strong.

"We should get out of here," I said finally, my voice steady despite the tremor in my hands.

"Yeah," Ryan agreed, glancing around as if searching for unseen threats. "Let's go home."

The ride back to his apartment was filled with an uneasy silence. The city that had once felt alive now pulsed with hidden dangers, a vibrant mask for the shadows lurking beneath. The streets blurred past us, each familiar turn now unfamiliar and fraught with tension. As we pulled into the parking lot, I noticed a figure loitering near the entrance, their face obscured by a hoodie. My heart raced, dread pooling in my stomach.

"Do you see that?" I pointed, my voice barely a whisper.

Ryan's expression darkened, his protective instincts flaring. "Stay close to me." He stepped out of the car, and I followed, anxiety gnawing at my insides. The figure turned, and for a fleeting moment, our eyes met before they slipped into the shadows, disappearing like a ghost.

We hurried to the building, the weight of our fears hanging in the air. I felt the tension between us, the unspoken words dancing just out of reach. Ryan opened the door, and as I stepped inside, the warmth of his apartment wrapped around me like a cocoon. But even here, I couldn't shake the feeling of being watched, the gnawing anxiety coiling tighter with every heartbeat.

I stood there, torn between fear and determination. I was in love with Ryan, and walking away was not an option. But the truth weighed heavily on my shoulders, and as the shadows deepened around us, I knew the battle was just beginning.

The apartment felt stifling as we stepped inside, the air heavy with unspoken words. Ryan leaned against the kitchen counter, arms crossed, the tension in his body an echo of my own. I stood at the threshold, half-tempted to retreat to the safety of the hallway, where the world felt just a little less complicated. My phone buzzed again, vibrating against my thigh, and I could almost hear the taunting laughter of the universe in that single sound.

I glanced at the screen, my heart thudding like a bass drum, and the message was there, as chilling as before: You should have stayed away. It's not too late to leave. I exhaled sharply, my breath hitching in my throat. Ryan looked up, catching the anxiety that had settled on my face.

"What is it?" he asked, the calm in his voice contrasting sharply with the storm brewing inside me. I wanted to be honest, to lay everything out on the table, but the weight of the threats bore down like a leaden shroud, suffocating any sense of clarity.

"Just... a text," I managed, forcing a smile that felt more like a grimace. "Some random spam. You know how it is." The lie tasted bitter, but I held onto it tightly, hoping it would protect him from the darkness that was clawing at the edges of my reality.

"Spam, huh?" Ryan arched an eyebrow, skepticism etched across his face. "I don't like that look. You're not one for random spam." He stepped closer, the distance between us diminishing as the air crackled with electricity. "Tell me what's really going on."

I opened my mouth, but the words tangled up, refusing to come out. Instead, I took a deep breath and attempted to redirect the conversation. "I was thinking we could cook something together. Something that makes us forget the outside world for a while." The idea sounded good, an escape wrapped in a home-cooked meal, but even as I said it, I could see the worry knitting Ryan's brow.

He hesitated, glancing out the window, as if searching for something beyond the glass. "You want to cook? Are you sure you're ready for that?" There was a hint of a smile in his voice, the playful sarcasm lightening the mood ever so slightly.

"Hey, I can handle a box of pasta and a jar of sauce," I replied, hands on my hips, feigning indignation. "But I might need a sous-chef. Do you have any experience with boiling water?"

Ryan chuckled, the sound resonating in the room, a small flicker of normalcy amidst the chaos. "I've been known to boil an egg or two. It's a skill, really."

As he started rummaging through the cabinets, I slipped my phone into my back pocket, determined to leave the ominous messages behind, at least for the moment. It felt good to reclaim a sliver of normalcy, even if it was just boiling pasta.

"So, what's on the menu tonight? Family recipe?" Ryan asked, peering into the depths of the pantry as if expecting to find hidden treasures.

"Definitely a family recipe," I said with mock seriousness. "You see, my family always adds a pinch of chaos and a dash of impending doom."

"Ah, the secret ingredient," he replied, feigning contemplation. "I should have guessed. I knew it was special."

We settled into a rhythm in the kitchen, the sounds of water boiling and the occasional clattering of pots filling the air. With each moment, the weight of outside pressures began to fade, replaced by laughter and light-hearted teasing. Ryan, with his too-big chef's apron—an old relic of a family reunion—looked absurdly adorable as he chopped garlic, a concentration etched into his features.

"Careful there, Gordon Ramsay. Those fingers are for holding hands, not chopping vegetables," I teased, earning a glare that was softened by the smile creeping at the corners of his lips.

"Just trying to impress my date," he said, glancing at me over the edge of the cutting board, mischief dancing in his eyes. "How am I doing?"

"On a scale of one to ten? About a solid seven, but you've still got time to impress me with your culinary skills."

As we stirred the pasta, the laughter flowed freely, yet I felt the flicker of unease beneath the surface. Each glance toward the window reminded me of the lurking threats outside, shadows creeping ever closer. A loud knock at the door jolted me from my reverie, the sound echoing through the apartment like a gunshot.

"Who the hell is that?" Ryan's smile faded, his expression turning serious.

I could feel my heart racing, every instinct screaming that something was off. "Maybe it's just a delivery?" I offered weakly, but deep down, I knew it was more than that.

"Stay here," he instructed, his voice firm as he moved toward the door. I wanted to argue, to insist I wouldn't be left alone, but the look on his face brooked no dissent.

I nodded, biting my lip as I hovered near the counter, the warmth of the stove contrasting sharply with the chill creeping into my bones.

Ryan opened the door slowly, and I caught a glimpse of a man standing there, his silhouette framed by the dim light of the hallway.

He wore a hood that obscured his face, and even from where I stood, I could feel the tension radiating from Ryan as he faced this stranger.

"Can I help you?" Ryan asked, his voice steady but edged with wariness.

The man stepped forward, revealing sharp features and an unsettling grin that sent a chill down my spine. "I'm just here to deliver a message," he said, the words sliding out like a sinister whisper.

I couldn't hear everything, but my breath caught when I saw Ryan's expression shift from confusion to anger. "What do you mean a message? From who?"

The stranger shrugged, the action almost casual, but there was a calculated glint in his eye. "You know who it's from. You should have listened. Now you're both in over your heads."

Before Ryan could respond, I dashed forward, adrenaline propelling me as I stood beside him. "Who sent you?" I demanded, my voice shaky but fierce.

He turned his gaze toward me, and for a moment, I felt an unsettling connection. "You should go home," he said, voice low and dangerous. "This isn't where you belong."

"Home?" I echoed, incredulous. "This is my home now, and I won't let anyone threaten me or him."

Ryan's hand tightened around mine, grounding me as the air thickened with tension. "Get out. Now," he commanded, the heat of his fury cutting through the anxiety that had built like a pressure cooker.

The stranger's smile widened, an expression of amusement dancing in his eyes. "You think you can keep her safe?" He chuckled, the sound hollow. "This is just the beginning."

Without another word, he turned and vanished into the hallway, leaving us standing in the doorway, hearts racing and breaths shallow.

The echo of his words hung between us, ominous and heavy, and I knew in that moment that everything had changed.

"We need to talk," Ryan said quietly, the gravity of the situation settling over us like a dark cloud. I nodded, a silent agreement to face whatever came next together.

The moment Ryan closed the door, the air shifted, thickening with unsaid fears and uncharted territory. I could feel the storm inside him, a tempest of protectiveness mixed with an underlying current of panic. "We need to figure out what's happening," he said, running a hand through his hair as he paced the room. I watched him, each step he took feeling like a beat in a song that was rapidly approaching its crescendo.

"Figuring out what?" I said, my voice sharper than I intended. "That someone is trying to intimidate us? That your family is breathing down our necks? What else is there to figure out?"

Ryan paused, his eyes locking onto mine, dark and stormy. "There's more at play here. It's not just random threats; it's organized. It's personal." He took a deep breath, grounding himself, but I could see the anxiety bubbling just beneath the surface.

"Personal?" I echoed, feeling the hair on the back of my neck stand on end. "What do you mean? Do you think this is coming from your family?"

He ran a hand down his face, the frustration palpable. "They've always been controlling, but I never thought they'd resort to this."

"Do you really think they'd go this far?" I asked, skepticism tinged with disbelief.

Ryan hesitated, his gaze distant as if he were recalling painful memories. "They've always had a way of manipulating situations to get what they want. Maybe they think I'm too far gone, that I'll never come back to them."

A chill crawled down my spine, the reality settling uncomfortably in my gut. "And what do they want? You back? You to end this?"

"Both, I suppose. But it's more than that. They don't want anyone to disrupt their image, to tarnish the perfect family portrait they've spent years crafting. They think I'm ruining everything."

I stepped closer, feeling the urgency of the moment crackling in the air. "And what about what we have? What do you think that is to them?"

"An inconvenience, a blight on their reputation," Ryan replied, his voice low, simmering with anger. "But to me, it's everything."

My heart soared at his words, but the specter of danger loomed large, darkening the corners of my mind. "We can't let them drive us apart," I insisted, determination fueling my voice.

"Then we need to be smart," he said, taking my hands in his, warmth and strength radiating between us. "We have to figure out who sent that guy and what they really want. This isn't just about us anymore."

Before I could respond, my phone buzzed again, an unwelcome intrusion. I hesitated, dread pooling in my stomach, but I knew I had to look. I pulled it out, the screen illuminating my face with the latest threat. You've made a mistake. You won't get another chance. Leave before it's too late.

My heart raced, and I swallowed hard, forcing the bile back down. "They're not backing down, Ryan," I whispered, my voice trembling. "What do we do?"

He took a step closer, his brow furrowing as he processed the weight of the words. "We gather information. We go on the offensive."

"Offensive?" I repeated, incredulous. "How exactly do we do that?"

"By investigating. There has to be a way to find out who's behind this. Maybe there are records, or..." He trailed off, deep in thought, and I could see the gears turning behind his eyes.

"What if we talk to your family?" I suggested, hoping for some semblance of normalcy to return, even if just for a moment. "Maybe they know something."

He shook his head vehemently. "No way. If I confront them, they'll only dig their heels in further. This is our fight now, not theirs."

"Okay," I replied, biting my lip, feeling the weight of uncertainty crash over me. "So we're playing detective, then?"

"Exactly." He pulled away, moving toward the small desk in the corner of the room. "I'll need my laptop. Let's see if we can dig up anything on threats like this."

As he turned his back, I caught my reflection in the window—a shadow of the person I used to be, consumed by fear yet unwilling to cower. This wasn't just about me; it was about Ryan, about standing up against the tidal wave of his family's expectations. "I'll look for any online traces," I said, tapping my phone.

I felt a spark of hope as we began working side by side, the air buzzing with our shared purpose. The dim glow of the laptop screen illuminated our faces as we clicked through endless search results. I could see Ryan's brow furrow deeper as he scrolled through articles about stalking and harassment, his jaw clenched in concentration.

"Here," he said suddenly, pointing to a forum post discussing similar threats, a community rallying against anonymous harassment. "People have been documenting their experiences. Maybe we can find a common thread."

"Good idea," I said, leaning closer, excitement bubbling within me. We dove into the information, each click unveiling stories of resilience and tenacity.

As we sifted through the posts, I felt a shift in the atmosphere—a vibration, like a storm gathering strength just beyond the horizon. My phone buzzed again, the sudden intrusion jolting us both.

"Another message?" Ryan asked, his voice laced with concern.

"No," I said, glancing down. "It's a call. From an unknown number." My heart raced as I debated answering, the instinct to run overwhelming. But curiosity won out, and I swiped to answer.

"Hello?" I said, my voice shaky.

A voice crackled on the other end, low and distorted. "You should have left while you had the chance."

"Who is this?" I shot back, my pulse quickening.

"Does it matter? You're in way over your head. Get out now, while you still can."

The line went dead, leaving me breathless and reeling. I looked at Ryan, my pulse thrumming in my ears. "They're serious. This isn't just some prank."

He stepped closer, his expression darkening, a mix of concern and determination igniting in his eyes. "Then we have to take this seriously. No more playing nice."

I nodded, feeling a fierce adrenaline surge as we both stood in solidarity against the looming shadows. "So what's the plan?"

Ryan hesitated, then smirked, that boyish charm igniting a flicker of courage within me. "First, we need to gather intel. We need to talk to the people who've posted in that forum and find out if they have connections. They may know something."

"Brilliant. We'll be the modern-day Bonnie and Clyde," I said with a laugh, feeling a flicker of defiance.

"More like Bonnie and Clyde with a side of caution," Ryan replied, his voice teasing, but there was an undercurrent of seriousness.

Just then, there was a loud crash outside the window, making us both jump. I rushed to the glass, heart racing as I peered into the street below. My stomach dropped as I spotted a figure lurking near the entrance of the building, their dark hoodie pulled tight against the fading light.

"Ryan," I said, my voice a breathless whisper. "We're not alone."

He rushed to my side, and together we watched as the figure shifted, casting a long shadow that felt impossibly close. "What do we do?" I asked, panic rising like a tidal wave.

"Stay here," he instructed, his voice low but steady. "I'll go check it out."

"No!" I protested, grabbing his arm. "You can't just go out there. It's too dangerous."

"Trust me," he said, meeting my gaze with a fierce intensity. "I can handle this."

And just like that, he was gone, slipping into the hallway, leaving me with the deafening silence and the growing dread that something terrible was about to unfold. I stood there, my heart pounding, torn between wanting to follow him and the instinct to stay hidden.

As I waited, the figure outside shifted again, moving closer, until the sharp outline of a familiar face came into view. My heart raced, confusion spiraling within me.

"Ryan?" I called, my voice trembling, but the figure didn't respond.

The moment stretched, the air thick with tension. I stepped closer to the door, the chill of fear coursing through my veins. The figure turned, and for a fleeting second, I caught sight of his eyes—a glint of recognition that sent shivers down my spine.

I didn't have time to think. The door swung open behind me, and Ryan stepped in, looking pale and shaken. "What's happening?" he asked, glancing nervously at the window.

"I... I think I saw someone," I stammered, my heart racing as I pointed outside.

But before I could finish, the power suddenly flickered, plunging us into darkness. The soft hum of the city faded, replaced by an unsettling silence that felt suffocating.

Ryan moved instinctively to shield me, but the sound of footsteps echoed ominously from the hallway. Panic surged within me, and I squeezed his hand, my heart pounding in my ears. "What's happening?"

And then, a voice rang out from the darkness, chilling and familiar. "Did

Chapter 8: Into the Fire

The air was thick with tension as I navigated the maze of opulent marble floors and extravagant chandeliers hanging from the gilded ceilings of Ryan's family estate. It was a labyrinth designed to impress, but all it did was trap me in a web of privilege and power that threatened to choke me. I could hear the laughter echoing through the hallways, an unsettling blend of joy and malice that twisted my stomach. Each peal of laughter felt like an unspoken challenge, daring me to step further into the fray.

Ryan moved close, his presence a reassuring warmth against the chilly atmosphere that surrounded us. His hand found mine, fingers entwining in a way that felt both intimate and precarious, as if we were two flames dancing too close to the fire. "Just stick by me," he murmured, his voice low and steady, but I could sense the undercurrents of uncertainty that laced his words.

"Easier said than done," I shot back, my tone teasing but my heart racing. I glanced around, catching sight of his family members flitting between groups, their smiles polished but their eyes sharp, scrutinizing every interaction with the precision of hawks. There was a sense of grandeur to their malice, a polished cruelty that made me feel like an unwelcome guest at a banquet of betrayal.

As we approached a lavish sitting room, I overheard snippets of conversation, words laced with subtle insinuations that pricked at my skin. "Did you hear about the article? It's going to shake things up, that's for sure," one voice purred, dripping with intrigue. My heart sank. The article. The one I had poured my soul into, capturing the essence of the city and its underbelly, unknowingly tethering myself to a looming disaster. The truth was a double-edged sword, and I was holding it by the blade.

"Who's writing it?" another voice chimed in, and the laughter that followed felt like shards of glass piercing the air. I turned to

Ryan, searching his face for answers, but he was already staring into the distance, his expression unreadable.

"Ryan?" I pressed, anxiety bubbling in my chest.

He hesitated, and I could almost see the gears turning in his mind. "It's a... sensitive topic. My family doesn't take kindly to having their dirty laundry aired." The gravity of his words hung between us, a weight I could barely comprehend. I was standing at the precipice of a choice that felt both monumental and terrifying.

"Then we have to do something," I said, my voice rising slightly, adrenaline rushing through me. "You can't let them—"

"They'll come for you, you know." His voice was harsh, almost desperate. "If they find out who you are, what you've written..."

I swallowed hard, the implications of his statement settling in. It was a reality I hadn't fully processed, the concept of being a target in a world where power wielded its influence like a finely honed weapon. "And what about you?" I countered, frustration bubbling beneath my skin. "What happens to you if I go through with this?"

"Let's not make it about me right now," he replied, pulling me slightly closer, his breath warm against my ear. "We have to focus on the bigger picture."

"Bigger picture? Ryan, you're talking about a family that destroys lives for fun." I clenched my jaw, feeling the heat of anger rise within me. "What if that life is mine?"

Just then, a figure emerged from the crowd—a woman draped in a stunning crimson dress that clung to her like a second skin, her hair cascading in waves around her shoulders. She glided toward us, an air of authority radiating from her every move. I recognized her immediately; she was Ryan's sister, Elise, the one rumored to have a flair for manipulation that rivaled the finest chess players.

"Ryan," she cooed, a saccharine sweetness in her voice, yet the undertone was unmistakable. "What a lovely evening. I see you've found yourself... a distraction." Her eyes flickered to me, and in that moment, I felt like a prize caught in the crossfire of a rivalry I didn't want to be a part of.

"She's just getting acclimated to the family," Ryan replied smoothly, but the way he positioned himself between us spoke volumes. I could practically hear the tension sizzling in the air.

"Is that what you call it?" Elise's smile was sharp, cutting through the atmosphere like a knife. "I do hope she's not too curious about our affairs. Curiosity can be dangerous, you know." Her eyes bore into mine, and I could feel the weight of her scrutiny. I wanted to shrink back, to disappear into the opulent wallpaper that seemed to envelop us, but I stood my ground.

"I'll keep my curiosity in check, thank you," I shot back, surprising even myself with the defiance that spilled from my lips. There was something exhilarating about pushing back against the force of her gaze, an unspoken challenge that flared between us.

Elise laughed, a sound devoid of genuine amusement. "Oh, darling, you have no idea what kind of fire you're playing with." She leaned closer, lowering her voice conspiratorially. "Remember, in this family, loyalty is everything. Betrayal? It's unforgivable."

I felt Ryan tense beside me, his grip tightening as if to pull me closer to him, to shield me from the onslaught of Elise's words. But there was something in her tone, a warning tinged with amusement that made my skin prickle.

"You'll find your footing, I'm sure," she continued, stepping back, a satisfied smile playing on her lips. "Just be careful not to trip over the lies we've built our lives upon." With that, she glided away, leaving an unsettling silence in her wake.

"Wow," I breathed, my heart racing. "That was... something."

"Welcome to the family," Ryan replied, a wry smile touching his lips, but I could see the flicker of concern in his eyes. The unspoken threat lingered between us, heavy and intoxicating.

"I have to write this article," I said, the determination bubbling within me. "I have to tell the truth. They can't keep hiding behind their walls of deception."

"But at what cost?" Ryan countered, his voice steady but edged with desperation. "What if the truth isn't worth your safety? Or mine?"

In that moment, I realized the stakes were higher than I'd ever anticipated, and the path ahead twisted into shadows I wasn't sure I could navigate. But one thing was clear: I couldn't back down now. I was in too deep, and the fire was already raging.

The night deepened around us, a velvet cloak draped over the mansion, obscuring the sharp edges of its grandeur. I felt the weight of unseen eyes watching every move I made, their scrutiny curling like smoke around my ankles, threatening to trip me at any moment. Ryan and I stepped away from the gilded chaos of his family's celebration, seeking refuge in the farthest corner of the estate, a small balcony overlooking the garden. The moonlight painted everything in shades of silver, and the air was laced with the sweet fragrance of blooming jasmine, masking the tension that crackled between us.

"Are you sure you want to do this?" Ryan asked, his voice low, almost lost in the soft rustle of leaves. He leaned against the balcony railing, his posture relaxed but his eyes betraying a storm of emotions. "I can't stand the thought of you getting hurt because of my family."

"I'm not afraid of your family," I replied, surprised at the conviction that surged within me. "What scares me is what they'll do if I don't write this article. What kind of hold do they have over everyone? How many lives have they ruined?"

Ryan's expression shifted, a flicker of admiration blending with concern. "They're not just my family. They're powerful people in this city. You have no idea what kind of influence they wield. They'll stop at nothing to protect their secrets."

I drew in a sharp breath, the reality of my situation crashing over me like a cold wave. "But if I don't expose them, who will? They can't keep hiding behind this façade. There has to be accountability."

He ran a hand through his hair, the frustration palpable. "Accountability? They have a way of making that word disappear, trust me." He paused, his gaze drifting to the garden below, where shadows danced under the trees. "I don't want to lose you, not to them. You have to promise me you'll be careful."

"Promise?" I scoffed, the tension in my shoulders easing slightly. "I'm not making promises to a man whose family has an arsenal of deception at their disposal. It's like promising not to get wet in the rain."

Ryan's lips twitched into a smile, and for a moment, the heaviness of our reality lifted. "Fair point. But if it comes down to it, I'll protect you."

"By hiding behind me?" I shot back, grinning despite myself. "I'd like to see you try."

He laughed softly, the sound warming the air around us. "Not my proudest moment, I admit. But I'm serious. I'll do whatever it takes."

"Okay, okay," I relented, my heart swelling with affection for him. "But what if I end up needing saving from you? Your family is a force of nature, Ryan. And I'm standing right in the eye of the storm."

"Then I'll be your umbrella," he replied, his eyes sparkling with mischief. "A very fancy, designer umbrella, I promise."

Just as I was about to respond, a sharp voice cut through the night, yanking me back into the cold reality. "Ryan! There you are!" It was Elise, her silhouette emerging from the shadows like a vengeful specter.

"Speak of the devil," I muttered under my breath, rolling my eyes as she approached with that predatory grace.

Ryan straightened, a tension returning to his frame. "Elise, can't you see we're busy?"

"Busy? Is that what we're calling it?" she teased, her eyes narrowing with a mix of amusement and disdain. "I'm sure the entire family would love to know what secrets you're sharing with our guest."

I felt my cheeks flush under her scrutiny, a mix of embarrassment and defiance bubbling beneath the surface. "Just discussing the weather," I said with a straight face, earning a chuckle from Ryan.

Elise raised an eyebrow, unimpressed. "Right. Because we all know that's what you talk about in a place like this." She leaned closer, lowering her voice conspiratorially. "I hope you're not getting any wild ideas. You might find the truth is much more dangerous than you realize."

Her words hung in the air, heavy with a veiled threat that sent a chill racing down my spine. I met her gaze, unwilling to back down. "What kind of truth are we talking about, Elise? The kind that your family buries under all that wealth and influence?"

"Oh, darling, you're clever, I'll give you that," she purred, her smile sharp as glass. "But cleverness only gets you so far in this world. It's the strong who survive."

"Good thing I'm not afraid of a little strength," I shot back, unable to suppress the fire in my words. The tension between us crackled, and for a moment, I felt like a gladiator facing off against a lion in a grand arena.

Elise's lips curled into a smile that didn't quite reach her eyes. "Just remember, it's a family affair, sweetheart. And families don't play fair." With a flick of her wrist, she turned on her heel and sauntered away, leaving behind a lingering sense of unease.

"What a piece of work," I breathed, leaning against the railing for support as the weight of her words pressed down on me.

"She thrives on intimidation," Ryan replied, his voice low. "But don't let her get to you. You have to keep your focus on the story."

"Right," I said, shaking off the remnants of the confrontation. "The story. Just a little expose on a crime family. No big deal."

Ryan's expression darkened, the playful glimmer replaced by a seriousness that unnerved me. "I'm serious, though. This isn't just about an article; it's about survival. They'll do anything to keep their reputation intact."

"Do you think they would hurt me?" My heart raced at the thought, a sickening knot forming in my stomach.

"I don't know, but it's a possibility." His eyes locked onto mine, filled with an intensity that made me shiver. "You need to be careful. If they find out what you're planning... if they discover your intentions..."

"Then what? I run and hide?" I challenged, my voice rising with the swell of my emotions. "That's not who I am, Ryan. I can't just sit back and let them continue their reign of terror. I refuse to live in fear."

"Fear isn't a weakness; it's a survival instinct," he replied, his tone softer now, almost pleading. "You're brave, but bravery doesn't mean being reckless. It's a tightrope walk, and you're dancing on it."

I could feel the resolve in my chest tightening, as if the very air around me was being compressed into a single, undeniable truth. "Then let's walk it together. I can't do this alone. If I'm going to expose them, I need you by my side."

He hesitated, searching my eyes for a flicker of doubt. "You're asking a lot, you know that?"

"I'm asking for honesty," I said firmly. "And for you to help me navigate the fire you've grown up in. If we're going to face this, we face it together."

A tense silence stretched between us, the kind that crackled with unspoken words and shared fears. Finally, he sighed, the weight of his family's legacy bearing down on his shoulders. "Okay. Together, then. But you need to promise me one thing."

"Anything."

"Promise me you'll think before you act. The moment you step into this world, there's no going back."

"I promise," I whispered, even as a flicker of doubt danced in the corners of my mind. Together, we faced the abyss, the fire already raging at our feet, and I couldn't shake the feeling that the dance had only just begun.

The night unfolded around us like a well-orchestrated symphony, but I felt more like a discordant note playing against the harmony of Ryan's world. The party raged on behind us, laughter and clinking glasses resonating with a false cheerfulness that only amplified the tension simmering between us. I leaned against the cool metal railing of the balcony, the cold biting into my skin as if it were a reminder of the stakes at play. "I can't help but feel like we're standing on the edge of a volcano," I said, my eyes scanning the opulent grounds below. "One misstep, and we're toast."

"Welcome to my life," Ryan replied, his voice laced with a blend of humor and exasperation. "Except in this scenario, it's more like I'm the one holding the match." He gestured toward the distant flicker of lights, the city sprawling beneath us like a glittering ocean. "This isn't just any family; it's a dynasty. My mother built this empire on secrets, and my father... well, let's just say he's got a few skeletons in his closet that would make a graveyard look like a garden party."

I turned to him, intrigued despite the tension that surrounded us. "And what about you? Are you just a pawn in this game?"

Ryan chuckled, but there was a bitter edge to it. "I'm more of a reluctant knight. I didn't choose this life; it chose me. But I refuse to play the part they've scripted for me."

"Then let's write our own script," I suggested, a spark igniting within me. "What if we turned the tables? Expose the truth together, expose them before they can crush us."

He met my gaze, the intensity in his eyes sparking a flicker of hope mixed with trepidation. "That's a dangerous game, you know. If we do this, there's no turning back."

"Would you rather be a spectator in your own life?" I shot back, my voice sharper than I intended. "Because I sure as hell won't be one. I'm ready to step into the fire if it means coming out on the other side stronger."

Ryan sighed, running a hand through his hair as he weighed my words. "I admire your bravery, really. But bravery can be naive. It's easy to say you'll stand tall until you're the one being shot at."

"Then let's prepare for battle," I insisted, feeling the adrenaline surge through my veins. "Let's arm ourselves with the truth, however dangerous it might be. If we go down, we go down swinging."

He studied me, the resolve in my eyes sparking something deep within him. "Alright. Together, then," he said finally, the weight of his agreement settling between us. "But we'll need a plan, and we have to be smart about this. My family doesn't just fall apart under scrutiny. They've weathered storms before."

I nodded, my heart racing with both excitement and anxiety. "I've been gathering intel—every bit of gossip, every whisper I've heard. There's a network of people who want to see them held accountable. We just need to connect the dots."

"Connecting dots sounds all well and good until you realize the dots are made of explosives," Ryan replied, his humor creeping back in, but there was an underlying seriousness to it that grounded us. "But I'm in. Just... let's be cautious."

We were pulled from our strategizing by a sudden commotion from inside the mansion. A shrill voice echoed through the halls, cutting through the lively chatter. "Where is she? I want her found!"

My heart dropped. "Is that your mother?"

"Seems like it," Ryan muttered, his brow furrowing as he stepped closer to the balcony's edge, straining to catch a glimpse of the chaos unfolding inside.

"Can't you just hide behind one of those fancy curtains?" I suggested, attempting to lighten the mood, though the impending confrontation loomed like a storm cloud.

He shot me a sidelong glance, a hint of a smile playing on his lips despite the rising tension. "Hiding is not exactly a family trait."

Before we could make another move, the glass doors to the balcony swung open with a flourish, and in strode his mother, elegantly furious, her designer dress shimmering in the dim light. "Ryan! There you are! Why is your phone off? I've been trying to reach you!"

The way she pronounced his name was like a soft whip crack, full of authority and disappointment.

"Just getting some air, Mom," he replied, his voice casual but his posture stiff.

"Air?" She glanced past him, her eyes landing on me with laser-like precision. "And who is this?"

I felt the warmth drain from my face, the confidence I had mustered suddenly dissipating like fog in the morning sun. "I'm—"

"Her name is Hannah," Ryan interjected smoothly, stepping in front of me as if to shield me from the scrutiny of his mother's piercing gaze. "She's a friend."

"Friend," his mother echoed, her voice dripping with skepticism. "You have a curious way of making friends, Ryan. Is she aware of the company she's keeping?"

I cleared my throat, forcing myself to step forward. "I'm aware, Mrs. Blackwood. And I assure you, I'm not here to disrupt your family. Just visiting."

A small, barely perceptible smirk tugged at the corners of her lips, but her eyes remained hard as marble. "Visiting? How quaint. Just know that this family has its own rules, and you would do well to learn them. Consider this a warning."

A chill ran down my spine, the weight of her words sinking in like stones. "I appreciate the heads-up," I managed to say, my voice steady despite the fear swirling within me.

"Good. Because in our world, the stakes are high," she replied, her gaze flicking between Ryan and me, a silent challenge lingering in the air. "And I won't hesitate to protect what's mine."

With that, she turned on her heel, striding back into the mansion with an air of finality that left my head spinning.

Ryan let out a long breath, tension rippling off him like a wave. "That went well," he muttered, sarcasm dripping from his words.

"Remind me never to cross her," I said, trying to mask my unease with humor. "She could probably sink a ship with that glare alone."

Ryan shook his head, a smile ghosting his lips. "You have no idea. But she's right about one thing. This family plays for keeps."

"I'm not scared," I asserted, my voice more firm than I felt. "I won't back down."

"We'll see about that," Ryan replied, but there was a glimmer of admiration in his eyes that bolstered my confidence. "But we need to act fast. If we're going to expose them, we can't waste any more time."

Suddenly, the shrill tone of Ryan's phone shattered the charged air. He pulled it from his pocket, glancing at the screen before his expression shifted from casual concern to palpable dread. "It's my father," he said, his voice dropping to a whisper.

"Answer it," I urged, feeling the stakes rise higher than ever.

He hesitated for a heartbeat, a shadow crossing his face. "I don't know if I can."

"Ryan," I pressed, urgency bubbling in my chest. "This could be critical. We need to know what they're planning."

With a reluctant nod, he answered, the tension in his body coiling tighter as he lifted the phone to his ear. "Dad," he said, his tone strained.

The words on the other end were muffled, but I could see the color drain from his face, the weight of the conversation pressing down like a heavy fog.

"I'll be right there," Ryan finally said, his voice tight as he ended the call.

"What did he say?" I asked, heart racing.

He looked at me, eyes wide with a mix of fear and resolve. "They're onto us, Hannah. They know what you're writing about. They're coming for us."

In that moment, the fire I had thought we could control roared to life around us, and I realized we had stepped into the heart of the inferno, with no way of knowing how it would all end.

Chapter 9: The Betrayal

The door creaked as I pushed it open, the familiar smell of old wood and lingering cologne wrapping around me like an unwelcome embrace. I had expected to feel something—anger, disappointment, perhaps even a smattering of hope. But instead, an icy chill washed over me the moment I crossed the threshold of Ryan's apartment. It wasn't just the cool air that sent shivers down my spine; it was the sight that greeted me.

He was standing there, relaxed and at ease, like the world hadn't just upended itself. And beside him was a woman who radiated an unsettling confidence, her dark hair cascading over her shoulders like a silk waterfall. She wore a sleek black dress that hugged her figure, paired with heels that seemed to elevate her not just physically but in every conceivable way. Her hand rested possessively on Ryan's arm, the kind of gesture that spoke volumes without a single word being exchanged. I stood frozen for a heartbeat, my pulse thrumming in my ears as the revelation struck me like a rogue wave crashing against the shore.

"Ryan," I managed, though it felt as if the name was clawing its way out of my throat, raw and ragged. He turned to me, and for a moment, his face flickered with something—regret, maybe? But it vanished as quickly as it had appeared, replaced by an expression so carefully crafted that it might as well have been a mask.

"You should have stayed away," he said, his voice steady, laced with a coldness that made my stomach twist. It felt like a punch to the gut, the wind knocked out of me. Had I really thought we could just talk? That the warmth we had shared could withstand this? I clenched my fists, the nails biting into my palms as I fought against the tide of emotion threatening to sweep me under.

"And you should have called," I shot back, my tone sharper than I intended, though the truth was that I had prepared for every possible scenario except this one. I hadn't anticipated the way she leaned against him, the way her laughter seemed to dance in the air, light and effortless while my heart felt like it was dragging me to the floor.

The woman turned to me, a faint smirk playing on her lips. "Is this the girl you've been talking about, Ryan?" Her voice was smooth, almost syrupy, as she spoke. It dripped with a condescension that made my skin crawl. "I didn't realize you had a pet."

"Not a pet," I replied, my voice steadier now, fueled by indignation. "Just someone who thought she meant something to him." I forced myself to hold her gaze, even as my heart raced.

"Good to know," she said with a tilt of her head, her eyes sparkling with amusement. "But it's always charming to see someone cling to their delusions." There was a mirth in her tone that only made my resolve harden. I didn't just feel exposed; I felt like an intruder in my own life, watching everything I had built crumble before me.

"Why are you here, really?" I demanded, turning back to Ryan. "Was it all a game to you?" The words tasted bitter on my tongue, the accusation hovering in the air like a thick fog.

He hesitated, a flicker of something genuine crossing his face—was it guilt?—but then the wall went back up. "You don't understand," he said, his voice firm. "This is complicated."

"Complicated?" I scoffed. "You mean like lying to me, pretending we were building something real while you were cozying up with her?" My finger jabbed toward the woman, who looked entirely unfazed, as if my words were nothing but a faint breeze ruffling her hair.

"Maybe I should have told you earlier," Ryan admitted, but his tone lacked conviction. "But it wasn't what you think. I was trying to protect you."

"Protect me?" I laughed, but it was a hollow sound that echoed back in mockery. "From what? The truth? Because this feels like betrayal, Ryan, not protection." Each word fell from my lips like a stone, heavy and weighted with all the hurt he had piled onto my shoulders.

He stepped toward me, his expression shifting, but the distance between us felt monumental. "You're making this worse than it is. You don't know her like I do."

"Maybe I don't," I shot back, "but I know you, and right now, I don't recognize you at all."

Silence stretched between us, a chasm filled with unspoken words and what-ifs. The woman, still lingering beside him, finally spoke, her voice dripping with a playful mockery that grated on my nerves. "Oh, honey, you really should have seen this coming. Ryan has always had a type." She leaned in closer, her lips curving into a predatory smile as she added, "And it looks like you don't quite fit the mold anymore."

My heart raced, a tempest of emotions swirling inside me—hurt, anger, a flicker of desperation. "And you? What do you know about me?" I challenged, forcing myself to stand tall, even as my legs trembled.

"Enough to know you're the one holding on to a lost cause," she replied, a dismissive wave of her hand as if I were merely an annoyance rather than a person.

I felt a swell of strength rise within me, fueling my resolve. "Maybe I'm the only one who still believes in what we had. Maybe I'm the only one who isn't afraid to fight for it." My eyes found Ryan's, searching for any hint of the man I had once known.

In that moment, the room crackled with tension, a storm of emotions swirling around us, each of us grappling with our truths. I had entered this space seeking clarity, only to find myself ensnared in a web of lies, betrayal, and fierce competition for a heart that once felt like home.

The air hung heavy with unspoken words, tension electrifying the space between us. Ryan's gaze flickered between me and the woman beside him, his face a carefully crafted mask of indifference that felt more like a betrayal than anything else. I could practically feel the ground shift beneath my feet as I struggled to regain my footing, the world around me warping into a distorted reflection of what I thought I knew.

"You know, I came here expecting a conversation," I said, forcing a wry smile that didn't quite reach my eyes. "Instead, I find a scene straight out of a bad romance novel. Is this the part where I'm supposed to grab my heart and run?" The words dripped with sarcasm, a flimsy shield against the vulnerability threatening to engulf me.

The woman laughed softly, a sound like glass shattering, and leaned closer to Ryan, her eyes sparkling with a mischievousness that sent a jolt of irritation through me. "I like her spunk, Ryan. It's adorable." Her tone was patronizing, and I fought the urge to roll my eyes.

"Spunk isn't the word I would use," I replied, crossing my arms, feeling the urge to hurl an insult but biting back just enough. "Desperation might fit better, but it seems that's more your area of expertise."

"Cute," she shot back, her smile unyielding. "But really, you're barking up the wrong tree if you think you can win him back with snappy comebacks."

"Who says I'm trying to win him back?" I countered, although even I could hear the faint tremor in my voice. "I'm just here to collect the pieces of my dignity, thanks."

Ryan shifted, clearly uncomfortable under the weight of our verbal sparring. "This isn't helping," he muttered, casting an annoyed glance at both of us. "Can we not turn this into a spectacle?"

"Too late for that," I quipped, my heart racing as I relished the chaos of it all. "Besides, you're the one who brought the showgirl to the performance. I'm just here for the front-row seat."

"Enough!" Ryan snapped, and I flinched, the volume of his voice cutting through the charged atmosphere. "You don't understand what's going on here."

"Enlighten me," I shot back, crossing my arms defiantly. "Because I can't tell if this is a soap opera or a poorly scripted rom-com."

"It's complicated," he said again, but the way he spoke, with a hint of desperation, made it sound like he was trying to convince himself as much as me.

"Complicated," I repeated, my voice thick with incredulity. "Is that the excuse we're going with? Because from where I stand, it looks a lot like betrayal wrapped in a pretty bow."

The woman leaned back against the couch, an imperious look on her face. "Oh, sweetie, it's much more than that. You really don't want to get involved in our lives. It's messy."

"I'm already messy," I shot back, "and I'm tired of cleaning up after your theatrics."

"Your passion is admirable," she said, her tone dripping with faux sympathy, "but perhaps you should redirect it. Like, I don't know, into something productive? Maybe gardening? You seem to have a green thumb for drama."

"Careful," I warned, my eyes narrowing, "you might just sprout a thorn."

In that charged moment, Ryan sighed heavily, dragging a hand through his hair as if the weight of our words were too much for him to bear. "Can we just take a breath?"

"I didn't come here to negotiate a peace treaty," I said, my frustration spilling out. "I came here to confront you. This is my heart we're talking about, not a business deal."

His expression shifted, and for a brief moment, vulnerability cracked through his façade. "I never wanted to hurt you."

"Really?" I scoffed, the disbelief palpable in my voice. "Because it certainly feels like you've got a knack for it."

"Maybe I do," he replied, an edge creeping into his tone. "But you don't know what's at stake here."

"Try me," I dared, leaning in closer, the fire in my chest refusing to die out.

"It's about more than just us," he said, his voice dropping to a near whisper. "There are consequences to everything we do. I was trying to protect you—"

"Protect me? By lying?"

He took a step forward, desperation lining his features. "By keeping you away from a world you don't understand. She's not just some girl; she's part of something bigger."

"What, a cult?" I interjected, unable to suppress my incredulity. "Because I'm not interested in signing up for anything."

The woman laughed again, and this time it sounded like a warning. "Oh, it's more than a cult. It's an entire lifestyle, darling. One that you couldn't possibly grasp."

"Enlighten me, then. What's so fascinating about playing second fiddle?" I retorted, my voice thick with bitterness.

Ryan shot her a look, one that suggested this conversation was veering into dangerous territory. "Let's not get into details."

"Why? Are you afraid of what the truth might reveal?"

He hesitated, and in that moment, the mask slipped just a little further. "You deserve better than this."

"Better than you?" I shot back, the words tasting bitter on my tongue. "Because honestly, this version of you is barely recognizable."

He opened his mouth, perhaps to protest or offer some defense, but the silence stretched on, heavy and thick with the weight of unsaid truths.

"Listen, it's clear we're both holding onto different stories," I said, my tone softening despite the anger simmering beneath the surface. "But I'm not going to sit here and pretend this doesn't matter. I refuse to let you walk away with my heart like it's a trophy."

The woman rolled her eyes, and I could almost see the gears turning in her mind as she prepared her next volley. "Isn't it cute how she thinks she has a say in this?"

But before I could respond, Ryan turned to her, his voice firm. "Stop. This isn't about you."

The tension in the room thickened, the air practically crackling with unresolved feelings and bitter memories. It felt like we were standing at the edge of a cliff, each of us too afraid to leap into the abyss below, yet drawn to the precipice nonetheless. My heart raced with a mix of anger and a desperate need for closure, for answers I wasn't sure Ryan was ready to give.

"Then tell me," I pressed, forcing the words out, as if speaking them might shatter the fragile silence. "Tell me what this is really about."

His gaze locked onto mine, searching for something in my expression—understanding, maybe? Regret?

"It's about survival," he finally admitted, his voice barely above a whisper, "and I never wanted to pull you into it."

"Survival?" I echoed, incredulity creeping back into my voice. "You mean you were just trying to save yourself at my expense?"

"Not at your expense," he insisted, stepping closer, desperation etched on his face. "At your protection. I thought I could keep you safe from all of this. But I see now how that looks."

"Does it feel good?" I asked, my heart pounding as I wrestled with the tumult of emotions swirling within me. "To stand here and justify your choices while I'm left to pick up the pieces?"

"I never meant to hurt you," he said again, his voice cracking, and in that moment, I could see the storm brewing behind his eyes.

"Intentions don't change the damage done, Ryan."

As the weight of his gaze bore into me, I felt a shift in the air, a recognition of the path we had both chosen, however unwittingly. And I realized, in that charged moment, that some battles would never truly be won.

The silence that filled the room felt like a taut wire, vibrating with the tension of unspoken words, lingering truths, and an emotional storm threatening to unleash its fury. I could feel every second stretch into eternity as Ryan's gaze bore into mine, flickering with an intensity that promised revelations I wasn't sure I was ready to hear. The woman beside him stood like a silent sentinel, her presence a constant reminder that I was an intruder in my own life.

"What do you mean by that?" I finally managed, my voice steadier than I felt. "What could possibly justify your decision to shut me out?" The frustration bubbled within me, a simmering pot on the verge of boiling over.

Ryan took a deep breath, his features momentarily softening before hardening again. "I thought I was doing the right thing. I thought you'd be better off without knowing what I'm tangled in."

"Tangled in?" I echoed incredulously, as if the very word had a secret meaning I was yet to grasp. "What, exactly, are you tangled in? Because all I see is a guy who's played games with my heart while you play house with your new friend."

"Stop," he said sharply, his voice cutting through the tension. "You're being unfair."

"Unfair?" I laughed, the sound harsh and bitter. "How do you define fairness? By pulling the rug out from under me while you play puppet master? Newsflash, Ryan: I'm not a marionette."

The woman's smirk faltered, replaced with a glint of annoyance. "Honestly, you should take a hint and move on. You're clearly not his type anymore."

"Funny coming from you," I shot back, the sting of my words dancing in the air. "But I have to wonder—are you even aware of how utterly transparent you are?"

"Enough!" Ryan's voice boomed, reverberating against the walls. "This isn't helping anyone. We're just going in circles."

"Maybe it's time to cut the circle and find a straight line," I snapped, my anger morphing into something more profound, a sense of betrayal that curled tightly in my gut. "Because it seems to me that you've both made your choices."

"Choices?" The woman raised an eyebrow, crossing her arms as she leaned against the wall, a predator reveling in the chaos. "Is that what you think this is about? Choices?"

"Enough with the cryptic remarks," I said, my voice unwavering. "You're not in some mysterious drama. This is my life, and I deserve clarity, not riddles."

"Clarity?" Ryan shook his head, his expression shifting to one of resignation. "You want clarity? Fine. But know that you might not like what you hear."

"Try me," I challenged, my heart racing with a cocktail of anticipation and dread.

"I'm involved in something dangerous," he admitted, his voice lowering, almost conspiratorial. "And I didn't want you caught in the crossfire. There are people involved who—"

"Who what?" I pressed, my curiosity piqued despite the trepidation curling in my stomach. "Who will hurt me? Who are you trying to protect me from?"

He hesitated, glancing at the woman who was now silently observing us, a calculating smile playing at her lips. "It's not just people. It's a situation. A network that I got drawn into, and I didn't know how deep it went until it was too late."

The room seemed to tilt on its axis, the gravity of his words pulling me into an uncharted territory of fear and confusion. "What do you mean? What kind of network?"

"Listen, you have to understand," Ryan said, his voice strained, "it's complicated and dangerous. You're better off forgetting me and moving on. This is a world you don't want to step into."

"I refuse to let you dictate the terms of my life," I retorted, my heart pounding with the adrenaline of defiance. "I'm not walking away without knowing the truth."

"Sometimes ignorance is bliss," he shot back, frustration leaking into his tone.

"Is that your grand excuse? Hiding behind this façade of 'I'm protecting you'? It sounds a lot like cowardice."

"Cowardice?" He stepped closer, and I could see the storm brewing behind his eyes. "You think you have any idea what I've faced? I'm not afraid of the danger; I'm afraid of what it would do to you."

"And here we are again," I replied, a sharp edge to my voice, "with you placing me on this pedestal like I'm some delicate flower. I'm not. I'm stronger than you give me credit for."

The tension hung thick in the air, and for a moment, neither of us spoke. The woman watched with a predatory gleam, her expression a mix of amusement and annoyance, as if we were merely entertainment in her twisted play.

"I'm not going to stand by while you make decisions for me," I declared, the fire in my chest igniting anew. "I want to be part of your life, not some ghost you hide away."

Ryan's gaze darkened, and I could feel the pull of his emotions, the fear and confusion battling for dominance. "You don't know what you're asking for," he said, his voice low and raw.

"Then tell me," I insisted, my heart racing as I searched his eyes for the truth, a truth I was desperate to uncover. "I can handle it."

"You really think you can?" he asked, a challenge in his tone that made my heart lurch.

"I know I can," I replied, unwavering.

His expression shifted, a flicker of doubt crossing his features, and I felt an unexpected rush of hope. "There are people watching," he said finally, his voice low. "People who don't take kindly to... complications."

"Complications?" I laughed bitterly. "Like your little friendship here?"

"It's bigger than that," he said, his tone earnest. "You don't know the half of it."

"I think you're right," I said, my heart pounding in my chest. "But I want to know. I'm done waiting."

Suddenly, the woman interjected, her voice sharp. "Enough of this. You're wasting your time here, Ryan. She's not worth it."

"Shut up," he snapped at her, the sudden intensity in his voice surprising me.

"You don't get to talk to me that way," she hissed, her façade of cool confidence beginning to crack.

"Maybe I do," he retorted, his gaze locked onto mine, the battle in his eyes palpable. "Maybe I finally see that this is not just about me. It's about you, too."

"Ryan—"

Before I could finish, the door swung open violently, slamming against the wall with a force that echoed like a gunshot in the tense atmosphere. My heart raced as a tall figure stepped into the room, a shadowed silhouette framed against the hallway light.

"What the hell is going on here?" the newcomer demanded, their voice low and dangerous.

A wave of dread washed over me as I recognized the voice, the sharpness cutting through the lingering tension. My breath caught in my throat as I realized we were no longer just players in a complicated game; we were caught in the crosshairs of something far more sinister. The room felt small, claustrophobic, as I braced for the inevitable storm that was about to unfold.

"Who are you?" the woman snapped, stepping back slightly, her confidence faltering.

Ryan's expression shifted, a mixture of dread and resignation crossing his face as he looked back at me. "This is exactly what I was afraid of."

My heart raced, every instinct screaming at me that the true threat had just walked through the door.

Chapter 10: The Other Woman

I stumble into the neon glow of a diner, the scent of fried food and burnt coffee wrapping around me like a comforting blanket. The place is a patchwork of retro decor: checkered floors, chrome stools, and a jukebox playing soft country tunes, the kind that evoke a sense of longing. I slide into a booth, feeling the plastic seat stick slightly to my skin as I plop down. The waitress, a no-nonsense woman in her sixties with a beehive of hair and a pencil skirt that could probably stand on its own, gives me a quick once-over. She raises an eyebrow, clearly assessing whether I'm worth her time.

"Coffee?" she asks, her tone blunt yet curious, as if she's privy to the melodrama that just unfolded outside.

I nod, the word lodged in my throat. My eyes dart to the window, where the rain begins to dance against the glass, each drop a reminder of the tears I didn't shed. I wrap my fingers around the warm cup when she finally sets it down in front of me, the steam curling up and catching the fading light like a ghost of a memory I wish I could forget.

"You don't look like you're from around here," she comments, taking a seat across from me without waiting for an invitation. Her eyes are sharp, probing. "You're not in some kind of trouble, are you?"

"No," I reply, almost too quickly. "Just... visiting." My voice sounds hollow, even to my ears. The truth is I'm lost in a labyrinth of my own making, caught in the throes of a heartache I didn't see coming.

"Visiting? Is that what they call it nowadays?" She smirks, a hint of mischief in her eyes. "Honey, you're not fooling anyone. Looks like you just got thrown off a merry-go-round."

I can't help but chuckle, the sound a little too loud for the quiet diner. "More like a rollercoaster I didn't sign up for."

"Tell me about it," she replies, crossing her arms as if settling in for a story. "You know, we all have our moments. Last summer, my husband decided it was a good time to leave me for a woman named Bambi." She rolls her eyes, the name dripping with disdain. "Turns out, Bambi was just a stage name for a woman who couldn't cook to save her life. What a time that was."

Her laughter is infectious, pulling me out of my spiraling thoughts. It reminds me that life goes on, even in the wake of chaos. "I don't think I've reached that level yet," I confess, a wry smile tugging at my lips. "But it feels like a bad rom-com. The kind where everyone gets hurt but somehow ends up laughing about it."

"Life is one big, twisted rom-com, sweetheart. You either laugh or cry. Sometimes, both." Her gaze softens, and for a moment, I feel a flicker of camaraderie in this stranger. "What's the deal with the guy? He sounds like a piece of work."

"Ryan," I say, testing the name on my tongue like a bitter pill. "He's... charming, ambitious, and apparently, involved with someone else." The weight of those words crushes my chest anew, a fresh wave of hurt crashing over me. "Vivian. She's everything I'm not."

She narrows her eyes, leaning in conspiratorially. "Let me guess. She's got the looks, the money, and the kind of connections that make you feel like a bug under a shoe."

"Pretty much," I sigh, rubbing my temples as if I can massage away the headache of reality. "She has that effortless elegance, like she's been trained to glide through life without a care. And there I was, just trying to keep my balance in a world of stilettos."

"Sounds like you need to get yourself a pair of those," she quips, her laughter brightening the dim diner. "You've got to play the game, honey. Don't let some fancy lady make you feel small. You've got something she doesn't."

"What's that?" I ask, curiosity piqued.

"Personality. Heart. Grit. You know, the stuff that doesn't come with a price tag." She leans back, her tone shifting to one of knowing wisdom. "You'll be surprised how far a good heart can take you. Just remember, even the fanciest dresses can't hide a rotten core."

As the conversation unfolds, I realize how much I crave this sense of connection. It's like a lifeline thrown into turbulent waters, pulling me back from the edge of despair. I take a deep breath, feeling the coffee warm me from the inside, slowly nudging my thoughts back to the surface.

"What if I told you I'm not even sure I want him back?" I murmur, surprising myself. The admission feels foreign yet liberating. "I thought he was my forever, but maybe I was just a stop along his way."

The waitress nods, her expression softening as if she sees more than just a lost girl. "Sometimes, the universe has a funny way of steering us in the right direction, even when it feels like we're headed for a crash. Maybe it's time for you to find your own path, away from the rollercoaster."

I nod slowly, the realization washing over me like a gentle tide. It's not just about Ryan anymore; it's about reclaiming my story. I might not know what lies ahead, but for the first time in a while, I feel the faintest spark of hope. The rain outside begins to soften, each droplet becoming a promise rather than a reminder of what was lost. I can choose to rise from the wreckage, to step into a world where I'm more than just a side character. Perhaps it's time to write my own script.

The diner's fluorescent lights buzz softly overhead as I sit in my booth, a half-eaten slice of pie neglected on the plate before me. The waitress, sensing I'm not going to touch it, scoops it up with a smirk. "You sure you don't want to save room for dessert? This is the best piece of cherry pie you'll find south of the Mason-Dixon."

I manage a weak smile, but my mind is still tangled in the mess of Ryan and Vivian. "Thanks, but I think I've had my fill of bittersweet flavors for one day."

"Bittersweet, huh? Sounds like a soap opera. You ever think about auditioning for one?" She quirks an eyebrow, her sarcasm laced with genuine intrigue. "What's his deal, anyway? The pretty boy with the perfect hair?"

"Pretty boy, indeed," I mutter, rolling my eyes. "He's more like a well-packaged riddle I can't solve. Just when I thought I knew all the answers, he rewrote the questions."

"Ah, the classic case of a handsome idiot," she chuckles, shaking her head as she retreats to the counter, leaving me to my swirling thoughts. I take a sip of coffee, its bitterness grounding me.

Lost in contemplation, I barely notice the door swing open until a gust of cool air swirls around me. A figure enters, drenched from the rain and shaking off droplets like a dog fresh from a bath. I squint, my heart racing slightly as recognition sets in. It's him. Ryan.

He's scanning the diner, his expression a mix of determination and confusion. My stomach twists, a cruel reminder of how easily he can turn my world upside down. Just when I think I've gathered my composure, I feel that familiar pull of gravity as he strides toward me. The beehive-haired waitress glances between us, her lips twitching as if she's a spectator at a particularly juicy play.

"Can I sit?" he asks, and the words catch in my throat, trapping any clever retorts I might've had. It feels absurdly intimate, yet painfully awkward. I nod, watching as he sinks into the seat across from me, the scent of rain and something distinctly Ryan enveloping the space between us.

"What are you doing here?" I manage to say, keeping my voice steady as though we're merely discussing the weather.

"Came looking for you." He runs a hand through his damp hair, glancing around as if he expects the diner to hold the answers to everything. "I didn't know what to say back there, and then I realized I didn't want to lose you without a fight."

"A fight?" I scoff, my heart twisting with the absurdity of it all. "That's rich. You didn't even put on the gloves before you let Vivian have a swing at me. You could've at least warned me that you were playing in the big leagues."

He leans closer, his expression earnest, almost desperate. "It's not like that, Jess. Vivian... she's part of my past. A complicated one, but I'm not—"

"Not what?" I cut in, my voice rising slightly as my frustration bubbles to the surface. "Not choosing her? Not wanting to go back to whatever life she represents? You think I'm going to buy that? You can't just waltz in here and expect me to feel like everything's okay again."

His face falls, and I see the pain in his eyes. "I came to explain," he says quietly, almost as if he's afraid to raise his voice. "You deserve that much."

"Explain what? How you've strung me along while keeping her in the background? I want to understand how you could look at me with those big, soulful eyes and pretend everything was fine."

The silence stretches between us, heavy and suffocating. My heart races as I wait for him to respond, the reality of our situation sinking deeper into my bones.

"I thought I was done with her. I thought I'd closed that chapter," he finally admits, his voice low. "But she showed up out of the blue, and it felt like a whirlwind. One moment we were laughing, and then I turned around, and there you were, and everything changed."

"A whirlwind? Really?" I shoot back, incredulous. "Is that how you justify it? You act like you didn't know what you were doing. You knew, Ryan. You've always known."

He takes a breath, like he's preparing to dive into deep waters. "I can't deny that, but Jess... I care about you. I want to figure this out, but I'm stuck in a mess that's not just mine. I thought I could handle it alone."

"Handling it alone? You didn't think maybe I deserved a say in this? A warning?" I say, the heat of my words catching the attention of a couple at the next booth. Their wide eyes and hushed whispers only fuel my anger.

"I didn't want to hurt you," he insists, his voice dropping to a whisper, his sincerity palpable. "I know it's not an excuse, but I thought I could keep it all together without dragging you into the chaos."

"You mean you wanted to keep me in the dark while you danced with your ex?" I shoot back, my voice trembling with hurt. "How noble of you."

His expression twists, the weight of my words hitting him. "I know I messed up. I'm sorry, truly. But I've never felt this way about anyone before. Not with her. You're different, Jess."

"Different how?" I challenge, folding my arms. "Because I'm not some trophy on your arm? Because I don't come with a designer label?"

"Because you challenge me," he says, his gaze steady. "You make me laugh. You make me want to be a better person. I didn't realize how much I wanted that until I met you."

The sincerity in his voice tugs at something deep within me. There's an honesty that feels like an anchor amid the storm swirling around us. But can I trust him? Can I trust anything he says after all the lies wrapped in pretty bows?

Before I can respond, the waitress saunters over, eyebrows raised, her presence an unspoken reminder that we're in a public space, not a confessional. "Y'all want to hash this out, or are we going to order some food?"

Ryan's lips twitch, and I can't help but laugh despite myself. "Maybe just coffee for now," he replies, and I see the corner of his mouth lift, a glimmer of hope in his eyes.

"I could use a slice of pie," I add, my heart still heavy, but at least momentarily distracted.

As the waitress walks away, I find myself studying Ryan, trying to read the expression etched into his features. The intensity in his eyes suggests a depth I had never seen before. Could it be possible that beneath the surface of this complicated situation, there was still a chance for something real? Something that could rise from the ashes of betrayal?

Before I can decide, he leans in closer, his voice barely above a whisper. "I'm not asking you to forgive me right now, but I need you to know that I want to try. I don't want to lose you, Jess. Not to her, not to anyone."

The words hang between us, fragile yet filled with a tentative promise. The world outside continues to rain, but in this moment, I realize that perhaps the storm is only just beginning.

I'm startled back to reality as the waitress sets down a steaming mug of coffee in front of me, the rich aroma briefly distracting me from the tempest swirling in my heart. Ryan watches me closely, the weight of his gaze both reassuring and unnerving. I take a deep breath, the coffee warming me from the inside, a stark contrast to the icy dread pooling in my stomach.

"I can't keep doing this," I say, my voice steady but laced with a quiver of uncertainty. "You say you want to try, but what does that even mean? Are we just going to pretend Vivian doesn't exist? That this whole mess didn't happen?"

He looks like I've slapped him, shock widening his eyes. "I'm not asking you to pretend anything. I want to face this. Together."

"Together." The word hangs between us, tempting yet daunting, like a thin rope suspended over a bottomless pit. "What does that even look like? Do we just ignore the fact that she's part of your life, your past? I don't want to be the 'other woman' in our own story."

He leans back, visibly shaken. "Jess, I don't see you that way. You're not a side note. You're the main event. I didn't expect to feel so strongly about you."

"Clearly," I reply, unable to suppress the bitterness creeping into my tone. "You didn't expect to find yourself tangled in this little love triangle, did you? You made your choice, and I was left holding the pieces."

"Hold on," he counters, his voice rising. "I never chose her over you. Not like that. It was complicated."

"Complicated? That's an understatement." I can't help the sarcasm lacing my words. "You were on the verge of having a dinner with her when I thought we were on our way to something real. You can't just drop that kind of revelation on someone and expect them to be cool with it."

The waitress returns with a slice of cherry pie and sets it down in front of me, her expression wry as if she's overheard our exchange. "You two sound like my last marriage," she says, a smirk dancing on her lips. "Suffice it to say, it didn't end well. Best of luck, kids." She winks and walks away, leaving Ryan and me to stare at each other in disbelief.

"Great, now we're being compared to failed marriages," I mutter, forcing a forkful of pie into my mouth. The sweetness feels like a false comfort, a deceptive layer hiding the tartness beneath.

Ryan breaks the silence, his voice softer this time. "I'm not here to rush you, Jess. But I need you to understand that this isn't just a fling for me. I want to figure out how to make this work."

"Make this work?" I echo, incredulous. "You make it sound so simple, like we can just wave a magic wand and erase everything that's happened." I can feel the heat rising in my cheeks, a blend of frustration and sorrow flooding through me. "What if I can't just forget?"

"Then don't," he insists, leaning forward. "But don't shut me out either. Give me a chance to show you that I can be better, that I can be the man you thought I was. I've been a fool, and I'm willing to prove that I can change."

"Prove it," I challenge, crossing my arms defiantly. "What does that even look like? Words are just words, Ryan. I need actions."

He bites his lip, his expression pained as he considers my request. "Alright, how about this? Let's start fresh. We'll take it slow, no expectations. Just two people trying to figure it out, one day at a time."

I take a deep breath, the offer hanging tantalizingly in the air. Part of me wants to leap into this new world he's proposing, but another part warns me to tread carefully. "And what about Vivian?"

"Let's deal with her as it comes," he replies, his voice steady. "For now, I want to focus on us."

As we share a tense moment of silence, I can't help but admire the vulnerability in his eyes. There's a sincerity that feels real, but can I truly trust him again? My heart is still raw, and the remnants of doubt gnaw at my insides.

"You know," I begin, trying to lighten the mood, "I was really looking forward to spending some time alone at the fair. Cotton candy, Ferris wheels, maybe even a game of whack-a-mole. You're messing with my plans."

"Whack-a-mole?" He raises an eyebrow, a hint of laughter breaking through the tension. "Now that sounds like a serious commitment."

"Hey, it's not easy to whack those pesky little critters," I retort, a smile creeping onto my face. "It takes skill. But here's the thing: if you really want to prove yourself, you might just have to join me for some cotton candy after all."

"I'm in," he says, leaning back with a grin that lights up his face. "But only if you promise not to judge me when I eat it all in one go."

"Deal." I can't help but laugh, the air lightening as we navigate the complexities of our newfound connection.

But as quickly as it came, the laughter fades, and I feel a weight settling in my chest again. The thought of Vivian looms like a storm cloud, ready to unleash its fury. I glance at Ryan, uncertainty swirling in my gut. "And if she comes after me? What then?"

His smile falters, replaced by a steely resolve. "Then we face her together. You're not alone in this, Jess. I won't let her come between us."

Before I can respond, the bell above the diner door jingles again, and my heart sinks as I see Vivian enter. She's soaking wet, her hair slicked back, exuding an aura of cold confidence that feels like a slap in the face. The moment she spots us, her eyes narrow, the gears of her mind turning as she surveys the scene.

Ryan stiffens across from me, his expression shifting from hopeful to wary in an instant. "Jess—"

But it's too late. Vivian strides over, her heels clicking ominously against the floor, each step echoing like the toll of a bell. "Well, well, what do we have here?" she says, her voice smooth as silk but laced with a venom that sends shivers down my spine. "Didn't expect to find you two playing house. How quaint."

The tension in the diner thickens, wrapping around us like a noose. Ryan opens his mouth, but I shoot him a warning glance, unwilling to let him take the fall for what's about to unfold. I can feel the adrenaline surging through me, a mixture of fear and defiance igniting a fire in my belly.

"Vivian," I say, my voice steady despite the chaos inside. "I think we need to talk."

Her smile widens, a predator circling its prey. "Oh, darling, I'm all ears."

As the storm brews, I brace myself, realizing this confrontation will determine everything. The stakes are higher than I ever imagined, and with each word exchanged, I feel the ground shifting beneath my feet.

Chapter 11: Into the Storm

The photo flutters to the floor as my heart races, a wild drum echoing in the silence of my apartment. My pulse pounds in my ears, drowning out the creaking of the floorboards beneath me. I blink hard, as if the motion might dispel the dark figure that lingers at the edges of my vision, but the cold, jagged edges of fear pierce deeper than mere shadows.

I crouch down to retrieve the photo, my fingers brushing the paper as if it might burn me. In it, Ryan and I are smiling, unaware of the watchful gaze lurking somewhere behind the lens. It feels like a betrayal, a perfect moment turned into a weapon, and I can't shake the icy tendrils of dread wrapping around my throat. Who took this? More importantly, why?

My mind races through the possibilities, each one more terrifying than the last. Maybe it's just a cruel prank. A misguided attempt at humor from a stranger. Or maybe it's something far worse—a threat meant to manipulate me, to push me into some unseen corner. But cornered animals fight back, don't they? I straightened my spine, trying to convince myself that whatever came next, I wouldn't go down without a fight.

I grab my phone, fingers shaking as I swipe through contacts until I find Ryan's name. My thumb hovers over the screen, hesitant, but I can't let fear dictate my actions. I need him. Just as I gather the courage to press call, my phone buzzes, jolting me from my thoughts. A message from an unknown number flickers across the screen: I know where you are.

I drop the phone like it's a live wire, pulse racing anew. I've always thought of myself as strong, the kind of woman who can face whatever storm comes her way. But this? This feels like quicksand, and no matter how much I fight, I can feel the darkness pulling me in.

The night stretches out before me, heavy and oppressive. I pace my small living room, the sound of my footsteps echoing against the stark walls. I glance toward the window, half expecting to see someone lurking in the shadows, watching my every move. I force myself to breathe, steady and calm, but with every breath, the realization settles in: I can't stay here. Not alone.

With a flick of determination, I grab my coat, slipping it over my shoulders, and venture out into the cool night air. The streets are quiet, the only sound being the rhythmic tap of my boots against the pavement. Each step echoes my resolve; I need answers. I need Ryan.

The city lights shimmer against the inky backdrop of the sky, illuminating the path ahead but casting dark shadows that seem to dance with each flicker. I can't shake the feeling that I'm being watched. I shake my head, scolding myself for being so paranoid. A moment of self-reflection slips in, nagging at my confidence. How did I become the type of woman who jumps at every corner? It's not like I haven't faced my share of challenges before.

As I approach Ryan's apartment building, the familiar structure looms like a fortress, its brick façade both welcoming and intimidating. I push through the entrance, heart racing as I head up the stairs, each creak underfoot amplifying my anxiety. But I refuse to let fear win tonight. I need him, and I need him now.

I knock on his door, the sound reverberating through the stillness. The seconds stretch out, each one heavy with anticipation. Just when I think he won't answer, the door creaks open, revealing Ryan, tousled hair and an expression that swiftly shifts from surprise to concern.

"Is everything okay?" His voice is low, laced with worry, and it cuts through the tension I've been holding. I can see the concern etched across his features, but it's the spark of something else that catches me off guard—a deep, unfathomable connection that stirs within me.

"No," I admit, my voice barely above a whisper. "I need your help."

The sincerity in my tone sends a flicker of urgency through him, and he steps aside, allowing me to enter his space. It feels like stepping into a cocoon, and for a brief moment, I let myself relax, letting the warmth of his presence wash over me. But the storm brewing within me isn't ready to settle just yet.

"I don't know how to explain this," I begin, pacing the small living room, the familiar scent of his cologne swirling around me, both comforting and disarming. "But I received a photo—a threat."

His expression darkens, eyes narrowing as he processes my words. "A threat? What do you mean?"

I pull the photo from my pocket, handing it to him as my hands tremble slightly. He examines it, his jaw tightening as he reads the scrawled message beneath the image. I watch as anger flashes across his face, a fierce protectiveness rising in him that sends warmth flooding through my chest.

"Who did this?" he asks, voice low and dangerous. "Did you see anyone?"

"No," I say, frustration lacing my words. "Just a man at my door. He didn't say anything. Just handed me this and left."

Ryan's gaze meets mine, the intensity in his eyes sending a rush of energy through me. "We need to figure out what's going on. You can't be alone right now."

His words offer a strange mix of comfort and concern. I want to believe that together we can face whatever is lurking in the shadows. It feels oddly comforting to have him by my side, the connection between us rekindling in the face of fear. For a moment, the world outside fades away, and all that matters is the two of us standing together against the encroaching darkness.

But even as I soak in his presence, the gnawing doubt creeps back in. How much can I really trust him? And as I look up into his eyes, searching for reassurance, I wonder if this is just the calm before an even greater storm.

The silence stretches between us, heavy like a wool blanket on a hot summer day, as Ryan examines the photo, his brows knitted in concentration. The tension in the room shifts, thickening with unspoken words. I can feel the gravity of the moment, the weight of everything I'm not saying pressing down on my chest. He looks up, his gaze sharp and unyielding, and in that moment, I know we're both teetering on the edge of something vast and unknown.

"Who would do this?" he asks, his voice low, almost reverent, as if he's afraid that saying it too loudly might bring the specter haunting me crashing through the door. "You didn't mention anyone who might have a reason to."

I huff out a breath, running my fingers through my hair in frustration. "You think I'd just casually throw around the names of my enemies? No one just hands someone a threatening note without a motive."

"Enemies can be subtle," he replies, stepping closer, the warmth of his presence enveloping me like a protective shield. "Sometimes they lurk in the most unexpected places."

I can't help but feel the heat radiating off him, igniting something deep within me, but I push the feeling aside. Now isn't the time for distractions, no matter how tempting they are. "Great. So now I have to worry about shadows and secrets too?"

Ryan takes a moment, his expression softening as he considers my words. "Look, we can figure this out. Together. I won't let anything happen to you."

The sincerity in his voice tugs at something inside me, but I can't afford to let my guard down completely. Trust is a luxury I'm not sure I can afford anymore. I cross my arms, leaning against the back of the couch, feeling the fabric's coarse texture beneath me. "Okay, but how? I don't want to just wait around for this person to make their next move. I want to take control of this situation."

His lips curve into a smirk that flickers like a flame. "You're definitely a stubborn one, aren't you? That's not always a bad thing. But maybe we should try a different approach."

I raise an eyebrow, intrigued despite myself. "And what exactly is your grand plan? Should we hold a séance? Call upon the spirits of my past to get some answers?"

Ryan chuckles, the sound breaking through my tension like sunlight piercing through a stormy sky. "I was thinking more along the lines of a little detective work. I might know a few people who can help us dig deeper into this."

I watch him, caught between gratitude and wariness. It's disarming how easily he can lighten the mood, but the undercurrent of unease still swirls around us like a fog. "And you trust these people? This doesn't feel like the kind of situation where we can afford any loose ends."

He leans back against the kitchen counter, his expression turning serious once more. "I wouldn't put you in harm's way. You have my word."

Somewhere in my gut, a small flicker of hope ignites, but I tamp it down. Hope can be dangerous. "Fine, let's do it. But if this blows up in our faces, I'm holding you responsible."

"Deal," he replies, a grin spreading across his face. "Just don't take it out on my cooking. I've been told it's quite good."

"Are you trying to charm me into compliance with promises of gourmet meals? Because it might just be working," I say, the teasing lilt of my voice surprising even myself.

As the conversation shifts, I can feel the tension of the last few hours loosening its grip, if only slightly. There's something oddly reassuring about having Ryan by my side, even as the specter of threat looms just outside the door.

"Okay, how do we start?" I ask, determined to keep this momentum going.

"First, we need to gather intel. I know a couple of guys who owe me favors," he says, pulling out his phone. "They can help us find out if there's anyone asking questions about you or anyone who might have been tailing you."

"Are you suggesting we create a sort of... unofficial surveillance network?" I ask, trying to ignore how thrilling the thought is.

"Think of it as a tactical response team. I'll handle the heavy lifting. You just focus on looking fabulous while we gather intel," he replies, winking.

"Now you're just trying to distract me," I say, but my heart flutters. "But I appreciate the vote of confidence.

Ryan begins to type furiously on his phone, and I can't help but watch the way his fingers fly over the screen, as if his thoughts spill out faster than he can process them. There's a focus in him that I admire, something intense and committed that makes me want to lean in closer, to find out what lies beneath that calm exterior.

"Okay, we have a couple of leads. Let's hit up the usual spots and see if we can pick up on anything," he says, finally putting the phone down and meeting my gaze.

I nod, swallowing the rising unease. "What if this goes sideways? What if whoever's behind this catches wind of what we're doing?"

He shrugs, an easy gesture that does nothing to quell the knots in my stomach. "Then we'll adapt. That's what we do, right? You're not afraid of a little chaos."

"Right, chaos is my middle name," I retort, trying to inject humor into the situation even as dread snakes its way through my veins.

"Let's see how much chaos we can stir up then," he says, his grin turning wicked.

As we head out into the night, I'm struck by the irony of our circumstances. Here I am, stepping into the unknown with a man who once seemed like a beautiful distraction, now transformed into a reluctant ally. My heart races, not just from the thrill of impending danger, but from the unexpected connection growing between us, weaving its way through the fabric of uncertainty that surrounds us.

The city hums around us, each light a flickering reminder of life moving on, oblivious to the tension building beneath the surface. I'm no longer merely a spectator; I'm stepping into the fray, ready to confront whatever shadows may lie ahead. With each step, the edges of fear sharpen, but so does my resolve. This is not just a fight for my safety; it's a chance to reclaim my narrative, to wrestle control from the hands of the unseen. And with Ryan beside me, I feel an unfamiliar but exhilarating sense of possibility, one that pushes me to lean into the chaos rather than shy away from it.

The streetlights flicker as we walk through the dimly lit streets, casting ghostly shadows that dance at our feet. My heart is still racing from the thrill of our plan, the rush of adrenaline intertwined with a deep, unsettling anxiety. It feels like we're on the brink of something monumental, though I'm not entirely sure if it's good or bad. Ryan strides ahead, his pace brisk and purposeful, and I struggle to keep up, lost in a swirl of thoughts.

"Okay, so what's the first stop on this little escapade of ours?" I ask, trying to keep my tone light even as my stomach twists in knots.

He glances back at me, a mischievous glint in his eyes. "We're heading to the dive bar down on Seventh. Trust me, it's the kind of place where secrets are as common as stale beer."

"Ah, the classic 'drunken wisdom' strategy," I reply, feigning mock enthusiasm. "So, I should prepare myself to hear tales of lost love and misunderstood genius?"

"Something like that," he says, laughing softly. "But more importantly, the bartender knows everyone and everything in this town. If anyone's got dirt on whoever's been watching you, it's him."

I nod, although my heart sinks a little. It's one thing to take action and another to confront the reality of why we're here. The weight of the threat lingers over me like a storm cloud, and I wish I could shake off the dread that clings to my skin.

As we approach the bar, the neon lights buzz and flicker, illuminating the worn sign that reads "The Rusty Anchor." The air is thick with the scent of old wood and spilled drinks, the kind of place where anonymity is a given, and patrons nurse their secrets like old wounds. The door swings open with a creak, and the noise inside swells, a chaotic mix of laughter and clinking glasses.

"Welcome to the underbelly of the city," Ryan says with a dramatic flourish as we step inside. "If we're lucky, we might even find a friendly face among the scoundrels."

As we navigate through the dimly lit interior, I catch glimpses of worn leather booths and grizzled men nursing their drinks, stories etched into their faces. The bartender stands behind a wooden bar that looks like it's seen better days, a tattooed arm resting casually on the countertop as he wipes a glass with a rag that probably hasn't seen soap in years.

"Let me do the talking," Ryan says, nudging me forward as we approach the bar. "And try to look inconspicuous. We're just two people enjoying a night out, not potential victims of a stalking scenario."

"Right," I say, trying to suppress a smile. "Just a casual rendezvous in a bar full of strangers while I'm being watched. No pressure at all."

Ryan chuckles as he leans against the bar, flashing the bartender a smile. "Hey, Charlie. Long time no see. You still serving up the best whiskey in town?"

"Ryan! You're a sight for sore eyes," the bartender replies, his deep voice carrying warmth and familiarity. He sets down the glass and wipes his hands on a towel. "What can I get you?"

"Just a couple of shots for now. We need some liquid courage for a bit of a chat," Ryan says, glancing back at me. "And, um, we're looking for some information."

Charlie raises an eyebrow, intrigued. "Information, huh? You know I don't usually play that game unless the price is right."

"Let's just say this is a special case," Ryan says, his voice lowering slightly. "We're looking for someone who might have been following a friend of mine."

Charlie's expression shifts, seriousness washing over his features. "Following? You sure you want to get involved in that kind of business?"

"Trust me, we've already been involved," I interject, trying to sound more confident than I feel. "I just need to know who's behind it. I'm tired of living in the shadows."

He studies me for a moment, weighing my words. "Alright, I'll bite. What do you have for me?"

Ryan slides a couple of crumpled bills across the bar, and Charlie narrows his eyes, pocketing the cash with a nod. "I might know a thing or two about some unusual faces lurking around lately. You'll want to pay attention to the guy who comes in after the midnight crowd. He's got a reputation for being... well, let's say, he knows a thing or two about unwanted attention."

"What do you mean?" I ask, a chill running down my spine.

Charlie leans in, lowering his voice as if sharing a secret. "He's a known associate of some not-so-friendly types. If he's sniffing around you, it's not for your sparkling personality."

"What's his name?" Ryan asks, his tone sharp.

"Goes by the name of Lex. Be careful. He's not the kind of guy who takes too kindly to questions."

"Sounds charming," I say dryly, but the seriousness of the situation is weighing heavily on me.

"Just keep your eyes open," Charlie warns. "And if you feel like you're being watched, you probably are. This town has eyes everywhere."

I share a glance with Ryan, a silent understanding passing between us. "Thanks, Charlie. We'll keep our heads down," Ryan replies, throwing back his shot like a seasoned pro.

As we make our way toward the exit, I can feel the tension building, a sense of urgency swirling around us. "What do we do now?" I ask, my mind racing with possibilities.

"We wait," Ryan says, his expression focused. "We keep an eye out for Lex and see if he leads us to whoever is behind those threats."

"Waiting doesn't exactly sound thrilling," I say, crossing my arms.

"True, but we can't jump into a lion's den without a plan," he replies, his eyes scanning the crowd as if looking for danger. "Let's grab a booth and blend in. If he shows up, we'll know."

We slide into a booth in the corner, shadows cloaking us like a protective barrier. I take a deep breath, trying to steady my racing heart. The atmosphere around us feels electric, charged with a sense of foreboding.

"So, tell me more about this Lex," I say, trying to keep the conversation flowing despite the tension tightening around us. "Is he as charming as his name suggests?"

Ryan smirks, a playful glint in his eyes. "Oh, absolutely. He's the type who could charm the pants off a statue—if you're into that kind of thing."

"Good to know," I say, rolling my eyes. "And what's your plan? Ask him for a friendly chat over drinks?"

"Not quite. More like a 'what the hell do you want from me' kind of conversation," he replies, his tone shifting to seriousness again.

Time stretches as we sit in silence, waiting for Lex to appear. The bar fills and empties around us, laughter and music blending into a haze, but I can't shake the feeling that something is off. The clock on the wall ticks away, each second amplifying my anxiety.

Finally, the door swings open, and in walks a figure that commands attention. Lex is tall, his presence magnetic yet menacing, with sharp features and an easy confidence that radiates danger. He scans the room, a predatory glint in his eye that sends a shiver down my spine.

"There he is," Ryan whispers, tensing beside me.

"Great. Now what?" I ask, my voice barely above a whisper.

"We watch and wait," he says, his gaze fixed on Lex as he approaches the bar, but my instincts scream that waiting might not be the best option.

Just then, as if sensing our scrutiny, Lex glances in our direction. His eyes narrow, locking onto mine with an unsettling intensity. Time freezes, the air thick with tension, as I realize that in this moment, I'm not just another face in the crowd.

"Uh-oh," Ryan mutters, shifting closer to me. "I think we've been made."

Before I can respond, Lex's lips curl into a sly smile, and he starts walking toward us, each step deliberate, like a predator closing in on its prey. My heart races, panic clawing at my chest as I wonder how deep into the darkness we've just stepped.

"Maybe waiting wasn't such a good idea after all," I whisper, dread curling in my stomach as Lex closes the distance, his gaze burning with something that feels dangerously close to a challenge.

"Let's put on our bravest faces," Ryan replies, tension threading through his voice.

The world around us fades as Lex approaches, and I can't shake the feeling that this moment could change everything. My breath hitches as he stops at our booth, leaning in, the shadows wrapping around him like a cloak, and I know, without a doubt, that the real storm is just beginning.

Chapter 12: Falling Apart

I should leave Nashville. I know that now. But something keeps me here, a tether that pulls tighter with every day. Perhaps it's Ryan, that charming enigma who feels more like a puzzle than a person sometimes, a puzzle I can't quite seem to solve. He carries the weight of secrets behind those expressive eyes, and I find myself wanting to delve deeper into his world. Or maybe it's the story that's ensnared me—like a siren's call, luring me to the rocky shores of truth. The secrets are unraveling, thread by delicate thread, and I can't bring myself to abandon the tapestry I've begun weaving.

With each step I take through this city, I sense the threads pulling at me—compelling, yet dangerous. The vibrant energy of Nashville pulses around me, a rhythm that is intoxicating yet ominous. The scent of warm, buttery biscuits wafts through the air, mingling with the distant sound of country music spilling from a nearby bar. I can almost taste the sweetness of the moment, but underneath, a sour note of anxiety simmers.

The other day, I was in line at the grocery store, the fluorescent lights buzzing overhead, when I felt that familiar prickling sensation at the nape of my neck. It was as if the air had thickened, charged with an electric current. I turned, half-expecting to find someone staring at me, but instead, I was met with the indifferent gazes of bored shoppers. I shook it off, chalking it up to a momentary lapse in sanity, but deep down, I knew better. The man from the hotel room lurked in the periphery of my life, shadowing me like a ghost I couldn't exorcise.

Every time I leave my apartment, I scan the streets for him—tall, with a sun-kissed complexion and a smile that could charm the devil. He blends seamlessly into the crowd, his presence a phantom that slips through my fingers every time I try to grasp it. Yet I can feel him watching, just beyond the corner of my vision, a dark cloud that looms closer with each passing moment. I should have left Nashville the second I spotted him. Instead, I find myself looking over my shoulder and questioning my sanity.

The police won't help me. I tried, once, clutching my phone as I reported my suspicions. "You can't just accuse someone without evidence, ma'am," the officer said, glancing up from his paperwork with a tired sigh, as if my fears were merely an annoyance in his otherwise mundane day. My stomach twisted into knots as he dismissed me, treating my anxiety like an inconvenient fly buzzing around his head. "Try to keep your distance. Maybe it's just your imagination." Imagination. I'd like to see him navigate through the haze of my reality, where shadows take on shapes and every sound feels like a threat.

So, I turned back to Ryan, my unexpected confidant, though doubt now casts a long shadow over our friendship. The last time we were together, the atmosphere shifted like the unpredictable Nashville weather—one moment warm and welcoming, the next, a storm brewing on the horizon. It was that night in the bar, surrounded by laughter and music, when I saw Vivian. I should have turned away, should have shielded myself from the truth that her presence threatened to unravel, but curiosity propelled me forward, and I caught a glimpse of something I wish I hadn't.

Vivian was radiant in the dim light, her laughter like the tinkling of glass, but beneath it all was a tension that made my skin crawl. She was an old friend of Ryan's—someone I'd heard about but never met—and there was an unsettling familiarity in the way she leaned into him, her fingers brushing against his arm as if it were the most natural thing in the world. I stood frozen in place, the weight of betrayal sinking into my bones. Ryan had let me believe that we were building something more, but here was Vivian, a reminder of the past I wasn't a part of, weaving her way back into his life.

When I finally approached them, feigning a smile that felt more like a grimace, I could see the flicker of surprise in Ryan's eyes, quickly masked by his charming façade. "Hey, there you are!" he said, but the enthusiasm in his voice felt forced, as if he were trying to convince both of us that everything was fine. I forced laughter that didn't quite reach my heart, the distance between us growing like a chasm.

"What a surprise to see you here," I said, my voice too bright, my mind racing. Did he plan this? Did he want me to see them together? Or was it an innocent encounter that I was twisting into something sinister? But I couldn't shake the feeling of being an interloper in a scene I didn't belong to.

The conversation shifted awkwardly, the air thickening with unspoken words as I tried to glean meaning from their interactions. I could sense Ryan's hesitation, the tension in his shoulders as he navigated between the two of us. It was a delicate dance, one that felt all too familiar yet uncomfortably foreign. My heart sank deeper with each passing moment, knowing that the very foundation of trust we were building was on the verge of crumbling.

As we parted ways that evening, Ryan walked me to my car, the silence stretching between us like a taut wire. I could feel the words teetering on the edge of my tongue, begging for release, but the weight of uncertainty kept them locked away. What was left to say? Would he tell me the truth about Vivian, or was I destined to remain an outsider in my own story?

The engine roared to life beneath me, the familiar hum grounding me in reality. I could feel the weight of his gaze as I pulled away, the shadow of his presence lingering long after I turned the corner. I couldn't shake the feeling that I was standing on the precipice, teetering between two worlds—one with Ryan, where possibilities shimmered like the warm glow of streetlights, and the other, dark and foreboding, where the man from the hotel room lurked just out of sight.

The city whirred around me as I drove, its lights sparkling like a constellation of unfulfilled dreams. In that moment, I realized that Nashville was no longer just a backdrop for my story. It had become a character in its own right, one that challenged me at every turn. The uncertainty prickled at my skin, making every street corner feel like a choice, every shadow a potential threat. But I wasn't ready to let go. Not yet.

The sun was barely peeking over the horizon when I woke up, its light spilling through the gaps in my curtains like a cautious intruder. I lay there for a moment, tangled in sheets that felt more like a protective cocoon than a comforting embrace. Outside, the city was beginning to stir, the sounds of traffic and distant chatter seeping into my apartment, but my mind was trapped in a loop of anxiety and uncertainty. I rolled over, glancing at the time. It was too early for coffee, yet my heart craved it like a child craves a secret treat.

As I shuffled to the kitchen, the reality of my situation washed over me like a cold wave. My fingers trembled slightly as I poured the grounds into the filter, the familiar ritual providing a fleeting sense of normalcy in a world that felt anything but. I couldn't shake the nagging sensation that something was very wrong. Maybe it was the man from the hotel room or maybe it was the ghost of Vivian hovering over my thoughts like a dark cloud, but my gut told me I was teetering on the edge of something precarious.

I had managed to suppress the memory of that night at the bar, yet now it replayed in my mind like a movie stuck on a loop. Ryan's face when he saw me, the slight frown that flickered across his features before he masked it with that disarming smile. I could still hear the laughter echoing in my ears, an unwelcome reminder of the fragility of our connection. Was it all a facade? Had I been the one blind to the reality that everyone else could see?

The coffee machine gurgled, drawing me from my thoughts, and I inhaled the rich aroma as it filled the air. A moment of warmth spread through my chest, soothing the jagged edges of my anxiety, if only for a heartbeat. I took a sip and leaned against the counter, letting the bitterness mingle with the sweetness of my swirling emotions.

I needed to confront Ryan. Not just about Vivian, but about everything—the man in the shadows, the secrets woven into our lives, the trust that had frayed around the edges. But how do you confront someone when your heart thrums with both affection and suspicion? The truth hung in the air, thick and suffocating, and I could feel it beckoning me to take action.

Later that day, I found myself at a little café downtown, one of those places with mismatched furniture and an ambiance that thrummed with creativity. It was a perfect spot for an impromptu confrontation, as long as I could suppress the wave of nerves threatening to send my heart into overdrive. I settled into a corner booth, the scent of cinnamon wafting through the air, mingling with the soft notes of acoustic guitar strumming in the background.

Time ticked by, each minute feeling like an eternity. I fidgeted with my phone, a thousand texts unsent lingering in the void between us. The bell above the door chimed, and in walked Ryan, his presence lighting up the room even before his eyes found mine. There was a part of me that melted at the sight of him—the tousled hair, the easy smile that made my heart flip. But beneath that warmth lay the cold tendrils of doubt, and I steeled myself as he approached.

"Hey!" he said, sliding into the seat opposite me, his voice a melodic balm against my rising tension. "You look... deep in thought."

"Maybe I am," I replied, arching an eyebrow, the corner of my mouth twitching into a half-smile. "Or maybe I'm just contemplating my coffee order. Do you think I should get a pastry? I mean, life is short, right?"

His laughter rang out, genuine and bright, yet there was an undercurrent of apprehension swirling between us. "I mean, if we're being philosophical about pastries, I think you have to go for it. They're like tiny hugs for your taste buds."

"Exactly," I said, the wryness in my tone a thin veil over the seriousness of the conversation I needed to initiate. "So, speaking of hugs... how are things with Vivian?"

The laughter faded from his eyes, replaced by a flicker of surprise that morphed into something more serious. "Vivian? I mean, she's an old friend. We ran into each other. It wasn't... anything like you might think."

I leaned back, studying him, letting the weight of my words settle between us. "You know, when I saw you two together, it felt like a punch to the gut. I thought we were building something real, and there you were, reconnecting with someone from your past."

"Jess, it wasn't like that," he insisted, his voice steady but tinged with urgency. "She's part of my past, sure, but we're not... whatever you're imagining. It was a coincidence. I promise."

"Right. Coincidences," I scoffed, the tension in my chest tightening. "Because it's totally normal for someone to drop back into your life just when things start to get serious with someone else."

He sighed, running a hand through his hair, frustration evident in the movement. "I'm not trying to downplay how you feel. But can't you see how this looks? How it looks like you're reading into things that aren't there?"

"What am I supposed to think, Ryan?" I shot back, my voice rising, drawing glances from other patrons. "I'm not sure if I'm just paranoid or if my instincts are trying to warn me. You were the one who told me to trust my gut."

His gaze softened, the edges of his frustration melting into concern. "I know you've been through a lot, and I want to help, but you have to let me in. If you don't trust me, this isn't going to work."

And there it was, the unspoken truth hanging in the air—my trust was the fragile thread holding us together. "I want to trust you, Ryan. But how can I when I keep seeing shadows lurking around every corner?"

"What shadows?" he pressed, his expression shifting from concern to confusion. "You're not making sense, Jess. What are you talking about?"

"I keep seeing that man. The one from the hotel. He's been following me, and I can feel him watching me. He's always just... there." The words spilled out of me in a rush, desperation curling around each syllable. "I thought I was being paranoid, but I can't shake the feeling that I'm not safe."

Ryan's face shifted, the playful demeanor replaced by something heavier, an understanding dawning in his eyes. "What do you mean, following you?"

"I don't know! But every time I leave my apartment, I feel him—like he's right there, waiting. I thought I was just imagining it, but now... now I'm not so sure."

"Jess, why didn't you tell me this sooner?" His voice dropped to a whisper, urgency lacing every word. "We need to figure this out. You shouldn't be going through this alone."

The warmth of his concern wrapped around me, pushing back the shadows that had been crowding my mind. But still, doubt lingered like a ghost, refusing to let me fully embrace his support. "You're not the one I'm worried about, Ryan. It's me. I can't help but think that if he's out there, maybe it has something to do with you."

"I swear, it has nothing to do with me," he insisted, his eyes earnest. "I don't know what's going on, but we'll figure it out. Together."

Together. The word hung between us, a fragile promise wrapped in uncertainty. And for the first time in days, a glimmer of hope flickered in my chest, fighting against the encroaching darkness. I wanted to believe him, to trust that we could navigate through this together. But as the shadows loomed ever closer, I couldn't help but wonder if the real danger was yet to be unveiled.

The café's ambiance buzzed with a nervous energy, the chatter of patrons mingling with the clinking of cups and the soft strumming of a guitar in the corner. I could see it in Ryan's eyes, the determination that flickered like a flame—a warmth that cut through the chill of my anxiety. But even as he leaned forward, his expression earnest, shadows danced at the edges of my vision, and a nagging feeling settled in my gut.

"Jess, we can't ignore this," he said, his voice low but steady. "If someone's following you, we need to take it seriously. Maybe we should get you a lawyer, or at least look into some self-defense classes."

"Self-defense?" I laughed, though the sound was hollow. "You think that's going to stop a guy who's already in my head? Besides, I can't afford a lawyer." I motioned dismissively with my hand, but the thought of getting a restraining order crossed my mind, chilling me to the bone.

Ryan frowned, his brow furrowed. "Look, it doesn't have to be a big deal. We could just look into it, see what our options are. And I can help with the costs. I'm not letting you deal with this alone."

The offer hung in the air, tantalizing yet suffocating. The last thing I wanted was to feel dependent on anyone, especially not when my instincts were screaming that something deeper was at play. "You don't understand," I replied, lowering my voice. "It's not just about the money. It's about feeling safe, about feeling... I don't know, secure? I can't even do that when I'm second-guessing every move."

"Okay," he said, his tone shifting to something softer. "Then let's do something about it. Tonight, I'll stay at your place. We can keep an eye out together."

The suggestion sent a cascade of warmth through me, the kind that whispered promises of safety and solidarity. Yet, a layer of uncertainty danced beneath that warmth. What if having Ryan there only brought more complications? I didn't want to overanalyze every gesture or word. I was tired of feeling like a detective in my own life.

"Are you sure that's a good idea? I mean, what about Vivian?" The name felt like a thorn in my side, sharp and irritating.

"Vivian isn't my priority right now," he said, his gaze unwavering. "You are. I'll deal with her later. Right now, I'm just focused on keeping you safe."

A part of me wanted to argue, to push back against the tide of his concern, but as I looked into his eyes, I found sincerity there. "Alright," I finally conceded, trying to infuse my tone with confidence. "But you might regret it. I'm not exactly the easiest person to be around these days."

"I thrive on chaos," he quipped with a grin, lightening the mood, and just like that, the tension between us eased. For a brief moment, it felt like we could find comfort in the shared battle against the uncertainty that loomed like a storm cloud.

As evening approached, the sun dipped below the horizon, painting the sky in hues of orange and purple. I felt an unsettling sense of dread settle in the pit of my stomach as we prepared for the night. My apartment felt like a sanctuary and a prison all at once, the walls echoing with memories I was desperate to escape.

When Ryan arrived, I tried to shake off the lingering unease. We settled onto the couch, the familiar warmth of his presence pushing back against the shadows creeping in from outside. A movie flickered on the screen, but I could hardly focus, each creak of the building or rustle from outside sending my heart racing.

"Why don't you try to relax?" he suggested, his voice laced with gentle humor. "You know, not every noise means there's a stalker lurking outside your window."

I rolled my eyes playfully, but the laugh that escaped me felt forced. "I just want to keep my eyes open, you know? The moment I let my guard down, I'll probably regret it."

"Fair enough," he said, leaning back into the couch. "But if you're going to keep watch, at least let me know if you see anything that looks like a demon. I'd like to be prepared."

"Just so you know," I replied, smirking at his jest, "I don't know how I'd differentiate between demons and bad pickup artists. There's a fine line, after all."

We both chuckled, but my laughter faded when the feeling of being watched crept back in.

A sharp knock echoed through the apartment, silencing the playful banter. My heart leapt into my throat as I shot a look at Ryan. "Did you hear that?"

"Yeah," he replied, his expression turning serious. "You expecting someone?"

"No," I whispered, my breath hitching in my throat. "No one."

"Stay here," he said, his voice low and commanding. I watched as he stood, moving toward the door with a confidence that belied the tension thickening the air around us.

"Ryan—"

"Just stay behind me," he said, glancing back, a reassuring smile that barely reached his eyes. He reached for the doorknob, pausing for a brief moment. "Ready?"

I nodded, though I felt anything but. He opened the door a crack, and for a split second, the world outside was nothing but darkness. Then a figure stepped into the light, and my breath caught in my throat.

It was a woman—a striking silhouette framed by the dim light of the hallway, hair cascading down her back like a waterfall of midnight. "I know this is weird," she began, her voice smooth yet edged with urgency. "But I need to talk to you, Jess. It's important."

"Who are you?" Ryan interjected, his protective instincts flaring, the tension in his body radiating like heat from a flame.

"I'm a friend," she said, glancing at me, her gaze piercing and full of intent. "And I know about the man watching you. We don't have much time."

Confusion flooded my senses, and I glanced at Ryan, searching for answers in his eyes. But before I could speak, the woman pressed on. "You need to come with me. I can help you understand what's happening. There's so much more at stake than you realize."

The urgency in her voice sent a chill down my spine, and before I could formulate a response, I noticed the shift in Ryan's demeanor. "Wait," he said, stepping forward, his voice firm. "You can't just barge in here and—"

"Ryan," I interrupted, the weight of my instincts overwhelming the fear. "I think... I think we should listen to her."

In that moment, the tension in the room thickened, anticipation crackling like static electricity. I could see the internal struggle on Ryan's face, the desire to protect me clashing with the undeniable need to uncover the truth.

"Jess, this could be dangerous," he warned, his eyes narrowing in concern.

"Or it could be the answer we're looking for," I countered, my heart racing with an exhilarating mix of fear and curiosity. I looked back at the woman, my resolve solidifying. "I'm listening. What do you know?"

Before she could respond, a loud crash reverberated through the hallway, followed by a deep, angry voice that sent shockwaves of fear coursing through me. "Jess! Open up! I know you're in there!"

My blood ran cold. My instincts screamed at me to hide, but the words of the woman echoed in my mind—so much more was at stake than I realized. As the door shuddered under the force of the voice outside, I felt the room pulse with impending chaos, and I knew I was on the precipice of a truth that would change everything.

Chapter 13: The Confrontation

I find Ryan at a charity event, surrounded by Nashville's elite, their laughter echoing off the gilded walls of the banquet hall like a prelude to a symphony composed in superficiality. Crystal chandeliers cast a warm glow, and the air is thick with the cloying scent of expensive perfume and the sharp tang of overpriced hors d'oeuvres. Everyone pretends to care about the cause, but I know the truth: they're here for the Instagram stories, the whispered rumors, and the chance to rub elbows with the city's glitterati.

Ryan stands at the center of this manufactured glamour, a dapper figure in a tailored navy suit, his dark hair perfectly tousled. He looks every bit the part of a man in control, his smile polished to perfection, but when our eyes lock, something in his demeanor shifts. For a fleeting second, the mask slips. I see the man I once knew, the one who poured out his secrets to me over midnight coffee, the one who made me believe in the possibility of something real between us.

A rush of emotions sweeps over me—nostalgia, anger, and an inexplicable ache that gnaws at my insides. I don't care about the crowd, the glitzy decor, or even Vivian, who stands across the room, her smile sharp enough to slice through the air between us. The sight of her, perfectly poised in a shimmering dress that hugs her like a second skin, ignites a fire in my chest. She may think she's won, but I refuse to play the role of the defeated.

I stride toward Ryan, my heels clicking purposefully against the polished marble floor. With each step, the clamor of laughter and chatter fades into a dull roar, and all I can focus on is him. I pull him aside, into the shadow of a potted palm, where the warmth of the room turns to the coolness of uncertainty.

"Ryan," I demand, my voice low and steady, "I need answers."

His brow furrows as he glances around, his eyes flitting nervously like a deer in headlights. "Not here," he whispers, the tension in his voice palpable. But I refuse to back down.

"Too bad," I shoot back, my words sharp as shards of glass. "You think I'm going to stand here and watch you smile at Vivian while I'm being threatened?"

His expression darkens, the façade of calm slipping further. "Threatened? By who?"

"Someone who has a photo of us," I say, my voice barely above a whisper. It's a risk, revealing this information, but it's my only bargaining chip. "They said they'd use it if I don't stay away from you. What the hell is going on?"

At the mention of the photo, fear flickers behind his eyes, a stark contrast to the bravado he'd put on for the cameras. I watch him swallow hard, the air between us thick with unsaid words and hidden truths.

"Listen," he says, his tone shifting, the bravado fading. "You need to leave the city. It's not safe for you anymore."

His insistence strikes a nerve, igniting a fire in my chest that I can't ignore. "No. I won't run away. Not from you, not from whoever this is." My heart pounds in my ears, the rhythm of defiance echoing through my body. "I need to know the truth, Ryan. I need you to trust me."

His eyes narrow, assessing me with a look that makes my skin prickle. "You don't understand what you're asking. I never meant for you to get involved. But now you're in deeper than you think."

The weight of his words hangs heavy between us, each syllable laden with implications I'm not ready to unpack. I catch a glimpse of the boy I once loved, the one who had dared to dream, hidden beneath layers of concern and regret. "Then help me," I implore, desperation creeping into my voice. "Help me understand. I deserve that much."

Ryan hesitates, and I can almost see the gears turning in his mind. He glances over his shoulder at Vivian, who's now laughing too loudly at some joke that likely wasn't even funny. Something twists in my gut, a mixture of envy and determination. "What does she have that I don't?" I think bitterly. But I shake it off; this is about more than jealousy—it's about survival.

"I can't," he finally says, voice low and strained. "I wish I could, but the moment I let you in, you become a target. I can't let that happen."

My resolve hardens. "I'm already a target, Ryan. If they have that photo, I'm already in danger. You can't protect me by shutting me out."

He runs a hand through his hair, frustration evident in the clench of his jaw. "You don't understand. This goes deeper than you realize. There are people who—"

"Who what?" I interrupt, feeling the panic rise. "Who want to hurt us? Or who want to keep us apart?"

"Both," he admits, his voice dropping. The truth in his words lands like a punch to the gut. "I've made enemies, and those enemies are not just after me—they'll hurt anyone close to me."

The revelation sinks in, an icy tendril wrapping around my heart. "Then let me help you fight them," I say, the intensity of my determination surprising even myself. "I won't back down."

Ryan's gaze softens, and for a brief moment, I see the flicker of hope reflected in his eyes. "You have no idea what you're asking."

"Then enlighten me." My heart races as I step closer, closing the distance between us, emboldened by the fire burning within me. "Whatever it is, I'm ready."

He hesitates, and for the first time, I see the cracks in his armor. The vulnerability behind the bravado, the fear of letting me in. "Are you sure?" he finally asks, his voice barely above a whisper.

"Yes." I stand firm, the word a promise—a tether binding my heart to his. The chaos of the event fades into the background, leaving only us and the unspoken understanding hanging in the air. It's a dangerous game we're playing, but it's one I'm willing to engage in, and if Ryan won't take the leap, I'll drag him along with me. The stakes are high, but so is my determination to uncover the truth and protect what remains of us.

The moment hangs between us, thick with unspoken truths and the kind of tension that can only blossom in the shadows of a crowded room. Ryan's expression shifts, caught between concern and something more like desperation, and for a heartbeat, I feel the pull of all those late-night conversations we shared, where dreams felt tangible and the world outside faded into a comforting blur.

"Listen," he says, lowering his voice further, "you have to understand. The people I'm dealing with—" he hesitates, searching my eyes as if trying to gauge my readiness for what he might reveal. "They're not just interested in the photo. They want leverage, and they won't stop until they get it."

A chill runs down my spine at the weight of his words. "Leverage?" I repeat, feeling the ground beneath me shift slightly. "You mean they'll use me against you? Like a pawn in some twisted game?"

He grimaces, nodding slowly, the implication clear and terrifying. "Exactly. They know how much you mean to me, and that makes you a target."

I take a deep breath, attempting to steady my racing heart, but the air feels charged, alive with danger and unfulfilled promises. "Then we need to turn the tables," I declare, stubbornness igniting a spark in my chest. "If they think I'm a pawn, then let's make them think twice."

A flicker of admiration crosses his features, quickly masked by worry. "You're not thinking straight. This isn't a game, and I won't let you become collateral damage."

"And I won't let you play the martyr," I counter, crossing my arms defiantly. "You can't just decide what I can or can't handle. I'm not some damsel in distress waiting for a knight in shining armor. I'm in this with you."

His eyes soften, and the resolve begins to crack, revealing a glimpse of the vulnerability beneath his bravado. "You have no idea what they're capable of," he murmurs, the desperation threading through his words like a fraying rope.

"And you think I care more about my safety than finding out the truth?" I take a step closer, the energy between us palpable. "Whatever this is, whatever danger we're facing, I can handle it. But you have to let me in."

He runs a hand through his hair, the gesture so familiar it pulls at something deep within me. "This isn't about you being brave, Claire. It's about protecting you. I won't risk your life for a truth that might break us both."

And there it is—the unacknowledged fear that has haunted both of us since the moment things spiraled out of control. I see it now, the thin veneer of control he clings to while everything around him threatens to crumble. "If we don't confront this together, we'll never know what we could have had," I say, my voice softer, almost pleading.

Just as he's about to respond, the piercing sound of clinking glasses draws our attention. Vivian has approached, her smile bright but her eyes glinting with mischief. "Oh, Ryan! There you are," she chirps, her tone dripping with sweetness that feels anything but genuine. "I've been looking everywhere for you."

I roll my eyes, the need for her to intrude feeding the fire in my belly. "Perfect timing, as always," I say under my breath, not caring whether Ryan hears me.

He shifts uncomfortably, a tension knotting his shoulders as he straightens his posture. "Vivian, this isn't the best time," he says, his voice low but firm.

"Isn't it?" she retorts, not backing down. "It's a charity event, darling. We're all about being seen and making connections, right? I'd hate for you to miss out on mingling."

I shoot Ryan a look that says, This is your fault. He meets my gaze with a mixture of apology and frustration, clearly caught in a web of his own making.

"Vivian, I really need to talk to Claire," he says, trying to keep his voice steady, but I can hear the slight tremor beneath it.

"Oh, I get it. You need to discuss your little secrets." Her laughter rings out, sharp and unforgiving, as she leans in closer, a gleam of challenge in her eyes. "Just make sure you don't get too lost in your conversation. You wouldn't want anyone to overhear something... compromising."

Her words hang in the air, heavy with implication, and a rush of anger surges through me. "What's your game, Vivian?" I demand, stepping forward. "You think you can scare me away from him? Because let me assure you, it won't work."

Ryan's gaze flits between us, concern etched into his features. "Claire, don't—"

But I'm already on a roll, fueled by indignation. "I won't let you bully me. You think playing your little mind games will keep me from figuring this out? You're mistaken."

Vivian smirks, clearly enjoying the tension. "Oh, darling, you're the one who's mistaken. You're playing with fire, and I promise you, this is a game you won't win."

I glance at Ryan, searching for reassurance, but all I see is the shadow of regret cast over his face. "This isn't how it should be," he murmurs, his voice heavy with realization.

"No," I agree, my voice steadying. "But we're already here, and I refuse to back down now."

Vivian raises an eyebrow, amusement sparkling in her gaze. "Well, good luck, sweetie. I hope you have a fire extinguisher handy."

She glides away, her laughter trailing behind like a distant echo, leaving a chill in the air. The moment she's gone, I feel the weight of uncertainty settle in, thick and oppressive.

"I'm sorry about her," Ryan says, running a hand through his hair again. "She doesn't know when to back off."

I shake my head, feeling the fire of determination simmer just beneath the surface. "This isn't just about her, Ryan. We need to confront whatever's lurking in the shadows, and we can't do it half-heartedly."

He takes a deep breath, the weight of our situation settling in. "You're right," he admits, his gaze steady. "But promise me you'll be careful. If we're going to face this together, we need to be smart about it."

"Smart is my middle name," I reply with a grin, the tension easing just slightly. "Okay, maybe it's not, but you get the idea. We'll figure this out together, one way or another."

As the party continues around us, the laughter and music fading into a dull hum, I know we're teetering on the edge of something monumental. It's a gamble, a leap into the unknown, but for the first time in a long time, I feel alive—ready to take back the narrative that someone else tried to write for us. The stakes have never been higher, and I'm determined to play this hand until the very end.

The tension lingers in the air between us, thick and electric, as I refuse to back down from the path we've chosen. I can see the conflict in Ryan's eyes—a mix of desperation and the undeniable spark that always simmered beneath the surface between us. It's that spark that ignites my resolve, making me feel invincible, even in the face of uncertainty.

"Fine, let's be smart," I say, folding my arms and leaning against the palm tree, my resolve hardening like tempered steel. "But let's also be proactive. If they want to play, then we'll play. And if they think they can intimidate us, they've got another thing coming."

Ryan studies me, his expression shifting as he weighs my words. "You're not scared at all, are you?"

"Scared?" I laugh lightly, the sound almost foreign in the midst of the gathered crowd. "I mean, who doesn't love a little danger with their champagne? It's practically a Nashville cliché."

A small smile flits across his lips, but it's quickly replaced by the grimace of reality. "This isn't a joke, Claire. These people don't play nice, and they have resources we can't even begin to understand."

"Then let's outsmart them," I reply, a rush of adrenaline coursing through me. "What do we know about our adversary? Let's start with the facts."

He takes a deep breath, clearly torn between caution and admiration for my determination. "Okay. But we need to keep our heads down and not attract attention."

"Not my forte," I quip, flipping my hair over my shoulder and casting a glance at the throng of well-dressed attendees. "But I'll do my best."

With an uneasy truce hanging in the air, we make our way to a quieter corner of the room, away from the curious eyes that seem to follow Ryan like moths to a flame. The soft strains of a string quartet filter through the hall, creating a surreal atmosphere that feels almost out of place given the brewing storm.

"So, who's our shadowy figure?" I prompt, taking a seat on a plush velvet couch that feels far too luxurious for the crisis at hand.

He hesitates, glancing around as if checking for eavesdroppers. "It's someone I thought was an ally," he says, his voice lowered. "A business associate. But I recently discovered they've been working against me—feeding information to someone who wants to see me fall."

"What? Are you serious?" The gravity of his revelation sends a jolt through me. "Do you know who it is?"

"I have my suspicions." His jaw tightens. "It's a colleague named Mark. He's always been a little too eager to please and a little too friendly with the wrong crowd."

"Wow, how original. A backstabbing colleague? It's like we're in a bad corporate thriller." I roll my eyes, trying to lighten the mood, but the weight of reality sinks in. "So what's the play? Do we go after him directly?"

He shakes his head, a grim smile barely touching his lips. "Going after Mark would be reckless. He has connections that could complicate everything. We need to gather information first, find out who else he's involved with."

"Fine. Let's play the long game." I lean forward, excitement bubbling beneath my skin. "Let's become the best spies this city has ever seen. We'll infiltrate his life, make him think we're on his side."

Ryan raises an eyebrow, intrigued yet cautious. "You really think you can pull that off?"

"Oh, please. I've spent years navigating the treacherous waters of social media influencers and wannabe Nashville stars. I can charm the socks off anyone," I say with a wink, puffing out my chest in mock bravado.

He chuckles, the sound like a breath of fresh air. "Okay, Agent Claire. Let's devise a plan. We need to start digging through his connections, see if we can find anything useful."

"Consider it done," I declare, the thrill of the chase sending shivers down my spine. "And if we need to blend in, I can always throw on a disguise. Maybe a classic 'girl next door' look."

"Or a 'mysterious femme fatale,'" Ryan suggests, his eyes twinkling with mischief.

"Now you're speaking my language," I retort, feeling the electricity in the air shift from anxiety to anticipation.

But just as I start to outline my grand plan, my phone buzzes violently against the velvet couch. My heart leaps into my throat as I fumble for it, the name on the screen causing the world around me to momentarily blur.

Unknown Number.

"Should I answer?" I glance at Ryan, who shrugs, clearly on edge.

"Only if you want to risk a potential bombshell."

"Great. My favorite kind of conversation." I swallow hard and press the green button. "Hello?"

"Claire," a voice croons, smooth like honey but laced with menace. "I hear you've been asking questions. Very curious, aren't we?"

My pulse races, the weight of his tone sinking in like a stone. "Who is this?"

The laugh that follows is chilling, an echo of mockery. "Someone who knows exactly what you're digging for. And I suggest you stop before you uncover things that aren't meant to be found."

"Is that a threat?" My voice quivers slightly, but I steel myself against the fear creeping in.

"Just a friendly warning. You really don't want to get involved in this game."

"Funny. I thought I was already playing," I retort, the bravado I'm trying to project flickering.

"You have no idea what you're dealing with," the voice replies, a low rumble that sends chills down my spine. "Consider this your last chance to walk away. Or else the consequences could be... dire."

The line goes dead, leaving an eerie silence hanging in the air. My hands tremble slightly as I lower the phone, the reality of the situation crashing over me like a cold wave.

Ryan's eyes narrow, concern etching deep lines across his brow. "What did they say?"

"Something about consequences," I whisper, my heart racing. "They know I'm involved. They know everything."

"Okay," he says, his voice steady despite the chaos around us. "We'll figure this out. Together."

But even as he speaks, a shadow flickers at the edge of my vision—an ominous figure in a tailored suit, a knowing smile playing at the corners of his lips. My breath catches as recognition washes over me, and I realize we're far from safe.

I grip the couch's armrest, the fabric digging into my palm as I look at Ryan, terror flooding my senses. "We have to move. Now."

Just as we stand to escape, a loud crack reverberates through the room, followed by the startled gasps of the guests. I turn toward the source, my heart plummeting as I see it: the doors swinging wide open, a swarm of dark figures entering, each one cloaked in shadow and intent.

And as their gazes land on us, I know—this isn't just a warning anymore. This is the beginning of something far more dangerous than I ever imagined.

Chapter 14: Beneath the Surface

The air at the lake house was thick with the scent of pine and damp earth, a stark contrast to the sterile chill of the city. I could almost taste the freedom here, sweet and fresh, mingling with the sharp tang of the water splashing against the weathered wood of the dock. Ryan and I sat with our feet dangling over the edge, the soft sunlight reflecting off the lake in shimmering patches, casting a magical spell around us. I was torn between the beauty of the moment and the turmoil in my chest.

"What are we doing here, Ryan?" My voice was steadier than I felt. "You shouldn't have brought me."

He turned, his expression a mix of regret and defiance. "I didn't have a choice. You deserve to know the truth."

His words hung in the air like a heavy fog. I glanced at him, trying to reconcile the boy who made me laugh over coffee and the man who now carried the weight of secrets that threatened to crush us both. His brown hair caught the sun, casting soft shadows across his cheekbones, and I felt the pull of my heart against the reality of our situation. Beneath the laughter and easy banter, a storm brewed, one that had been gathering momentum since the moment I'd first stumbled into his orbit.

Ryan took a deep breath, and the sound of the water lapping at the dock filled the silence between us. "My father's not just some businessman, Chloe. He's involved in things that... that go beyond what you can imagine." His eyes searched mine for understanding, and I knew then that whatever came next, it would change everything. "He makes deals with people who don't just want to build towers. They control the city from the shadows."

As he spoke, his voice dropped, almost conspiratorial, laced with a tension that set my nerves on edge. I leaned closer, drawn into the gravity of his words. "What do you mean? Who are these people?"

"They're powerful," he said, looking out across the water as if the answers floated just beneath the surface. "They've got their hands in every industry, every corner of this city. Real estate, politics, you name it. And my family—my father in particular—he's at the center of it all. Money flows through our family like blood, but it's tainted, Chloe. It's dirty."

A chill crept up my spine. "And what does that mean for us? For me?"

Ryan shifted, his jaw tightening. "It means you're in danger."

The weight of his words crashed over me like a wave. I wanted to recoil, to deny the truth that loomed over us, but the anger that had been brewing inside me pushed back. "You think I'm scared of your father's empire? You think I'm scared of this mess?"

He ran a hand through his hair, frustration bubbling beneath the surface. "You should be. I wish you could see it the way I do. It's not just about me; it's about the whole city. You've uncovered something that they won't let go of easily."

I scoffed, my voice sharper than I intended. "So what now? We just sit here and wait for the storm to come crashing down?"

His eyes locked onto mine, a spark of something—determination, perhaps—flickering in their depths. "No. We fight back."

A laugh bubbled out of me, incredulous and tinged with bitterness. "Fight back? Against a shadowy empire? Ryan, this isn't a movie. We can't just wave a magic wand and make it all go away."

"Maybe not a magic wand," he said, a slight grin breaking through the tension. "But we can dig deeper. You're a journalist, Chloe. You know how to uncover the truth. We can expose them."

I paused, considering his words. The thrill of the chase—the spark that had first ignited my passion for journalism—pulsed through my veins like a heartbeat. But was I ready to dive into a world where the stakes were so high? "And what if they find out? What if they come after us?"

He leaned closer, his intensity palpable. "Then we'll be ready. Together."

The promise hung in the air, charged with potential. My heart raced, caught in the tug-of-war between fear and excitement. What if we could do something? What if this was the moment that defined us?

"Fine," I said, the defiance in my tone taking shape. "Let's expose your family's empire. But if we're doing this, we do it right. No half-measures."

His smile widened, a glimmer of hope illuminating the darkness that threatened to envelop us. "That's the spirit. We'll start with what we know. Your research, my connections—it's a powerful combination."

"Powerful," I echoed, still wary of the enormity of our undertaking. The realization that I was stepping into a battle against forces far beyond what I'd ever faced weighed on me, but I couldn't deny the adrenaline surging through my veins. "And dangerous."

"Dangerous is my middle name," he said, his tone lightening the heaviness in my chest. "But we'll do this together. I promise."

As we sat there, the sun dipping lower in the sky, casting golden rays over the lake, I felt the weight of the world shift ever so slightly. This was more than just a quest for the truth; it was a plunge into uncharted waters. The path ahead was fraught with uncertainty, but the bond forming between us—stronger than either of us realized—was a beacon in the dark. Together, we would face whatever lay beneath the surface.

We spent the evening on the dock, the sunlight bleeding into a tapestry of orange and pink across the sky, as if the world was drawing the curtains on an elaborate performance. I could hear the frogs croaking their evening song, their voices harmonizing with the gentle lapping of the lake, creating a soundscape both soothing and surreal. But the serenity felt as fragile as the fleeting twilight, and I couldn't shake the weight of the truth we'd unearthed.

"I can't believe your family is involved in this," I said, my voice barely above a whisper, as if saying it too loudly would conjure the shadows lurking just beyond our sight. "How did you get mixed up in all this?"

Ryan sighed, leaning back on his palms, his gaze fixed on the horizon where the sun melted into the water. "It's a family business, I guess. When you grow up in it, you don't see the red flags; you just accept it. But then you start to see things differently. The moment I realized my father wasn't just a businessman, everything changed."

"And now you want to take him down?" I asked, raising an eyebrow. "That's a tall order. Don't you think it's a little risky?"

He chuckled, the sound low and filled with a hint of defiance. "Risky? Oh, honey, risky is my middle name. If you want to survive in this world, you've got to be willing to gamble. And I'm not talking about poker nights with friends." He looked at me, his eyes serious now. "I've watched him destroy lives without a second thought. I'm done standing by. It's time to flip the table."

The fire behind his words ignited something in me. I had always chased stories that mattered, but this was different. This was not just another article; it was a crusade. "Okay, let's say we expose him. What then? We waltz into the police station with a shiny piece of evidence and say, 'Look, here's the real estate mogul who's not just selling condos but also selling souls?'"

Ryan smirked, his expression teasing but his eyes gleaming with conviction. "Well, when you put it that way, it sounds downright delightful. But no, we need something concrete. We'll gather evidence—emails, contracts, anything we can find that ties him to these shady deals. We'll take it to the right people."

"Right people? You mean the people who are probably in his pocket?" I rolled my eyes, frustration creeping into my tone. "This isn't some movie where the hero always wins, Ryan. This is real life, and in real life, the bad guys don't always lose."

He leaned forward, intensity etched into his features. "I get it, Chloe. But it's time to play the game differently. If we can get enough proof, if we can show the public what he's really doing... maybe we can create a shift. Maybe we can pull the mask off the monster."

The fervor in his voice sent a thrill coursing through me. What we were contemplating felt monumental, like igniting a spark in the dark. Yet beneath that exhilaration lay a nagging doubt, a voice whispering that we were risking everything—our safety, our lives.

"Let's assume we pull this off," I said, my skepticism creeping back in. "What if they retaliate? What if they come after us?"

Ryan's expression softened, and he reached out, brushing his thumb against my knuckles, a gesture so simple yet profound. "I won't let anything happen to you. I promise."

The sincerity in his eyes sent a wave of warmth through me, but I couldn't help but feel the absurdity of it all. Here we were, two ordinary people embroiled in a deadly game that was larger than life. "You know, I never imagined my life would take a turn like this. One minute I'm writing about city events, and now I'm talking about taking down crime syndicates."

Ryan laughed, a sound like bubbling water. "Welcome to the real world. It's messy, unpredictable, and absolutely wild. You wanted a story, right?"

"I wanted a good story, not a death wish," I shot back, but a smile tugged at my lips despite myself.

The laughter lingered in the air, but as the sun dipped lower, casting long shadows across the dock, I felt the weight of uncertainty creeping back in. Just as I opened my mouth to voice my fears, a rustling from the nearby trees made us both freeze.

"Did you hear that?" I whispered, my heart racing.

Ryan's eyes widened, the playful atmosphere dissipating instantly. "Yeah, I did. Stay quiet."

We strained to listen, the usual sounds of the lake now swallowed by a tense silence. Then, just as suddenly, a figure stepped into view, silhouetted against the dying light. My heart plummeted.

It was a man, tall and broad-shouldered, wearing a dark jacket that looked out of place in the serenity of the lake house. His eyes scanned the area, sharp and calculating. The hairs on the back of my neck stood up, and I instinctively inched closer to Ryan, who tensed beside me.

"Who is that?" I murmured, dread pooling in my stomach.

"I don't know," Ryan said, his voice low and tense. "But I think it's time we get inside."

As we quietly slipped off the dock and crept towards the cabin, the adrenaline surged through me, a heady mix of fear and anticipation. What had started as a quest for truth was morphing into a dangerous game, and suddenly, it felt very real.

The man continued to scan the dock, his expression unreadable, and I knew we had crossed a line we could never uncross. Whatever shadows lurked in Ryan's past had found us, and now we were tangled in their web.

I glanced back at the figure, heart pounding, and as darkness settled in around us, I couldn't help but wonder just how deep the secrets ran—and if we would make it out unscathed.

The moment we stepped inside the lake house, the atmosphere shifted. The scent of aged wood and lingering smoke hung in the air, wrapping around us like a comforting but deceptive blanket. The walls, adorned with faded photographs of long-ago summers, whispered tales of joy, laughter, and secrets. I could almost picture Ryan as a boy, carefree and blissfully unaware of the shadows his family cast. But now those shadows loomed larger than ever, and the stillness felt like a trap waiting to spring.

"What do we do now?" I asked, my voice barely a whisper as I leaned against the door, keeping my eyes on the window. The rustling outside was replaced by a deep silence that hung like a fog, suffocating in its intensity.

Ryan ran a hand through his hair, frustration tightening his features. "We need to figure out who that guy is. If he's here because of me—because of what we're about to do—then we need to be smart about this."

"Smart? You mean more than just hiding like deer in the headlights?" I shot back, my heart racing. "What if he's one of your father's goons? What if he's here to silence you—us?"

He stepped closer, his expression serious, almost fierce. "Then we can't let him catch us off guard. We need a plan. Let's see if we can gather any supplies."

I took a deep breath, willing my heartbeat to settle as I nodded. Ryan began rummaging through the small kitchen, tossing aside a few mismatched dishes and old utensils. I moved to the window, peering out at the fading light. The man was still outside, lingering just beyond the tree line, the outline of his figure blending into the growing dusk.

"There's got to be something we can use," Ryan said, frustration lacing his words. "What about those old camping supplies? They must be in one of these cabinets."

I turned my attention back to him, watching as he opened a cupboard that creaked in protest. "You know, this place could use some TLC. I can't believe your family just left it to rot like this."

"Not everyone can be as meticulous as you," he quipped, shooting me a grin that momentarily lit up the tension in the room. "Besides, my dad doesn't care about this place. He only cares about what he can control."

As he searched, I glanced outside again, my eyes narrowing at the figure. Something about him felt too familiar, but I couldn't place it. A shiver ran down my spine, and I turned back to Ryan, my voice low. "I think he's coming this way."

"Hide," Ryan hissed, darting towards the only other room in the cabin. I followed him, pressing myself against the wall as we slipped into a small bedroom filled with dusty furniture and forgotten memories. Ryan gestured towards a large wardrobe in the corner, and we crouched behind it, hearts pounding in unison.

The door creaked as it swung open, and we held our breath, listening as footsteps approached the cabin. The soft crunch of leaves and twigs echoed ominously, and I felt the blood drain from my face. "Who is he?" I whispered, feeling the weight of uncertainty in the air.

"Not sure," Ryan replied, his voice barely above a murmur. "But we're about to find out."

The footsteps stopped just outside the door. I could almost hear the man's breath, measured and steady, as if he were assessing the situation. My mind raced, and I could feel the tension building like a pressure cooker ready to explode. A sudden thud against the door sent shockwaves through my body, and I stifled a gasp.

"Open up!" the voice barked, gravelly and authoritative.

Ryan's eyes widened, and in that moment, I could see the gears turning in his head. "We can't stay here," he whispered, his tone urgent. "We have to find another way out."

As we edged toward the window, the man's voice rose again, more insistent this time. "I know you're in there, Ryan. You can't hide from me."

My heart dropped. I knew that voice—had heard it in hushed conversations, always laced with danger. It belonged to someone who should have been a ghost in Ryan's life, a figure he had desperately tried to escape.

"Your father sent me," the man continued, and I could hear the menace threading through his words. "He wants to know what you're up to. You'd better open this door before things get messy."

Ryan's expression turned grave, and I felt a rush of determination surge through me. "You can't let him in," I said, urgency creeping into my voice. "We have to get out now."

He nodded, and we moved quickly to the window, peering through the grimy glass. The fading light made it difficult to see, but I caught a glimpse of the man's face—sharp features, dark hair, and eyes like cold steel. I could feel a knot tightening in my stomach. "What's the plan?" I asked, glancing back at Ryan, whose face had hardened with resolve.

"We go out the back and circle around the house," he replied, determination igniting in his eyes. "If we can make it to the trees, we'll find a way to get to the car without him seeing us."

The man's voice boomed again, punctuating the air with a threat. "Don't make this harder than it has to be, Ryan! You know your father won't be pleased if I have to come in after you."

Ryan took a deep breath, his expression set. "Let's move."

We slipped out the back door, my heart racing as we darted across the porch and into the thickening shadows. The trees loomed like sentinels, and I could feel the night closing in around us. As we navigated the underbrush, I kept glancing over my shoulder, half expecting to see the man charging after us.

The cool night air stung my lungs as we stumbled through the darkness, but we pressed on, hearts pounding in sync. Just as we reached the edge of the tree line, a loud crash erupted from the cabin.

"Ryan!" I hissed, fear surging through me as we ducked behind a large oak tree. I peered back toward the cabin, and my breath caught in my throat.

The man was inside now, stalking through the rooms with a predatory grace, scanning for any sign of us. The tension hung thick, a palpable entity that filled the night.

I turned to Ryan, who was pale but resolute, his jaw set with determination. "We need to find the car. Now."

We started moving again, adrenaline fueling our steps as we weaved between the trees, hearts racing with every crunch of leaves beneath our feet. But as we crested a small hill, the headlights of a vehicle suddenly pierced the darkness, cutting through the trees like a knife.

"Chloe!" Ryan's voice broke through the chaos, his eyes wide with panic. "It's them! We have to go back!"

Before I could respond, the vehicle's engine roared to life, illuminating the space around us. The headlights swung in our direction, and I froze, fear wrapping its icy fingers around my throat.

"Chloe!" Ryan shouted, pulling me back into the cover of the trees as the headlights continued their search.

Panic surged as the figures emerged from the vehicle, their intentions clear. They were here to hunt us down.

My mind raced with possibilities as the realization struck hard: we weren't just running from Ryan's past anymore; we were caught in a game where the stakes had skyrocketed. And the only thing left to do was to find a way to fight back—or risk losing everything.

"Where do we go?" I whispered, desperation edging my voice.

"Follow me," he urged, his eyes scanning for a route as the weight of the situation pressed heavily on both of us.

As we turned to move deeper into the forest, a sudden crack echoed behind us, and the realization hit me like a freight train.

We weren't just being watched. We were being hunted.

Chapter 15: Lines Crossed

The soft glow of my phone screen illuminated the small apartment, casting shadows that danced against the peeling paint of the walls, like specters in a haunted house. I had just settled onto my worn-out couch, the springs creaking in protest beneath me, when the familiar chime of a message broke the silence. My heart sank as I recognized Vivian's name at the top. I felt a rush of adrenaline; her texts had a way of making my pulse race, not from excitement but from a primal sense of dread.

"Leave Ryan alone, or you'll wish you hadn't." The message was succinct, void of the coyness that had marked our earlier exchanges. It was a threat, stark and brutal, like the autumn wind that rattled the bare branches outside. I stared at the words, an uncomfortable mix of anger and fear bubbling in my chest. She wasn't just a rival; she was a storm, and I was standing in its path, drenched and unprepared.

I dropped the phone onto the coffee table, feeling the need for some space, some distance from her words that felt like ice. My reflection in the window caught my eye, the way my hair fell in messy waves, the dark circles under my eyes painted a picture of sleepless nights haunted by thoughts of Ryan and Vivian. But the fear was a veil I was ready to rip away. Vivian had ruled my thoughts for too long, but it was time to reclaim my narrative.

With determination igniting my senses, I leaned forward, grabbing my laptop. The air around me crackled with the electricity of purpose. If Vivian wanted a battle, I was ready to dig into the shadows she cast, to unearth the secrets buried beneath the polished facade she so carefully maintained. I opened a search engine, fingers poised over the keys, heart racing with a thrill that bordered on reckless.

Her life unfolded on the screen like a web of intricacies and lies. She was more than Ryan's business partner; she was the puppeteer, her strings entwined in every corner of his world. I uncovered articles about her impressive ascent in the corporate world, her charming smile melting hearts and convincing the skeptical. But behind that smile lurked the chilling fact: she was the architect of Ryan's entrapment, her machinations ensuring he remained ensnared in the gilded cage of his family's expectations.

A jolt of indignation surged through me. How dare she treat him like a pawn in her game? Ryan wasn't just a figure on her chessboard; he was a person with dreams, desires, and a spirit that yearned for freedom. I felt the swell of anger, like a tidal wave crashing against the shores of my resolve. It was time to act, to dig deeper, and reveal the hidden layers of Vivian's carefully crafted life.

As I sifted through the information, my determination morphed into a strategy. I needed to understand the nuances of her power, the way she manipulated not just Ryan but the entire network of people around her. I stumbled upon an old article, detailing a charity gala she hosted, a night framed in glitz and glamour. Beneath the surface, whispers hinted at shady dealings, the way she had leveraged charitable donations to advance her interests. It was the first crack in her flawless armor.

I printed the article, a tangible piece of ammunition. With every word, the tension coiled tighter in my chest. I could almost feel Vivian's presence, her cool demeanor slipping as I chipped away at her facade. As the printer whirred to life, my phone vibrated again, another message from Vivian. "You think you can play with fire and not get burned?" The words dripped with venom, and a strange exhilaration coursed through me.

"I'm already burned, Vivian," I muttered to myself, a defiant grin creeping onto my lips. "But I'll be damned if I let you stoke those flames."

I turned my focus back to the screen, my fingers flying over the keyboard, uncovering anything that might illuminate her dark corners. Hours melted into the night, punctuated by the low hum of the city outside, a world oblivious to my one-woman crusade against a formidable foe. My eyes strained, fatigue gnawing at the edges of my resolve, but the thrill of uncovering more kept me tethered to the glow of the laptop. Each new discovery felt like a victory, a small rebellion against the shadows Vivian cast.

The air thickened with anticipation as I pieced together a timeline of Vivian's rise to power. Connections emerged like threads woven into a tapestry, each one hinting at a hidden agenda, a ruthless ambition veiled by a disarming smile. I felt an odd mix of empathy and resentment for her, the way she had been forged in the fires of ambition but now wielded that fire as a weapon.

But that wasn't enough. I needed to confront her, to unmask her in front of Ryan. As the sun began to rise, casting a golden light through my window, I felt a surge of clarity wash over me. I would no longer be the pawn in her game; I would become the queen.

With a plan forming in my mind, I grabbed my phone, heart pounding as I texted Ryan. "Can we meet? I need to talk to you about Vivian." The message sent, I leaned back against the couch, breathless with anticipation. The stakes had never been higher, and for the first time in a long time, I felt a flicker of hope ignite within me. This was just the beginning, and I was ready to play my hand.

The clatter of the coffee shop's door chimed as I stepped inside, the familiar aroma of freshly ground beans wrapping around me like a warm hug. I spotted Ryan at our usual corner table, his brows knitted together in thought, a latte forgotten beside him. He looked up, and for a fleeting moment, the storm clouds brewing between us evaporated in the sunlight streaming through the window. But that warmth faded quickly; the weight of my message hung heavily in the air.

"Hey," I greeted, sliding into the seat opposite him. "You look like you're pondering the meaning of life."

His lips curved into a half-smile, but the concern in his eyes betrayed him. "More like trying to solve a Rubik's Cube blindfolded." He gestured at his untouched drink, a hint of humor in his voice. "I guess I'm not as good at multi-tasking as I thought."

I chuckled lightly, but my heart raced, a dissonant rhythm against the gentle background chatter. "I hope you're not going to take that approach to our conversation." I leaned in, lowering my voice. "I really need you to focus."

Ryan's gaze sharpened. "What's going on? You sounded serious in your text."

I took a deep breath, the moment stretching like taffy. "It's about Vivian." The name slipped from my lips like poison, leaving a bitter aftertaste. I watched as his expression shifted, the easy camaraderie replaced by a guarded tension.

"What about her?" he asked, his tone carefully neutral, but I could see the flicker of concern in his eyes.

"I've been looking into her," I said, each word feeling like a pebble dropped into a still pond, creating ripples of uncertainty. "She's not who you think she is, Ryan. She's been manipulating everything, pulling the strings behind the scenes. You're not just her business partner; you're part of her game."

He stared at me, disbelief etched across his features. "What do you mean? She's... she's been supportive. I thought we were building something together."

I couldn't help but notice the way his voice faltered, a mix of admiration and confusion. "Supportive? Or controlling? Vivian doesn't do anything without a reason, and you've been so wrapped up in your work with her that I fear you haven't seen the larger picture."

Ryan's brow furrowed as he processed my words. "I just don't understand. Why would she want to manipulate me?"

"Because you're her ticket to something bigger," I said, urgency creeping into my voice. "You're her way of maintaining a grip on this family business and its secrets. She's woven you into this web of corruption, and now you're stuck."

His expression shifted from skepticism to realization. "But she's always been so... charming. I just assumed—"

"Charm is her weapon," I interjected, my heart pounding in my chest. "The moment you start questioning her, that charm turns into something sharper. I got a text from her this morning, warning me to back off. It's a threat, Ryan."

The warmth in his eyes dimmed, replaced by a chilling resolve. "You didn't mention this earlier. What exactly did she say?"

I pulled my phone from my pocket, scrolling through our conversation, and handed it over. "Read it."

He frowned at the screen, and when he looked up, the light of disbelief had shifted into a darkness that ignited a fire of anger. "She can't just intimidate you like this! We have to do something."

"It's not just about us, Ryan. She's playing a much larger game," I replied, trying to steady my racing thoughts. "If we confront her without a plan, we're just setting ourselves up as targets."

"But ignoring it isn't an option either," he said, the steel in his voice palpable. "What if she's using your past against you? What if she's already got something on you?"

I swallowed hard, recalling the memories I'd buried deep. "I won't let her use my past to hurt us. I'll expose her. We can outsmart her, but we need to be strategic. Think like she does."

Ryan leaned back, fingers rubbing his temples as if trying to ease the tension pooling in his mind. "Okay, so what's our first step?"

I felt a surge of adrenaline at his willingness to fight alongside me. "We need to gather evidence. I've found some articles hinting at her shady dealings. If we can connect her to something illegal, we can go to the authorities. But first, we need to ensure we're safe."

"Safe?" His brows shot up. "How do we do that? You've seen how she operates."

"We'll get ahead of her. We need to strategize our next moves, watch our backs. I have a few contacts in journalism who might be able to help us dig deeper. If she's as dirty as I suspect, we can expose her."

Ryan nodded slowly, the fire in his eyes reigniting. "I can reach out to some of my contacts in the business world. If anyone knows about her, it's them."

A small grin tugged at my lips, a spark of hope illuminating the looming darkness. "Exactly. Together, we can shine a light in her shadows. We'll put her on the defensive."

The tension between us began to shift, transforming into a kind of electric camaraderie that buzzed in the air. "So, what's our battle cry?" Ryan joked, his usual charm resurfacing, lifting the heaviness between us.

"Maybe something like, 'Don't mess with the underdogs'?" I quipped back, smirking.

He chuckled, but the laughter quickly faded as he glanced out the window, his expression turning serious. "I just can't shake the feeling that she's always one step ahead. What if she already knows we're onto her?"

"Then we outsmart her," I replied, feeling the determination solidify in my bones. "We act like everything's normal. She can't use our suspicions against us if she doesn't see them coming."

"Okay," Ryan said, nodding as if he were cementing a pact. "Let's do this. I'm in."

As we settled into planning, the coffee shop buzzed around us, oblivious to the brewing storm just outside its doors. I felt an unexpected rush of exhilaration, the world suddenly vibrant and electric, as though the caffeine-infused air had awakened something dormant inside me. It was a dangerous game we were playing, but with Ryan by my side, the stakes felt different. They felt attainable.

Just then, the bell chimed again, and my heart skipped a beat as I caught a glimpse of Vivian's silhouette through the glass door. The world outside had darkened, but we were ready. We were no longer just players in her game; we were now contenders, and it felt exhilarating.

The atmosphere in the coffee shop had shifted, the air thick with tension that crackled like static electricity. My heart pounded in my chest, not from the caffeine coursing through my veins, but from the realization that our lives had transformed into a high-stakes chess game. I glanced at Ryan, who sat across from me, his fingers nervously tapping against the table. The cozy café, once a backdrop for our lighthearted banter, now felt like a stage for an impending showdown.

As we discussed our plans to uncover Vivian's secrets, the barista passed by, her hands full of steaming cups, oblivious to the storm brewing at our table. I sipped my latte, its warmth grounding me, but the unease gnawed at my insides like a hungry predator. My mind raced with possibilities, each more harrowing than the last. What if Vivian anticipated our every move? What if she had already turned the tables?

"Let's not waste time," I said, trying to shake off the creeping dread. "We should start reaching out to my contacts today. The sooner we get moving, the better."

Ryan nodded, his expression a mix of determination and concern. "I'll message some people who might know more about her connections. If she's been involved in anything illegal, someone will have seen something."

"Good idea," I replied, feeling a flicker of hope. "And I can contact that journalist friend of mine. She has a knack for digging up dirt."

The plan began to crystallize, a tangible sense of purpose wrapping around us like a protective shield. As we leaned into our roles, plotting out our next steps, the world outside the café window blurred into a backdrop of bustling pedestrians and honking cars, mere noise against the intensity of our focus. We were allies now, two warriors in a battle against a cunning adversary.

After we had formulated our approach, I felt a slight shift in the energy around us, as if the universe had suddenly tilted. I glanced up, my heart sinking. Vivian stood at the entrance, her striking figure framed by the light filtering in from the street. She scanned the room, her gaze honing in on our table, and my blood ran cold.

"What's the plan now?" Ryan whispered, eyes wide.

"Act natural," I replied, the command sounding more like a prayer than a strategy. My stomach twisted as Vivian glided toward us, her smile bright enough to light the entire room, but I could sense the darkness lurking just beneath the surface.

"Ryan! What a delightful surprise!" she exclaimed, her voice dripping with sweetness that made my skin crawl. She turned her gaze toward me, her eyes narrowing slightly. "And you're here too. How charming."

"Vivian," Ryan greeted, trying to sound casual, but the tension radiating off him was palpable. "What brings you here?"

"Oh, just grabbing a coffee. It's such a lovely day, isn't it?" Her smile didn't quite reach her eyes, and I felt an icy shiver crawl down my spine. "You know, it's funny running into you two together. I had the strangest feeling I might see you."

"Funny how that works," I managed, forcing a smile that felt like it might shatter. "So... coffee, huh? You must be really busy."

"Always busy," she replied, leaning slightly closer, her voice lowering conspiratorially. "But I can always make time for friends. Especially when they're planning something."

I caught the undertone of her words, the threat wrapped in sugary sweetness, and I fought the urge to shiver. "Planning? We're just enjoying a casual chat," I said, forcing a lightness into my tone that felt completely unnatural.

"Casual, of course," she echoed, her smile unwavering. "But you know, some conversations can lead to complications."

"Is that so?" Ryan interjected, an edge of defiance creeping into his voice. "I think we can handle complications just fine."

Vivian's expression shifted, the flicker of amusement replaced by something darker. "Oh, I have no doubt about that, Ryan. But complications have a way of coming back around, don't they?"

A beat of silence passed, thick and suffocating, as the unspoken tension crackled between us. I felt a chill ripple through me, like the prelude to a storm, as her gaze darted between Ryan and me. "I'll leave you to your chat," she said finally, her voice dripping with false cheer. "But remember, it's a small world. Be careful where you tread."

As she walked away, I released a breath I didn't realize I had been holding. Ryan ran a hand through his hair, frustration etched on his face. "She's playing with fire, and she knows it."

"We need to be careful," I replied, my voice low. "She's right about one thing: we're not just in a small world; we're in her world now. We have to tread lightly."

Before we could regroup, my phone buzzed in my pocket, pulling my attention away from the chaos of the moment. I fished it out and stared at the screen, my heart dropping as I read the message.

"Don't think I won't be watching you. Consider this a warning. You have no idea what I'm capable of."

I felt the blood drain from my face, the reality of Vivian's threat sinking in like a stone in water. "Ryan," I whispered, my voice barely above a breath. "She knows."

"What do you mean?"

"She just sent me a message." I showed him the screen, my fingers trembling slightly. "She's onto us."

Panic flashed across Ryan's features, his brow furrowing as he processed the implications. "We need to regroup, come up with a new plan."

Before I could respond, a loud crash echoed through the café, cutting through the tension like a knife. The door swung open violently, and a figure stumbled inside, a familiar face twisted in panic. It was my friend Jess, her usually bright demeanor replaced by a look of sheer terror.

"Guys! You need to get out of here!" she shouted, breathless and wide-eyed.

"Jess, what are you talking about?" I asked, the chaos around us suddenly intensifying as patrons turned to stare, their expressions a mix of confusion and alarm.

"Vivian!" she gasped, pointing back toward the door. "She's not just watching you; she's coming for you!"

Before I could comprehend the gravity of her words, I caught a glimpse of movement outside. A black car had pulled up to the curb, its engine roaring ominously. I felt my heart stop as the realization hit me like a punch to the gut.

"Run!" Jess yelled, her voice cutting through the noise as she grabbed my arm, pulling me toward the back exit.

Ryan was right behind us, his face set with determination, but I could feel the weight of Vivian's presence bearing down on us, a shadow creeping closer. My mind raced as we darted through the café, adrenaline pumping through my veins, the fear of what lay ahead propelling us forward.

We burst through the back door, the cool air hitting us like a splash of ice water. My pulse pounded in my ears, drowning out everything else as we sprinted down the alley, the shadows elongating behind us. I couldn't shake the feeling that Vivian was only a step behind, her eyes watching, calculating.

"Where do we go?" Ryan shouted, glancing back at the café, the chaos we left behind already beginning to fade into the distance.

"I don't know!" I gasped, searching for any hint of safety.

As we turned a corner, a screeching of tires echoed, and I dared to look back. The black car was speeding down the street, its headlights cutting through the darkness like a predator closing in on its prey.

"Jess, keep running!" I yelled, my heart racing as I urged her forward. But as I turned, a cold hand grasped my shoulder, yanking me back.

I was trapped in a nightmare, the realization crashing over me as I found myself face-to-face with the very person I had hoped to outsmart. Vivian stood there, her smile as sharp as a blade, her eyes glinting with something wickedly triumphant.

"Did you really think you could escape me?" she purred, and as the darkness closed in around us, I knew this was only the beginning.

Chapter 16: Caught in the Crossfire

Every time I hear the creaking of the floorboards beneath my feet, I brace myself, half-expecting them to snap under the weight of my resolve. The hotel room, dimly lit by the flickering neon sign outside, feels like a cage. It used to be my sanctuary, a place where I could drown out the world with a glass of wine and the rhythm of my laptop keys. But now, with each passing day, it morphs into a war zone, with me as the reluctant soldier, trapped in a battle I never signed up for.

I push the door open, the heavy wood swinging with a reluctant groan, and the sight that greets me is more than just disheartening—it's a stark reminder that I've crossed a line, and there's no going back. My belongings are strewn across the floor, pages of my notes fluttering like wounded birds in the draft. The laptop, once a trusted companion in my quest for truth, lies shattered, its screen a spider web of despair. It's as if my entire world has been turned upside down, and I can't help but wonder who orchestrated this chaos. Vivian's shadow looms large in my mind, a sinister puppet master tugging at the strings of my unraveling life.

My heart races as the adrenaline surges through my veins. This wasn't just a random act of vandalism; it was a message. They know I'm getting too close, and they want me to feel the weight of their threats. I sink to my knees, scrambling to gather the scattered pages, desperate to salvage whatever I can of my work. Each ripped sheet is a fragment of hope, a piece of my stubborn determination to expose the truth behind Ryan's family—their secrets, their lies. But every time I piece my narrative back together, I feel the sharp edge of anxiety creeping in, gnawing at my confidence.

"Let me guess, your day has been nothing short of delightful?" Ryan's voice cuts through the haze of my thoughts. He appears at the door, a towering figure framed by the dim light, his brow furrowed with concern. His presence is a balm to my frayed nerves, yet it also tightens the knot in my stomach. I can't let him bear the weight of my troubles, not when he's already wrestling with his own demons.

"Delightful is one way to put it," I say, forcing a smile that doesn't quite reach my eyes. "Just your average Tuesday evening of devastation." I wave my hand dramatically at the chaos around me, trying to inject some levity into the situation, but the forced cheer falls flat.

He steps further into the room, his gaze scanning the wreckage with a mix of horror and anger. "What the hell happened here? Did you see anyone?"

"No, just the ghosts of my sanity." I'm not even sure I'm joking anymore. I can see the tension tightening in his jaw, the muscles working overtime as he processes what's unfolding. "I think it's safe to say that Vivian is escalating her tactics."

Ryan's fists clench at his sides, and for a moment, I can almost hear the gears in his mind grinding against each other. "This can't keep happening. You shouldn't have to go through this alone." His voice is fierce, a blend of protectiveness and frustration that makes my heart flutter in a way that both comforts and complicates things.

"I don't want to drag you deeper into this mess," I insist, though the warmth of his concern is intoxicating. "You have your own battles to fight, Ryan. Your family—"

"My family can deal with the consequences of their actions," he interrupts, the steel in his voice slicing through my hesitance. "And if they think they can scare you into silence, they've underestimated you. I won't let that happen."

The determination in his eyes ignites something within me—a flicker of hope against the backdrop of chaos. I can't help but admire the way he stands tall, a beacon of strength amidst the wreckage of my life. "You're not scared?" I ask, the disbelief coloring my tone.

"Of them? Not even a little," he smirks, but there's an edge to his bravado that tells me he's not entirely convinced. It's a vulnerability I find endearing, even as it pulls at my heartstrings. I can see the conflict within him, the tug-of-war between familial loyalty and the undeniable connection we've forged.

We stand there in silence, the air heavy with unspoken words. I want to reach out, to bridge the gap between us, but the fear of dragging him further into this treacherous quagmire holds me back. Instead, I settle for a half-hearted chuckle. "So, what's the plan? Call in the cavalry? Maybe hire a private investigator?"

Ryan rolls his eyes, a grin breaking through the tension. "I could call my uncle. He's got a few shady connections, but I'm not sure I want to go that route. I'm more of a 'take the bull by the horns' type of guy."

"More like 'take the bull by the horns and hope it doesn't gore you in the process,'" I counter, unable to suppress a smile. The banter flows naturally, like a lifeline thrown in the turbulent sea of uncertainty.

"Exactly," he nods, his eyes sparkling with a mischief that briefly distracts me from the gravity of our situation. "And I'm not backing down from this fight, especially when I know you're in it."

The words wrap around my heart, a warm embrace in a world growing colder by the minute. But as quickly as the warmth spreads, I feel the chill of reality creeping back in. I can't let him bear the weight of my struggles. I've always been the one who solves problems, who carries the burden of others' chaos without complaint. But now, as Ryan stands beside me, I'm beginning to wonder if perhaps it's time to share the load, to allow someone else to shoulder the darkness that threatens to consume me.

"Alright then," I say, feigning bravado even as a storm brews beneath the surface. "Let's figure out a way to untangle this mess without becoming collateral damage."

And as the two of us huddle together amidst the wreckage of my world, I can't shake the feeling that we are on the precipice of something monumental—a collision course with destiny that might either free us or plunge us further into chaos.

The next morning dawns with a strange kind of heaviness, the sun pushing its way through the curtains like a timid guest who's just learned about my night of chaos. The light reveals the wreckage of my room, illuminating the scattered pages like lost souls awaiting rescue. I should feel defeated, but instead, a fire ignites within me. There's something intoxicating about being on the brink of something explosive—something dangerous—and it makes me giddy, even as I glance at the remnants of my work.

Ryan's call cuts through the murky haze of my thoughts, his voice steady yet laced with an urgency that pulls me from my reverie. "Are you alright?" he asks, concern threading through the words. I can picture him pacing, his brow furrowed as he tries to piece together the fragments of our reality.

"Just living the dream," I reply, trying to inject a hint of humor. "Room service has taken a slight detour into demolition."

There's a brief pause on the line, then he exhales sharply. "Meet me at the café down the street. I need to see you."

My heart races at his tone. It's a mixture of authority and worry, like he's about to dive into uncharted waters. "I'll be there in ten," I say, my resolve settling around me like armor.

The café is a cozy little nook that smells of roasted beans and freshly baked pastries, the kind of place where laughter floats like confetti and strangers share tables without a second thought. It's a world away from the turmoil I left behind, and as I enter, the warmth wraps around me like a well-worn blanket. But even the inviting atmosphere cannot mask the tension coiling in my stomach.

Ryan sits at a corner table, his fingers tapping rhythmically against the wood, a habit he has when he's anxious. His eyes scan the entrance, searching, and when they finally land on me, a hint of relief washes over his face. I slide into the chair opposite him, my breath catching at the sight of him. It's as if he's been cast in a different light, the tension and determination sharpening his features, making him look almost regal.

"Did you sleep?" he asks, his voice low, his concern palpable.

"Not exactly. I was too busy plotting my revenge against the interior decorators who clearly have a vendetta against my sanity."

A flicker of amusement dances in his eyes, but it quickly vanishes. "You know, there's only so much you can do on your own. You need someone watching your back."

His words hang in the air, and I shift uncomfortably, my thoughts spiraling back to the mess that is his family. "I appreciate it, really, but I can't involve you further. You're already caught in this whirlwind because of me."

"I'm involved whether I like it or not. You're not getting rid of me that easily." There's an edge to his voice that sends a thrill down my spine. "Besides, I think my family needs a reality check, and who better to deliver it than you?"

I raise an eyebrow, unsure whether to be impressed or concerned. "You're advocating for me to go toe-to-toe with your family? That sounds like a recipe for disaster."

He leans forward, intensity radiating off him. "If we're going to unravel their web, we need to approach this strategically. Vivian's not going to back down. She'll only double down on her tactics."

As I contemplate his words, the café's lively chatter fades into the background. The idea of confronting Vivian sends a jolt of adrenaline through me. "What do you propose?"

"Gather intel," he suggests, his gaze piercing mine. "Find out everything you can about their business dealings. I know some people who could help—people who owe me favors."

"I don't know, Ryan. That feels like walking straight into a lion's den."

"Exactly. But if we don't go in with a plan, we're just waiting for her to strike again."

The weight of his conviction pulls me closer, and I nod slowly, feeling the shift in our dynamic. This wasn't just about me anymore; it was about us, a shared mission that could either break us or bond us closer together.

"Alright," I finally concede, the thrill of the unknown dancing in my veins. "What's the first move?"

He smirks, that familiar glint in his eye that has the power to turn my unease into excitement. "Let's start with a little reconnaissance. I have a meeting with my father later today. I'll casually drop in a few questions and see what kind of response we get."

"And if that response is less than welcoming?" I challenge, leaning back in my chair.

"Then we adapt," he replies with a shrug, unfazed by the prospect of familial backlash. "We're not amateurs, remember? We've already made it this far."

As we share a conspiratorial smile, I can feel the tension lifting, replaced by an unspoken understanding that we are in this together. My heart swells with a mix of fear and exhilaration, the thrill of the chase binding us in a way I hadn't anticipated.

"Do you think your father will be cooperative?" I ask, intrigued by the labyrinth of family politics we are about to navigate.

"Cooperative is a strong word," he chuckles, shaking his head. "But I know how to push his buttons. I just need to keep my cool, not let him see how much this is affecting me."

Our banter continues, each exchange weaving a thread of camaraderie between us, but just as I'm about to let my guard down completely, a shadow passes over his face.

"Wait," Ryan says suddenly, his eyes narrowing as he scans the café. "I think someone's watching us."

I instinctively turn my head, and my stomach drops. Across the room, a figure is leaning against the wall, their gaze locked on us with an intensity that sends shivers down my spine. It's a woman, her sharp features framed by dark hair, and even from a distance, I recognize her. Vivian.

"What the hell?" I whisper, adrenaline flooding my veins.

Ryan's expression hardens, the playfulness evaporating in an instant. "We need to go, now."

Before I can respond, he's standing, grabbing my wrist and pulling me with him. The café that felt like a sanctuary moments ago now transforms into a potential trap, and I follow him out into the street, the chill of reality hitting me like a slap.

"Do you think she saw us?" I ask, glancing over my shoulder, my heart pounding like a drum in my chest.

"Definitely," Ryan replies grimly, his grip tightening. "But we'll handle this. Together."

And as we move further into the chaos of the city, I realize that every step forward brings us closer to the precipice, the edge of a confrontation that could unravel everything we've worked for—or bind us closer than ever before.

The city pulses with an energy that feels electric, a stark contrast to the chaotic thoughts swirling in my head. With Ryan at my side, we weave through the bustling streets, our footsteps echoing like a heartbeat against the concrete. Every face we pass blurs into anonymity, but I can't shake the feeling that Vivian's gaze is still on us, lurking like a shadow at the corner of my vision.

"Let's find a place to regroup," Ryan suggests, his voice steady despite the undercurrent of tension. "Somewhere quiet."

I nod, grateful for his calm, yet the weight of uncertainty drapes over us like a shroud. We turn down a side street lined with quaint boutiques and cafés, the kind of charming spots that feel like they've sprung from the pages of a storybook. The aroma of fresh pastries and coffee wafts through the air, tempting my senses even as my stomach knots with apprehension.

After a few minutes, we settle into a cozy nook at a small café with mismatched chairs and fairy lights strung above us like stars. I order a latte, my fingers trembling slightly as I cradle the warm mug, hoping it will steady my nerves. Ryan's gaze roams the café, assessing the patrons as if he's scanning for threats.

"Okay," he says, finally turning his attention back to me, "let's talk strategy. Vivian will be looking for any sign that we're onto her."

I take a sip, savoring the rich flavor as I consider his words. "You think she'll make a move soon?"

"Absolutely. She thrives on control, and she won't take kindly to us poking around."

A knot forms in my stomach at the realization. "What if she goes after your family? Or you?"

Ryan leans forward, his expression fierce. "Then we ensure that whatever she does backfires. We need to be one step ahead."

I admire his determination but also feel the gnawing worry that accompanies such a bold plan. "You make it sound so easy."

"It's not easy, but it's possible. And we're in this together, remember?" His reassurance warms me, a flicker of courage igniting beneath my unease.

"Right," I say, drawing a deep breath. "So, what's our first step?"

"We start with what we know. Gather evidence against her—financial records, anything that hints at the family's shady dealings."

I nod, the wheels in my mind turning as I mentally catalog the bits and pieces I've collected. "I have some contacts who might help. I'll reach out to them."

"Good," Ryan replies, his eyes shining with a fierce determination that makes my heart race. "And we need to keep communicating. If Vivian suspects anything, it could spell trouble."

"Trouble seems to be our middle name these days," I quip, trying to lighten the mood.

"True, but I'd prefer something a little less dramatic," he replies, a playful smirk tugging at the corners of his mouth.

Just as I'm about to respond, the door swings open with a jingle, drawing my attention. A gust of wind follows a newcomer into the café, but it's not the chill in the air that makes me shiver; it's the person who steps in. Vivian strides in with an air of confidence that makes my stomach drop.

"Speak of the devil," Ryan mutters under his breath, his body going rigid beside me.

I sink lower in my seat, desperately wishing I could disappear into the fabric of the chair. "What is she doing here?"

"Just act natural," he whispers, eyes narrowed as he watches her approach the counter. "We can't let her know we're onto her."

Vivian is a force of nature, her presence dominating the small space. She orders a coffee with a practiced grace, the barista visibly intimidated by her commanding demeanor. I can't help but notice how effortlessly she commands attention, her every move precise and calculated.

"What do we do?" I whisper, feeling the panic clawing at my throat.

"We stay put and don't make eye contact. The moment she realizes we're here, all hell could break loose."

I force myself to nod, though every instinct screams at me to flee. The tension in the air is palpable as Vivian takes her drink and scans the room. My heart pounds in my chest, and for a moment, I swear time stands still.

Then, without warning, her gaze locks onto ours. I can't help but hold my breath as her lips curl into a predatory smile.

"Interesting to see you here," she calls out, her voice dripping with feigned sweetness. The room falls silent, eyes flickering between us and her, and I feel the heat of embarrassment flood my cheeks.

Ryan stiffens beside me, but I can't afford to let her see fear. "Just enjoying some coffee," I reply, attempting to sound casual despite the tremor in my voice.

"Ah, coffee," she muses, stepping closer, her heels clicking against the wooden floor. "A delightful beverage. So comforting, don't you think?"

"Very comforting," I reply, forcing a smile that feels more like a grimace.

Her gaze darts between us, sharp and calculating. "I trust you're still working on that little article of yours? Would be a shame if it went unpublished."

Ryan's grip on the table tightens, and I can sense the tension radiating off him like heat waves. "Why would you care about my work, Vivian? I thought you didn't read small-time journalism," I retort, my voice firmer than I feel.

"True, but I've developed an interest in your... activities. Let's just say the last thing I want is for you to get hurt." Her eyes glint with something dark, a predatory thrill that sends a shiver down my spine.

"Thanks for your concern," I reply, sarcasm dripping from my tone.

"Just looking out for your well-being," she says, a chilling smile spreading across her face. "After all, there are some truths better left buried."

As she turns to leave, a jolt of fear surges through me. "What do you mean?" I call after her, my voice ringing out, startling a few patrons.

She glances back over her shoulder, the smile never leaving her lips. "You'll find out soon enough." With that, she strides out of the café, leaving behind a silence that feels like a dam waiting to break.

Ryan's expression is a mixture of anger and frustration, the tension between us palpable. "We need to act quickly. If she's this confident, she knows something we don't."

I nod, my heart racing, but the fear is palpable. "What if she's right? What if I'm too deep into this?"

"You're not too deep, and you won't back down now," he insists, his voice firm.

"Maybe we should just get out of this mess, Ryan. Walk away."

He leans in, his eyes fierce. "And let her win? No. We fight. Together."

Just as I open my mouth to respond, my phone buzzes violently against the table, slicing through the thick tension in the air. I glance down, and my blood runs cold.

A message flashes on the screen: "You're running out of time. Consider this your final warning."

I look up at Ryan, panic surging through me. "What do we do now?"

But as I search his face for answers, I realize we've just crossed a line. And there's no going back.

Chapter 17: Breaking Point

The city hummed with the usual late-night chatter, the kind that felt like a low-level buzz in my bones, an almost comforting reminder that I was alive amidst chaos. Streetlights flickered like weary guardians, illuminating the damp pavement, reflecting a kaleidoscope of colors that danced at my feet. I pulled my jacket tighter, wishing it could wrap around my heart too. The chill in the air seemed to mimic the distance growing between Ryan and me, each step I took a reminder of how close I was to losing him entirely.

I had parked my car a few blocks away from the café where we often met. The familiar scent of roasted coffee beans wafted toward me, but tonight, it was tinged with something acrid, a hint of anxiety that curled around me like smoke. As I approached the door, a sense of foreboding settled in the pit of my stomach, as heavy as a stone. The bell jingled as I stepped inside, and my heart raced at the sight of him. Ryan sat in our usual corner, his fingers wrapped around a steaming cup of coffee, but his gaze was far away, lost in the murky depths of his thoughts.

"Hey," I said, sliding into the seat across from him. The warmth of the café enveloped me, but it couldn't thaw the ice that had formed between us.

"Hey," he replied, his voice barely above a whisper, laced with the weight of unspoken words. His dark hair fell across his forehead, shadowing his eyes, but I could feel his tension radiating like heat from a flame.

I tried to break through the wall he had built around himself. "I was thinking we could brainstorm some ideas for the article. Maybe even bring in some fresh angles?" My voice wavered, laced with hope, but it hung in the air, unacknowledged.

He glanced at me then, his eyes flickering with something akin to regret. "We need to talk."

The knot in my stomach tightened. Those four words could unravel everything. "About what?" I leaned forward, desperate to breach the chasm growing between us.

"About us," he said, finally meeting my gaze. "About my family."

I held my breath, bracing for the impact. "What about them?"

"I don't think we can win." His voice was steady, but there was a crack in it, an echo of vulnerability that made my chest ache. "Vivian has too much power. My family... they've built an empire on secrets. They're not going to let us expose them without a fight."

I swallowed hard, the reality of his words crashing over me like cold waves. "So you want me to just walk away? To give up?"

"It's not about giving up. It's about being smart." The edge of frustration crept into his tone. "I'm trying to protect you."

I leaned back, a mix of disbelief and anger bubbling within me. "Protect me from what? The truth? Ryan, we've come too far to back down now. We're onto something big, and you know it. We can't let them win."

He ran a hand through his hair, the gesture both familiar and heartbreaking. "What if I'm wrong? What if we're just putting you in more danger?"

"I'd rather face danger with you than live a lie without you." The words tumbled out before I could stop them, and for a moment, the flicker of connection returned, as if we were back in the sunlit days of hope rather than this dimly lit café that felt like a cage.

He sighed heavily, the weight of his family's legacy pressing down on him. "You don't know them like I do. They won't hesitate to ruin us, and I can't let that happen to you. You deserve better."

A bitter laugh escaped me. "What, like a life without you? Is that what you think is better? Because I don't know how to do that."

Ryan looked down at his coffee, his expression unreadable. The steam curled up like tendrils of smoke, a silent witness to our unraveling. "Maybe that's what you need to do. Just... forget about me."

I felt the ground shift beneath me, the world tilting on its axis. "How can you even say that? You're the one who wanted to uncover the truth. You're the one who dragged me into this mess."

He finally looked up, a fire igniting in his eyes. "And you think I'm enjoying it? Watching you get dragged into my family's darkness? I can't stand the thought of you getting hurt because of me. I won't let it happen."

"And I won't let you push me away," I shot back, the words like a lifeline tossed into turbulent waters. "I'm not afraid of your family, and I'm not afraid of what they might do. If we stand together, we have a fighting chance."

"Together?" he echoed, a bitter smile tugging at his lips. "You don't even know the extent of what they're capable of."

"Then let me learn," I said, my heart racing as I leaned forward. "I won't back down. I refuse to let fear dictate my life. We'll figure this out together."

For a heartbeat, I saw the flicker of hope in his eyes, but it was extinguished almost immediately. "You don't understand. This isn't just about us anymore. They've started making calls. I've been getting threats—"

Before he could finish, my phone buzzed violently in my pocket, interrupting the tension. I fished it out, and the sight of an unknown number made my heart plummet. The caller was persistent, and I hesitated, caught between the weight of Ryan's words and the unsettling urgency of the call.

"Who is it?" he asked, concern washing over his features.

"Just... a number I don't recognize," I said, the unease clawing at my throat. "I'll call them back later."

"Are you sure?"

"Yeah, just some telemarketer or something." But deep down, I felt the pull of something sinister lurking beneath the surface, like a storm gathering on the horizon, ready to break.

Ryan shifted in his seat, his eyes narrowing. "No, don't brush it off. It could be important."

I nodded, trying to suppress the growing fear. "Right. I'll answer."

The moment I pressed the green button, a cold voice slithered through the receiver. "You need to leave the city. You're in danger, and we're not kidding."

I felt Ryan's presence intensify across the table, his expression darkening.

"Who is this?" I demanded, my voice shaking despite my best efforts to sound resolute.

"Just a concerned citizen. You're digging into things you shouldn't. Walk away now, or there will be consequences." The line went dead, leaving an echo of fear in its wake.

I looked up at Ryan, panic spilling over. "Did you hear that?"

His eyes were fierce, a storm brewing behind them. "We can't ignore this. They're watching us."

"Then let's not give them what they want. Let's fight back."

I felt the familiar spark of determination ignite within me. But as Ryan's expression hardened, I realized we were standing on the precipice of a decision that could change everything.

The café, with its chipped paint and mismatched furniture, had always been our refuge, a place where we could pour out our thoughts like the coffee we shared. But now it felt like a stage set for a tragedy, the weight of unspoken fears pressing down like a heavy fog. I could see the lines of tension etched into Ryan's face, the furrow in his brow deepening as he grappled with the gravity of our situation.

"Maybe you should think about it," he said quietly, his voice barely carrying over the soft hum of conversation around us. "Leaving, I mean. For your own safety."

I folded my arms across the table, leaning in closer. "And what, let them win? Let Vivian and your family dictate my life? That's not happening." My voice held a steely determination, one I hoped would seep into him.

His gaze darted around the room, searching for something—perhaps a way to escape the reality that enveloped us. "You think this is just about you and me? This is bigger than both of us. I can't bear the thought of you getting hurt because of my mess."

"Then let's make it our mess." I sighed, frustration bubbling beneath the surface. "We've got to stick together. If we're going to take them down, we need each other."

His lips pressed into a thin line, and the fire in his eyes dimmed. "What if it's already too late? What if the calls are just the beginning? I don't want to see you in the crosshairs."

An uncomfortable silence settled between us, thick and suffocating. My heart raced as I fought against the tide of doubt creeping in. Just as I opened my mouth to push back, my phone buzzed again, vibrating insistently on the table. I snatched it up, half-expecting another ominous message, but the number was the same as before. A wave of anger surged through me; whoever was on the other end was relentless.

"Answer it," Ryan urged, his intensity making the air around us crackle.

I hesitated, glancing at his furrowed brow before pressing the green button again. "Hello?"

"Don't ignore what I said," the cold voice returned, devoid of empathy. "You need to leave. Now."

"Why should I listen to you?" I shot back, each word laced with defiance. "You're just some coward hiding behind a phone."

"Coward? Maybe," the voice sneered. "But I'm not the one playing with fire. You have no idea who you're dealing with."

"Then enlighten me," I countered, though my heart raced with unease.

The line went silent for a beat before the voice spoke again, sharp and clear. "You think you're safe, but you're not. The moment you stepped into the world of secrets and lies, you became a target. You're just a pawn in their game."

The revelation landed like a heavy stone in my chest. "A pawn? That's rich coming from someone too afraid to reveal their identity."

"You'll regret this." The call ended abruptly, leaving only the dull beep of the disconnected line in my ear. I set the phone down slowly, the gravity of the situation wrapping around me like a vice.

"Are you okay?" Ryan's voice sliced through my thoughts, concern etched across his face.

"No," I said flatly, trying to ground myself. "But I will be." I took a deep breath, steeling my resolve. "They want to intimidate me, but they don't know who they're dealing with. I won't back down."

Ryan's eyes widened, a mixture of admiration and fear flashing across his features. "You really think you can take them on alone?"

"I'm not alone," I replied, leaning in closer. "I have you. And together, we can figure this out."

He seemed to consider my words, the tension between us softening slightly. "You're not like anyone I've ever met," he said, a hint of a smile breaking through his worries. "You've got this fire inside you. It's both terrifying and intoxicating."

"Just like a double espresso," I quipped, trying to lighten the mood. "Strong, a little bitter, and guaranteed to keep you awake at night."

Ryan chuckled softly, the sound soothing the frayed edges of my nerves. "And just as dangerous."

As we exchanged witticisms, I could feel the connection weaving its way back, knitting together the torn pieces of our conversation. But just as quickly as the warmth returned, a shadow flitted through the café window, causing me to look up. My heart dropped when I saw a figure standing outside, shrouded in the dim light—a silhouette that felt all too familiar.

"Do you see that?" I murmured, my voice tight.

Ryan followed my gaze, and his expression hardened. "What the hell?"

The figure turned, revealing the unmistakable features of Vivian, her eyes glinting with malice. I could feel my pulse quicken, the weight of her presence heavy in the air. She seemed to sense the tension, her lips curling into a mocking smile before she turned and walked away, disappearing into the night.

"Damn it," Ryan muttered, fists clenched on the table. "She's getting bold. This is not good."

"What do we do?" I asked, anxiety creeping in again.

Ryan's eyes narrowed, a spark of determination igniting within him. "We confront her. She thinks she can intimidate us, but we can't let her dictate the terms. Not anymore."

"Are you sure? She's dangerous, Ryan. We have to be smart about this."

"I'm tired of being smart. I'm tired of playing their games," he said, his voice rising. "We need to stand up for ourselves, even if it means facing her head-on."

I felt the adrenaline course through me at his words. "Then let's do it. But we have to be strategic. We can't just charge in blindly. We need a plan."

"Fine. Then let's gather everything we have. The documents, the evidence. We'll expose her and your family for what they are."

"Together?"

"Always."

The heat of resolve enveloped me, banishing the creeping doubt that had threatened to overwhelm. "Then let's go."

We left the café, the brisk night air invigorating. The city felt alive, its pulse echoing in our steps as we made our way back to my apartment. The streetlights flickered above, a constellation of determination guiding our path. With every step, the weight of the world on our shoulders felt lighter, buoyed by the strength of our shared purpose.

Once inside, the familiar chaos of my living space greeted us—papers strewn across the table, the faint smell of takeout clinging to the air. I turned to Ryan, a sense of urgency sparking between us. "We need to organize everything we have. We can't let them intimidate us. Not anymore."

As we spread out the papers, the tension in the room shifted, morphing into something electric, crackling with possibilities. Ryan leaned closer, his shoulder brushing against mine, igniting an unexpected warmth that sent my heart racing. "Let's figure out how to hit them where it hurts," he said, a wicked glint in his eye.

"Yes, let's," I replied, matching his intensity. "Time to shake things up."

In that moment, with determination coursing through our veins, the darkness felt a little less daunting, and the battle ahead, though fraught with uncertainty, shimmered with the promise of something fiercely beautiful.

The flickering overhead light cast erratic shadows across the room as Ryan and I sifted through the chaos of papers scattered across my coffee table. The air was thick with urgency, and I could almost taste the tension hanging between us, a palpable mix of adrenaline and fear. Every scrap of evidence we unearthed felt like a potential weapon, each document a key that could unlock the doors to the truth we so desperately sought.

"This is it," Ryan said, holding up a folder thick with documents. The corner of his mouth quirked up in a ghost of a smile, a reminder of the hope we clung to. "This could be the break we need."

I leaned in, my heart racing at the sight of names and dates, connections that made my head spin. "If we can prove what's going on behind the scenes, we might have a fighting chance. We need to make copies of everything."

He nodded, the glint of determination in his eyes sparking a fire in my belly. "Let's do it now, while we still have time. I don't want to risk them showing up and catching us off guard."

As I rifled through the papers, a sense of urgency crackled in the air. "Have you thought about where we'll go if things go south? We need a backup plan."

Ryan's expression shifted, shadows darkening his features. "We'll cross that bridge when we come to it. For now, we need to stay focused on this."

I couldn't shake the unease creeping in. "You know I'm not a fan of leaving things to chance. This isn't just a story anymore; it's our lives on the line."

He leaned closer, his voice dropping to a conspiratorial whisper. "You don't need to worry about that. Just trust me. We'll be fine."

With a reluctant nod, I forced myself to concentrate on the files, but my mind kept flickering to the calls, the ominous warnings that had become all too familiar. I glanced at Ryan, his jaw clenched, his brows furrowed in thought. I wished I could ease the burden he carried, the weight of his family's legacy pressing down on him like a leaden blanket.

The minutes ticked by as we organized the papers into neat stacks, each one representing a thread in a larger tapestry of corruption. My heart raced with every name we uncovered, the realization of the network of deceit that lay hidden beneath the surface. It felt like peeling back the layers of an onion, each one revealing something sharper, something that could make us cry.

Just as I began to feel a sense of accomplishment, the sharp ring of my phone shattered the tension in the room. I grabbed it, my stomach knotting as I glanced at the caller ID—another unknown number. I shot a quick look at Ryan, whose eyes widened in alarm.

"Answer it," he urged, leaning closer as I hesitated.

Taking a deep breath, I pressed the green button. "Hello?"

"Still digging, I see," the voice dripped with mockery, sending a chill down my spine. "You're really determined to get yourself hurt."

"Who is this?" I snapped, a mix of fear and anger bubbling to the surface. "You have no idea who you're dealing with."

"Oh, but I do. And I must say, I admire your tenacity. It's quite endearing. But let's get one thing straight—you need to stop. This isn't a game."

"What do you want?" I demanded, my heart pounding like a war drum. "I'm not afraid of you or your threats."

"Is that so?" The voice laughed, a chilling sound that echoed through the line. "You should be. I'm only giving you a chance to back down. This is your final warning."

"Final warning?" I scoffed, anger igniting my bravado. "You think you can scare me into submission? I've faced worse than you."

"Is that right? Like what? The wrath of Ryan's family? They'll bury you and your precious story without a second thought."

The call dropped, leaving the eerie silence of my apartment ringing in my ears. I glanced at Ryan, my pulse racing. "They're serious, Ryan. They're not backing down."

His eyes were stormy, filled with determination. "Neither are we. We can't let them intimidate us. We have to show them we're not afraid."

I nodded, the tension between us crackling like electricity. "Let's finish what we started. We need to get this evidence out there."

We worked in a frenzy, the adrenaline coursing through us as we made copies, printed everything we could, our hands moving with an urgency born of desperation. Each sound—the whir of the printer, the rustle of paper—felt amplified, as if the walls themselves were listening.

But just as I thought we were making headway, the quiet of the night was shattered by a loud crash outside my window. My heart lurched, and I exchanged a glance with Ryan. "What was that?"

"Stay here," he commanded, his expression hardening.

"No way. I'm not hiding while you check it out. We're in this together."

"Just—" he started, but I cut him off.

"Ryan, please. If they're here, I want to know."

With a heavy sigh, he nodded, and together we crept toward the window. Peering through the curtain, the streetlights cast an eerie glow on the scene below. I gasped as I caught sight of two figures lurking in the shadows, their silhouettes barely visible against the flickering light.

"Do you see them?" Ryan whispered, his breath hot against my ear.

"Yeah," I replied, trying to steady my racing heart. "What are they doing?"

Before Ryan could respond, the figures turned, and my breath caught in my throat. One of them was Vivian. She seemed to sense our gaze, her head snapping up to meet our eyes. A malicious smile spread across her face, and in that moment, something primal surged through me—a mixture of dread and defiance.

"They know we're here," Ryan said, his voice barely a whisper.

"We need to get out. Now," I urged, adrenaline pushing me into action.

"Wait, not yet." He grabbed my arm, pulling me back as I felt my heart thundering against my ribcage.

"Why not?"

"Let's see what they're planning."

The weight of his words hung heavy in the air as we watched, our breaths held tight in our throats. Vivian spoke to the second figure, gesturing animatedly, her demeanor oozing confidence. My mind raced as I tried to make sense of the situation, the pieces falling together in an unsettling mosaic.

"Do you think they know about the documents?" I whispered, panic rising in my chest.

"Maybe," Ryan replied, his eyes locked on the scene unfolding below. "But if they do, we need to be one step ahead."

Suddenly, the second figure stepped closer, and the moonlight illuminated his face. My blood ran cold. It was someone I recognized—someone I never thought would be in league with Vivian. "No," I breathed, horror flooding my senses.

"What?" Ryan asked, his voice a low growl.

"That's..." My mind raced, disbelief clawing at my thoughts. "That's my editor."

Ryan's expression darkened, his grip tightening around my arm. "This just got a whole lot more complicated."

As if sensing our discovery, Vivian turned abruptly, her gaze piercing the veil of darkness that separated us from the street. I stepped back instinctively, heart racing, but it was too late. The window creaked ominously, betraying our presence as she shouted, "They're up there! Get them!"

Chaos erupted as footsteps thundered toward the building, and in that moment, all our plans unraveled like the threads of a fraying tapestry. We scrambled, adrenaline surging as I grasped Ryan's hand, our eyes locking in silent understanding.

"Run!" I yelled, and we burst away from the window, our breaths quickening as we hurtled toward the door, uncertainty nipping at our heels. With each step, I could feel the weight of our choices crashing down, and all I could think was that the game was far from over.

Chapter 18: Shattered Trust

I was hunched over Ryan's laptop, the soft glow of the screen illuminating the darkened corners of the room. The late-night quiet wrapped around me like a heavy blanket, stifling the frantic thoughts spiraling in my mind. My fingers moved hesitantly across the keyboard, betraying the turbulence that roiled within. I had promised myself I wouldn't invade his privacy, but desperation had clawed at my resolve, and now I was knee-deep in a world I had never signed up for.

Each click of the mouse echoed like a drumroll, punctuating the suffocating silence. I navigated through layers of folders and files, my heart racing with each new discovery. As I unearthed the hidden folder, an involuntary gasp escaped my lips, breaking the stillness like a glass shattering on a tiled floor. Documents spilled forth, revealing the labyrinthine connections of Ryan's family—the deals, the betrayals, the tangled web of power and greed that loomed over our lives like an ominous storm cloud.

"Ryan," I murmured to myself, feeling a pit of disappointment gnawing at my insides. The air turned heavy with the scent of betrayal, an acrid flavor that coated my tongue. I had seen him struggle with the weight of his family's legacy, but I had never imagined how deep the roots ran, intertwining with the very essence of who he was. Each document painted a portrait of a young man torn between loyalty and the desire for freedom, a silent war raging beneath his handsome façade.

Suddenly, the door creaked open behind me, and I whipped around to see Ryan standing there, his silhouette outlined by the soft light of the hallway. The way he hesitated—caught between the desire to confront me and the instinct to retreat—made my stomach lurch. "What are you doing?" he asked, voice low and gravelly, thick with an emotion I couldn't quite decipher.

"Finding out what you've been hiding," I replied, my tone sharper than I intended. The documents lay sprawled across the desk, unmasked and vulnerable, the truth laid bare for both of us to see.

His brow furrowed as he stepped closer, a mix of concern and something darker shadowing his features. "You shouldn't be looking at that," he said, his voice dropping to a whisper as if the very words were a sacred incantation. "It's not what you think."

"Then enlighten me," I shot back, crossing my arms defiantly. "Because from where I'm standing, it looks like you've been playing both sides." The heat of anger surged through me, a tidal wave crashing against the shores of my trust. "You could have told me. We could have faced this together."

Ryan ran a hand through his hair, a gesture I had come to recognize as a sign of his anxiety. "It's complicated," he said, frustration lacing his voice. "You don't understand what they're capable of."

"Oh, I think I do." The words slipped out before I could rein them in, a bitter truth I hadn't meant to expose. "Vivian warned me about this, about you. And I wanted to believe she was wrong. But now—" My voice faltered, the weight of my own heartbreak pressing down like a vice.

"Vivian doesn't know anything," he said, stepping closer, eyes pleading. "She doesn't understand what it means to be part of this family. The stakes are higher than you realize."

"But you kept it from me," I countered, the hurt rising in my throat like bile. "How do I know you're not still trying to protect them? To protect yourself?"

Ryan's jaw tightened, the muscles working beneath the surface as if he were holding back a flood of emotions. "Because I'm trying to protect you!" His voice raised, but there was an urgency beneath the anger, a raw vulnerability that made my heart ache. "I thought I could handle it alone, but I was wrong. I thought I could shield you from this life, from the dangers it brings."

"Shield me?" I echoed, incredulous. "By lying to me? By shutting me out?" Each word felt like a dagger, and I didn't care how much it hurt to say them. The truth needed to be said, needed to be laid bare. "I thought we were in this together, but now…" I swallowed hard, my throat tight with unshed tears. "I feel like I'm standing on the edge of a cliff, and you're the one who pushed me there."

"Please," he said, reaching out, his fingers brushing against my arm. The warmth of his touch ignited a war inside me—a battle between love and betrayal, trust and doubt. "Let me explain. I never meant to keep you in the dark. I thought it would be safer for you, for both of us. You don't know what they'll do if they find out I'm trying to break free."

"Maybe I'm tired of being protected," I snapped, pulling away from his touch, the warmth fading like sunlight behind a storm. "Maybe I deserve to know the truth." The finality of my words hung in the air like a fragile promise. I wanted to believe in our connection, in the strength of our love, but the chasm of secrets between us felt insurmountable.

He stepped back, hands clenched into fists at his sides, and for a moment, the air crackled with tension. My heart pounded, a relentless drum echoing the fear that coursed through me. I could see the storm brewing in his eyes, a tempest of regret and longing, but how could I trust him again? How could I navigate this treacherous path when the ground beneath us felt so unstable?

"I need time," I finally said, the words leaving me like a whisper of a prayer. The silence that followed was deafening, filled with unspoken apologies and the weight of shattered trust. I turned away, unable to meet his gaze any longer, feeling the distance between us grow like a shadow stretching across the floor. The truth lay heavy in the air, a murky fog that wrapped around my heart, threatening to suffocate me.

As I stared at the flickering screen, illuminated with the secrets of his past, I felt a flicker of hope extinguished. The battle lines were drawn, and I was left standing in the crossfire, unsure of where to go next.

The quiet lingered long after Ryan's footsteps faded down the hallway, leaving me with a churning mix of anger and sorrow. I sat in his dimly lit room, surrounded by the ghostly glow of the computer screen, its light flickering like the uncertainty that clouded my mind. The documents lay scattered like fallen leaves in autumn, each page holding secrets that twisted like vines around my heart.

How had it come to this? Moments ago, we were two souls tangled in a shared dream, and now we were adversaries in a silent war. I rubbed my temples, feeling the tension pulsate like a dull ache. I couldn't shake the thought of Ryan—his face torn between desire and fear. The same expression I had come to adore had morphed into something unrecognizable, and it left a bitter taste on my tongue.

I stood and paced the room, each step a futile attempt to outrun the chaos in my head. The walls seemed to close in, echoing memories of laughter and whispered secrets, each one now tainted by the shadow of deception. I had imagined a future with him, one filled with hope and shared dreams, but now it felt like a mirage, slipping through my fingers like sand.

The door creaked open again, and I turned to see Ryan's silhouette against the hallway light. This time, I steeled myself, ready to confront the man who had become both my anchor and my storm. "Can we talk?" he asked, his voice low, the weight of unspoken words hanging in the air between us.

I crossed my arms, my heart pounding in my chest, unsure of whether I wanted to hear what he had to say or if I simply wanted to hurl accusations until I felt better. "What is there left to talk about?" I shot back, my voice sharper than I intended.

"I get it," he said, stepping closer, a flicker of desperation in his eyes. "But please, just listen to me."

With a resigned sigh, I nodded, curiosity creeping in despite my anger. "Fine, but make it quick. I have a busy day of contemplating life choices ahead of me."

"Fair enough," he said, a hint of a smile breaking through the tension, though it quickly faded. "I should have told you everything sooner. You deserve to know what I've been dealing with." He rubbed the back of his neck, a nervous habit I found endearing despite the situation. "It's not just family drama. It's... complicated."

"Complicated? Try more like a telenovela on steroids," I replied, folding my arms tighter. "You could have spared me the heartache. How long have you been hiding this from me?"

He inhaled deeply, as if the words were lodged somewhere deep in his throat. "It's been a part of my life for so long that it felt impossible to bring it into ours. I didn't want to burden you with it."

"Too late for that now," I quipped, unable to help myself. "I'm knee-deep in your family's skeletons, Ryan."

He took a step closer, his expression earnest. "They're not just skeletons. They're dangerous. I've seen what they're capable of, and I thought if I kept you away from it all, you'd be safe. But I realize now that it only pushed you away."

My heart softened slightly at his admission, the sincerity in his eyes a reminder of the warmth we had once shared. "You should have trusted me enough to let me decide what I could handle," I countered, though my tone had lost some of its bite. "I'm not made of glass, Ryan. I can take the truth, even if it's ugly."

He nodded, the weight of my words sinking in. "You're right. You are so much stronger than I ever gave you credit for. But you don't understand the depth of my family's ties. They're like a dark cloud that's hung over my entire life. If I spoke out, it could mean losing everything."

"Everything?" I echoed, my brows raised. "What do you mean by that? Your privilege? The family name? Or something deeper?"

He hesitated, looking like he was wrestling with demons. "It's more than just the name," he said, finally. "It's loyalty. It's the threat of losing not just the comforts of my life, but also my family. There are things I've done—things I've had to do—to keep them at bay. I never wanted you to get caught in the crossfire."

A shiver ran down my spine at the thought of Ryan being dragged into whatever murky depths his family was mired in. "And what if they come after you? What if they come after us? I can't just stand by while you try to fight your family's war alone."

"I'd never let them touch you," he said fiercely, his gaze locking onto mine with a fire that ignited something deep within me. "That's why I've kept you out of it. I wanted to protect you."

"Protect me? By keeping me in the dark?" I laughed bitterly, shaking my head. "That's like putting a blindfold on someone while they're standing on the edge of a cliff."

"I know, I know," he sighed, running his hands through his hair in frustration. "I messed up. I thought if I could figure it out, if I could just make enough moves to escape, then we could start fresh. Together."

"Together," I echoed, the word feeling heavy and loaded between us. "But can we really be together if there's this chasm of secrets separating us? How do I know you won't just retreat into the shadows again?"

"Because I'm here now," he insisted, desperation creeping into his voice. "I won't run anymore. I promise. I'll share everything, even the parts that terrify me. I'll let you in. Just please, give me the chance to make it right."

I searched his eyes, looking for sincerity, for a glimpse of the boy I had fallen for—the one who had shown me kindness and laughter amidst the chaos. But there was also a darkness lurking there, a reality that felt as palpable as the air around us. "And what if it's too late?" I whispered, my voice cracking.

"Then we'll figure it out together," he said, stepping even closer, the warmth of his presence wrapping around me like a safety net. "But I need you to trust me. I can't fight this alone."

The tension in the room swirled around us, heavy with unspoken fears and desires. I could feel the lines between love and betrayal blurring like ink on wet paper. As I looked into Ryan's eyes, the storm swirling between us shifted, teetering on the brink of something profound. It was a risk—one I was terrified to take, yet desperately wanted to explore. The path ahead was littered with uncertainty, but the promise of connection flickered like a candle, inviting me to step closer.

The silence between us felt like a fragile dam, barely holding back the flood of emotions threatening to pour out. I could feel my heart racing, each thump echoing in the stillness of the room, a rhythm that mirrored the anxiety coursing through me. Ryan's gaze was steady, searching mine for a flicker of understanding, but all I could feel was the uncertainty weighing heavy on my chest.

"Okay," I said, forcing myself to breathe through the tension. "Let's say I believe you. Let's say you're really ready to tell me everything. Where do we even begin?"

He took a step back, the hint of a smile breaking through the storm clouds of our conversation. "How about the part where I admit that I'm terrified?" The vulnerability in his tone softened my defenses, if only slightly. "This whole thing is bigger than I thought, and it's spiraling out of control. But I can't keep running."

"Running isn't really an option at this point, is it?" I replied, a wry smile tugging at my lips. "Seems like you've been running for a while now."

He chuckled softly, the sound breaking some of the tension. "Touché. But I can't keep dragging you into my mess, either."

"Right," I said, crossing my arms as I leaned against the desk. "Because what's a little emotional turmoil compared to family drama, right? I mean, who doesn't want a little danger in their life?"

His expression turned serious again, the flicker of humor extinguished. "This isn't just danger; it's life and death. I've seen things. My family's dealings aren't just shady—they're illegal, and they'll do anything to protect their interests. That includes me."

I swallowed hard, the weight of his words settling heavily in the pit of my stomach. "What do you mean by 'do anything'? Are we talking about threats? Violence? Because if that's the case, I need to know exactly what we're dealing with here."

"Exactly that," he said, his voice dropping to a whisper. "I was too naïve to think I could distance myself from it all. They think they can use me as leverage, as if I'm just a pawn on their board. But I'm not. I refuse to be."

"Then let's expose them," I said, surprising myself with the fierceness of my own resolve. "If they think they can control you, we'll turn the tables. We can gather evidence, go to the police, whatever it takes."

Ryan shook his head, the frustration etched deep into his features. "It's not that simple. The people we're dealing with have connections everywhere. They can make problems disappear. I can't put you in danger like that."

"Oh, please," I scoffed, unable to keep the sarcasm out of my voice. "You've already put me in danger by keeping me in the dark. What's a little more?"

He stepped forward again, his expression softening, and for a moment, it felt like we were wrapped in a bubble, cut off from the world. "I'm trying to protect you," he insisted, his voice low and earnest. "But I can't keep lying to you. I know it's too late for that."

"Then let's find a way to fight back together," I said, my voice firm. "I won't stand by and watch you drown in your family's mess. We're stronger as a team, right?"

He looked torn, his brows knitted together as if he were weighing the consequences of what we might be getting into. "I don't want to put you at risk. You have no idea what they're capable of."

"Neither do you," I shot back, my pulse quickening. "And that's precisely why we need to face this head-on. If we're going to move forward, it has to be together. No more secrets. No more half-truths."

He sighed heavily, the tension in his shoulders visible as he looked away for a moment, grappling with my words. "Okay, okay. But we have to be smart about this. If we do it, we do it right."

"Smart is my middle name," I replied with a grin, but it faded as reality crept back in. "What's our first move?"

"We start by gathering information. I need to get access to more files—things that my family has hidden away. If we can find proof of what they're involved in, we can use it as leverage. But I need your help to get in there."

"Consider it done," I said, a thrill of adrenaline coursing through me. "I'm in."

As we began to outline our plan, my mind whirled with the possibilities. I had never considered myself particularly brave, yet here I was, ready to dive headfirst into a dark world I barely understood. The stakes were high, and my heart raced at the thought of what could happen next.

"Just promise me one thing," I said, biting my lip as a sudden seriousness swept over me. "If things start to go sideways, you'll let me walk away. I won't pretend that this is all okay if it's not."

Ryan's gaze softened, the weight of our shared understanding hanging in the air. "I can promise you this: I'll never put you in a position where you have to make that choice."

"Good. Then let's get to work," I said, feeling the surge of determination rise within me.

But just as we were about to dive deeper into our plans, a loud crash echoed from the living room, startling us both. My heart raced as I exchanged a glance with Ryan, confusion and alarm flooding our expressions.

"What was that?" I whispered, my throat dry with apprehension.

"I don't know," he replied, his eyes wide with concern. "Stay here. I'll check it out."

Before I could protest, he slipped out of the room, leaving me in the dim light, the air thick with unease. I glanced around, my heart pounding in my chest, every instinct screaming that something was very wrong. I moved to the doorway, straining to listen for any sounds, any indication of what awaited us.

Suddenly, a voice boomed from downstairs—deep and menacing, sending chills down my spine. "Ryan! You're in over your head, and it's time to come home!"

The realization hit me like a cold wave. Whoever that was, they weren't just here for a chat. A sick knot of dread formed in my stomach as I stood frozen, torn between the instinct to run and the need to stay and protect him. Just as I turned to call out, the sound of footsteps rushed up the stairs, echoing ominously as they closed in.

My pulse quickened, and I had a fleeting moment to decide: fight or flight? But the only thing I knew for sure was that whatever lay ahead could change everything.

Chapter 19: Turning the Tables

The smell of rain-soaked asphalt and freshly brewed coffee hung in the air as I stepped into the small café on the corner of Elm Street. It was a modest little place, the kind of coffee shop where the barista knew your name and your favorite drink—an almond milk latte with just a hint of cinnamon. I had claimed this spot as my sanctuary during my turbulent investigations. As I settled into a corner table, the familiar sounds of the espresso machine whirring and soft chatter from the regulars provided a comforting backdrop to my stormy thoughts.

Sipping my latte, I glanced through my notes scattered across the table—my latest attempts to untangle the web of deception surrounding Ryan's family. The name "Ryan" twisted my heart. The man I had fallen for was now a specter of what I once believed him to be, a truth buried beneath layers of lies. As the steam from my coffee curled upward like the haze of uncertainty clouding my mind, I felt the weight of my decision pressing down. I had drawn a line in the sand; I couldn't go back. There was a revolution stirring in my chest, fueled by the whispers of whistleblowers and the deepening shadows of corporate corruption.

Each person I met had a story, a piece of the puzzle that unveiled a landscape of greed and betrayal. I'd become a ghost in their stories, hovering at the edges as they recounted their experiences with Ryan's family business. Old employees, embittered by broken promises and shattered dreams, spoke of fraudulent contracts, of funds mysteriously disappearing into shadowy accounts. The more I heard, the more I realized that exposing this network of deceit could bring everything crashing down—not just for Ryan, but for me too. I was teetering on the brink of a precipice, and the view was both exhilarating and terrifying.

My phone buzzed, jolting me from my thoughts. It was a text from Liz, my best friend and my rock, whose unwavering support had been my lifeline during this chaotic whirlwind. "I'm worried about you. Are you safe? Call me." The text was laced with concern, a reminder that I was walking a tightrope between ambition and self-preservation.

"Hey, you okay?" the barista asked as she refilled my cup, her eyes searching mine for signs of turmoil. I forced a smile, knowing it didn't quite reach my eyes.

"Just diving into some heavy stuff," I replied, my voice softer than I intended.

"Gotcha. Remember to breathe," she said, winking before returning to the counter.

Breathe. It was the one thing I found increasingly difficult to do, especially when I thought of what lay ahead. As I gathered my notes, the café door swung open, and a gust of wind swept through, rustling my pages and momentarily blinding me with rain. I squinted through the mist and, just for a fleeting moment, I thought I saw Ryan standing there, his hair slicked back against the rain, an expression of concern carved into his handsome features. But as quickly as he had appeared, he disappeared, leaving me with only my racing heart and swirling thoughts.

Determined to chase away the phantom of his presence, I plunged back into my research. Each piece of information drew me deeper into a quagmire, and I could feel the shadows of uncertainty creeping closer. My laptop chimed as an email notification popped up, the subject line catching my eye: "Urgent: Meet at the Old Warehouse." My pulse quickened; this could be the lead I needed. I was on the verge of uncovering something monumental.

The old warehouse was a relic of a bygone era, its brick façade weathered and cracked, standing in stark contrast to the sleek modernity surrounding it. As I pulled into the empty lot, the air thickened with tension, and the echo of raindrops on metal reverberated through the stillness. I stepped inside, greeted by the dim light filtering through dusty windows, illuminating the faces of the few brave enough to confront the truth alongside me.

"Glad you made it," said an older man, his voice gravelly and lined with years of frustration. "This isn't going to be easy, but you're on the right path."

I nodded, sensing the gravity of his words as he laid out the documents he had brought—financial records that painted a damning picture of Ryan's family. My heart raced as I scanned the pages. This was the evidence I needed to expose the depth of their corruption. Yet, in the back of my mind, the realization gnawed at me like a persistent ache: this would shatter Ryan.

We discussed the implications of what we had found, each piece interlocking with the next, forming a grotesque mosaic of betrayal. I felt a cocktail of determination and dread bubbling in my stomach, each word spoken tightening the knot of conflict within me.

"Publishing this will ruin lives," one woman said, her brow furrowed. "But it will also save others from the same fate."

"Are you willing to live with that?" another added, their voice heavy with the weight of the decision.

As the conversation ebbed and flowed around me, I felt the ground shifting beneath my feet. The duality of truth and love clashed violently in my chest, each vying for dominance. I could see the headlines, the articles tearing apart the façade of a family I had come to know intimately. The thought of Ryan's reaction—a mixture of fury and heartbreak—made my breath hitch.

"I can't just turn away," I finally said, my voice steady despite the turmoil inside. "If I don't do this, who will? We can't let them keep hurting people."

Their nods were almost imperceptible, yet they filled the room with a shared understanding—a silent pact formed in the gloom of the warehouse. I glanced down at my phone, half-expecting a text from Ryan, an urgent plea for me to stop. But nothing came. Maybe it was better this way; the silence was deafening, and my resolve solidified in its absence.

As I left the warehouse, the rain had eased into a gentle drizzle, the clouds beginning to part. The evening air was cool and crisp, invigorating, as if it sensed the tumult of my thoughts and sought to clear the storm. I took a deep breath, filling my lungs with the scent of damp earth and hope. I was ready to turn the tables, to reclaim my power, even if it meant sacrificing my heart.

The cool evening air wrapped around me like a comforting shawl as I made my way to my apartment. The rain had ceased, leaving behind glistening streets that reflected the neon lights of the city, creating a kaleidoscope of color that danced beneath my feet. Each step felt heavier than the last, laden with the weight of what I had learned, but also buoyed by a newfound sense of purpose. The confrontation at the warehouse had ignited something deep within me—a fierce determination that burned brighter than my doubts.

I entered my building and was greeted by the familiar creaks of the wooden floors, the comforting scent of old books mixed with a hint of jasmine from the plant I had somehow managed to keep alive. I kicked off my shoes, letting them land haphazardly by the door, and plopped down on the couch, my heart racing as I pulled my laptop onto my lap. The screen flickered to life, illuminating my face in a pale glow as I opened a new document titled "The Truth About Martin Industries."

The blinking cursor taunted me, urging me to dive in. Each word I typed felt like a step closer to dismantling the fortress that Ryan's family had built, but it also felt like a betrayal of the man I loved. A man who had charmed me with laughter, his playful jabs about my obsession with true crime resonating in my memory. I could almost hear him teasing, "You're not going to get yourself into trouble, are you?"

Trouble? I was already neck-deep in it.

As I began crafting my narrative, the coffee table littered with papers became a battleground of my thoughts. I had pages filled with interviews, notes on financial discrepancies, and the haunting testimonies of those who had lost everything. I recalled the woman with tears in her eyes, recounting the moment she lost her job—the moment she realized the company she had devoted her life to was built on lies. Her words echoed in my mind, a chorus of anguish that fueled my resolve.

Suddenly, a loud knock on the door startled me, a jolt of adrenaline coursing through my veins. My heart raced as I jumped up, heart hammering against my ribcage. I glanced through the peephole, half-expecting to see Ryan standing there, an earnest look on his face, ready to sweep me off my feet and away from this chaos. Instead, I was met with the slightly disheveled yet undeniably familiar figure of Liz, my best friend.

I flung open the door, relief flooding me as she stepped inside, the scent of her coconut-scented shampoo trailing in after her.

"Okay, spill," she said, planting her hands on her hips and narrowing her eyes at me. "You look like you've been wrestling with a bear. Or, you know, Ryan's family."

I laughed, a sound that felt foreign amidst the tension. "It's more like wrestling with a whole circus of bears. How did you know I needed a lifeline?"

"Your face," she replied, plopping down onto the couch beside me. "It's a mix of fury and fear. You're scaring me a little."

"Just doing some digging," I said, gesturing to the papers sprawled around us. "You know, to find the truth and save the world or whatever."

Liz picked up a page, scanning it quickly, her expression shifting from concern to intrigue. "This is... heavy. You're really going through with this?"

"Do I have a choice?" I replied, the weight of the question hanging in the air. "If I don't, who will? I can't let them keep hurting people."

"Fair point," she conceded, looking back at me with an intensity that made my heart clench. "But what about Ryan? How are you going to handle that?"

I met her gaze, feeling the lump in my throat grow. "I don't know. But I can't let my feelings for him cloud the truth. What if I let him convince me to back down, and then he goes back to his family and... what? Just goes on with his life?"

Liz sighed, leaning back against the couch, her fingers tapping against the armrest as she considered my words. "You're right. But it's not just about you anymore. You have to think about the fallout, the way this will change everything."

"I know," I admitted, rubbing my temples as if I could massage away the anxiety curling around my brain. "But what if this is the only chance I have to expose them? What if they just keep getting away with it? I can't be the person who stands by and does nothing."

The room fell silent, the tension thickening the air between us. I could feel the weight of her scrutiny, the way she wrestled with the enormity of my choices, but it was clear we were on the same page. After all, we had been through so much together.

"Okay, let's think this through," she said finally, her voice steady and calm, the kind of clarity I desperately needed. "What's your next step? Do you have a plan for how you'll publish this?"

"I do," I said, a flicker of determination igniting within me. "I'm going to reach out to the local paper. They're always looking for breaking stories, and this could shake up the whole community. If I present it right, they won't be able to ignore it."

"Sounds ambitious," she replied, a teasing glimmer in her eyes. "But that's you, right? Always trying to save the world one article at a time."

"Exactly," I grinned, buoyed by her encouragement. "But I'm not doing this alone. I'll need your help—someone to keep me grounded when I inevitably spiral into a puddle of self-doubt."

She chuckled, nudging my shoulder playfully. "Oh, I can do that. Just promise me you'll think of yourself in this too, okay? You deserve to be happy, even if it means making tough choices."

"Agreed," I said, a hint of conviction in my voice. "But I can't be happy knowing I turned a blind eye. Not anymore."

Liz gave me a solemn nod, her gaze unwavering. "Then let's get to work. You can't do this all on your own."

We dove into the details together, her presence filling the room with a warm energy, the tension shifting as we crafted a plan. Each idea exchanged felt like a spark, igniting a fire that drove away the darkness. We dissected the facts, plotted timelines, and crafted potential narratives as the evening unfolded, laughter and determination blending seamlessly in the air.

As we stood on the precipice of something monumental, I felt an exhilarating mix of fear and anticipation coursing through me. The path ahead was fraught with danger, but the light of truth beckoned me forward. I might be turning the tables, but this time, I wouldn't be standing alone.

The sun peeked through my apartment window, casting long shadows across the floor, the golden light dappling the pages of my scattered notes. The air felt charged with possibility, the kind of energy that thrums just before a storm, the sky outside a canvas of ominous gray. I leaned back in my chair, staring at the screen as the blinking cursor seemed to mock me, a reminder that I was at a crossroads where each choice felt heavier than the last.

Liz had left earlier that morning, her words still ringing in my ears. "You have to think about yourself too." The reminder was meant to ground me, yet it echoed in a different light now. Could I afford to think of myself when the stakes had grown so high? I poured another cup of coffee, allowing its rich aroma to envelop me, momentarily drowning out the swirling thoughts of betrayal and consequence. I needed clarity, and caffeine was the lifeblood of my brainstorming sessions.

As I sipped, the thought of Ryan clawed at the back of my mind. He was out there, oblivious to the storm brewing around him. Would he see me as the heroine of this tale or the villain who shattered his world? I longed to speak to him, to confront the man I had fallen for, yet the thought of revealing what I had learned left me breathless. My fingers hovered over the keyboard, ready to pour out my emotions, but the words clung stubbornly to my throat.

A sudden knock at the door broke my reverie, sharp and insistent. I nearly spilled my coffee as I scrambled to my feet, heart racing with an odd blend of dread and anticipation. Who could it be? I peered through the peephole again, half-expecting Ryan's familiar silhouette. Instead, my stomach dropped as I caught sight of the last person I ever wanted to see: Mia, Ryan's sister.

Mia was everything I despised about Ryan's world—polished, ambitious, and wrapped tightly in the family legacy. Her long, blond hair fell in perfect waves, and her designer clothes looked like they were tailored by an elite squad of seamstresses. I opened the door just a crack, bracing myself for whatever onslaught awaited.

"Hello, darling!" she chirped, her smile bright but her eyes glinting with something darker. "I hope I'm not interrupting."

I narrowed my eyes, debating whether to slam the door in her perfectly manicured face. "What do you want, Mia?"

"Oh, just wanted to have a little chat," she said, feigning innocence. "You know how family is. Always keeping tabs."

"Family?" I scoffed, crossing my arms. "Since when do you care about family?"

"Touché," she replied, an amused grin breaking through. "But I'm here to help, actually. I heard you've been busy—meeting people, gathering intel. I thought I might offer my expertise."

"Your expertise?" I repeated, incredulous. "What do you know about my investigation?"

Her expression shifted, seriousness creeping in. "More than you think. I know what's happening within Martin Industries, and trust me, you're walking a fine line. You might think you're the one holding the pen, but you're not the only one who knows how to write a story."

I stepped back, considering my options. Did I trust her? The answer was a resounding no, yet the curiosity gnawed at me. "Why should I believe anything you say?"

"Because, sweetheart, I'm on your side," she purred, stepping closer, her voice lowering to a conspiratorial whisper. "You're not the only one who's tired of the family secrets, and I'd hate to see you caught in the crossfire. You're too good for that, really."

I eyed her suspiciously, my mind racing. "And what's in it for you?"

"Ah, see, there it is," she replied, a smirk forming. "The skeptical journalist. Just like Ryan. But I'm different. I'm willing to burn bridges if it means clearing the path for you. This family is rotting from the inside, and if you can help me take it down, then I'm all in."

Her proposition hung in the air, heavy and palpable. I couldn't shake the feeling that she was playing a game, her own agenda simmering just beneath the surface. But then again, perhaps there was a sliver of truth in her words. The thought of having someone inside the family willing to turn against them was intoxicating.

"What do you want from me?" I asked, narrowing my eyes.

Mia leaned closer, her voice barely above a whisper. "You need leverage, and I can provide it. I have documents—things that could blow this whole operation wide open. But you need to trust me."

"Trust you?" I scoffed again. "You're Ryan's sister. How do I know this isn't a trap?"

"Because I've been trapped in this family long enough. And I'm tired of wearing a smile while the world crumbles," she said, her voice steady, devoid of the playful tone from moments earlier. "You've got a chance to change everything, and I can help. But you have to let me in."

Her sincerity pierced through my defenses, and for a fleeting moment, I considered the possibilities. But then I thought of Ryan—the pain it would cause him, the damage it could do to our fragile relationship.

"Let me think about it," I finally said, unwilling to commit just yet.

"Fine. But don't take too long," she replied, her eyes glimmering with ambition. "You don't want to miss the moment when everything goes down. It might be your only shot."

With that, she turned on her heel and walked away, her heels clicking against the tile floor like a metronome marking the passing seconds. I stood frozen in the doorway, the weight of her proposition hanging heavy in the air. My heart raced as I closed the door, the quiet thud echoing through the silence that enveloped me.

I paced my small living room, my mind a tornado of thoughts. Could I really partner with Mia? What did she know that I didn't? The stakes had never felt higher, and every instinct told me I was about to tip the balance of power in a game I barely understood.

As I sat back down at my laptop, fingers poised over the keys, the phone buzzed on the table, jolting me from my thoughts. I glanced at the screen, my breath hitching as I saw Ryan's name flash. My heart raced, and I hesitated, torn between answering and what I might have to say. I could feel the room spinning, the walls closing in as I pondered the possibilities of this moment.

Just as I picked it up, a notification pinged on my laptop. I glanced at the screen, heart sinking as I read the words: "Emergency Board Meeting Scheduled: 2 PM Tomorrow."

A chill crept down my spine. This was it. The clock was ticking, and everything was about to change. I needed to decide quickly—whether to trust Mia, whether to risk everything I had with Ryan, and whether to dive headfirst into the chaos waiting on the other side of that meeting.

The stakes had never been higher, and I could feel the ground shifting beneath me as I braced for the fall. Just as I pressed 'answer' on my phone, ready to confront Ryan, another notification chimed, this time from an unknown number: "You're in over your head. Don't say a word to him."

My breath caught in my throat, the words striking a match in the darkness, igniting a fire I hadn't anticipated. The room spun around me, every decision closing in like the walls of a collapsing tunnel, and I knew there was no turning back now.

Chapter 20: The Price of Truth

The sun slices through the slits of the hotel blinds, casting thin, angular shadows across the room, each one a reminder of the precarious balance I'm about to disrupt. The city hums softly, as if anticipating the fallout of my decision. Outside, the world stirs slowly to life; the clatter of an early delivery truck echoes faintly, while the distant sound of laughter floats in from a nearby café. I breathe in deeply, the air thick with the scent of damp pavement and stale coffee, grounding me in this moment before I take the plunge.

The weight of my phone still lingers in my hand, a small device that now feels like a weapon. I replay the conversation with my editor, her voice sharp and eager, punctuating the silence of my hotel room. "This could change everything," she had said, but the tone of her excitement had felt more like a lead weight settling deep in my chest. I stare at the pile of notes scattered across the small table—jotting down half-formed thoughts and chaotic ideas was easier than dealing with the heart of the matter. The truth I've unearthed, wrapped in layers of deceit, is a fragile thing, and I fear that exposing it will only serve to shatter what little peace I've found.

I lean against the cool glass of the window, my reflection staring back at me—a woman on the verge of a reckoning, with a tangled mess of hair and eyes shadowed by sleepless nights. I've spent so many hours trying to find the right angle, the perfect words that will unravel the years of silence surrounding Ryan's family. Beneath the surface, their lives are a tapestry of secrets and lies, but now, I hold the scissors, ready to snip through the threads. My fingers fidget with the fraying edges of a napkin, where I've scribbled bits of dialogue and poignant moments from my conversations with Ryan, the fragments that made him human to me. Each note represents a moment shared, a laugh exchanged, and now they feel like a betrayal, each one pulling me away from the connection we've fought to forge.

I can still hear Ryan's laughter, vibrant and warm, wrapping around me like a blanket. The way his smile would light up the dimmest of rooms, transforming even the most mundane moments into something magical. Just last night, we sat across from each other at that corner table in Café Étoile, the atmosphere heavy with the smell of fresh pastries and rich coffee, our conversation flowing freely as we navigated our thoughts and fears. He'd leaned in, eyes sparkling with mischief, and told me how he was ready to confront the ghosts of his past, how the burden of truth was beginning to feel lighter. But what he didn't know was that I had already stumbled into that darkness, and it was deeper than either of us anticipated.

A sharp knock at the door jolts me from my thoughts, and I freeze, the very air around me suddenly electric with tension. My heart races as I open it, revealing a young woman with tousled hair and oversized glasses, clutching a stack of papers to her chest like a shield. She's my neighbor, or at least I think she is; we've exchanged polite smiles in the elevator but never really spoken. "Um, I was wondering if you could help me," she says, her voice tinged with urgency. "I lost my phone charger, and I think it might have slipped under your door."

I blink, momentarily disarmed by her presence. "Sure, let me check," I reply, forcing a smile that feels oddly forced. As I crouch down, rummaging beneath the edge of the bed, I can't shake the gnawing feeling that this encounter is a distraction—one I can't afford. I finally pull out a tangled mess of cords and hold them up triumphantly. "Found it!"

Her eyes light up, relief flooding her features. "Oh my God, thank you so much! I thought I was going to have to go all day without my phone." She reaches for the charger, but I hesitate, the weight of my decision pressing heavily on my chest. A part of me wants to ask her what she would do in my situation, if she would choose to protect the truth or unleash it upon the world. Instead, I simply hand over the charger and force a smile.

"Good luck," I say, a quiet blessing for a stranger embarking on her own journey. As the door clicks shut behind her, I'm struck by the juxtaposition of our lives—hers, full of simple, immediate needs, while mine spirals into the complex web of repercussions that await me.

I return to my desk, the notes a chaotic swirl of thoughts that refuse to coalesce into anything coherent. With every second that ticks away, the gravity of my decision settles deeper into my bones. This isn't just about a story; it's about lives irrevocably altered by the truth I'm about to expose.

Gazing at my reflection, I murmur, "What would Ryan say?" I can almost hear his voice, teasing yet understanding. "Just do it, Margo. The truth is worth it, even if it hurts."

As I draw in a breath, my fingers hover over the keyboard. The blank screen beckons me like a canvas, waiting to be painted with words that might change everything. The sun continues its rise, bathing the room in a warm, golden hue, and I know I can't turn back now. It's time to decide what kind of story I want to tell—not just about Ryan and his family, but about myself, the woman willing to risk it all for the sake of truth.

With each keystroke, I can feel the tension simmering just below the surface. I'm crafting a narrative, one that could unravel a family's carefully constructed facade and alter the course of my life forever. My heart races at the thought, a mixture of fear and exhilaration propelling me forward. It's a dangerous game, but the stakes have never felt more real.

The sun's rays spill into the room like a promise, illuminating every shadowy corner and revealing the chaos that is my mind. I sit at the small table, my fingers drumming anxiously against the wood, tapping out a rhythm that feels both frantic and desperate.

The weight of the decision lingers, heavy as the worn hotel curtains that flutter ever so slightly in the morning breeze. Each passing moment feels like an echo of my choice, a reminder that the truth can be as messy as it is liberating.

After that call, silence enveloped me, and for a fleeting moment, the quiet felt reassuring, like a lullaby soothing a frightened child. But as I sit there, the reality crashes over me like a wave, pulling me under with thoughts of Ryan—his kind eyes, the laughter that felt like sunlight breaking through the clouds. How could I expose the family secrets he's carried for so long, secrets that have etched pain into his very being? The thought of hurting him churns my stomach, a cauldron of fear and regret simmering just beneath the surface.

With a deep breath, I pull my laptop closer, the screen flickering to life as I remind myself why I'm here. The truth demands to be told, doesn't it? But even as I type, I can hear Ryan's voice in my mind, teasing me about my chronic need to uncover the hidden layers of people's lives. "It's like you have a built-in detective chip," he'd say, half-joking, half-admiring. I can almost see the playful smirk on his lips, and it makes my heart ache.

Before I can dive deeper into my thoughts, my phone vibrates on the table, the familiar sound cutting through the tension. It's a message from my best friend, Clara, and I can't help but smile at the way she seems to sense when I need a distraction. Her texts are like sunlight on a gloomy day, always brightening my mood.

"Hey, superhero! Just checking to see if you've saved the world yet. Or are you still mulling over that deliciously scandalous story?"

I chuckle softly, knowing she's well aware of my tendency to dwell on the darker sides of my work. "Not yet," I text back, "but I'm pretty sure the world is plotting against me."

A few seconds later, my phone chimes again. "Don't worry! Just think of all the lives you'll save once you expose the truth. Or at least, the drama. Maybe start a podcast while you're at it? 'Tales of a Truth-Seeker' or something equally cheesy."

Her playful banter brings warmth to my chest, and for a moment, I allow myself to imagine how cathartic it would feel to let everything out in the open, to speak my truth without hesitation. But then the image of Ryan's face surfaces in my mind, and the warmth quickly dissipates. What good is truth when it comes at such a cost?

Determined to shake off the creeping dread, I turn back to the screen, where a blank document sits in front of me, begging for words that refuse to flow. I decide to scroll through my notes, searching for a glimmer of inspiration amid the mess of scribbles and half-formed sentences. But as I read, my heart sinks. It's all there—the tangled web of deceit woven by Ryan's family, a narrative that could very well bring them to their knees. The implications swirl in my mind, clouding my judgment. What if I'm not just unveiling a story but tearing apart the very fabric of their lives?

Suddenly, a knock at the door yanks me from my spiraling thoughts. I pause, heart racing as I wonder who it could be. My first instinct is to hide, to bury myself under the weight of my worries, but I remind myself that avoidance never solved anything. Tentatively, I open the door, revealing a tall man dressed in a well-fitted suit, his hair slicked back as if he just stepped out of a magazine.

"Excuse me," he says, voice smooth like honey but with an edge that sends a chill down my spine. "I'm looking for a Miss Margo Jennings. I have something important to discuss with you."

My heart skips a beat as I step back, instinctively scanning the hallway for anyone else. "Who sent you?" I ask, suspicion lacing my words.

"Let's just say I'm here on behalf of someone who cares about your well-being," he replies, his eyes narrowing slightly as he leans closer, lowering his voice. "It would be in your best interest to hear me out."

A jolt of fear flares within me, and I wonder if this is what I've been waiting for—a message from Ryan's family, perhaps? A warning against exposing their secrets? "I'm not interested in whatever you're selling," I snap, trying to sound braver than I feel.

His lips curl into a faint smirk, as if he relishes my defiance. "Oh, but you should be. There are things at stake here that go far beyond your little story. The truth has a way of catching up to people, Margo. You might not want to be the one holding the knife."

I glare at him, my heart racing. "I don't appreciate threats."

"I'm not threatening you," he replies smoothly, crossing his arms as he leans against the doorframe. "I'm merely offering a piece of advice. You have no idea what you're getting yourself into."

A million questions flood my mind, but I focus on the instinctual urge to slam the door shut. Yet, there's something magnetic about him—a dangerous allure that makes me hesitate. "Who sent you?" I ask again, my voice steadier this time, and his expression shifts, a flicker of something akin to respect shining in his eyes.

"Let's just say I'm a messenger. You don't want to become collateral damage in a battle you didn't even know existed."

I take a deep breath, forcing myself to remain calm. "What do you want?"

"Just a friendly warning. Think long and hard about your next move, Miss Jennings." With that, he turns and strides down the hallway, leaving me standing in the doorway, breathless and bewildered.

I close the door slowly, my heart thundering in my chest. The warning lingers in the air, heavy and foreboding, as I retreat to the safety of my room. The truth that I believed I could wield now feels like a double-edged sword, and I can't shake the feeling that the stakes have just been raised in a game I didn't even know I was playing.

Sinking back into my chair, I run a shaky hand through my hair, trying to process what just happened. The walls feel closer now, pressing in around me as I contemplate the depths of the rabbit hole I'm about to plunge into. My fingers hover above the keyboard, hesitating as I fight against the wave of doubt crashing over me. This wasn't just about my story anymore; it was about survival, both for myself and for Ryan.

The weight of the man's warning clings to me like an unwanted scent, lingering even after he's vanished down the hallway. I can still hear his words echoing in my mind, a relentless refrain that raises the hairs on the back of my neck. "Collateral damage." What a lovely phrase to wrap around the core of my anxiety, making it all the more palpable. I lean back against the chair, the leather cool against my skin, and close my eyes for a moment, willing my heartbeat to slow. The morning sun bathes the room in golden light, but it feels more like a spotlight illuminating the chaos within me.

I pull my laptop toward me, the screen glaring like a beacon in the burgeoning day. I can almost convince myself that if I just start typing, if I put my fears into words, they might dissipate. But every thought feels heavy with consequence, each word a brick I'd be stacking onto a wall that might one day come crashing down on me. I glance down at my notes again, each scribble a jigsaw piece to a picture I'm no longer sure I want to complete.

Suddenly, my phone buzzes again, and I snatch it up with a mix of hope and dread. Clara's name blinks on the screen, a reminder of normalcy. "You okay?" her text reads. Simple, yet loaded with concern.

I pause before replying, trying to summon the right words. "Just having an existential crisis over here," I type back, a weak attempt at humor. "You know, the usual."

"Can't be a superhero without the drama," she shoots back almost immediately. I can almost see her rolling her eyes at my melodrama. "Wanna talk?"

"No," I reply, biting my lip. I don't want to burden her with my swirling thoughts or the dark specter of Ryan's family that hovers over me now like an uninvited guest at a party. "I'm good. Just... working through some stuff."

"Fine, but I'm here if you need me," she replies, and I can picture her leaning back, arms crossed, a playful pout on her lips. Her unwavering support is a balm, yet I still hesitate to share the reality of what I'm facing. What could I even say? "Hey, Clara, I'm about to write a piece that could ruin a man's life, and by the way, I might be in over my head."

I throw my phone aside and glance out the window, where the world bustles by, blissfully unaware of the storm brewing in my mind. A couple strolls past, hand in hand, their laughter spilling up toward me like an invitation to a life I momentarily yearn for. I can't help but feel like a voyeur, watching a scene I'll never be a part of.

Determined to reclaim my focus, I begin typing. Words pour onto the page, raw and unfiltered, each sentence a release of tension that's built up like steam in a kettle. The outline of my story takes shape—Ryan's family, their history, the whispers that shadow their name—but then I hit a wall, the familiar dread creeping back in. What am I doing?

A soft knock at the door jolts me from my spiral, and I sit up straight, my heart racing. Who could it be this time? Hesitantly, I rise and move toward the door, a mix of curiosity and apprehension bubbling within me. I open it, half-expecting to find the suited man again, but instead, I'm greeted by the unmistakable figure of Ryan himself, standing there, windswept and frazzled, as if he's just run a marathon.

"Margo," he breathes, his voice barely above a whisper, tinged with urgency and something else—fear? I'm taken aback by the sight of him, disheveled yet striking, a stark contrast to the polished persona I've come to admire. "We need to talk. Now."

My stomach knots. "What's wrong?" I ask, my heart lurching at the worry etched across his face.

"Can I come in?" he replies, glancing nervously down the hall, as if expecting someone—or something—to emerge from the shadows. I step aside, my mind racing with possibilities. Is this about my story? Has he somehow found out what I'm planning?

He strides past me into the room, the scent of him—citrus and something distinctly him—filling the space and instantly throwing me off balance. "I was trying to reach you," he says, his voice low, edged with a sense of urgency that sends shivers down my spine. "You shouldn't be here, Margo. It's not safe."

"What do you mean?" I ask, bewildered. "What's going on?"

Ryan takes a breath, running a hand through his hair, revealing the vulnerability in his eyes. "It's my family. They're—" He pauses, collecting his thoughts as if they're scattered puzzle pieces he's struggling to put together. "They're hiding something, and it's worse than I thought. I didn't want to believe it, but now... I can't ignore it."

My heart sinks. The truth I've been holding could end up destroying him. "I have to write this, Ryan. I can't just sit back and let it go."

"No," he interrupts sharply, his voice rising slightly. "You don't understand. They're not just some family with secrets. They're dangerous, Margo. And if they find out you're digging, they won't hesitate to protect themselves."

The chill of his words snakes through me. "What do you mean 'protect themselves'?"

He steps closer, lowering his voice. "I've been getting messages too, threats. They're watching you. They know you're involved."

I feel the ground shift beneath me, a cold panic gripping my chest. "What? No one told me anything about this!"

"That's why I came," he insists, his expression fierce, desperate. "You need to leave this alone. Walk away before it's too late."

"I can't!" I exclaim, my voice rising in frustration. "I need to uncover the truth, Ryan. It's the only way to bring light to what they've done!"

"Is it worth your life?" he counters, his eyes blazing with an intensity that's both frightening and captivating. "What if they come after you? What if I can't protect you?"

The fear in his voice sends a tremor through me, unraveling the bravado I've held on to. I swallow hard, forcing myself to meet his gaze. "So what? We just let them get away with it?"

A heavy silence settles between us, the air thick with tension as we both grapple with the enormity of our choices. It feels like standing on the edge of a cliff, teetering dangerously close to a fall.

Suddenly, Ryan's phone buzzes in his pocket, and he pulls it out, his expression darkening as he reads the screen. "Shit," he mutters, his face paling. "I have to go."

"What? Why?"

"There's no time to explain," he says, grabbing my hand, his grip fierce and desperate. "But you need to promise me something."

"Anything," I reply, my heart racing.

"Stay away from them. Just promise me."

Before I can respond, he turns to leave, and I grasp his arm, desperation fueling my words. "Ryan, don't go! You can't just leave me like this!"

His gaze softens, but there's a fear in his eyes that makes my blood run cold. "I have to, Margo. Trust me. I'll figure this out. Just—please, promise me."

"I promise!" I say, voice trembling.

And then he's gone, slipping out of the door and leaving me standing alone in the room, the silence suddenly deafening. The weight of his absence is palpable, wrapping around me like a shroud.

I look back at my laptop, the blinking cursor taunting me, the story unwritten but looming larger than life. Ryan's warning echoes in my mind, but I can't shake the feeling that I'm too deep in now. With the adrenaline still pumping through my veins, I grab my phone, preparing to do what I should have done before—reach out to Clara. But just as I'm about to dial, the lights flicker overhead, plunging me into darkness for a heartbeat before they flicker back on.

My breath catches in my throat as a figure appears in the doorway, silhouetted against the light, a shadow that makes my heart race. I squint, trying to make out who it is, when a voice cuts through the air, low and dangerous. "Well, well, Margo. I believe we need to have a little chat."

And just like that, the ground beneath me shifts again, the weight of the truth now threatening to pull me under as the figure steps forward into the light, revealing a face I recognize all too well.

Chapter 21: Ryan's Silence

The rain starts to patter against the window, its rhythm a soft lullaby that contrasts sharply with the storm brewing in my chest. I wrap my arms around myself, as if I can hold together the fragments of my heart that seem to be slipping through my fingers. Each drop is a reminder of his absence, a countdown of sorts, echoing in my mind. I can't shake the feeling that the storm outside mirrors the tempest inside me—a clash of emotions I can't quite name.

It's been days since I hit "send" on my story, days since Ryan's face lit up my world with that crooked smile. I had spent countless nights with my fingers poised over the keyboard, pouring out everything I knew about him, about the choices he made that landed him in a world he desperately tried to escape. Each keystroke had felt like an act of love, a way to tell his truth. But now, I wonder if it was love at all or just reckless ambition masked as virtue.

I take a deep breath, the stale air of the hotel room suffocating me. I should be working on something else—revisions for my upcoming article, maybe—but the words swim away from me, like fish darting beneath the surface, too quick to catch. My phone lies abandoned on the bedside table, the screen dark and still, mocking me with its silence. I can't decide what hurts more: the absence of Ryan's calls or the certainty that I may have lost him for good.

That morning, I had ventured out to grab coffee, hoping that the warm brew would melt away the chill settling into my bones. The café down the street was a cozy nook, its windows fogged with the warmth of conversation and laughter. I pushed through the door, the bell tinkling above me, a cheerful sound that felt out of place. A barista with a beaming smile took my order, and I found a small table by the window, attempting to drown out the thoughts swirling in my mind with the aroma of freshly brewed coffee.

But even surrounded by people, I felt isolated, as if an invisible wall separated me from the rest of the world. Conversations bubbled around me, snippets of laughter and gossip swirling like leaves in a brisk autumn wind. My heart ached for connection, for someone to understand the weight I was carrying. I watched as couples shared intimate glances, their fingers intertwined, while I sat alone with a cold cup of coffee that had long since lost its warmth.

The tension I felt was palpable, gnawing at me like a hungry beast. I replayed our last encounter, each moment etched in my mind like a tattoo. His voice had been steady, but the hurt in his eyes was undeniable—a deep, raw wound that throbbed with every heartbeat. I had wanted to tell him that my intentions had been pure, that I thought I was helping him by giving his story a voice, but how could he ever believe that? To him, I was just another journalist seeking the truth, and the truth was a fickle thing.

Just as I was about to drown myself in another sip of bitter coffee, I spotted a familiar figure crossing the street, his gait unmistakable even from a distance. My heart raced, and I squinted, hoping it was some sort of mirage. But there he was—Ryan, with his dark hair tousled by the wind and that signature leather jacket that always made him look effortlessly cool. He paused under the awning of the café, glancing around as if searching for something—or someone.

A rush of hope surged through me, but just as quickly, it was followed by a wave of dread. Would he even want to see me after everything? I had torn down the walls he had so carefully built around his heart, and I feared he would find me standing there with a microphone in hand, ready to dissect every piece of his life like a specimen under glass.

But before I could decide on a course of action, he turned on his heel and started to walk away, back toward the shadows of the city. A sudden impulse shot through me, igniting a fire I thought had long been extinguished. I jumped from my seat, abandoning my cold coffee and the blanket of melancholy that had settled over me. I pushed through the café door, the bell chiming in protest, and stepped into the damp chill of the day.

"Ryan!" I called, my voice shaking but resolute, cutting through the soft patter of rain like a lifeline.

He paused but didn't turn. My heart raced; I felt like a marionette on strings, the urge to run toward him battling the weight of my fear. "Please," I added, desperation creeping into my voice. "Just... just let me explain."

Finally, he turned, the expression on his face unreadable. I took a few tentative steps forward, the ground slick beneath my feet, as if the universe conspired to trip me up at this pivotal moment. But I wouldn't be deterred. He stood there, a statue carved from shadow and rain, and I could see the war raging behind his eyes—hurt, confusion, anger.

"I didn't mean to hurt you," I said, my breath hitching as I finally closed the distance between us. "I thought... I thought you wanted your story told."

His lips pressed into a thin line, and I could see the flicker of pain in his gaze. "My story?" he echoed, the incredulity almost painful to hear. "Or your story? There's a difference, you know."

I swallowed hard, feeling the weight of his words settle into my stomach like a stone. "I wanted to help you. To give a voice to the things you've been through."

"And now?" He crossed his arms, the rain beading on his jacket, framing him in a sorrowful silhouette. "What's your excuse for selling me out?"

Each word cut deep, a jagged edge of truth I couldn't escape. I searched his face for a glimmer of understanding, a crack in his armor, but all I saw was a fortress, unyielding and cold. My heart raced as I prepared to fight for the space between us, to find a way back to the warmth we had shared.

"Because I care about you, Ryan! I didn't want to hurt you, I swear!" My voice broke, the vulnerability spilling out like a long-buried secret. "I thought that maybe... maybe you'd want to share this burden, but I see now that I didn't give you a choice. I crossed a line."

The rain picked up, drenching us both as the world around us faded into a blur of gray. But in that moment, beneath the downpour and the weight of our unspoken truths, I could feel the tension shifting, a delicate dance of hope and despair hanging in the air between us.

The rain falls heavier now, each droplet a stinging reminder of the distance between us, as if the universe has conspired to drench my heart in despair. I stand there, shivering not just from the cold but from the weight of words left unsaid, each moment stretching into an eternity. It's as if time itself has folded, trapping me in this liminal space of regret and longing, where every heartbeat reverberates with what-ifs and might-have-beens.

I can't let this be the end, can I? The thought spirals through my mind, punctuated by the relentless sound of rain hitting the pavement. I take a hesitant step forward, half-tempted to call out to him again, but I bite my lip instead, fearing that another attempt to reach him might only push him further away. The world feels unbearably vast without him, the city's cacophony blending into a dull roar, while I'm stuck here in this microcosm of our last encounter.

Turning back toward the café, I scan the room for any sign of solace, but laughter bounces off the walls like mocking echoes. I need to breathe, to think. I weave through the tables and slip out the door, where the rain welcomes me like an old friend, its chill wrapping around me. I navigate the slick streets, my feet carrying me almost of their own accord, as if my body knows the way to somewhere safe, somewhere I can figure out how to bridge this chasm between us.

The nearby park looms ahead, its once-vibrant greenery dulled by the storm. I push through the wrought-iron gates, the smell of damp earth filling my lungs, grounding me as I take refuge beneath the sprawling branches of an ancient oak. The tree stands tall, a sentinel against the storm, and I envy its strength. I can almost hear its roots deep in the earth, whispering secrets of endurance and resilience.

Sitting on a bench, I pull my knees to my chest, thoughts swirling like the autumn leaves caught in the wind. What had I done? I thought I was giving Ryan a chance to reclaim his narrative, to shine a light on the shadows that haunted him. Yet here I was, drowning in the very darkness I tried to illuminate. The sting of betrayal lingers, but I can't shake the feeling that I may have underestimated him, his strength, and our connection.

I close my eyes, picturing his face—those dark, stormy eyes that once held warmth now cloaked in disappointment. I can't erase the memory of his gaze when he said he thought I was different. It slices through me, igniting a familiar fire. Was I really just another person in his life seeking to exploit his story? The self-loathing floods in, overwhelming and suffocating, and I can't bear the thought of being that person.

The wind rustles through the leaves, and I feel a jolt of determination surge within me. I won't let fear dictate my actions. If Ryan needed space, I'd give him that, but I wouldn't back down. I need to show him that I didn't mean to hurt him—that I was on his side, despite my choices.

A sudden noise breaks my reverie, and I turn to see a young couple strolling by, their laughter spilling into the air like music. They walk hand in hand, sharing whispers and inside jokes, oblivious to the storm surrounding them. I wonder if Ryan and I had ever been that carefree, if we'd ever danced in the rain instead of standing in its shadows, hesitant and uncertain.

With a sigh, I dig my phone out of my pocket and scroll through our previous messages. Each text is a lifeline to the past—moments filled with shared secrets and laughter that feel like distant memories now. I hover over his name, my heart racing at the thought of reaching out, of crossing that divide. But what could I possibly say?

As I sit there, wrestling with my thoughts, the rain begins to taper off, the clouds parting just enough to let slivers of sunlight pierce through. It's as if the world is reminding me that storms don't last forever, that even the heaviest downpour will eventually give way to clearer skies.

I'm jolted from my thoughts when I feel my phone buzz in my hand. My heart leaps, and I fumble to unlock the screen, hoping against hope that it's Ryan. Instead, it's a notification from my editor, demanding a follow-up on the article I had submitted. My stomach twists at the thought; I can't face that right now. The words feel like poison on my tongue, and I toss my phone back into my bag, unwilling to let the outside world invade this fragile moment of clarity.

But just as I resolve to focus on myself, a familiar figure appears at the edge of the park. My heart lurches as I see Ryan standing there, his hair slicked back from the rain, the jacket clinging to his frame like armor. He looks hesitant, unsure whether to step into the sanctuary of the park or retreat back into the storm.

I can't breathe, my pulse racing as I search for words, but they're tangled in the net of my throat. He glances around, taking in the scene—the couples, the lingering rain, and then, finally, he meets my eyes. A moment stretches between us, thick with unspoken tension. I can see the conflict warring behind his gaze, a tempest of emotions that makes my heart ache.

"Why are you here?" he finally asks, his voice a rough whisper that cuts through the air like the chill from the clouds.

"I... I needed to think," I stammer, my voice small against the weight of the moment. "And then I saw you."

"I didn't mean to come back." His admission surprises me, his honesty raw and disarming. "I thought I'd just keep walking."

"Maybe we both did," I reply, trying to keep the tone light despite the gravity of our situation. "But here we are. Seems like the universe has other plans."

He takes a step closer, and I can see the tension in his shoulders, the way his jaw tightens. "I don't understand how you could do this. I let you in, and then you... you turned around and sold me out."

"I didn't sell you out," I plead, desperation lacing my words. "I thought I was helping you. I wanted people to see you for who you really are, not just the headlines."

His gaze softens slightly, but the storm behind it is still brewing. "And how do you know what I want? You think you can just write my story without even asking me?"

My heart races, a mixture of panic and anger igniting within me. "I thought you wanted to share it! I thought you wanted to let people know the truth."

"Truth?" he scoffs, running a hand through his hair, frustration radiating off him like heat. "What do you know about my truth? What makes you think you can define it for me?"

I take a deep breath, feeling the sting of his words. "I know it's complicated. I know you're complicated."

For a moment, silence envelops us, heavy and suffocating, like a thick fog that makes it hard to breathe. But I refuse to back down. "Ryan, I care about you. I don't want to lose you over this. I need you to see that I wasn't trying to hurt you. I was trying to give you a voice."

His expression shifts, the anger melting away into something more vulnerable. "And now? What do you expect me to do with that?"

I take another step forward, closing the distance between us. "I want to try again. I want to hear your story, to understand it the way you want it to be told. But I can't do that if you shut me out."

He looks at me, and for a moment, I see a flicker of the man I fell for—the warmth, the passion, the undeniable connection that had pulled us together. But just as quickly, the shadows flicker back, and I'm left wondering if I've ruined the chance we had.

"Just... give me time," he finally says, his voice softening as the rain begins to fall lightly again, a gentle reminder of the storm that had brought us together.

"I can do that," I reply, my heart swelling with hope, even as uncertainty lingers in the air. The road ahead is uncertain, but in that moment, the storm feels a little less daunting. We stand there, both drenched, yet somehow lighter—two souls caught in a rainstorm, trying to find our way back to the light.

As the rain tapers off, the air around us feels charged, heavy with unsaid words and unresolved emotions. I can see the tension in Ryan's shoulders, the way his fingers twitch at his sides, as if he's fighting an internal battle I can't quite comprehend. There's a flicker of something in his eyes, a ghost of the warmth that once connected us, but it's quickly masked by shadows of doubt and hurt.

"Time?" he repeats, a mix of incredulity and weariness lacing his tone. "Time is what we're out of, isn't it? You put my story out there, and now it's out of my hands. It's too late for time."

I take a step closer, the ground beneath me slick and uncertain, mirroring the fragile ground we're standing on. "It's never too late to talk, Ryan. I want to understand. I want you to tell me what you need."

"You think it's that simple?" He shakes his head, the frustration crackling in the air like static electricity. "You put me on display for the world to pick apart. How can I trust you again?"

I want to reach out, to bridge the chasm between us with a touch, a gesture, something to show him I'm still here, still fighting for us. "Because I'm standing here. Because I didn't run away when things got tough. I'm not asking for a pass for what I did, but I'm here to make it right. If you give me a chance, I'll make sure your story is told in a way that honors you."

For a moment, he seems to waver, his resolve cracking ever so slightly. I can see the conflict within him, the pull between the walls he's built and the longing for connection that has always drawn him to me. I wish I could reach into his mind, unravel the thoughts that torment him, and lay bare the truth that we are more than just our pasts.

"You don't get it," he finally says, his voice a low rumble, almost lost to the sound of water trickling off the leaves overhead. "You think I want to relive it all? That I want to sit down and dissect my life like it's some fascinating case study? This isn't a game to me, Julia."

"I know," I whisper, swallowing hard against the swell of emotion. "But it's not a game for me either. I'm not some heartless journalist trying to get a headline. I wanted to tell your story because I believe in it. Because I believe in you."

His eyes flash with something—anger, pain, perhaps hope—but it's quickly overshadowed by a wall of uncertainty. "And what if I don't want to be part of your narrative anymore? What if I want to walk away and leave it all behind?"

The question hangs heavy between us, and I feel my heart sink. "Then you walk away," I say, my voice steadier than I feel. "But let me show you what I could have done. Let me rewrite it, give you control over your truth."

There's a long pause, a thick silence punctuated only by the soft patter of rain. I can see the gears turning in his mind, the struggle between his instinct to retreat and the pull toward the connection we once had.

"Do you even understand what you're asking?" he finally asks, his voice low, almost vulnerable. "You're asking me to trust you after you shattered everything we had."

"I know I broke your trust," I say, my heart racing. "But I'm not asking for forgiveness right now. I'm asking for a chance to prove that I'm still on your side."

Ryan searches my face, his expression unreadable, and for a moment, it feels as if the world around us has faded into insignificance. It's just the two of us, standing in the remnants of the storm, caught in a web of emotions that both binds us together and threatens to tear us apart.

"Fine," he finally says, his voice steady but layered with uncertainty. "Let's say I give you this chance. How do we even start?"

"Let's take a walk," I suggest, my heart lifting slightly at the prospect of moving forward. "I know a quiet place where we can talk. Somewhere that feels... safe."

He hesitates, but then nods, and together we venture down the rain-slicked path that leads us away from the park. As we walk side by side, I can feel the tension still thrumming between us, but there's a shift in the air, a tentative hope that hangs just out of reach, waiting to be grasped.

We head toward the river, where the trees create a natural canopy, the sound of the water rushing past drowning out our quiet footsteps. The sun breaks through the clouds, casting a warm glow that dances across the surface of the river, illuminating the beauty of the moment. It feels surreal, almost like we've stepped into a dream where everything is beautiful but fragile.

I choose a small clearing by the water, a secluded spot where we can finally talk without the chaos of the world intruding. The gentle murmur of the river flows beside us, a constant reminder of the passage of time, of life moving forward even when we feel stuck. I take a seat on a moss-covered rock, and Ryan sinks down next to me, the tension between us shifting, if only slightly.

"I don't want to hide from what I've been through," he starts, his gaze fixed on the water. "But I'm terrified of how people will react. It's one thing to tell a story; it's another for people to judge you for it."

"I get that," I reply, feeling the gravity of his words sink in. "But what if, by sharing your truth, you help someone else? What if they see themselves in your story?"

He turns to me, his eyes searching mine. "What if they don't? What if all they see is the mistakes I made?"

"Then they're missing the bigger picture," I say, my voice steady. "Your story isn't just about the past. It's about who you are now, and the strength you've found to move forward."

Ryan lets out a long, slow breath, and for a moment, I can see the conflict in his eyes. It's a battle between vulnerability and the instinct to protect himself. "You really think people will see it that way?"

"I know they will," I insist, feeling a spark of conviction ignite within me. "You have a chance to inspire others, to show them that even in darkness, there's hope. You're not defined by your past; you're shaped by it."

A flicker of something shifts behind his eyes, and I can tell he's contemplating my words, weighing them against his fears. "And what if I fail? What if I open up and it backfires?"

"Then you dust yourself off and try again," I reply, unable to keep the fire from my voice. "You're not alone in this, Ryan. I'm here with you, and I won't let you fall."

He looks away, the river reflecting the sunlight like a thousand tiny diamonds, each one shimmering with possibility. "You say that now, but what if I become a liability?"

"Then we'll figure it out together," I answer, the conviction in my heart burning brighter. "That's what this is about, right? Building trust. Finding a way to be honest without losing each other in the process."

His silence stretches, and I can see the wheels turning in his mind. I want to reach out, to bridge that final distance, but something keeps me grounded, waiting for him to take that leap of faith.

Suddenly, a loud crash pierces the tranquil atmosphere, making us both jump. I turn to see a tree branch fall nearby, splashing water as it lands on the riverbank. The momentary distraction jolts us back to reality, and I glance at Ryan, who's staring at the fallen branch, his face pale.

"See?" he mutters, the tension reasserting itself. "That's what happens when you take risks. You get blindsided."

Before I can respond, he stands abruptly, eyes locked on the water. "Maybe it's time for me to go," he says, his voice steady but strained. "I need to think."

"Ryan, wait—"

But he doesn't stop. The distance between us stretches again, and I watch, helpless, as he turns away, retreating from the connection we just began to forge. My heart races, a rush of panic flooding through me as I scramble to my feet.

"Please!" I call after him, but my voice is lost in the rustle of leaves and the sound of rushing water. "Don't walk away!"

But he keeps going, each step further away sending ripples of despair through my heart. And just as he reaches the edge of the clearing, a sudden shout echoes from the other side of the riverbank—an unfamiliar voice, sharp and panicked.

"Hey! You! Stop!"

I turn, confusion flooding my mind as I try to make sense of the interruption. Ryan freezes mid-step, looking back at me, his expression a mix of fear and uncertainty. And then, before I can fully process what's happening, I see two figures emerge from the trees, their silhouettes sharp against the fading light.

In that moment, everything freezes. The air thickens with tension, and I can see the unmistakable flash of something metallic glinting in the sunlight—an unmistakable threat that sends chills down my spine.

"Ryan!" I scream, my voice breaking the fragile calm

Chapter 22: Fallout

The news spread like wildfire, igniting every corner of our sleepy town with the ferocity of a summer storm. I could feel the world around me shift, a palpable tremor echoing through the streets and hallways of my once-quiet life. Every channel, every headline blared my revelations like some kind of twisted victory anthem. The pictures of Ryan's family—their smiling faces now juxtaposed with the dark, brooding headlines—haunted me, each frame a reminder of the storm I had set in motion.

I strolled through the crowded streets, the crisp autumn air biting at my cheeks, but I hardly felt it. My thoughts were too entangled in the aftermath of my findings. The coffee shop that usually buzzed with laughter and casual banter was muted, whispers bouncing off the walls like a rubber ball. "Did you hear about the Mortensens?" "I can't believe it." "Scandalous!" The words ricocheted around me, clinging to my skin like the leaves swirling down from the trees overhead.

I pushed open the door of Café Noire, the familiar bell chiming, but the comforting scent of coffee failed to wrap around me like a hug. Instead, it felt like a shroud. I ordered my usual—an oat milk latte with just a hint of vanilla—and slid into a booth by the window. Outside, the world went on as usual, but inside my head, the chaos raged. My heart hammered in my chest, not from excitement, but from an unsettling mix of guilt and fear. Did I really want this? Was exposing the Mortensens worth the destruction it wrought?

As I sipped my coffee, I stared blankly at the window, watching the leaves dance to the ground, oblivious to the chaos swirling just beyond their vibrant golden hues. I pulled my phone from my pocket, staring at the barrage of notifications that flooded my screen. Friends checking in, acquaintances sharing their thoughts on the scandal, but nothing from Ryan. It gnawed at me, a deep, unsettling ache in the pit of my stomach. He had been my anchor in this wild ride, and now? Now he was missing, lost in a sea of controversy, perhaps drowning in a storm of his own making.

I glanced at my reflection in the window, the girl looking back at me appearing more a stranger than ever. My messy bun had surrendered to the whims of the wind, loose strands framing my face like wild tendrils of doubt. I looked tired—exhausted from sleepless nights fueled by caffeine and anxiety. The fight in me felt like it had dimmed, but there was no room for retreat. The stakes were too high, and yet, here I was, ensnared in an emotional labyrinth I hadn't anticipated.

A sudden rush of laughter pulled my attention, breaking through my haze. I turned to see a group of familiar faces—Ryan's friends, gathered at a nearby table, their expressions a mixture of disbelief and excitement. They were discussing the scandal like it was the latest blockbuster hit. "I can't believe she did it!" one girl exclaimed, her voice a melody of surprise. "I mean, how did she even find out?"

The heat in my cheeks flared, the sharp jab of their words piercing through my insecurities. "Who even is she?" another chimed in, laughter bubbling between them like champagne. They had no idea—no idea what it felt like to take down a titan, to watch everything you thought you knew crumble around you. But then again, did I really know what I was doing?

My phone buzzed again, a jarring intrusion. My heart raced as I glanced at the screen—Lucas, Ryan's younger brother. His name was a flash of color against the dull backdrop of my thoughts.

Can we talk?

The text was simple, unadorned, yet it felt like a lifeline thrown into the turbulent waters of my mind. I hesitated, fingers hovering over the keyboard. What was there to say? I had done what I thought was right, what I believed needed to be done, but the aftertaste of my choices lingered, bitter and unyielding.

Sure, I replied, my stomach twisting into knots. Where?

The old park. 4 p.m. Don't be late.

As I pocketed my phone, a wave of anxiety washed over me. The old park, where Ryan and I had shared countless laughs, where secrets had been exchanged like currency. Would this conversation shatter whatever remnants of our connection remained? I watched the clock on the wall, the minute hand ticking away the seconds, each one a reminder that I was spiraling deeper into a vortex I had unleashed.

By the time I arrived at the park, the sun was beginning its descent, casting long shadows across the faded playground. The air was thick with the scent of damp earth and decaying leaves, a melancholic reminder of what was to come. I spotted Lucas sitting on a swing, his silhouette framed against the dying light. He looked smaller than I remembered, like a child caught in a world too big for him.

"Hey," I greeted softly, the word hanging between us like a fragile thread.

"Hey," he replied, his voice barely above a whisper. The tension was palpable, swirling around us, thick enough to choke. I took a seat on the swing beside him, the creaking chains echoing the heaviness of our hearts.

"What's it like?" he asked, his eyes darting to the ground, as if the answer lay buried beneath the damp grass. "Knowing you've ruined everything for my family?"

"Lucas, I didn't ruin anything. I just—"

"You exposed them," he interrupted, his voice rising with emotion. "You made it impossible for them to hide. Do you understand what that means?"

"Yes, I do," I shot back, the defensive edge creeping into my tone. "But they were hiding things that shouldn't have been hidden. People deserve to know the truth."

"But at what cost?" His voice cracked, raw with pain. "What about Ryan? He didn't choose this. None of us did."

The mention of Ryan sent a pang through my chest. I couldn't shake the image of his face—the way his eyes sparkled with mischief, the warmth of his laughter that had become my refuge. "I don't know where he is," I admitted, my voice trembling. "I can't help but think… maybe I pushed him away. Maybe I—"

"Maybe?" Lucas scoffed, a bitter laugh escaping his lips. "You did more than push him away. You set off a bomb, and now we're all standing in the fallout. You need to understand that."

His words landed heavily, each one a stone thrown into the still waters of my resolve. The world had become a cacophony of consequences, and I was caught in the eye of the storm.

Lucas's words lingered in the crisp air, a tangible weight pressing down on my chest. I could feel the shift beneath me, the earth trembling in response to the upheaval I had caused. "You think I wanted this?" I shot back, my voice sharper than I intended. "Do you think I was sitting there with my laptop, gleefully typing away, imagining the chaos that would ensue? I didn't want to hurt anyone."

"Then what were you trying to do?" he countered, arms crossed, a protective barrier against the vulnerability that threatened to spill over. "Because it sure doesn't look like you were thinking of the fallout."

I could see the hurt in his eyes, a reflection of my own uncertainty. He was right. The consequences had mushroomed like smoke from a detonated bomb, leaving nothing but wreckage in its wake. My heart raced as I searched for the right words, the ones that could bridge the gap between his pain and my resolve.

"I was trying to do the right thing," I admitted, feeling a wave of exhaustion wash over me. "I thought—maybe foolishly—that if I exposed them, if I brought the truth to light, something good would come of it. That it would matter."

His expression softened, just a fraction, enough for me to see the boy beneath the bravado. "You think your truth is worth ruining lives? My brother—he's not some criminal mastermind. He's just trying to survive like the rest of us. You think he knew? He was blindsided. We all were."

The sincerity in his words pierced through my defenses, cutting deeper than I cared to admit. "I never wanted to hurt Ryan," I murmured, the weight of guilt curling around my heart like a snake ready to strike. "I thought he deserved to know the truth about his family. I thought... I thought maybe it could save him."

"Save him?" Lucas's voice cracked, a mixture of anger and disbelief. "From what? A family that has been a part of his life since he was born? You've turned everything upside down, and for what? Some misguided sense of justice?"

Silence enveloped us, the tension palpable as the sun dipped lower, casting an eerie glow across the park. I searched for words, my throat dry, but nothing came. The truth was, I had acted impulsively, driven by a sense of righteousness that now felt naïve and reckless.

The sound of crunching leaves echoed behind us, and we both turned to see a figure emerging from the shadows. It was Ryan, his silhouette framed against the dusky backdrop, eyes dark with something I couldn't quite decipher—anger, disappointment, confusion?

"Lucas," he said, his voice hoarse, as though he had just woken from a long nightmare. "What's going on?"

"Just talking about your favorite subject," Lucas replied, his tone laced with bitterness. "You know, your family's spectacular fall from grace."

Ryan's gaze shifted to me, the weight of his stare cutting through the air like a blade. "And you? What's your role in this delightful conversation?"

"I was just explaining to Lucas how I didn't mean for any of this to happen," I said, my voice trembling slightly. "I thought you should know what your family was involved in."

He stepped closer, and the air thickened with the tension crackling between us. "What I should know?" His voice dripped with sarcasm, but beneath it, I could hear the hurt. "You think this was your choice to make? You think you can play the hero without consequences?"

"I didn't want to play the hero," I shot back, frustration bubbling to the surface. "I wanted to do what was right! Your family was hurting people, Ryan. Don't you see that?"

"And what about the people you're hurting?" he retorted, his tone sharp as a knife. "What about my family? You've torn us apart! I don't even recognize them anymore."

The air grew thick with unresolved emotions, swirling like the autumn leaves around us. I opened my mouth to protest, but the words caught in my throat. I was standing at the precipice of something terrible, and I could feel the ground shifting beneath my feet.

"I didn't want this for you," I whispered, feeling vulnerable, laid bare under his scrutinizing gaze. "I just wanted you to be safe. To know the truth."

Ryan's expression softened, just a flicker, but it was there—a moment of vulnerability amidst the anger. "Safe? From what? You don't get it, do you?" His voice broke slightly, revealing a crack in his carefully maintained facade. "The truth you think you uncovered is just another layer of lies. You don't know how deep this runs."

"Then tell me," I urged, desperation creeping into my voice. "Help me understand."

He ran a hand through his hair, a gesture that spoke volumes. "You don't want to know. You think you're ready, but you're not. My family—what you found? It's just the surface. The truth is darker, more twisted. It's a family secret that's been buried for years, and now? Now you've unearthed it, and it's going to consume everyone."

Lucas shifted uncomfortably, the tension palpable as he glanced between us. "Maybe we should all just take a step back—"

"No," Ryan cut him off, his voice firm. "We need to face this head-on. It's not going away just because we pretend it doesn't exist."

I nodded, the reality of our situation crashing over me like a wave. "What do we do?" I asked, my voice small amidst the rising tide of uncertainty.

Ryan's eyes bore into mine, filled with a storm of emotion. "We figure it out together. Because if we don't, it'll tear us apart."

A sense of solidarity washed over me, a flicker of hope amid the wreckage. I knew the path ahead would be treacherous, but facing it together felt like a lifeline. The world outside the park continued to bustle, blissfully unaware of the tempest brewing within our little triangle.

"Okay," I said, steeling my resolve. "Together."

As the three of us stood there, the shadows lengthening around us, I felt the beginnings of a fragile alliance form—one that could either heal the wounds I had inadvertently inflicted or plunge us deeper into chaos. But for the first time since the storm began, I sensed that perhaps we might have a chance.

The weight of those words settled heavily between us, a living thing pulsing with the energy of unresolved tension. The park, once a sanctuary of laughter and youthful secrets, now felt like a battlefield littered with the remains of shattered trust. Ryan stood before me, his expression a complex tapestry of hurt and anger, and I was suddenly acutely aware of how much was at stake.

"Together," I repeated, the word tasting foreign on my tongue. It felt brave and foolish all at once, but I meant it. Whatever lay ahead, we needed to tackle it as a unit, an odd trio brought together by the shrapnel of my recklessness.

Lucas sighed, his shoulders sagging under the weight of our collective burdens. "So, what's the plan? Are we going to sit here and share marshmallow-roasting stories about the Mortensen family's impending doom?"

"Funny you should mention marshmallows," I shot back, a hint of sarcasm creeping into my voice. "I could really use a s'more after all this."

Ryan ran a hand through his hair, his frustration palpable. "Jokes aside, we need to get a handle on this. We can't just let the narrative be dictated by the headlines. There are people out there—reporters, investigators—who will stop at nothing to dig deeper."

"I know," I said, feeling the urgency of the moment grip me. "But what if we counteract it? What if we get ahead of this?"

"Get ahead of it how?" Lucas asked, skepticism threading through his voice. "We're not exactly a crime-fighting superhero team."

"Not yet," I replied, allowing a grin to break through the tension. "But I've got some ideas. We can start by gathering intel, talking to people who might have the real story."

"Great, like you and your laptop can turn this into a headline story, too?" Ryan said, but there was an edge of curiosity in his tone. "What exactly do you propose?"

"I've been thinking about the other families involved. The ones who were hurt by the Mortensens. There has to be a way to reach out to them, maybe even convince them to go public with their stories. If we can show how their actions affected real lives, it might shift the focus off you guys."

Ryan considered this, his brow furrowing as he weighed the implications. "And what if they refuse? Or worse—what if they don't even care? This town thrives on gossip, and we're standing in the center of a wildfire."

"We'll burn it down and start anew," I said, my voice steady as I locked eyes with him. "But we can't do anything if we're sitting here in this park. We need to act."

Lucas chimed in, his expression brightening slightly. "Okay, so we gather our little ragtag crew and start digging. If we can find evidence of their wrongdoings that shows how corrupt they really are, it might just sway public opinion."

"Exactly!" I said, my heart racing as we spun this plan into motion. "If we're proactive, we take back some of the power. We can shift the narrative from one of scandal to one of accountability. We're not out to destroy them, but we won't let them hide behind the smoke and mirrors."

"Alright then," Ryan said, finally cracking a reluctant smile. "Let's give this a shot. But we have to be careful. If we're going to do this, we need to cover our tracks. I can't afford to lose everything just because we want to play detective."

Lucas laughed, the sound lighter now, "The Mortensens won't know what hit them. And we can grab some snacks while we're at it. Who's with me?"

We made our way through the park, the fading light of dusk casting a warm glow over our small but determined group. It was ridiculous how something that started as a reckless quest for truth had morphed into a covert operation—one that felt exciting yet terrifying. I could feel the pulse of adrenaline begin to thrum through me again, a welcome reminder that perhaps I hadn't lost all of my courage.

As we wandered back towards the edge of the park, a sharp rustling in the nearby bushes made us all jump. "Did you hear that?" I whispered, instinctively stepping closer to Ryan.

"Probably just a squirrel," Lucas shrugged, but there was an unease in his tone that made my heart race.

"No, it sounded like—"

Before I could finish, a tall figure emerged from the shadows, his presence startling us into silence. It was Jackson, Ryan's father, his face twisted with a mix of anger and desperation. He looked older than I remembered, lines etched deep into his forehead, eyes alight with a fierce intensity.

"What are you three doing here?" he demanded, his voice low but commanding. "You shouldn't be here. Not now, not ever."

The air turned electric, charged with tension. I took a step back, instinctively moving closer to Ryan, who stood rigid beside me, his expression unreadable.

"We're just—" I started, but Jackson cut me off.

"You don't want to get involved in this, trust me," he warned, his tone serious. "This isn't a game. You're playing with fire, and you'll get burned."

Ryan stepped forward, his posture defensive. "Dad, we're trying to figure this out. You can't just threaten us."

Jackson's gaze shifted from Ryan to Lucas and then to me, the weight of his scrutiny palpable. "You think you can fix this? You're out of your league. The world isn't black and white. There are consequences to every action, and you three are standing at the edge of something much larger than you realize."

"Then help us understand!" I exclaimed, the frustration spilling over. "If this is about something deeper, then tell us! Don't you care about what's happening?"

He hesitated, a flicker of uncertainty flashing across his face, but then the walls came crashing down once more. "You think you want the truth, but the truth can destroy you. You're better off walking away while you still can."

With that, he turned abruptly, striding back into the shadows, leaving us reeling in the wake of his warning.

"What just happened?" Lucas asked, bewildered.

"I think he just gave us a glimpse into the abyss," Ryan murmured, his voice filled with a mixture of anger and worry. "And I'm not sure we want to look any deeper."

The night air turned heavy around us, and as we stood there, uncertainty gnawed at my insides. I had wanted answers, had sought to uncover a truth that felt vital, yet the stakes were climbing higher, and the path ahead became murkier by the second.

Suddenly, my phone buzzed violently in my pocket. I fished it out, heart racing as I read the notification. The message was from an unknown number.

I know what you're doing. Stop now, or you'll regret it.

My stomach dropped, a chill creeping up my spine as the implications settled in.

"What is it?" Ryan asked, eyes narrowing as he peered over my shoulder.

I turned to him, the reality of our situation hitting me like a punch to the gut. "We're in deeper than I thought."

The shadows seemed to stretch around us, closing in, and in that moment, I realized this was only the beginning.

Chapter 23: Backlash

My phone buzzes relentlessly, each vibration a tiny grenade detonating in the quiet of my living room. The flickering screen illuminates messages that feel less like communication and more like a barrage of bullets. "You've ruined lives," one reads. "How does it feel to destroy a family?" The digital taunts slice through the air with an unnerving clarity, each word wrapped in a layer of anonymity that somehow makes them all the more menacing. I let out a shaky breath, casting a furtive glance around the room as if expecting a tangible entity to emerge from the shadows, taunting me in flesh and blood.

I used to believe I could handle anything that came my way—like a modern-day Joan of Arc, armed with a keyboard instead of a sword, ready to champion the truth against the fires of deceit. But now, as I sink deeper into the couch cushions, that image feels ridiculous. The weight of my choices presses down like a thick fog, smothering me in doubt.

Just a few weeks ago, I stood triumphant, having uncovered a web of corruption that stretched across city council meetings and charity galas. My article, a carefully woven tapestry of betrayal and greed, was meant to shine a light on injustices too often buried under the gloss of civility. Yet here I am, grappling with the fallout, the reverb of my actions echoing around me like the remnants of a bomb blast.

The second wave of discomfort hits when I see the name "Ryan" pop up in yet another notification. His family's anger is almost palpable, like a predator closing in on its prey. I never thought I'd be on the receiving end of their ire, but here we are. I can almost picture them gathered around their living room, eyes filled with righteous indignation as they plot their revenge. I had heard whispers of Ryan's father, a man who could charm a snake out of its skin with his golden tongue, rallying the troops against me. His silver hair glinting under the warm glow of a chandelier as he deftly orchestrates their narrative—a media witch hunt against the reporter who dared to expose his son's misdeeds.

I stare at my laptop, the screen showcasing a small sea of comments, each more venomous than the last. It's exhausting, a chorus of digital detractors with their pitchforks raised high, ready to skewer me for daring to expose the truth. The irony gnaws at me: they'd rather defend a man whose family had orchestrated a lifetime of deceit than confront the reality of his actions. How did I become the villain in a story I believed was so clearly a fight for justice?

As I delve deeper into the comments, I catch glimpses of familiar names—former classmates, acquaintances from coffee shops, even my old barista, who always gave me an extra shot of espresso when he saw I was burning the midnight oil. They're all here, aligning themselves against me like soldiers choosing sides in a battle I never intended to fight. "Why would you do this?" one friend asks, his words tinged with disappointment. "You were always better than this."

I slam my laptop shut, the sound echoing in the silence of my apartment. I can't breathe. My sanctuary, once a refuge filled with the scent of freshly brewed coffee and stacks of half-read novels, feels like a cage now. The walls close in, adorned with framed photographs of happier times: beach trips, laughter echoing in the wind, carefree smiles frozen in time. It all feels so far away.

A knock at the door breaks the spell, sending a jolt through me. I'm not expecting anyone, and the pit of anxiety in my stomach grows heavier as I cross the room. I peek through the peephole, half-expecting the shadows of Ryan's family or an army of lawyers, ready to drag me into the light of their accusations. Instead, I find Lena, my best friend since grade school, her face a mixture of concern and determination.

"Let me in," she demands, her voice a blend of frustration and warmth. I open the door, and she breezes past me, filling the space with her familiar energy. "You're a mess," she states bluntly, a statement not of judgment but of care.

"Thanks for the compliment," I reply dryly, forcing a smile as I step aside to let her take stock of my chaotic living room. She eyes the discarded takeout containers and piles of laundry like a detective surveying a crime scene.

"I'm serious. What are you doing to yourself?" she asks, arms crossed over her chest, her brow furrowing in concern. "You can't let them get to you like this. You did what you thought was right."

"I thought I was doing what was right," I mutter, my voice low. "But what if I just set off a chain reaction that'll ruin everyone's lives?"

"Is that what you believe? That you're the one ruining lives?" she counters, her voice rising slightly. "You didn't pull the strings here. You just reported the truth."

The words hang in the air, heavy with the weight of accountability and responsibility. I want to believe her. I want to believe that my intentions matter more than the backlash echoing around me, but doubt is a suffocating blanket. It wraps around me, blurring the lines between right and wrong, truth and lies.

Lena moves closer, her eyes locking onto mine, the intensity there demanding my attention. "Listen, this isn't just about you. You've ignited a conversation, one that needs to happen. And yeah, it's messy, but that's life. Don't let their noise drown out your voice."

Her words cut through my fog of uncertainty, sparking a flicker of determination within me. Perhaps the battle was worth fighting, and perhaps it was time to armor myself for the war ahead.

The afternoon light seeps through the curtains, casting long shadows across the room as Lena remains steadfast, her eyes never wavering from mine. I take a deep breath, trying to muster the courage to respond, but the air feels thick with unspoken words, all tangled up in a mess of anxiety and self-doubt.

"Right," I finally say, forcing a laugh that sounds more like a choked sob. "Because having my name plastered on every 'you won't believe what she did' list is exactly what I had in mind when I signed up for this job." My voice is laced with sarcasm, a thin shield against the rising tide of panic.

Lena's expression softens, and she takes a step closer. "You know I'm not saying it's easy. But you have to look at the bigger picture. You've sparked something that can't be ignored. Not just for Ryan, but for everyone affected by this."

"Great, I've sparked a firestorm of hatred and threats. That'll look wonderful on my résumé," I retort, rolling my eyes in a manner that barely masks the tension bubbling beneath the surface.

"Okay, Miss Drama Queen," she shoots back, smirking as she crosses her arms. "How about instead of wallowing, we come up with a plan? You know, like in those action movies where the protagonist rallies her friends to take down the bad guys?"

I can't help but chuckle at the absurdity of it all. "So, I should grab a leather jacket, assemble a team, and do a dramatic monologue while storming the gates of the enemy?"

"Why not?" she replies, her playful tone shifting into something more serious. "You're a fighter, and you know it. You just need to remember what you're fighting for."

Her words resonate, awakening something dormant within me. I wasn't merely a journalist; I was an advocate for the voiceless. I had ignited a conversation that needed to happen, regardless of the backlash. But the thought of facing another day of online vitriol sends chills down my spine.

Before I can respond, a soft ping draws my attention to my phone lying forgotten on the coffee table. My heart races as I see yet another notification pop up, a comment from a user I'd never encountered before: "It's easy to tear people down from behind a screen. What are you really afraid of?"

My fingers tremble as I read and reread the message, its ambiguity clawing at my brain. Is this someone standing up for me, or yet another jab from a faceless critic? "I think they're onto something," I mumble, mostly to myself.

Lena leans over to read the comment. "Sounds like someone's trying to poke at your insecurities. Forget them. You're not afraid of the truth. You're afraid of being alone."

"Maybe I don't want to be alone," I admit, the admission slipping out before I can swallow it back down. "Everyone I thought would stand by me has either turned on me or gone silent."

"That's not true," she insists, shaking her head. "I'm here. Your editor might be acting distant, but you know why she wanted to run the story. You've got people who care about you; it just doesn't feel like it right now."

"Right now," I echo, the weight of the phrase settling heavily in the air between us. It's not just a passing moment; it's a reality that seems to stretch on indefinitely, casting a long shadow over every decision I've made.

"Let's take a break," Lena suggests, her voice a soothing balm against the tension thrumming through the room. "I can't remember the last time we did something fun. A little distraction might be just what you need."

"What do you have in mind? A trip to the grocery store? Maybe a rousing game of 'Dodge the Phone Call'?" I say, half-joking, but the corners of my mouth tug upward at her enthusiasm.

"Better. I know just the thing." She whips out her phone, tapping away with fierce determination. "Get ready to wear some ridiculous costumes because we're going to karaoke night at The Rusty Nail."

"The Rusty Nail?" I snort, trying to stifle laughter. "That dive? Do you want me to completely lose my dignity?"

Lena grins, the sparkle in her eyes promising mischief. "Absolutely! Dignity is overrated. Plus, I hear they have the best nachos in town. And if anyone deserves cheesy comfort food right now, it's you."

I hesitate for a moment, the lure of an evening spent lost in laughter and music battling against the anxiety coiling tightly in my chest. "What if I run into someone from Ryan's family? Or worse, a journalist looking for dirt on me?"

"Then you channel your inner rock star and own the night!" Lena exclaims, her excitement infectious. "If they see you living your life, they'll think twice about coming after you."

The idea tickles at my heart, the prospect of freedom and laughter a welcome contrast to the shackles of dread I've been wearing like a second skin. "Okay, you've convinced me. Let's do this."

As we prepare for the night, I can't help but feel a flutter of anticipation. It's been too long since I've indulged in carefree moments, the kind that let me forget the weight of the world for just a little while. I slip into a dress that feels both daring and comforting, a vibrant blue that reminds me of summer skies. Lena, ever the master of theatrics, emerges from the bathroom clad in sequins, her hair styled like a starlet from a bygone era.

"You look like a disco ball!" I laugh, twirling around to admire her ensemble.

"Exactly!" she beams, adjusting her faux fur wrap. "I'm here to shine, and so are you. Now let's go show those wannabe critics what real fun looks like!"

As we step into the warm embrace of the night, I feel a shift within me, the tension loosening its grip just a fraction. The world outside my apartment has a life of its own, filled with laughter, music, and people oblivious to the storm brewing in my mind. I grip Lena's hand, and together, we wade into the vibrant chaos that promises to be a welcome distraction.

Maybe, just maybe, I can find a moment of reprieve amidst the chaos, a moment where I can reclaim a part of myself that feels lost in the fray. As we approach The Rusty Nail, I can already hear the distant hum of music spilling out into the street, a siren's call that lures me into its embrace, urging me to dance, to sing, and to forget the world for just a little while.

The energy at The Rusty Nail is electric, a warm current flowing through the packed room as laughter and music intertwine. Lena and I step inside, instantly engulfed by the scents of sizzling nachos and spilled beer—a fragrant welcome that feels like stepping into a cherished memory. The walls, draped in faded band posters, seem to vibrate with stories of wild nights and spontaneous decisions. I feel a small smile creeping onto my face, the heaviness of the day slipping away like an old coat.

"Let's get you a drink first," Lena says, leading the way to the bar, where the bartender is busy tossing bottles into the air with the flair of a magician. "We need liquid courage if we're going to get you on that stage."

"Liquid courage?" I raise an eyebrow, already feeling the familiar flutter of nerves return. "What happened to just enjoying nachos?"

"Nachos are for the soul," she replies with a wink. "But a cocktail is for the spirit. Trust me, you'll thank me when you're belting out show tunes."

I roll my eyes but can't help chuckling. "If by 'show tunes' you mean off-key renditions of the latest pop hits, then sure."

The bartender slides two bright blue cocktails our way, garnished with colorful umbrellas that feel ludicrously cheerful. I raise my glass to Lena, the glint of mischief in her eyes contagious. "To a night of regrettable decisions!"

"Regrettable decisions that we'll laugh about for years to come!" she clinks her glass against mine with a flourish, the sound ringing like a promise in the air.

With our drinks in hand, we make our way to a small table near the stage. Lena hops up on the chair, her energy infectious as she surveys the crowd. "Look at them! They're having the time of their lives! You'll be up there in no time."

"Right, because nothing says 'great journalist' like karaoke," I joke, but the warmth in my chest grows, embers of excitement igniting beneath the surface. For once, I'm not mired in the chaos of online backlash. Instead, I'm enveloped by laughter and the prospect of a night where my biggest worry is whether I can hit the high note in "I Will Survive."

As the first act steps onto the stage, the crowd erupts into cheers. A woman with wild curls and a sparkly dress launches into a rendition of "Dancing Queen," her voice soaring through the room. I lean back, letting the music wash over me, each note a reminder of the joy that exists beyond the digital chaos of my life.

"Okay, my turn," Lena announces, jumping off her chair with a dramatic flair. "Hold my drink!"

She practically skips to the stage, and I can't help but laugh as she shakes her hips to the music, fully embracing the moment. Her enthusiasm is contagious, and as she begins to sing, I find myself cheering louder than anyone else, caught up in her joy.

When she finishes, the applause is thunderous, and I feel a surge of pride wash over me. "You're next!" she calls, stumbling back to the table, breathless and radiant. "You're going to crush it."

"Maybe after another drink," I reply, pretending to eye my half-empty cocktail with deep contemplation. "Or two."

"Excuses, excuses," she teases, nudging me. "I've seen you in action. You have it in you. Just think of it as writing your next story but with more glitter."

"Fine! Just don't expect a standing ovation," I say, though I feel the excitement bubble within me, pulling me toward the stage like a moth to a flame.

As the next singer finishes, I stand, my heart pounding like a drum in my chest. Lena's encouraging shout propels me forward, and as I step onto the small platform, the crowd cheers in an electrifying wave. I can feel the warmth of their attention wrapping around me, lifting me higher.

"Alright, folks!" the host calls, grinning as he hands me the microphone. "We've got a brave soul up here! What will it be?"

I glance at the setlist and pause, my eyes catching a glimpse of a song that feels like a burst of nostalgia—"Total Eclipse of the Heart." With a grin, I nod, the crowd murmuring in approval.

As the music starts, the familiar piano intro sends a thrill down my spine. I launch into the first verse, my voice shaky at first, but the magic of the moment grips me. The audience leans in, swaying along, and soon I'm lost in the melody, pouring my heart into each lyric. The world around me fades, and for a moment, I forget about the backlash, the accusations, the shadows looming in the background.

But as I reach the chorus, the energy shifts. A murmur ripples through the crowd, drawing my attention away from the music. I catch sight of a familiar face near the bar, and my heart plummets—Ryan's sister, Emily, her expression a mix of fury and disbelief as she clutches her phone tightly.

Suddenly, the room feels smaller, the spotlight hotter, and my voice falters mid-note. Memories of our shared childhood flash through my mind, the laughter, the secrets, the bonds that now seem frayed beyond repair. I falter, the words slipping from my grasp as the crowd's energy dissipates, replaced by a growing tension.

"Keep going!" Lena shouts, but my mind is racing, caught in a whirlwind of guilt and fear.

Emily's eyes blaze with accusation, and I realize that she must have seen the fallout unfold online, the very backlash that has been haunting me since the article dropped. What did I do? The question circles like a vulture, waiting for the perfect moment to strike.

I take a shaky breath, trying to regain my footing, but my confidence is wavering. The music continues, but the weight of Emily's stare feels like a noose tightening around my neck. Suddenly, I'm struck by the realization that this moment could spiral into something far beyond embarrassment.

With a quick glance at Lena, who looks both concerned and supportive, I try to rally myself. I need to finish this song, but now it feels like a battle—not just against the crowd's expectations, but against the demons lurking in my own mind.

I dive back into the chorus, pouring everything I have into the words, hoping to drown out the chaos swirling in my chest. But just as I reach the climactic peak, my phone buzzes again, a frantic vibration that cuts through the music.

Against my better judgment, I glance at it, my heart sinking as the screen lights up with a message from an unknown number. "You'll regret this. We're just getting started."

The room spins, and I can barely hear the fading notes of the song as the air grows thick with anticipation. I feel a chill creep up my spine, the sense of unease coiling tighter as I realize that the true fallout has only just begun.

Chapter 24: Vivian's Revenge

The city wrapped itself in a blanket of twilight, the fading sun bleeding out across the horizon like a forgotten watercolor painting. I pushed through the glass doors of the hotel, the cool air inside hitting me like a gust of relief. It was the kind of day where the heat clung to the skin, wrapping around my shoulders with an unwelcome familiarity. My heels clicked on the marble floor, echoing my unease as I approached the elevator. Each ding was a reminder of how far I'd come, but also of how precariously perched I felt on the edge of a cliff, about to tumble into chaos.

When the elevator doors slid shut, I leaned against the polished metal wall, inhaling the faint scent of lemon cleaner mixed with something floral. It should have felt comforting, but instead, it was suffocating. My thoughts spiraled like leaves caught in a whirlwind, and every twist brought me back to Vivian, the maestro of this disturbing symphony. Her touch was everywhere—like a specter whispering threats just out of earshot.

As the elevator lurched upward, I couldn't shake the chill of that note tucked beneath my door. This isn't over. The words burned in my mind, each syllable a dagger aimed directly at my resolve. What did she mean by that? I clenched my fists, feeling the tremors of fear and adrenaline play a dangerous duet. It was one thing to face her in a boardroom, armed with facts and truth, but this was war on another front—one that hid in shadows and skirted legality.

When I reached my floor, I stepped out, my heart thudding against my ribs as if it wanted to escape. I walked towards my room, each step heavier than the last, my mind racing through every scenario. Would she come after my career? My life? I fished the keycard from my bag, the thin piece of plastic feeling like a flimsy shield against an invisible army.

My room was dimly lit, the glow from a single lamp casting long shadows that danced like phantoms. I tossed my bag onto the chair and turned, intending to pour myself a much-needed drink, but the sight of the note on the table stopped me cold. It was as if it had materialized from thin air, taunting me, reminding me that I was still in the lion's den.

I approached slowly, picking up the white paper. It was crisp and almost pristine, but the words were inscribed in a scrawl that screamed of urgency. A sickly sweet scent wafted off it—like jasmine, too reminiscent of Vivian's perfume. My stomach churned. I had dealt with enough of her theatrics to know that she played the long game, each move calculated, every consequence anticipated.

With trembling hands, I flipped the note over, hoping for something more—some insight into her twisted mind. But there was nothing. Just that ominous declaration, lingering like smoke after a fire. I crumpled it into a ball, frustration bubbling inside me. The urge to retaliate, to play her game and twist the narrative back in my favor, sparked within me like a match striking against flint.

I poured myself a glass of bourbon, the amber liquid swirling like the thoughts in my head. It burned as it went down, a welcome distraction from the chaos outside. I sank into the plush chair, the fabric hugging me like a comforting friend, and tried to strategize. I'd have to be smarter, quicker. The stakes were higher now, and I couldn't let Vivian make me a victim.

Suddenly, my phone buzzed on the table, cutting through the silence. I grabbed it, the screen lighting up with Ryan's name. For a brief moment, a rush of warmth spread through me, but I quickly shoved it aside. This wasn't the time for distractions, even if I longed to hear his voice. He was part of this mess, too, tied to his family's tangled web.

"Hey," I answered, forcing my voice to sound light and untroubled.

"Hey, you," he replied, his voice a soothing balm against my fraying nerves. "I was thinking about you. How's it going?"

I took a deep breath, weighing the desire to confide in him against the risk of dragging him deeper into my troubles. "Just a normal day in paradise," I said, injecting a wry tone into my words. "You know, dodging bullets, trying to keep my head above water."

"Sounds like a lot of fun. Do you need backup?"

His concern twisted my heart, a surge of emotion I couldn't quite comprehend. "I'm good. Just some... administrative issues. You know how it is."

"Sure," he said, his voice flat. "But if you ever need someone to help you with those 'issues'..."

I could almost picture him, leaning against a wall, his brows furrowed in that adorable way when he was worried. "I appreciate it, really. But I need to handle this on my own."

"Fine," he replied, a hint of playful annoyance creeping in. "But if you get yourself into too much trouble, just remember I owe you dinner."

"I'll keep that in mind," I laughed, but the sound felt forced, almost hollow. "I'll let you know if I need anything. Promise."

After we hung up, the silence of the room wrapped around me again, thicker than before. I leaned back, staring at the ceiling, lost in thought. I needed a plan, but I also needed to think clearly. Vivian's threats loomed like storm clouds on the horizon, and I was trapped in the eye of her hurricane.

The sensation of being watched prickled at the back of my neck, a familiar discomfort that had followed me since I first crossed paths with Vivian. It wasn't paranoia; it was instinct. I rose from the chair, shaking off the remnants of our conversation, and made my way to the window. The city sprawled out beneath me, glittering with life, a stark contrast to the turmoil brewing within.

In that moment, I felt a flicker of resolve igniting deep within me. I couldn't let her win. I wouldn't let fear dictate my choices. Vivian may have played the game longer, but I had something she didn't—an unyielding spirit and the will to fight back.

I pulled the curtain back, the fabric heavy in my hands, and stared down at the bustling street below. The city hummed with life—cabs honked, couples laughed, and the distant murmur of a street musician floated up to me like a haunting melody. It was the perfect backdrop to my growing anxiety, a reminder that while the world moved on, I was trapped in a game where the rules were twisted and the stakes higher than I ever anticipated.

In the midst of this chaos, my phone buzzed again, breaking the moment. The screen lit up with a text from my sister, Nora. "You still breathing?" The message was a lifeline thrown into turbulent waters. I could almost hear her voice—sharp, witty, laced with concern.

"Barely," I typed back, my fingers flying over the screen. "Got a note from Vivian. She's plotting something."

"Do I need to come rescue you?" Her response was immediate, infused with the playful sarcasm that only sisters can share.

"Not yet. But maybe keep your cape handy." I laughed softly, picturing her in a superhero outfit, an apron tied around her waist and a spatula raised like a sword. She had always been my anchor, a bright light cutting through the storm clouds.

"Good. Just remember, if you need an alibi, I can whip up some wild story about you saving kittens or something."

"Perfect. I'll call you when I need my kitten-saving costume." I chuckled, but the weight of the situation pressed down on me.

After exchanging a few more playful messages, I tossed my phone onto the couch and sank back into the chair. I could hear the laughter and chatter from the street below, a stark contrast to the storm brewing inside me. Suddenly, a loud knock echoed through my room, jolting me from my thoughts. I froze, heart racing, every instinct screaming that it could only be one thing—Vivian's minions were already at my door.

I opened it cautiously, bracing myself for a confrontation, but instead found the hotel staff, holding a large bouquet of flowers. "Delivery for you, Miss," the attendant said, his voice cheerful, oblivious to the dread clawing at my insides.

"Flowers?" I said, incredulous, stepping aside to let him in. The sight of the vivid blooms—deep reds and cheerful yellows—struck me as surreal amidst my growing unease.

He placed the arrangement on the table, and I peered closer. A small card peeked out from between the petals. I snatched it up, tearing it open, half expecting another threat. But instead, it read, "Thinking of you. Let's talk soon." No signature. Just a chilling reminder that I wasn't the only one playing games.

"Are you all right?" the attendant asked, concern flickering in his eyes.

"Yeah, just... a little overwhelmed," I replied, forcing a smile.

"Well, if you need anything, just call down. Enjoy the flowers!" He left, closing the door behind him, and I was left alone with the bouquet and my swirling thoughts.

I tossed the card back on the table, staring at the flowers as if they might reveal some hidden message. Who sent them? Ryan? A potential ally? Or was it Vivian, playing her mind games yet again? The uncertainty gnawed at me, and I took a step back, needing space from the overwhelming scent of jasmine that wafted through the air, too reminiscent of my earlier encounter.

The walls of my hotel room began to close in on me. I had to get out, to breathe, to think. Grabbing my jacket, I headed for the door, determined to find some semblance of normalcy among the chaos.

As I stepped into the night, the city embraced me with its familiar rhythm. I wandered aimlessly for a while, letting the cacophony of sounds drown out my thoughts. Street vendors called out, their carts bursting with hot dogs and pretzels, the smell wrapping around me like an old friend. I passed by a small park, the lights twinkling overhead, illuminating the faces of people lost in their own worlds—laughter bubbling from a group of friends sprawled on the grass, a couple sharing a quiet moment on a bench.

In a sudden fit of impulse, I found myself at a nearby café, its warm light spilling onto the sidewalk. The aroma of freshly brewed coffee enveloped me as I stepped inside, and I welcomed the distraction. The barista, a young woman with vibrant purple hair, greeted me with a bright smile. "What can I get you?"

"Something strong," I replied, forcing a grin.

"Coming right up!" she chirped, her energy contagious.

I settled into a corner table, allowing the hum of conversation and the clatter of cups to settle around me. This was my sanctuary, a temporary escape from the storm that was Vivian.

As I sipped my espresso, the bitterness grounding me, I felt my phone buzz again. I glanced down, half-expecting a warning from Nora, but instead, it was Ryan. "You sure you're okay? I can come over if you need me."

I hesitated, fingers hovering over the screen. "I'm fine. Just taking a break. Getting some fresh air."

"Good. Just remember, I'm here if you need someone to kick Vivian's ass."

A laugh escaped me, surprising even myself. "I'll keep you in mind. Right after I finish this espresso."

"Fair enough. But seriously, don't hesitate. You're not alone in this."

His words lingered like a sweet balm, and as I looked around the café, I felt a flicker of hope. The world was still bright and alive, even if shadows lurked at the edges.

But just as I was starting to feel lighter, the café door swung open with a sharp creak, drawing my attention. I looked up, and time seemed to freeze as Vivian strode in, her presence a storm cloud darkening my oasis. She was stunning as always, dressed in a fitted blazer that highlighted her every curve, her hair cascading around her shoulders like a dark waterfall.

"Fancy meeting you here," she said, her voice smooth, laced with that signature sarcasm.

I felt my heart drop, panic rising as I sought a way out. "What do you want, Vivian?"

"Oh, just wanted to see how the other half lives." She scanned the café, her smile sharp, almost predatory. "It must be nice to sip coffee while plotting someone's downfall."

My pulse raced, and I fought to keep my voice steady. "I'm not plotting anything. Unlike you, I'm trying to live my life."

She chuckled, a sound that sent shivers down my spine. "You think you can walk away from this? My dear, you're already in too deep. You can't escape."

I took a deep breath, feeling the weight of the moment press down on me. "I'm not afraid of you."

Her laughter was rich, echoing off the café walls, and I felt every eye turn toward us. "Good. You'll need that courage, darling."

As she sauntered away, leaving a trail of tension in her wake, I realized the battle had only just begun. The city outside continued to pulse with life, but I felt the cold chill of her words settle deep into my bones. This wasn't merely a fight for survival; it was a war, and I had to be ready.

The café's atmosphere shifted after Vivian's unexpected entrance, morphing from a cozy refuge to a stage where I was the unwilling performer. I sat there, grappling with the aftermath of her taunting presence while the espresso sat cooling in front of me. The barista moved around the counter, oblivious to the invisible war brewing just a few tables away, and I could feel my heart racing as if I'd just sprinted a marathon.

As if to punctuate my anxiety, my phone buzzed yet again. This time, it was Nora. "Okay, spill it. What happened? You sound like you just faced a lion in a den."

"More like a lioness with a taste for blood," I typed back. I glanced over my shoulder, half-expecting Vivian to return. "She just showed up here. Talk about awkward."

"Did you throw your espresso at her?"

"I wish." I couldn't help but smile at the thought. "More like I sat there, stunned, like a deer in headlights."

"You have to get a grip, sis. You can't let her rattle you. Remember that one time we went camping, and you freaked out over a squirrel?"

"Hey, that squirrel was plotting something!"

"Sure it was," she replied, but I could hear the laughter in her words. "Just remember, you're tougher than you think. Channel your inner warrior princess."

Her text was a much-needed reminder, grounding me in reality. I downed the rest of my espresso, letting the bitterness wash away the remnants of panic. I wouldn't allow Vivian to dictate my feelings, to twist my narrative into something dark and twisted.

Taking a deep breath, I pushed my chair back and made my way to the door, shaking off the lingering unease. Outside, the city felt alive, the streetlights casting a warm glow on the sidewalks as people moved around me, blissfully unaware of the storm brewing in my life. I needed to regain control.

I headed toward a small bookstore nearby, a hidden gem where the scent of old paper mixed with fresh coffee lingered in the air. It was a sanctuary for me, a place where stories came alive and offered an escape from the chaos. As I entered, the soft jingle of the doorbell brought a smile to my face.

The cozy atmosphere wrapped around me like a warm blanket. I wandered through the aisles, trailing my fingers along the spines of books, the familiar titles inviting me into their worlds. I could lose myself here for hours, but I needed more than just an escape. I needed a plan.

As I reached the back of the store, a soft voice broke through my reverie. "Did you find anything interesting?"

I turned to find a tall man leaning against a bookshelf, his arms crossed casually, a knowing smile playing on his lips. It was Oliver, the owner of the store, a former journalist with a knack for spotting stories worth telling. His dark curls framed his face, and his deep-set eyes held a mixture of intrigue and empathy.

"I'm looking for something to keep my mind off...life," I replied, the words spilling out before I could catch them.

"Ah, the old escape route. I have just the thing." He stepped closer, his expression shifting from playful to serious. "But let me guess, this escape isn't just about books, is it?"

I sighed, knowing I couldn't hide the truth from him. "Vivian is out for blood. I need to figure out how to counter her next move before she strikes again."

He frowned, his brow furrowing with concern. "You know she's not just any opponent. She plays to win. What's your plan?"

"I don't know yet. I thought maybe if I could gather some intel, find a way to turn the tables...something." My voice trailed off, the weight of uncertainty settling back in.

"Intel, huh?" Oliver leaned against the bookshelf, a thoughtful look crossing his face. "I might have a contact or two who could help."

"Seriously?" My pulse quickened. "That would be amazing."

"Let me make a call. Stay put." He turned and headed to the back office, leaving me surrounded by the comforting walls of the bookstore. I wandered back to the fiction section, my mind racing with possibilities.

The sound of the bell jingled again, and I glanced toward the entrance, my heart sinking as I recognized the figure stepping inside. Vivian, in all her glory, glided back into the store, the energy in the room shifting like a storm front.

"Didn't expect to see you here, darling," she called out, her voice dripping with mock sweetness.

I tried to appear calm, though my stomach twisted in knots. "What do you want, Vivian?"

"Just browsing," she replied, her eyes scanning the shelves. "You know how it is—sometimes the best stories come from unexpected sources."

"Is that what you're after? A new plot twist?"

"Something like that." She leaned closer, lowering her voice to a conspiratorial whisper. "But you might want to be careful, dear. Not everyone can be trusted. Some are more likely to sell you out for a nice cup of coffee."

The threat hung in the air, a dark cloud threatening to swallow the room. I squared my shoulders, unwilling to show her any sign of weakness. "Is that what you think of me? That I would turn to the dark side just because you say so?"

Vivian's smile widened, revealing too much teeth. "Oh, I don't underestimate you. You're more resourceful than you give yourself credit for. But trust me, playing with fire can get you burned."

Before I could respond, Oliver returned, a frown creasing his brow as he spotted Vivian. "Can I help you with something?"

Vivian turned, her demeanor shifting as she locked eyes with him. "Oh, just enjoying the ambiance of your charming bookstore. It really does make a delightful hideout, doesn't it?"

"Not for the faint of heart," he shot back, his tone clipped. I felt a swell of gratitude for his protective instinct, but it was short-lived.

"True, but we're all a little brave in our own way." She flicked her gaze back to me, her expression challenging. "And sometimes, it takes a little push to find out just how brave we really are."

I clenched my fists, anger simmering beneath the surface. "I'm not afraid of you, Vivian."

"Then you're either very brave or very foolish." She leaned in closer, her voice a low whisper, barely audible above the low hum of the store. "Just remember, the game isn't just about the players on the board. Sometimes, it's about who's pulling the strings behind the scenes."

With that, she turned on her heel, her heels clicking sharply against the floor as she walked out, leaving behind a tense silence that echoed in the air. I felt the weight of her words settle like lead in my stomach.

"Are you okay?" Oliver asked, concern etched on his face.

I nodded, though my heart raced with a sense of impending dread. "I'll be fine. I just need to figure out how to outsmart her."

"Don't underestimate her," he warned. "She's dangerous."

"I know," I said, taking a deep breath. "But I have to try. I can't let her take me down without a fight."

Oliver nodded, his eyes softening. "Then let's find a way to turn the tide. You've got this."

As he began to outline a plan, my phone buzzed in my pocket, and I pulled it out to see a message from Ryan. "Can we meet? I have something important to discuss."

My stomach flipped as I looked up at Oliver, who was already deep in thought. "I think I might have to take this."

"Go ahead," he said, waving me off.

"Hey," I answered, trying to sound casual despite the knots in my stomach. "What's up?"

"Can we meet at the park? I need to tell you something."

"Sure, I'll be there in a few." I hung up, my heart racing with the prospect of seeing him. Would he have news that could help me?

As I stepped outside, the cool air hit me like a splash of water, bringing clarity to my thoughts. I began walking toward the park, but with each step, I felt the heavy presence of Vivian's threat looming above me.

The park was alive with the sounds of laughter and joy, a stark contrast to the turmoil swirling within me. I spotted Ryan sitting on a bench, his brows knitted together in concern. As I approached, his expression shifted from worry to relief.

"Hey," I greeted, forcing a smile that didn't quite reach my eyes.

"I'm glad you're here," he said, his voice low. "I've been hearing things...about your situation with Vivian."

I sat down, heart racing. "What have you heard?"

"I'm worried about you. I think she's planning something big."

Before I could respond, a loud crash echoed through the park, a sound that sent shockwaves through the crowd. My heart stopped as I turned to see chaos erupting at the nearby playground.

Screams filled the air, and I felt a rush of adrenaline as instinct kicked in. "We need to check it out."

Ryan nodded, and we rushed toward the source of the commotion, the world around us blurring into a hazy rush. As we pushed through the throng of people, a sense of foreboding washed over me.

Chapter 25: A Desperate Plea

The doorbell rang like a distant thunderclap, jolting me from the spiral of thoughts that had ensnared me all evening. I opened the door to find Ryan on the other side, his figure silhouetted against the dim light of the streetlamp. It felt surreal, as though time had warped and thrown him back into my life just when I thought I had finally put the pieces of my own existence back together.

He stood there, hands shoved deep into the pockets of a worn leather jacket, the kind that had once looked effortlessly stylish but now hung on him like a costume two sizes too big. His hair, usually perfectly tousled, hung limp, and his eyes—those once vibrant green orbs that had sparkled with mischief—now looked hollow, rimmed with shadows that spoke of sleepless nights and burdens too heavy for one man to bear. My heart twisted painfully at the sight of him, the memories of our past crashing in like waves against a rocky shore.

"Can we talk?" His voice was barely a whisper, a frayed thread of desperation woven through the syllables. There was something in the way he said it that tugged at the remnants of the connection we once shared, something that drew me in even though every rational part of my mind screamed to close the door and step back into the safety of my solitude.

I hesitated, a fleeting moment where the doorframe felt like a chasm between two worlds—my past and my present. But there was a crack in his armor, an unmistakable vulnerability that echoed through the space between us. I stepped aside, allowing him to enter. The scent of rain-soaked earth clung to him, mingling with the stale air of my apartment and igniting a thousand memories I had tried so hard to forget.

"Make yourself at home," I said, my tone laced with a sarcasm that masked my uncertainty. I motioned to the living room, which still bore the traces of my last half-hearted attempt at organization. A few books lay sprawled on the coffee table, their spines cracked from endless rereads, and an empty mug sat abandoned, remnants of cold tea staring back at me like an old friend I had neglected.

Ryan dropped onto the couch, his shoulders slumping as if the weight of the world had settled there. I watched him, my heart pounding with a mix of sympathy and skepticism. "What's going on, Ryan? You look like you've seen a ghost."

His laugh was hollow, devoid of humor. "If only it were just a ghost." He rubbed his eyes, then met my gaze, and for a moment, the barrier of time and hurt melted away. "I'm in trouble, and it's bigger than anything I ever imagined."

"Trouble? As in the kind where you accidentally send an embarrassing text to your boss or the kind that gets you tangled up in a crime ring?" I tried to keep the tone light, but my stomach twisted with concern.

He opened his mouth to respond, then closed it, his jaw clenching. The silence thickened around us, heavy with unspoken truths and unshed tears. Finally, he leaned forward, elbows resting on his knees, and exhaled like the air had been knocked from his lungs. "It's my family. The empire. It's crumbling, and I didn't know how deep the corruption went."

"Corruption? Are we talking about some shady investments or something much worse?" The sarcasm dripped from my voice, masking the way my heart raced. I wanted to believe he was innocent in all this, that he hadn't played a part in whatever mess he was wading through. But doubt lingered, a dark cloud that wouldn't disperse.

He ran a hand through his hair, his frustration palpable. "I had no idea what they were doing, Claire. I was so caught up in my own life, my own ambitions, that I didn't see the cracks forming around me. But now... now it's all coming to light, and I can't—" His voice broke, and for a moment, the façade slipped. "I can't let them drag me down with them."

"Why are you here, Ryan? What do you want from me?" I asked, though deep down, I knew. My heart had already begun to construct an elaborate fantasy of how we could right the wrongs together, how we could mend the past while navigating this new chaos.

"I need your help," he said, finally meeting my gaze with an intensity that sent shivers down my spine. "I'm not asking for much. Just... guidance. You're the only one who ever really understood me."

Those words hung in the air, heavy with implications. My mind raced through the years, through the laughter and the heartaches, through the moments we had shared that had somehow slipped through our fingers like grains of sand. But trust is a fragile thing, easily shattered, and our history was a tapestry of beautiful highs marred by devastating lows.

"I don't know if I can help you, Ryan," I replied, my voice firmer than I felt. "You've been a part of this world for too long, and I'm not sure you can disentangle yourself from it."

He shook his head, frustration flickering in his eyes. "You think I wanted this? I never wanted to be part of the empire or the games they play. I was naive, Claire, caught up in the glamour and the wealth. But now it's all falling apart, and I'm terrified of what they'll do if they realize I'm out."

The sincerity in his tone dug deeper into my heart. I hated that I could feel my defenses crumbling, that I could still see the boy I once loved beneath the weight of his mistakes. The air between us crackled with tension, a palpable reminder of the storm that had brewed in our lives, leaving scars on our souls.

"I don't know if I can trust you again," I admitted, feeling the weight of the truth settle like a stone in my gut. "Not after everything."

"I know. And I don't expect you to." He stood, pacing the small living room, a caged animal desperate for freedom. "But I wouldn't be here if I didn't think there was still a chance. Please, just hear me out."

And in that moment, as I watched him pace and plead, something shifted inside me. Maybe it was the glimmer of hope that maybe, just maybe, there was still a path forward for both of us—one riddled with obstacles and uncertainties, but a path nonetheless.

The room was thick with tension as I watched Ryan pace like a storm cloud trying to hold itself together. My mind swirled with the weight of his words, each one striking like a lightning bolt, illuminating the shadows of our shared history. He paused, hands on his hips, as if searching for the right words among the dust bunnies lurking in the corners of my apartment.

"Look, Claire," he began, his voice steadier now, "I wouldn't come to you if I had any other option. My family... they're not who they pretend to be." The earnestness in his tone almost made me want to reach out and touch his arm, to anchor him—or perhaps myself—in that moment. But I held back, afraid of where that connection might lead.

"So, you're saying they're not just a wealthy family with a penchant for overpriced art?" I quipped, trying to mask the concern with humor. "I'm shocked, really."

He shot me a look that was equal parts exasperation and something deeper—something that made my pulse quicken. "This isn't a joke, Claire. There are people in my family who would do anything to protect their interests. And now they know I'm onto them. I need to find a way to distance myself before it's too late."

The gravity of his situation began to sink in, twisting my stomach in a way that felt all too familiar. I had danced this waltz with him before, where the stakes were high and the music played on with a dissonance that echoed our troubled past. But now, the rhythm felt different. It was a race against time, and I wasn't sure if I could keep up.

"What do you expect me to do?" I asked, folding my arms across my chest in an attempt to shield myself from the rising tide of emotions. "I'm just a girl who knows how to make a mean cup of tea and binge-watch terrible reality shows. I'm not a spy."

"Exactly," he replied, his voice dropping to a near whisper as he stepped closer. "You're not part of this world. That's why I came to you. I need an outsider's perspective. Someone who won't be blinded by loyalty or family ties."

An outsider. I hadn't felt like that in a long time, not since he had swept me into his world of silk ties and champagne toasts. The thought made me bristle, a reminder of how far I had fallen from that shimmering existence. "And what if I decide not to help you? What if I want to protect myself?"

"Then I guess I'm just going to have to convince you," he said, a hint of a smile creeping onto his face, reminding me of the boy who used to charm me with his laughter and his knack for turning mundane moments into grand adventures.

"Is that a threat?" I shot back, my lips curving into an involuntary grin despite the weight of the situation.

He chuckled softly, the sound wrapping around me like a familiar blanket. "No threats, just persuasion. Maybe we could start with dinner? My treat. You know I can still cook a mean risotto."

"Oh, risotto," I scoffed, leaning against the wall, "the last bastion of men trying to win back their exes. How original."

"Hey, it's a classic! It never fails," he countered, a sparkle of mischief igniting in his eyes. "And besides, you love it."

"I did love it. Right up until you decided that my heart wasn't worth protecting."

The words slipped out before I could stop them, a raw truth spilling into the air like spilt wine on white carpet. I held my breath, expecting him to flinch. Instead, he just sighed, running a hand through his hair, a sign of vulnerability that made my heart ache.

"I messed up, Claire. I know that now. I was caught up in the chaos and lost sight of what really mattered," he admitted, his voice laced with regret. "But I'm trying to make it right. Not just for me, but for us."

"Us?" I echoed, the word tasting foreign on my tongue. "You mean 'us' as in your family's legacy, or 'us' as in the two of us standing here right now, tangled in this mess?"

"Both," he said, his gaze locking onto mine, an earnestness in his eyes that made my heart flutter against the logic of my mind. "I need you, Claire. Not just to help me untangle this. I need you because... because you make me want to be better."

I turned away, biting the inside of my cheek to suppress the swell of emotions battling for air. How could I trust him again? The heart can be a fool, yearning for connections long since broken. "Trust is a delicate thing, Ryan. I can't just pretend we haven't been through hell and back."

"I get that. But trust can also be rebuilt, layer by layer. I know I have to earn it back, and I'm willing to do whatever it takes." He stepped closer, the space between us humming with unspoken possibilities, nostalgia wrapping around us like an old, familiar coat.

I hesitated, considering the weight of his words. Could I really let him back in? The thought of opening that door, however slightly, sent chills down my spine, a mixture of excitement and fear.

"Okay, let's say I'm willing to hear you out. What exactly do you need from me?" I finally asked, crossing my arms, trying to project a confidence I didn't quite feel.

Ryan's face lit up, and I couldn't help but notice how his smile made my heart flutter against all better judgment. "I need your help gathering information. I have a lead on someone within the family who's been leaking information about our operations. If I can find out what they know, I can get ahead of this mess."

"Leaking? So, you're telling me that there's someone out there who wants to take your family down?" I raised an eyebrow, skepticism creeping into my voice. "That sounds like a plot twist in a bad thriller."

He chuckled again, that infectious laugh that danced through the tension. "I know it sounds crazy, but it's real. If I can expose this person before they turn the whole family against me, maybe I can escape this life for good."

"Okay," I said, my mind racing with the potential chaos ahead. "I'm in, but on one condition: you have to promise me that whatever happens, you'll be honest with me."

"Deal," he replied, and for a moment, it felt as if we were sealing some ancient pact, one that would either bind us together or tear us apart forever.

But even as I made that promise, I couldn't shake the feeling that the storm was far from over. Each step forward felt precarious, a tightrope walk over a pit of uncertainty. Little did I know that the very act of stepping into that chaos would lead us both down a path neither of us was prepared for, one lined with dark secrets and unexpected allies.

The air between us buzzed with a mix of nostalgia and trepidation, and as I agreed to help him, I felt the world tilt slightly on its axis. Ryan was back in my life, and with him came the delicious thrill of the unknown, tinged with the bitterness of our shared history.

That evening, we transformed my modest living room into a makeshift war room, scattered with papers and half-empty mugs of coffee that had long since cooled. I tried to focus on the mission at hand—finding the traitor lurking within his family's dark web of deceit—but every now and then, my gaze drifted to Ryan, who was so intent on the task that he didn't notice my lingering stares. There was something intoxicating about his determination, the way it flickered in his eyes like a candle trying to stave off the encroaching darkness.

"Okay, so who's our main suspect?" I asked, tapping my pencil against a notebook that was filled with my scrappy notes, each one a reminder of what had brought us to this point. The tension between us felt thick enough to slice, and I was torn between wanting to stay focused and wanting to drown in the chaotic waves of my feelings for him.

He leaned back, rubbing the back of his neck, a gesture that had always made me want to reach out and help relieve that tension. "There's a cousin, Lila. She's ambitious and has always resented me for getting more of the spotlight in the family. I wouldn't put it past her to take matters into her own hands."

"Right, the family's black sheep," I said, flipping through my notes to find a scrap of paper where I had jotted down details of their family dynamics. "Isn't that a classic trope? 'Jealous cousin plots against golden child?'"

"Perfectly scripted, isn't it?" He smirked, and for a fleeting moment, it felt like we were back in our old rhythm, the banter flowing like an old melody. "But this isn't a movie, Claire. This is real life, and I have to tread carefully. Lila's dangerous when cornered."

I raised an eyebrow, leaning forward. "Dangerous how? Is she packing heat, or is this more of a psychological warfare situation? Because if it's the former, I really hope you brought a gun to a knife fight."

He chuckled, but the humor faded as quickly as it had arrived. "It's more about the power she wields in the family. If she's working with someone outside the family, it could blow everything up. I need to get to her before she knows I'm onto her."

"Okay, so how do we play this?" My heart raced with the thrill of planning, but there was an undercurrent of fear that coiled tightly around my gut. This wasn't just about a potential family betrayal; it was about digging up secrets that could shatter lives, including my own.

Ryan pulled out his phone and scrolled through his contacts. "I think I have a way in. There's a meeting tomorrow night—one that's supposed to be top secret. Lila will be there, and if we can overhear her talking to whoever she's involved with, we might be able to piece this whole thing together."

"Sounds risky," I said, a shiver of apprehension running down my spine. "And what if you're wrong? What if she's just showing up to discuss family business?"

"Then we leave," he said, his voice steady, yet I could see the flicker of doubt in his eyes. "But I have a gut feeling about this. I wouldn't ask if I didn't think it was worth the risk."

"You've always had good instincts," I replied, the words tasting bittersweet on my tongue. "It's one of the things I loved about you."

His gaze locked onto mine, and I felt a spark of something electric ignite between us—a reminder of our past, of the way our lives had once intertwined so seamlessly. But I pushed it down, reminding myself of the stakes.

"Let's just be smart about it," I said, my voice almost a whisper. "We need a plan to ensure we're not caught. If she's as dangerous as you say, we can't just walk in unprepared."

"Right," he nodded, returning to the papers scattered across the table. "How about this? I can pretend to be meeting with her about a potential business deal, and you can be—"

"Wait, what? You want me to play the role of your business partner?" I interrupted, unable to suppress the laugh that bubbled up. "Do I look like I belong in your world of high-stakes negotiations and designer suits? I mean, I'm barely keeping my potted plant alive, Ryan!"

"You'll be fine! Just channel your inner tycoon," he shot back, the mischief dancing in his eyes. "You've got that whole 'charming yet aloof' thing down. Just act like you're in it for the money, and she'll play along. Women like her eat that up."

"Right, because nothing says 'trustworthy' like a potential millionaire's desperate plea for cash," I quipped, but a part of me was excited by the prospect. Stepping back into his world, even temporarily, felt like plunging into a cold lake—shocking yet invigorating.

As the evening wore on, we crafted a plan that felt equal parts ridiculous and daring, a whirlwind of possibilities swirling around us. Our laughter filled the room, but underlying it was a tension that hummed between us, a silent agreement that we were stepping into a dangerous game together.

The next night, I donned the best business attire I could scrape together—an old blazer that still had some semblance of style and a pair of heels that pinched my toes but made me feel fierce. Ryan arrived at my place looking every bit the part, sharp and confident in a tailored suit that hugged his frame like it was made for him.

"Wow," I said, taking a step back to admire the transformation. "You clean up nicely, Mr. Connors. Who knew you could look this good without the glow of your family's wealth lighting the way?"

He smirked, adjusting his cuffs with practiced ease. "And you look like you could negotiate a deal on Wall Street. I'm not worried about Lila not taking us seriously."

"I'm just hoping I don't trip and faceplant in front of her," I confessed, a flutter of nerves tumbling around in my stomach.

He stepped closer, his voice low and reassuring. "Just remember, you're the one with the power. You have the upper hand here, and if she suspects anything, just play it cool."

"Cool. Got it." I took a deep breath, trying to channel that essence of calm confidence, though my insides twisted in a deliciously chaotic knot.

As we drove toward the meeting location—a swanky bar tucked away in a hidden corner of the city—I couldn't shake the feeling that something was about to change. The air outside buzzed with the energy of the night, but it was laced with an undercurrent of tension that left me on edge.

We arrived and slipped inside, the ambiance a blend of dim lighting and murmurs of laughter mingling with clinking glasses. My heart raced as I scanned the crowd, searching for Lila among the sea of well-dressed patrons.

"There she is," Ryan said, nodding toward a table in the corner. Lila sat there, her dark hair falling in waves around her shoulders, a sly smile playing on her lips as she leaned toward a shadowy figure shrouded in mystery.

"Who's that with her?" I whispered, squinting to see through the haze of cigarette smoke and dim lighting.

"I don't know, but we need to get closer. It's now or never." His hand brushed against mine, a brief touch that sent a jolt of electricity up my arm, and for a moment, I forgot about the danger.

We maneuvered through the crowd, our hearts pounding in tandem. With each step, I felt the weight of my decision settle upon me—this wasn't just about Ryan; it was about facing the shadows of our past, stepping back into a world that had once felt like home but now felt alien and foreboding.

As we approached the table, my breath caught in my throat. The figure beside Lila turned, and my world shifted beneath my feet. It was someone I had never expected to see, someone whose presence sent a shockwave of realization crashing over me.

"Claire? What are you doing here?" the voice cut through the noise, sharp and unexpected.

Time froze as I locked eyes with the person I had thought was long gone from my life, and just like that, the ground beneath me opened up, revealing the chaotic path ahead.

Chapter 26: The Final Threat

The night air outside the hotel wrapped around me like a chilled blanket, the scent of rain-soaked asphalt mingling with the lingering perfume of jasmine from the nearby gardens. The streetlights flickered, casting a hesitant glow over the pavement, creating pockets of light that danced around the edges of shadows. I leaned against the cool stone of the building, my pulse steadying as I braced myself for the confrontation. But then, there she was—Vivian. She emerged from the darkness like a specter, her presence a jarring contrast to the quietude of the night.

"Vivian," I said, my voice steady despite the roiling dread in my stomach. She stood before me, draped in a sleek black coat that clung to her like a second skin. Her hair cascaded around her shoulders, framing a face that was both beautiful and terrifying. There was a glint in her eye that sent a shiver down my spine, a predator relishing the moment before the kill.

"You think you've won?" she purred, a smile spreading across her lips that reminded me of a cat toying with its prey. The threat in her words lingered, heavy like the humidity in the air. "This isn't over. You may have taken down my family, but I'm not going anywhere."

Her words hung between us, electric and charged. It was as if the world had narrowed down to just the two of us, the chaos of the city fading into a dull roar. I could feel my heart pounding against my ribcage, each beat a reminder of the stakes. Vivian was relentless, and the flames of her vengeance flickered dangerously close.

"I didn't take them down," I replied, forcing a confidence into my voice that I didn't quite feel. "They made their choices. And you can too. You could walk away from this."

A laugh escaped her, low and mocking. "Oh, sweetheart, that's adorable. You think you know me? I'm not some pawn to be played with. I'm the queen, and the game has just begun."

The weight of her words settled in my gut. I had thought I was untouchable, riding the wave of recent victories, but here she was, a tempest, ready to disrupt everything I had fought for. Her presence was suffocating, and the more I stared into those calculating eyes, the more I realized I was outmatched. She was chaos embodied, and I was clinging to the fragile threads of control.

"You're in over your head, sweetheart," she continued, a smirk twisting her lips. "And you don't even know it yet."

Her words, drenched in malice, ignited a fire within me. "Maybe," I countered, taking a step closer, refusing to let her intimidate me. "But I'm not afraid of you."

She tilted her head, curiosity piqued. "Fear is a funny thing. It can make you do foolish things, or it can keep you alive." Her gaze hardened, a dangerous glint sparking within those icy depths. "Which do you prefer?"

"Neither," I said defiantly, my heart racing with adrenaline. "I choose to fight."

Vivian stepped forward, invading my space, her breath a whisper against my skin. "Then fight, darling. Show me what you're made of. But remember, I play for keeps. You might just lose more than you bargained for."

With that, she turned on her heel and sauntered back into the night, the heels of her boots clicking against the pavement like the ticking of a clock counting down to my impending doom. My heart raced as I watched her silhouette disappear into the shadows. The threat she posed lingered like an echo, filling the air with a tension that seemed almost tangible.

I leaned against the wall, taking deep breaths to steady myself, my mind a whirlwind of thoughts. What did she mean? What more could she do? It was as if a storm had gathered on the horizon, ready to unleash its fury. The night felt heavier, charged with uncertainty, as I wrestled with the knowledge that Vivian was still out there, plotting her next move.

Deciding that I couldn't linger in this desolate space any longer, I turned and headed towards my car, the metal cool beneath my fingertips. As I drove away, the streets blurred past me, a hazy mix of lights and shadows. But no matter how fast I moved, the weight of Vivian's threat settled deeper within me, wrapping around my thoughts like a vine tightening its grip.

Arriving home, I flipped the light switch, flooding the room with a warm glow that fought against the encroaching darkness. I sank into the comfort of my couch, my mind racing with strategies and countermeasures. I was determined to find a way to counter her. A vision of her smile—a calculated, sinister expression—flashed in my mind, and I felt a rush of resolve.

The clock on the wall ticked steadily, each second echoing the urgency of my situation. I had to be proactive, to outsmart her. I picked up my phone and began scrolling through contacts, thoughts tumbling in my mind like leaves caught in a whirlwind. I needed allies, information, a way to turn the tide.

Suddenly, a name jumped out at me—Mark. He had been in the trenches with me during my recent battles. He was resourceful and sharp-witted, and while we'd had our share of disagreements, I knew he'd understand the gravity of my situation. My fingers hovered over the screen as I hesitated. Would he be willing to help me against someone as formidable as Vivian?

As I hit "call," the familiar ringing in my ear felt like a lifeline, pulling me back from the edge of despair. When he answered, his voice resonated with warmth, "Hey, what's up? You sound... intense."

"Vivian's back," I blurted, the words tumbling out like marbles spilling across a floor. "She's not done with me. We need to talk."

The silence that followed was heavy, punctuated only by the sound of my own breathing. I could almost hear the gears turning in his mind, the realization of the threat unfolding. "I'll be over in twenty," he finally said, and I felt a flicker of hope.

As I paced my living room, the shadows seemed to close in around me, but this time, I was ready to confront them. With every passing minute, the storm was building, and I was no longer the helpless prey. I would fight back.

The knock at the door jolted me from my thoughts, a sharp sound that sliced through the thick tension in the room. I glanced at the clock again, willing it to move faster, to somehow speed up the process of taking control of my life again. Mark's presence would either anchor me or send me spiraling deeper into uncertainty. I took a deep breath, steadied myself, and opened the door.

"Hey," he said, stepping inside, his usual easy smile replaced by a furrowed brow. He looked around, his eyes scanning for signs of distress, or perhaps, signs of Vivian's wrath. "What's going on? You look like you've seen a ghost."

"Not a ghost," I replied, shutting the door behind him. "Just a menace in designer shoes."

His eyes narrowed, the playful demeanor shifting to serious as I recounted the confrontation outside the hotel. Mark listened intently, his expression morphing from concern to disbelief as I detailed Vivian's threats. Each word felt like a weight I was dropping into the abyss, and I couldn't tell if it was relieving or just added to the growing dread.

"I always knew she was trouble," he muttered, running a hand through his hair. "What's her play? She can't just come at you like that and expect to walk away."

"Tell me about it," I said, pacing the small living room. "It's like she thinks I'm her favorite toy, and she's not ready to put me down yet." I stopped and faced him, my heart pounding. "I need to outsmart her, Mark. I can't let her have the upper hand."

Mark crossed his arms, the corner of his mouth twitching into a half-smile. "You're not exactly the toy type. More like the action figure—tough and ready for battle. What's your plan?"

"Honestly? I'm still brainstorming. I want to find out what she's really after. If it's revenge, there must be a weakness I can exploit." I plopped down on the couch, feeling the weight of my thoughts. "And if she's angry, she's going to make mistakes. I just have to find a way to make her slip."

Mark considered this, nodding slowly. "You could try to lure her into a trap. Get her to reveal more than she intends."

"Isn't that what she's already done to me? I can't afford to underestimate her," I replied, running a hand over my hair, frustration boiling beneath the surface. "I need something concrete, some kind of leverage."

Mark leaned back, his expression thoughtful. "You have friends in high places. What about calling in a favor? You know the local police have a record of her family's past dealings. Maybe they'd be willing to share something that could give you an edge."

"Are you suggesting I wade into that cesspool?" I raised an eyebrow. "That sounds like a surefire way to get caught in the crossfire."

"Only if you make a scene," he shot back, a playful glint in his eye. "You're good at staying under the radar."

I couldn't help but smile at his confidence. "Flattery will get you nowhere. But you might be onto something." My mind raced with possibilities, ideas sparking like fireworks. If I could find a thread to pull, a secret that could unravel her plans, it would give me the leverage I desperately needed.

The atmosphere shifted, the playful banter morphing into a serious strategy session as we plotted and brainstormed ways to outmaneuver Vivian. Our conversation flowed, the tension giving way to determination. But deep down, I couldn't shake the sense that time was slipping away, the clock's hands mocking me with each tick.

"Okay," I said finally, a decision crystallizing in my mind. "Let's start with your idea about the police. I know a few officers who might be able to help."

"Good. And we'll need a solid cover story," Mark added, his brow furrowing in concentration. "You can't just show up and ask them about a known criminal's dealings without drawing suspicion."

"Right," I muttered, chewing my lip. "I'll have to be clever about it. Maybe act like I'm gathering information for a piece I'm writing? Something to show I'm on the up-and-up."

Mark grinned, his eyes lighting up with mischief. "Now you're talking. Just remember, if you run into Vivian, it's not just your reputation on the line. You're playing a dangerous game."

"Since when have I ever backed down from a challenge?" I shot back, crossing my arms defiantly. "But I appreciate the pep talk. I'll add it to my mental list of things to consider while facing down a woman hell-bent on revenge."

Mark chuckled, shaking his head as he stood to grab his jacket. "Just make sure to keep your phone on you at all times. If you need backup, call me. I'm only a few blocks away."

"Deal." I walked him to the door, the tension still lingering in the air but now wrapped in a layer of camaraderie. As he stepped out, I felt a surge of confidence. Maybe I wasn't as alone in this fight as I thought.

The quiet of the house enveloped me once more, but I was determined to fill it with purpose. I grabbed my phone and began scrolling through contacts, my mind racing with potential leads. I needed to act quickly before Vivian made her next move. The stakes were higher than ever, and I couldn't afford to falter.

Hours later, as I sat at my kitchen table littered with notes and half-empty coffee cups, I could feel the adrenaline pulsing through me like a current. I was about to make a call that could change everything. Just as I dialed the number of an officer I trusted, the screen lit up with a text message from an unknown number.

You should watch your back. Vivian isn't the only one hunting you.

My breath caught in my throat, panic flaring up like an alarm in my chest. Who was this? Was it a warning or another threat? The words echoed in my mind, weaving into the fabric of my uncertainty. I couldn't afford to be caught off guard, not now when everything felt like it was on the precipice of chaos.

I stared at the screen, my heart racing as I typed a response, trying to decode the threat while keeping my composure. But before I could hit send, my phone buzzed again. Another message, this one from a familiar contact—an old friend from the police department.

Heard you're looking for info on the Hawthorne case. Let's meet.

The walls of my living room suddenly felt constricting, as if the very air had thickened around me. I knew this was it—the opportunity I had been waiting for. Yet the weight of the previous message loomed large, a reminder that my enemies were closing in, and every decision could mean the difference between safety and ruin.

"Guess I'm about to step into the lion's den," I muttered under my breath, a smirk crossing my lips at the irony. With resolve solidifying within me, I knew I had to keep pushing forward, to face whatever storm awaited. After all, I was done being the prey. The game had changed, and now I was ready to fight back.

The coffee shop hummed with the soft chatter of morning patrons, steam curling up from mugs and mingling with the scent of freshly baked pastries. I sat at a small table by the window, my hands wrapped around a warm cup, using it as a shield against the world outside. The sunlight streamed in, illuminating the pages of my notebook, filled with chaotic scrawls and frantic notes. My fingers tapped nervously against the ceramic, a rhythm that matched the pulse of anxiety thrumming beneath my skin.

As I waited for my contact, I replayed the message in my mind, the words haunting me: You should watch your back. Vivian isn't the only one hunting you. It felt like a shadow lurking just beyond the reach of light, a menace waiting for the perfect moment to pounce. The thought made my stomach twist uncomfortably, but I couldn't let it derail me. I had to stay focused, to dig deeper.

A chime above the door announced the arrival of a figure I recognized. Detective Jenna Torres stepped inside, her sharp gaze sweeping the room before landing on me. She was all business, with her dark hair pulled back into a tight bun and a tailored blazer that screamed authority. I gestured her over, heart racing in anticipation of what she might reveal.

"Sorry for the wait," she said, settling into the chair opposite me. "I had a hard time getting away. Busy morning."

"Understandable," I replied, forcing a smile. "You're the only detective I know who could make paperwork sound more thrilling than a rollercoaster."

"Don't flatter me. I might start expecting complimentary lattes." Jenna leaned in, her expression serious. "You said you were looking for information about the Hawthorne case. What exactly do you want to know?"

"Anything that might give me an edge against Vivian," I said, lowering my voice to a conspiratorial whisper. "I need to understand her motivations, what she might be planning next."

Jenna raised an eyebrow, skepticism lacing her features. "You do realize you're asking about a crime family, right? Their history is messy, and it's dangerous to get involved. You could end up on the wrong side of the law—or worse, in the crosshairs of someone who doesn't like you poking around."

I met her gaze, determination igniting within me. "I've already got a target on my back. I'd rather be proactive than reactive. If I don't find a way to deal with Vivian, it'll be too late for me."

She sighed, glancing around the bustling café as if weighing her options. "Okay, but you need to tread carefully. The Hawthornes were known for more than just their dealings in illegal activities. They had a network of informants, allies, and enemies all at once. If you expose yourself too much, you could inadvertently put yourself on their radar."

"Do you have anything concrete?" I pressed, my heart racing. "Some detail, some weakness I can use?"

"Rumor has it that Vivian's been trying to clean up her family's image since they fell from grace," she began, her voice barely audible above the clinking of cups and the sound of an espresso machine steaming. "She's made a few deals with some powerful players in the city, trying to distance herself from the criminal ties. But not all those deals have gone smoothly. There's friction. If you can exploit that..."

"What kind of friction?" I leaned forward, my curiosity piqued.

"Family disagreements," Jenna replied, her eyes darting to the door again. "You know how it is in these kinds of families—loyalty is a double-edged sword. Not everyone is pleased with her leadership. Some want to return to the old ways, and others are eager for a change."

That felt like a thread worth tugging. "You're saying there's a potential rift in her camp?"

"Exactly. If you can find someone on the inside who's willing to talk, it could give you an upper hand. But it's risky—betrayal runs deep in those circles."

Before I could respond, my phone buzzed on the table, the screen lighting up with a new message. I glanced down and felt my heart drop. It was from the unknown number again. Don't trust her. She's not what she seems.

"Everything okay?" Jenna asked, noticing my sudden stillness.

"Just a... reminder," I said, forcing a laugh to mask my unease. "So, how do I find this insider? Someone who might be willing to share secrets about Vivian?"

"Try reaching out to one of her old associates," Jenna suggested, leaning back as she considered the idea. "There's a bar downtown, The Rusty Nail, where some of them hang out. You might catch someone who knows more than they let on. But again, I can't stress enough how dangerous this could be."

"I've faced danger before," I said, determination lacing my words. "I can handle myself."

"Just promise me you'll be careful. I'd hate to see you get hurt over this."

I nodded, absorbing her words as a plan began to take shape in my mind. After Jenna left, I took a moment to collect my thoughts, mentally preparing myself for the encounter ahead. The Rusty Nail had always been a dive, known for its strong drinks and even stronger characters, but I wasn't about to shy away from a little grit.

As I stepped out into the bustling street, the sun hung high in the sky, casting long shadows across the pavement. I could feel the weight of the world pressing down on my shoulders, but I brushed it off. I had a purpose now, a direction. I just needed to tread carefully through the minefield that was Vivian's world.

Navigating through the crowd, I arrived at the bar, its neon sign flickering like an old heartbeat. Inside, the atmosphere was thick with the smell of stale beer and smoke. I scanned the room, taking in the dimly lit corners and the patrons who seemed to have stories etched into their faces.

After ordering a drink, I found a spot at the bar, positioning myself where I could observe without drawing attention. The laughter and clinking of glasses blended into a hazy soundtrack, but my focus remained sharp. I was searching for anyone who looked like they might have ties to Vivian—or who seemed willing to spill secrets for the right price.

A burly man in a leather jacket caught my eye, his face shadowed but familiar. He was an old associate of the Hawthornes, or at least, that's what the rumors said. I noticed him nursing a drink alone in a corner booth, his demeanor both wary and watchful. This might be my chance.

Gathering my courage, I approached him, my heart pounding in rhythm with my footsteps. "Mind if I join you?" I asked, forcing a smile.

He looked up, assessing me with eyes that held too many secrets. "Depends. You looking for trouble?"

"Depends on what you mean by trouble," I shot back, keeping my tone light. "I'm just hoping for some conversation."

He raised an eyebrow, skepticism mingling with curiosity. "You've got guts, I'll give you that. What's a girl like you doing in a place like this?"

"Trying to make sense of the chaos," I replied, leaning in closer, lowering my voice to a conspiratorial whisper. "Word is, you might know a thing or two about the Hawthornes."

His gaze hardened, the air between us thickening with tension. "Why would you want to know about them? You don't look like the type who wants to swim with sharks."

"Let's just say I have a vested interest," I replied, my heart racing as I gauged his reaction. "And I'm tired of being the prey."

For a moment, the bar faded away, leaving just the two of us in a world of uncertainty and unspoken danger. But just as he opened his mouth to respond, the door swung open with a bang, and in strode a figure that sent a chill down my spine.

Vivian.

Her presence lit up the room, a predatory grace in every step. She scanned the bar, her eyes narrowing when they landed on me. I felt my breath hitch in my throat, the weight of dread crashing down like an avalanche. It was as if time had slowed, the laughter and music fading into a muted backdrop.

The man beside me shifted, his posture suddenly tense. "You need to leave. Now," he hissed, eyes darting to the door.

But I didn't move. I couldn't. I was frozen in place as Vivian's gaze locked onto mine, a wicked smile creeping across her lips. The game had changed, and I was standing at the edge of a precipice, with no way of knowing whether I would fall or fly.

Chapter 27: A Return to the Past

The sun hung low in the sky, casting a warm, golden hue over the vast estate that lay before us, its grandeur dulled by years of neglect. Ryan stood beside me, his silhouette sharp against the fading light, a distant look in his eyes as he stared at the house he once called home. The sprawling façade, once alive with laughter and life, now seemed like a fortress of forgotten dreams, its windows dark and hollow. I could almost hear the echoes of his childhood—the clinking of glasses at lavish parties, the muffled laughter of friends, and the dissonant undercurrent of something sinister lurking beneath.

"Let's go inside," he said, his voice barely above a whisper, as if speaking too loudly would awaken the ghosts that seemed to linger in every corner. I nodded, a mixture of curiosity and apprehension flooding my senses. I was stepping into the remnants of a life that had shaped him, a life filled with shadows that I knew little about but felt weighed down by all the same.

As we crossed the threshold, the air grew heavier, laden with memories. The expansive foyer opened up like a cavern, and I instinctively stepped back, surprised by the chill that crept up my spine. The marble floors, once polished to a shine, were now coated in a fine layer of dust, and the grand staircase loomed ahead, its banister coated with neglect. It was as if time had forgotten this place, leaving it suspended in an eerie stillness.

"Where do you want to start?" I asked, trying to coax him out of his reverie. My voice felt foreign in the silence, but it seemed to pull him back from the abyss he was peering into. He turned to me, his expression a mix of determination and reluctance.

"The library," he said, motioning for me to follow. I felt a shiver of excitement mixed with fear; the library was where the stories were. Perhaps it held the keys to understanding his past—the laughter, the tears, the moments he had tried so hard to escape.

The room unfolded before us like a secret garden. Bookshelves lined the walls, their spines cracked and faded, filled with stories waiting to be told. A dusty leather sofa sat in the center, and a flicker of nostalgia crossed Ryan's face as he approached the nearest shelf. His fingers traced the titles lightly, almost reverently, and I couldn't help but wonder which stories had once captivated him, which ones had offered solace amidst the chaos of his family life.

"This was my favorite spot," he said, his voice now stronger, more resolute. "I spent hours in here, reading about worlds far away from this one."

"Did you ever imagine leaving?" I asked, unable to contain my curiosity. "Or was it just a dream that felt impossible?"

Ryan's gaze shifted to the window, where the last light of day painted the room in shades of amber and deep blue. "I think I always wanted to escape," he admitted. "But I was too afraid to actually do it. Fear can be a powerful cage."

I could feel the weight of his words, the truth resonating in the silence that enveloped us. It was as if he were peeling back the layers of his heart, revealing a vulnerability I had never encountered before. The playful banter we often shared felt miles away, replaced by this profound honesty that left me momentarily breathless.

"Do you want to know a secret?" I leaned closer, my voice dropping to a conspiratorial whisper. "I always thought you were brave. You put on this shield of confidence, and it's hard to see the cracks."

He turned to me, surprise flickering across his features, a hint of a smile tugging at the corners of his lips. "Brave? Me?"

"Absolutely," I insisted, feeling emboldened. "It takes courage to be who you are, to face your past head-on."

He chuckled softly, the sound warm and inviting, filling the vast room with a sense of familiarity. "You have a way of making things sound better than they are."

"Or maybe you just need to believe it," I shot back, the tension lifting as our banter resumed.

But as we settled into the comfort of our conversation, the atmosphere shifted. A distant creak echoed through the hall, a sound that didn't belong to the memories we were conjuring. Ryan's expression darkened as he paused, the humor fading from his eyes. "Did you hear that?"

I nodded, a knot tightening in my stomach. "What was that?"

"Probably just the house settling," he said, though his tone suggested otherwise. He hesitated, as if caught between dismissing the noise and exploring its source. "But let's check it out."

The air crackled with tension as we made our way through the house, each step reverberating with the weight of our shared fears. The darkness closed in around us, wrapping us in an unsettling embrace. I glanced at Ryan, whose jaw was set tight, his eyes scanning the shadows. It was a side of him I hadn't expected—one that revealed the depth of his struggles, the weight of his family's legacy pressing down on him like a shroud.

We reached a narrow hallway lined with faded photographs, each frame capturing moments frozen in time—smiling faces that hinted at a life filled with light and joy, now tarnished by the events that had unfolded. A chill raced down my spine, not from the cold but from the stark contrast between the past and the present. It was as if the walls themselves were whispering secrets, urging us to listen, to uncover the truth hidden in the silence.

And then, just as we approached the end of the hallway, a muffled sound broke the stillness, sending a jolt through me. It was a voice—soft yet unmistakable—seeping through the cracks of this decaying edifice. Ryan froze, his expression shifting from curiosity to alarm as the voice grew clearer. It wasn't just a whisper; it was a conversation, fragmented yet distinctly familiar.

"I didn't mean to—" the voice began, and I felt the ground shift beneath my feet.

"Who's there?" Ryan called out, his voice steady despite the tremor of uncertainty that rippled through him.

The response was immediate, abrupt, like a curtain falling. The voice cut off, replaced by the sound of hurried footsteps retreating down another corridor. My heart raced, a surge of adrenaline pushing me forward.

"Do you know who that was?" I asked, the words tumbling out before I could think better of them.

"I should," he said, his face a mask of confusion. "But... I can't place it."

Our world had shifted once again, a tangible tension knitting us together as we prepared to face whatever lay hidden in the shadows. As we ventured deeper into the heart of the estate, I felt the gravity of Ryan's past pressing down on us, the weight of secrets yearning to be revealed, and the promise of a reckoning that could reshape everything we thought we knew.

The silence that enveloped us after the voice faded was a tangible thing, thick and unsettling, like a dense fog that refused to lift. Ryan's gaze remained locked on the hallway ahead, a storm brewing in his eyes as he weighed the implications of what we had just heard. I felt the adrenaline coursing through my veins, the impulse to flee warring with an insatiable curiosity that urged me to press forward.

"Did you catch that?" I asked, the words rushing out in a breathless whisper. "That sounded like a woman."

"Yeah," he said, his voice steady yet laced with tension. "But who would be here?"

A thousand possibilities swirled in my mind, each more wild than the last. We had stumbled into a mystery, and while my rational side insisted that we should turn back, my adventurous spirit craved the thrill of discovery. "Maybe a squatter? Or an old friend?"

He shot me a look that blended disbelief with a hint of admiration. "An old friend? In my family's abandoned estate? That's quite the imagination you have."

"I'd say it's optimism," I countered, a playful grin creeping onto my face. "Always hope for the best, right?"

"Or prepare for the worst," he muttered, but there was a spark of amusement in his eyes. He took a step forward, his confidence returning, and I followed closely behind, a mix of dread and excitement bubbling in my stomach.

The hallway narrowed, the shadows deepening around us as we approached a door at the far end. It loomed like a portal to another world, and Ryan paused, glancing back at me. "Ready?"

"Are you kidding? I was born ready," I replied, adopting a mock-heroic stance that earned a soft chuckle from him.

With a firm hand, he pushed open the door, and a wave of stale air rushed out, wrapping around us like a shroud. The room beyond was a small office, its walls lined with bookshelves sagging under the weight of dusty tomes and forgotten accolades. A massive oak desk sat in the center, the surface littered with yellowed papers and old photographs.

"Welcome to my father's domain," Ryan said, his voice barely above a whisper. "This is where he plotted his empire—or whatever he thought he was building."

I stepped inside, the atmosphere heavy with secrets. The air was thick with the scent of old leather and paper, and I couldn't help but feel as if we were intruders in a place steeped in betrayal. My eyes fell on a photograph framed on the desk—a younger Ryan, smiling broadly alongside a striking woman with deep auburn hair.

"Is that your mother?" I asked, curiosity getting the better of me.

He nodded slowly, his expression shifting. "Yeah. That was taken before everything fell apart."

"What was she like?"

"Complicated," he said, a bitter smile forming on his lips. "She had this incredible way of making everything feel lighter, even in the darkest times. But she struggled—more than I realized until it was too late."

The words hung between us, a heavy reminder of the complexities of family ties. I wanted to ask more, to dig deeper, but just then, a glint of metal caught my eye beneath a pile of documents. I leaned closer and brushed away the dust, revealing an ornate box, its surface marred but still beautiful.

"Ryan, look at this." I turned it in my hands, admiring its intricate design. "What do you think it is?"

He stepped over, a mix of curiosity and caution etched on his features. "I've never seen that before."

"Maybe it's a treasure trove of family secrets?" I suggested, excitement dancing in my voice. "You know, like in the movies?"

His lips curved into a smirk. "If only there were gold coins and hidden maps inside."

With a shaky breath, I opened the box. Inside lay a collection of letters, neatly tied with a fraying ribbon. They looked decades old, their edges yellowed and delicate. "These look like they haven't seen the light of day in years," I murmured, glancing up at him.

"Read one," he urged, his voice a mixture of apprehension and intrigue.

I hesitated, the weight of the moment settling around us like a thick fog. "Okay, here goes." I carefully untied the ribbon and pulled out the top letter. The handwriting was elegant yet hurried, the ink slightly smudged as if the writer had been racing against time.

"Dear Eleanor," I read aloud, my voice steady. "If you're reading this, it means I'm no longer there to explain. I'm sorry for all the pain I've caused. You deserve to know the truth..."

I glanced at Ryan, his eyes widening as he took a step closer, the intensity of the moment electrifying the air between us. "What truth?" he whispered, almost to himself.

"The truth about your father," I continued, my heart racing as I processed the words. "He was never the man you thought he was."

Ryan's expression hardened, a mix of anger and disbelief flashing across his features. "This can't be good."

"Let's see what else it says," I urged, reading the next lines with bated breath. "He was involved in things far darker than you can imagine. The choices he made shattered our family, and for that, I will always carry the burden."

Ryan ran a hand through his hair, frustration evident in the movement. "This is insane," he muttered. "How could she know?"

"She might not know everything," I suggested gently. "But it sounds like there's more to uncover. This could be the key to understanding what happened."

"Or it could blow everything up," he replied, his voice low.

"Maybe," I conceded, "but isn't it worth finding out? You deserve to know what really happened."

His gaze flicked to the letters, then back to me, vulnerability cracking the armor he usually wore. "You're right. I just—I can't believe we're doing this."

I reached for another letter, my fingers trembling with anticipation. "Let's dive deeper then."

With each letter I unfolded, the truth layered itself more intricately, revealing a tapestry of choices, regrets, and hidden lives. The letters told stories of love lost and battles fought in silence, and with every word, I felt Ryan's world shift around us, the foundation of his family's legacy cracking under the weight of what had been concealed for so long.

"Every secret has its consequences," Ryan murmured as I read, the realization washing over him like a tide.

"But maybe those consequences can lead to healing," I countered, a quiet hope blossoming in my chest. "You don't have to carry this weight alone."

He met my gaze, and in that moment, I felt the connection between us deepen, a shared understanding of the tangled web we had stepped into. Together, we were unraveling a story that threatened to consume him, yet also had the power to set him free. And as we stood there, surrounded by whispers of the past, I knew that whatever lay ahead, we would face it together, ready to confront the shadows that loomed over his family, one letter at a time.

As I sifted through the letters, a heavy tension clung to the air, making it feel thick enough to cut. The words became a visceral connection to Ryan's past, an echo of secrets begging to be unveiled. Each letter told a tale of deception and regret, but the gravity of their content deepened with every page we turned.

Ryan stood beside me, a storm brewing in his eyes, as if he were grappling with the very foundation of his identity. "I can't believe my mother kept all this hidden. It's like she knew the truth but was too scared to face it."

"Or maybe she was trying to protect you," I replied, trying to find a silver lining amidst the shadows. "She might have thought keeping these secrets buried was for the best."

"Best for who?" he shot back, frustration spilling over. "The people who were hurt? Or just herself?"

A silence enveloped us, thick with unsaid words. I could see the conflict brewing within him, an internal battle between the desire for clarity and the fear of what that clarity might bring. I wanted to reach out, to offer comfort, but the weight of the moment held me back.

"Let's read another," I suggested, hoping to shift his focus away from the turmoil that danced in his eyes. I picked up another letter, and as I began to read, the words seemed to carry a different energy, a sense of urgency laced within the ink.

"Dear Eleanor," it began again, but this time, the tone was sharper, the handwriting trembling with emotion. "I'm writing this in the dead of night, unable to sleep as I think of the choices I've made. If you find this, know that I fought to protect you from the truth, but perhaps I've only succeeded in creating a larger web of lies."

Ryan's breath hitched as I continued. "The man you believe is your father is not who you think. I feared he would destroy everything if you knew. You must understand—I did what I thought was best."

His knuckles whitened as he gripped the edge of the desk, his body taut with tension. "What the hell does that even mean?" he muttered, pacing the small office as if the walls were closing in on him. "Who is she talking about?"

"I don't know," I said, my heart racing along with the weight of his emotions. "But it sounds like there's someone else involved. Someone who has been playing a much larger role in your family's life."

Ryan stopped abruptly, his eyes narrowing as if he were trying to piece together a puzzle with missing pieces. "Do you think it's my grandfather?"

"Maybe," I mused, flipping through the remaining letters, desperate for clarity. "But there could be someone else entirely."

Just as I reached for the next letter, an unexpected crash echoed from the back of the house, shattering the fragile silence that had settled around us. I jumped, the papers flying from my hands, a jolt of adrenaline racing through me. "What was that?"

"I don't know," Ryan said, his voice suddenly fierce, filled with a resolve that sent a shiver down my spine. "We should check it out."

He moved toward the door, and I quickly followed, adrenaline pushing me forward despite the sense of foreboding that hung in the air. We moved cautiously through the corridor, each creak of the floorboards amplifying the tension. The shadows danced ominously, stretching like fingers toward us, and I could feel my heart thrumming in my chest, a wild drumbeat of uncertainty.

As we approached the source of the noise, I could hear faint voices, muffled but undeniably present. I glanced at Ryan, who raised an eyebrow, silently urging me to stay quiet. He signaled for me to follow him as he crept closer to the door at the end of the hall.

I strained to listen, my heart pounding in sync with the murmured conversation. It felt surreal, standing on the threshold of what could be a revelation—or a nightmare. Ryan leaned closer, pressing his ear against the door, his body tense as if bracing for an impact.

"Can you hear anything?" I whispered, the words barely escaping my lips.

"Just whispers," he replied, his brow furrowing. "But it sounds like... arguments."

Before I could respond, he reached for the door handle, and my breath caught in my throat. "Wait—"

But the door swung open before I could finish, revealing a small, dimly lit room stacked with old furniture and boxes, the air thick with the scent of mildew. At the center, two figures stood silhouetted against the fading light filtering through the cracked window. One was a man with an air of authority, his posture rigid and tense. The other was a woman, her face partially hidden in the shadows, but there was something hauntingly familiar about her.

"Ryan?" she said, her voice a soft tremor that echoed in the silence.

I could see Ryan's expression shift, a mask of shock morphing into recognition. "What are you doing here?"

The woman stepped into the light, and my heart dropped as her features became clear. She was strikingly beautiful, with deep auburn hair that mirrored the photograph from the desk. It was as if I were looking at a ghost, a haunting specter from Ryan's past that had somehow stepped into the present.

"Ryan, I—" she began, her eyes wide with a mix of fear and relief. "I didn't think you'd ever come back."

"Why would I? You left!" he shot back, hurt and anger colliding in his voice. "You left me with him."

I felt the tension in the air shift, crackling like electricity as the woman's expression faltered. "I had no choice," she whispered, anguish lacing her tone. "You don't understand what he was capable of."

"What do you mean?" Ryan pressed, stepping into the room as if drawn by a magnetic force, his entire being brimming with rage and confusion. "What did you know? Who are you protecting?"

Her eyes darted to me, uncertainty flickering across her features. "I didn't want you to find out this way," she said, a deep sorrow entwined with her words. "I thought I could keep you safe. I never meant to hurt you."

I stood frozen, the tension between them thickening like smoke, choking the air from the room. This was more than just a confrontation; it was a reckoning—a moment where the past collided violently with the present, where secrets long buried were clawing their way to the surface.

As the room filled with silence, Ryan's expression darkened, and he took a step forward, his voice low and dangerous. "I need the truth. No more lies."

The woman hesitated, and in that moment, I could feel the weight of the world pressing down on her, as if she were teetering on the edge of a precipice. "If I tell you, you might not like what you hear," she finally said, her voice barely above a whisper.

"I don't care," Ryan replied fiercely. "I need to know."

And just as the air around us grew taut with anticipation, a loud crash erupted from the hallway behind us, making us all jump. Before I could react, the door slammed open, and a figure stepped inside, silhouetted against the fading light—a face I never expected to see, one that could change everything.

"Get away from her!" the newcomer shouted, eyes blazing with fury.

In an instant, the air became electric, a charged moment that shifted the dynamics entirely. I felt a mix of fear and confusion wash over me as the room descended into chaos. Everything we had unearthed, every secret we had chased, was about to unravel in ways I couldn't begin to fathom. And in that instant, the fragile threads of our reality were pulled taut, ready to snap, leaving us teetering on the edge of revelation—or destruction.

Chapter 28: Unforgiven

The afternoon sun filters through the dusty blinds of my bedroom, casting stripes of golden light across the floor. I sit at my worn-out desk, fingers hovering above the keyboard, yet I can't seem to type a single word. The blank screen stares back at me, taunting, but the real battle rages in my heart. Ryan's voice echoes in my mind, an unwanted reminder of all the moments we shared, tangled with the sharp edges of his betrayal. He said he loved me, and part of me clings to that declaration like a lifebuoy in a turbulent sea. The other part, however, floats in a murky depth of mistrust, swirling with doubt and hurt.

With a frustrated sigh, I push away from the desk and step into the small living room, where a faint scent of burnt coffee lingers in the air. I half-smile at the memory of my attempt to brew something more than instant. Just another reminder of how the ordinary turns chaotic when emotions run wild. I can hear Ryan's laughter in the back of my mind—a warm, rich sound that feels like home, yet stings like a fresh wound. He has this way of making the mundane feel magical, and now, in the aftermath of his choices, the magic feels like a cruel joke.

I glance out the window, the sky a vibrant blue, dotted with puffy white clouds that seem to mock my internal storm. The world outside continues its dance, oblivious to the chaos inside my heart. I wonder if the trees, with their branches swaying lightly in the breeze, ever feel the weight of betrayal. Probably not. They just stand there, rooted and resilient, while I feel like a leaf tossed about by the wind. I wrap my arms around myself, wishing I could find that same stability, that unwavering strength.

It's late afternoon when the doorbell rings, a sound so jarring it jolts me from my reverie. My heart races as I approach the door, the weight of uncertainty settling in my stomach. Ryan. I can almost

313

hear his voice whispering sweet nothings, and the thought sends a shiver down my spine. With every step I take, I mentally rehearse the possible conversations, each scenario more chaotic than the last. Finally, I open the door, and there he is, standing on the threshold, a mix of hope and apprehension etched on his face.

"Hey," he says, voice soft but firm, as if he's testing the waters. He looks good—too good. His hair is slightly tousled, and the stubble on his jaw gives him an edge that's as infuriating as it is alluring.

"Hey," I reply, crossing my arms over my chest, a shield against the vulnerability creeping back in.

"I brought coffee," he offers, holding up a steaming cup as if it's a peace offering. "Thought maybe you'd want to talk."

"Talk?" I raise an eyebrow, skepticism lacing my tone. "You mean like how you talked before?"

He flinches, the weight of my words hitting him squarely in the chest. "I know I messed up. I'm not asking for forgiveness right away. I just... I want to explain."

"Explain?" I scoff, taking a step back. "What is there to explain? You lied to me, Ryan. You manipulated everything we had."

"I know. And I hate myself for it. But please, just let me try to make it right." He takes a tentative step closer, and I can see the sincerity in his eyes, the desperation clinging to his every word.

"Make it right?" I echo, unable to keep the incredulity from my voice. "How do you make something like this right? You broke my trust. You shattered everything we built." The pain in my voice is palpable, a raw edge that both of us can't ignore.

"I want to help you rebuild it. One brick at a time," he says, his voice steady but laced with a hint of vulnerability. "I know I don't deserve a second chance, but I'm asking for one anyway."

For a moment, silence envelops us, the air thick with unresolved tension. I can see the flicker of uncertainty in his eyes, the way he hesitates, like a tightrope walker teetering on the brink. "And what if I'm not ready to start over?" I ask, the words tasting bitter on my tongue.

"Then we'll just stand here," he replies softly, the honesty in his gaze disarming me. "I can wait. I'll wait as long as you need."

I look at him, really look at him, and I feel the familiar ache in my heart—a longing for what we had. The connection that once felt unbreakable is now frayed at the edges, but beneath it all, the love lingers, stubborn and unyielding. "What if I can't ever trust you again?"

"Then I'll spend every day proving to you that I'm worth trusting." He steps back, giving me space, but his eyes never leave mine, holding me captive in that moment.

My heart races, battling between hope and doubt. I take a deep breath, weighing my options, grappling with the swirling emotions that threaten to drown me. "You have a lot of work to do, Ryan. I'm not some easy fix."

"I wouldn't dream of it," he replies, a small smile breaking through the tension. "I'm in for the long haul."

"Good," I say, finally stepping back to let him in, my mind still spinning with uncertainty but my heart pushing me forward. I'm not ready to forgive him, but maybe, just maybe, I can allow him to be part of my life again. With every step into the future, I know there will be obstacles to face, but I feel a flicker of something—a possibility that the broken pieces could one day fit together again.

The air inside my apartment feels heavy with unspoken words, the silence almost palpable as Ryan stands there, his gaze searching mine for any sign of hope. I can't help but wonder what we look like to the outside world—a mismatched puzzle, pieces stubbornly refusing to fit. He enters hesitantly, like a stray cat testing the waters of a home it once knew, afraid to step too far in case the door slams shut behind it.

"Want a seat?" I gesture towards the small couch, fighting the instinct to pace back and forth like a caged animal. He nods and settles in, the fabric of the couch creaking under his weight. I take a chair opposite him, a small but significant barrier between us.

"Okay," he says, rubbing the back of his neck, a nervous habit I used to find endearing. "So, I've been thinking about everything... and I know I don't deserve your time, but I want to explain why I did what I did."

"Explain?" I arch an eyebrow, skepticism draping over me like a thick blanket. "What makes you think I want to hear any of it?"

"Because maybe... maybe there's a chance I can help you understand?" His voice, smooth yet wavering, hangs in the air. "You deserve that much. You deserve to know the truth."

"Is it even the truth?" I shoot back, the bitterness in my tone sharper than I intend. "Or is it just another layer of deception to pile on top of everything else?"

Ryan exhales slowly, the frustration and regret spilling into the space between us. "I get it. I really do. But I promise you, I'm not trying to manipulate you anymore. I just... I want to be honest."

The honesty in his eyes gives me pause, a flicker of the man I fell for dancing at the edge of my consciousness. I fold my arms tighter, as if the gesture could contain the turmoil brewing inside. "Go on then. Tell me how you ended up hurting me so badly."

He shifts in his seat, his hands gripping his knees as if holding onto something that might slip away. "It all started with a misunderstanding—a bad decision, really. When I first met you, everything felt perfect. You were this light in my life that I didn't know I needed. But then... my past caught up with me."

"What do you mean?" I lean in, curiosity battling against my desire to keep him at arm's length.

"There were things I hadn't resolved—things I thought I could keep buried. But when you came into my life, I thought I could handle it, that I could be the man you deserved. I thought I was strong enough to push through it all."

"So you thought lying would help?" I counter, the anger boiling back to the surface. "How does that even make sense?"

He shakes his head, the shame washing over his features. "I know, it doesn't. But I was terrified of losing you. I didn't want to drag you into my mess. I convinced myself that if I just dealt with it on my own, I could protect you."

I scoff, my voice dripping with sarcasm. "Oh, great plan! Keep your girlfriend in the dark while you fight your demons alone. What a romantic notion."

"I see how that sounds now," he says, a wry smile creeping onto his lips. "But at the time, it felt like the only choice. I wanted to be your hero, not your burden."

"Heroes don't lie," I snap back, frustration tightening my throat. "They don't manipulate the people they claim to love."

"Fair point." His expression softens as he looks at me, and for a moment, the tension breaks like glass underfoot. "But that doesn't change how I feel about you. I should have been honest, even if it meant risking losing you. I was just... scared."

"Scared of what?" I challenge, trying to peel back the layers of his bravado. "Scared that I wouldn't love you if I knew the real you?"

"Scared that I wouldn't be good enough for you. That if you saw my flaws, you'd run away screaming."

A deep silence settles, wrapping us in an unexpected intimacy. I want to scream at him, to shake him until he understands the pain he's caused. Yet there's a part of me that wants to lean in, to connect the fragmented pieces of our lives. "Ryan, you don't have to be perfect for me to love you. You just have to be real."

"Real?" he echoes, his voice barely above a whisper. "What does that even look like after everything? Can we go back to that?"

"No," I say firmly, trying to quell the rising tide of hope in my chest. "We can't go back. But maybe we can start fresh? No lies, no masks. Just... honesty."

"Honesty," he repeats, like a mantra. "I can do that. I want to do that."

"Good." I swallow hard, the weight of my decision settling over me. "But understand, it's going to take time. Trust isn't built in a day, and I don't know how long it will take to heal."

"I'm willing to wait," he assures me, the earnestness in his voice palpable. "I'll show you that I mean it."

His gaze locks onto mine, and for a fleeting moment, the distance between us shrinks. Just as I begin to imagine a path forward, my phone buzzes loudly on the table, shattering the fragile bubble of our conversation. I glance down and see a notification from a mutual friend, one I haven't spoken to since everything unraveled.

"Is it important?" Ryan asks, his curiosity piqued.

"It's... complicated," I reply, trying to dismiss the knot tightening in my stomach.

"Complicated is my middle name," he quips, a glimmer of mischief in his eyes. "You can tell me. I promise I won't let it distract me from my speech on how to win back your trust."

I can't help but chuckle at his attempt to lighten the mood, but as I swipe to open the message, the smile quickly fades. It's a photo—one of me and Ryan, taken at a friend's wedding, carefree and blissfully unaware of the storm brewing ahead.

"What is it?" His tone shifts, concern creeping in as he leans forward.

"It's just..." I pause, searching for the right words. "It's a reminder of what we lost, I guess."

"Or a reminder of what we can still have," he suggests, his voice steady.

As I stare at the image, a pang of nostalgia washes over me. The laughter, the joy, the spark we once had feels like a lifetime ago. "Maybe," I whisper, feeling the weight of that single word.

Ryan's expression softens, and in that moment, the past and future intertwine like vines, unpredictable yet beautiful. The journey ahead is fraught with uncertainty, but perhaps together, we can navigate the tangled path. With a small, tentative smile, I set my phone down, ready to face whatever comes next.

The silence stretches between us, a fragile tension thick enough to choke on. I can see Ryan's uncertainty dancing behind his eyes, a mirror of my own conflicting emotions. The weight of unaddressed questions clings to the air, and I wonder if it's even possible to return to the ease we once had. The smile that once lit up his face now feels like a ghost haunting the edges of our conversations, reminding us of a past that feels both comforting and painful.

"I can't shake the feeling that this is all too good to be true," I admit, the words slipping out before I can stop them. "You standing here, trying to win me back, it's almost like something out of a romantic comedy—except the plot twist is that you've been lying to me the entire time."

Ryan chuckles softly, the sound tinged with an underlying sadness. "Yeah, well, maybe I should have hired a better screenwriter. Or at least read a few how-to guides on honesty."

"Don't be flippant," I say, frustration bubbling to the surface. "This isn't just some script you can rewrite on a whim."

"Okay, point taken. But maybe, just maybe, we can edit the scenes that follow?" He looks at me with an earnestness that pulls at the edges of my guarded heart.

I lean back in my chair, studying him. The way he fidgets with the hem of his shirt reminds me of when we first met, how he had that nervous energy that felt somehow charming. Now it feels like a reminder of everything he's hiding—or hid. "And if I don't like the direction of the new plot?"

"Then we'll work on it together," he replies, his voice firm yet soothing, like a gentle wave lapping at the shore. "I'm not asking for a quick fix. I want to do the work. I just need you to give me the chance to prove it."

The sincerity in his voice hangs in the air like a delicate thread, and I can't help but feel its pull. But just as hope begins to stir within me, a sudden sound shatters the moment—my phone buzzes again, louder this time, demanding attention. I grab it, my heart pounding in sync with the notification.

"It's from Anna," I say, my brow furrowing as I swipe to open it. She's been my rock through all of this, the friend who knows every sordid detail of my relationship with Ryan. "She says she has news. It sounds urgent."

"Maybe she's finally found the secret to life?" Ryan jokes, but there's a hint of nervousness in his tone.

I roll my eyes, trying to maintain my composure. "More like she's been digging into my life, which is honestly a little unsettling."

"Well, I'd prefer it if my friends weren't stalkers," he says, a teasing glint in his eyes. "But if it helps, I can break a few legs if she gets too nosy."

"Ryan!" I gasp, half-laughing despite myself. "You're supposed to be earning back my trust, not scaring off my friends."

"Okay, I'll tone it down. But in my defense, it's a little hard to navigate a situation where my life looks like a soap opera."

The levity vanishes as I read Anna's message. My heart races as I type back quickly, urging her to spill whatever it is she knows. The three dots dance on the screen for what feels like an eternity before she replies, and when the message finally comes through, my heart sinks.

"Meet me at The Blue Moon Café. I found something about Ryan's past. It's big. We need to talk."

I look up at Ryan, who's still sitting across from me, the easy humor fading from his expression. "What's going on?" he asks, eyes narrowing with concern.

"It's Anna," I say, my voice shaky. "She wants to meet. She said she found something about your past. Something big."

Ryan's face pales, the playful banter evaporating as if it were never there. "What kind of something?" he asks, his tone turning serious.

"I don't know," I admit, unease twisting in my stomach. "But if it's urgent enough for her to say this, it must be significant."

"Significant how?" he presses, a tension rippling through him.

I take a deep breath, grappling with the gravity of the situation. "I don't know, Ryan! But she's been on my side throughout this whole mess. If she thinks it's important, it probably is."

Ryan stands abruptly, his chair scraping loudly against the floor. "We can't let her dig into this. If there's something out there, something she can find..."

I cut him off, my heart racing. "You're the one who said you wanted honesty! If there's something I should know, you need to tell me now."

"I didn't think it would come to this," he says, running a hand through his hair, the stress evident in his posture. "I thought I had it all under control."

"Control?" I echo, disbelief thickening my voice. "You thought lying would give you control? This isn't just about you anymore, Ryan! It's about me too!"

"Then let me handle this. I don't want you getting hurt again," he pleads, stepping closer.

"You can't handle it if you're not being honest!" I shoot back, the frustration boiling over. "Maybe Anna knows something that could change everything."

Ryan's eyes flash with something that looks dangerously close to panic. "I can't let her find out. You don't understand what this could do!"

"What could it do?" I challenge, my heart racing faster than my thoughts. "What are you hiding?"

Before he can answer, my phone buzzes again, and this time, it's a call from Anna. I glance at Ryan, the gravity of the moment crashing down like a wave, leaving me breathless. With a hesitant hand, I answer the call, my heart pounding in my ears.

"Anna? What's going on?"

Her voice trembles on the other end, the urgency slicing through the air. "You need to get to the café now. It's about Ryan... and it's worse than I thought."

The weight of her words hangs between us, and I can feel Ryan's presence beside me, a mixture of desperation and dread enveloping us both. "What do you mean?" I ask, my pulse quickening.

"I can't explain over the phone. Just trust me. Get here!"

"Anna, wait—"

But the line goes dead, and I'm left standing in a whirlwind of emotions, caught between Ryan's pleading eyes and the storm brewing outside. I glance back at him, the tension so thick it feels suffocating. "What did you do, Ryan?"

His expression shifts, uncertainty mingling with fear. "I didn't mean for it to come to this."

And just like that, the walls I had begun to lower slam shut again, sealing off any chance of trust. The clock is ticking, and with every passing second, the unraveling thread of our fragile relationship feels more precarious. I take a step back, torn between the past I want to forget and the future that feels alarmingly out of reach.

"Let's go," I say, resolve hardening in my voice as I grab my keys. "We need to find out what she knows before it's too late."

As we rush out the door, the world outside feels charged with anticipation, like a storm ready to break. I can't shake the feeling that everything is about to change, but I have no idea how far the ripples will reach.

With each step toward the café, the weight of secrets looms larger, and I can't help but wonder if this is the beginning of the end—or the end of the beginning.

Chapter 29: The Ultimate Choice

The wind howls around me, a frigid gust that sends a shiver down my spine, yet it does nothing to extinguish the heat radiating from the moment. The cliff looms over the crashing waves below, the ocean churning in a frenzy, as if mirroring the tempest brewing inside me. I can almost taste the salt in the air, sharp and briny, mingling with the overwhelming weight of Ryan's gaze, piercing yet filled with an unspoken plea.

"Tell me you have something," Ryan's voice breaks through the chaotic symphony of nature, raw and laced with urgency. I can see his hands trembling at his sides, a subtle reminder of the monumental burden resting on my shoulders. It's almost comical how we've wound ourselves into this mess, like two moths spiraling toward a flame, drawn by our own flaws and fears. But now, standing here, I can see that flame flickering dimly, barely illuminating the path ahead.

"I have... options," I finally manage, my voice a hesitant whisper against the wind. The truth is a slippery thing, a double-edged sword that could slice through the fabric of our lives or leave us both bleeding. "But I can't decide for you, Ryan. You need to choose what you're willing to risk." My heart pounds, the rhythm syncing with the crashing waves below, echoing the tumult within me.

His brow furrows, a mix of confusion and frustration washing over his features. "This isn't just about me. It's about everything—about us. If I choose to confront my family, it could shatter the last remnants of my life as I know it. But if I don't... what do I have left?" His voice quakes, a blend of defiance and vulnerability that resonates deep within me.

The horizon bleeds into twilight, oranges and purples melding like a watercolor painting left too long in the rain. The world is a chaotic masterpiece, and I can't help but feel the weight of it all pressing down on my chest. Each color seems to scream at me, echoing the urgency of our situation, and I wish I could bottle this moment—this intersection of light and darkness, of hope and despair.

"What about the truth?" I ask, a hint of steel threading through my tone. "Isn't that worth fighting for?" It's a question I know the answer to, but I need him to vocalize it. The path to clarity is fraught with doubt, and I want him to find his own way through the haze.

Ryan exhales sharply, the sound heavy with the gravity of his thoughts. "The truth might destroy everything I've ever known, but living a lie... that's no way to exist." His eyes flash with determination, and I see the flicker of resolve spark to life. My heart lifts slightly at his admission, but the shadows of uncertainty still cling to us, threatening to pull us under.

"Then let's unravel it together," I suggest, stepping closer to him, the distance between us now a fragile thread. "You're not alone in this." I reach out, clasping his hand, feeling the warmth seep into my skin, a stark contrast to the chill surrounding us. The connection ignites a sense of hope, but with it comes an avalanche of fear. What if this choice drives us apart rather than unites us?

"Together." The word lingers in the air, a fragile promise hanging between us like a thin veil.

I scan the horizon, the waves crashing violently against the rocks, each surge a reminder of the chaos we're about to unleash. "We need to confront your family, but on our terms. No more hiding in the shadows. They've spun their web for too long." My voice is steadier now, fueled by the warmth of his grip and the intensity of the moment.

"What if they don't listen?" Ryan's expression darkens, clouds of doubt rolling back in. "What if they push back?"

A flicker of a smile tugs at my lips, a spark of mischief surfacing in the midst of the turmoil. "Then we give them something to really be afraid of."

He raises an eyebrow, curiosity piquing through his apprehension. "What are you thinking?"

"Let's blow the lid off their secrets. We can gather evidence, expose their lies, and reveal who they truly are. You'll have the upper hand." I can feel the adrenaline coursing through my veins, igniting a fire that had been dimmed for too long.

Ryan's expression shifts, the initial hesitation melting away. "You think we can do that?"

I squeeze his hand, determination thrumming between us. "If we don't fight for what's right, what's the point of any of this? We owe it to ourselves, Ryan. To uncover the truth, no matter how painful."

A moment of silence hangs heavy between us, as if the universe itself is holding its breath. Then, Ryan nods, a slow but steady movement that solidifies our pact. "Alright. Let's do this."

With that, the winds shift. The air crackles with a newfound energy, swirling around us like the beginning of a storm. I take a deep breath, savoring the metallic taste of anticipation, the thrill of stepping into the unknown. It's a moment laced with danger, but also with possibility.

As the waves crash below, I turn to face Ryan fully, my heart racing in tandem with the chaos around us. "We'll take it one step at a time," I assure him. "But no turning back."

He smiles then, a flicker of light breaking through the clouds of uncertainty. "No turning back," he echoes, his voice steady now, imbued with newfound courage.

Together, we step away from the edge of the cliff, moving toward the unknown, ready to confront the shadows of his past. As we embark on this perilous journey, I can't shake the feeling that we're not just unearthing secrets; we're also laying the foundation for something greater—a chance to redefine who we are in the chaos of truth.

The gravel crunched beneath our feet as we walked away from the cliff's edge, the roar of the ocean fading into the background, replaced by the rhythmic thrum of my heart. I glanced at Ryan, whose expression had morphed from a storm of uncertainty to a fragile determination, and I couldn't help but admire the fierce resolve blooming within him. Each step felt like we were peeling back layers of ourselves, shedding the fears that had weighed us down.

"What's our first move, Sherlock?" Ryan quipped, attempting a lightness that didn't quite reach his eyes. I chuckled softly, the sound a balm against the tension between us.

"First, we need a plan, and maybe a lot of coffee. I don't know about you, but I can't solve a mystery on an empty stomach." I glanced over at him, trying to lighten the mood. "Besides, I have a theory that caffeine may enhance our detective skills. I can't believe it's taken us this long to figure that out."

Ryan snorted, shaking his head, the corners of his mouth twitching upward. "Right, because nothing says 'let's confront family secrets' quite like a triple espresso."

"Exactly! They'll never see it coming," I replied, playful conviction lacing my voice. The absurdity of our situation collided with the gravity of our mission, a dizzying juxtaposition that made the thrill of it all even more intoxicating. I could feel the tension easing, our shared laughter stitching up the frayed edges of the day.

As we made our way back to my car, the sun dipped lower in the sky, casting a golden hue over the world. It felt like a moment suspended in time, the kind of magic that could only happen when life was on the cusp of a breakthrough. "Do you think they'll fight back?" Ryan's tone shifted again, the gravity returning as we reached the vehicle.

I shrugged, unlocking the door and sliding into the driver's seat. "If they do, we'll just have to be smarter and faster. But I doubt they expect you to fight. They think they own you, Ryan. That's where they're wrong."

He nodded slowly, the light in his eyes flickering with a blend of hope and fear. "Okay, so we take the fight to them. But where do we even start?"

I turned the key in the ignition, the engine purring to life as I pulled out of the gravel lot. "First, we need to gather intel. Your family has secrets, right? They've kept you in the dark long enough. We need to figure out what they are, and how we can use them."

"Yeah, secrets like where my dad hides the good whiskey," Ryan replied, a smirk dancing on his lips. "Or how my mother has a sixth sense about everything. Seriously, it's like she has eyes in the back of her head."

"Sounds like she's a pro at keeping secrets," I said, rolling my eyes dramatically. "But I'm talking about the big stuff—what they've done, what they've hidden from you. It's not just about the whiskey stash."

"Right. The, um, family business," he replied, the humor fading from his voice. "I've heard whispers, but nothing concrete."

"Then let's dig. I have a feeling that with a little digging, we can uncover more than just your mother's casserole recipes." The idea buzzed in my mind, each possibility flickering like fireflies in the night. "We could start with your family's old records, maybe even some public documents. I'm sure they've left a trail."

Ryan leaned back in his seat, a mixture of fear and excitement flaring in his eyes. "You're right. My family likes to play it close to the vest, but they're not infallible. If they've made mistakes, they'll have left evidence somewhere."

"And that's where we come in," I declared, enthusiasm surging through me. "We'll be the dynamic duo of family secrets, unraveling threads one by one until we've pulled at the whole tapestry."

The car sped down the winding road, trees flickering past like a blurred painting. I could feel the anticipation building between us, the electric charge of two people determined to take control of their destinies. With every mile we put between us and the cliff, the horizon opened up, a panorama of potential stretching out before us.

When we reached my apartment, I barely parked before jumping out, the thrill of the chase overwhelming. "Let's start with what we can find online. I have a hunch the family's financial records might hold some clues."

Ryan followed closely, a determined look on his face. "What are we looking for? Large transactions? Strange businesses?"

"Anything that looks suspicious. We want to know where the money goes and where it comes from. You'd be surprised at the skeletons that rattle when you shake a family tree."

We settled in front of my laptop, the dim light illuminating our faces as we began the search. The clicks of the keyboard echoed in the silence, a heartbeat of sorts that underscored our focus. "You ever think about how weird it is that you can learn so much about people just by typing their names into a search bar?" I mused, glancing over at Ryan.

"Welcome to the age of information," he replied dryly. "What's your plan? Type my parents' names and see what pops up? 'How to ruin your son's life in five easy steps'?"

"More like 'How to pretend everything's fine while chaos simmers beneath.'" I grinned as I continued typing, my excitement palpable.

Hours passed, the sunlight outside fading into twilight, but we were undeterred. Each document we unearthed felt like peeling away layers of varnish from a long-forgotten treasure. I could see the gears turning in Ryan's head as he processed each revelation, the flicker of anger igniting within him.

"There! Look at this," I said suddenly, my finger hovering over the screen. "This transaction—two hundred thousand dollars sent to a shell company. What the hell is that about?"

Ryan leaned in closer, his brows knitting together as he scrutinized the details. "That's... my father's signature. It's definitely his style—something he could hide behind."

The air thickened with tension, a palpable mix of excitement and dread. "This is huge, Ryan. We need to dig deeper. If we can find out what that money was for, we might be able to unravel the entire family façade."

He leaned back, running a hand through his hair, his expression a mix of disbelief and realization. "So they've been lying about their wealth all along? I knew they had money, but this... this is a whole different level."

"Just think, you could be sitting on the biggest family scandal in history," I teased, trying to lighten the mood. "Or at least in your family history."

His eyes sparkled with a blend of mischief and dread. "Let's just hope it doesn't turn into a reality show."

With newfound determination, we dove back into our research, the clock ticking away the hours as we navigated the murky waters of Ryan's family secrets. In the face of uncertainty, a shared sense of purpose bound us together, and I couldn't shake the feeling that we were on the brink of something monumental. The walls that had held Ryan captive were finally beginning to crack, and I was determined to help him break free.

The laptop screen glowed in the dim light of my apartment, casting a bluish hue on our determined faces as we immersed ourselves deeper into the labyrinth of Ryan's family secrets. Each click and scroll felt like stepping into uncharted territory, the thrill of discovery mingling with the unease settling in my stomach. I glanced at Ryan, who was still digesting the enormity of the information we had uncovered. His jaw was set, a line of tension carving deeper as we sifted through transactions and hidden connections.

"What if this changes everything?" he mused, his voice barely above a whisper, as if fearing the very words could summon the darkness we were hunting. "What if they retaliate? My family doesn't exactly take kindly to being exposed."

I leaned back in my chair, folding my arms. "Let them try. What's the worst they can do? Pretend to be a normal family? Please, Ryan, they've already got that act down pat." My sarcasm hung in the air, but beneath the levity, I felt the weight of his concern. I reached over, placing a reassuring hand on his arm. "You've got me, remember? We're in this together."

He offered a faint smile, the tension in his features softening. "Yeah, but I'm not sure how much longer we can hide what we're doing. My parents are good at sniffing out trouble. They might already know we're poking around."

"Then we need to pick up the pace," I replied, feeling a pulse of adrenaline. "The faster we get to the bottom of this, the less time they'll have to react. Besides, if they're as sharp as you say, we're not exactly hiding in the shadows. We're practically waving a neon sign."

"Right, the neon sign of impending doom," he said with a half-smile, but I could see the flicker of fear in his eyes. "Let's do it, then. Let's see what we're up against."

With that, we returned to the screen, the weight of our task looming before us. As we continued to dig, the hours slipped by, the world outside dimming into a starlit canvas. Each piece of data felt like a breadcrumb leading us deeper into the mystery of Ryan's lineage, unraveling the carefully crafted facade his family had maintained for so long.

"Okay, here's another transaction," I said, my eyes widening as I scanned the numbers. "This one's connected to a charity fund. Your parents have donated a lot over the years. Sounds altruistic, but why does it feel like a cover?"

Ryan leaned closer, his brow furrowing. "Charity? They've always liked to keep up appearances. But I never thought they'd use it to hide something. If there's a shell company involved, what else are they covering up?"

I quickly typed the charity's name into the search engine, hoping to dig deeper. "If they're funneling money through a charity, we need to find out what it's really funding." A list of projects and initiatives appeared, but none seemed to hold any red flags—at least, not yet.

"Look at this," Ryan pointed to the screen. "There's a gala every year. High-profile attendees, major fundraising. What if they're using this as a front to launder money or...?" His voice trailed off, the implications settling heavily between us.

"Or to cover up something much darker," I finished for him, the realization making my stomach churn. "We should find out who's on that guest list. Someone's bound to have seen something."

As I scrolled through the website, searching for previous gala records, a sudden thought struck me. "You know, your parents have a lot of connections. What if we could leverage that?"

Ryan raised an eyebrow, intrigued. "You mean like infiltrate their social circles?"

"Exactly. We could pose as guests at the next gala," I suggested, my mind racing with possibilities. "Blend in, gather intel. It's not like they'll expect you to be there, right?"

He considered this, rubbing the back of his neck. "It could work, but what if they recognize me? This is my family we're talking about."

"Then we make sure they don't. We can go incognito—disguises, fake identities. We're basically spies now." I grinned, enjoying the sudden rush of adrenaline. "Imagine the look on their faces when they see us waltzing through the door."

He chuckled, the tension easing slightly. "Spies, huh? I could get used to that."

"Great, then it's settled. We'll have to plan our outfits, though. No one's going to take us seriously in jeans."

"Or," he countered, leaning forward with a playful glint in his eye, "we could wear matching tuxedos. Really throw them off."

I laughed, shaking my head. "As much as I appreciate the visual, I think we should tone it down just a notch. We need to be subtle—chameleons among the peacocks."

But before we could continue our playful banter, the room was abruptly filled with a shrill ringing. My phone buzzed relentlessly on the coffee table, startling us both. I glanced at the screen, my heart racing as I saw the caller ID. It was my brother, Nathan.

"Do you want me to get it?" Ryan offered, sensing my hesitation.

"Yeah, but let's keep it brief." I swiped to answer, bracing myself. "Hey, Nathan. What's up?"

"Lia, you need to come home," he said urgently, his voice low and tense. "There's something you need to see."

"See what?" My pulse quickened, a sense of foreboding creeping in.

"Just come, please. It's important. I can't explain over the phone."

Ryan's eyes widened with concern as I nodded, though Nathan couldn't see me. "Alright, I'll be there soon." I ended the call, my heart pounding as I turned to Ryan. "I have to go. Nathan sounded serious."

"Do you want me to come with you?" he asked, concern etched on his features.

"No, it's okay. I'll handle it. I think it's best if I go alone. I'll call you when I know more."

He nodded, but I could see the worry lingering in his gaze. "Just be careful, alright? Something feels off."

With a final nod, I grabbed my jacket and headed for the door, my heart racing. The night felt heavy with uncertainty as I drove home, each passing streetlight casting fleeting shadows against my thoughts. What could Nathan possibly want to show me?

As I pulled into the driveway, my mind churned with possibilities. I hurried inside, the familiar warmth of home juxtaposed with the chill that wrapped around me. Nathan was waiting in the living room, his expression taut, a stark contrast to the usual ease of our banter.

"Lia, thank you for coming," he said, urgency bubbling just beneath the surface.

"What's going on?" I asked, my pulse quickening as I took a seat across from him.

He hesitated, glancing at the door before speaking. "You're not going to believe this, but I found something. Something about our family."

"About our family?" My breath caught in my throat as dread pooled in my stomach. "What do you mean?"

He leaned forward, lowering his voice. "It's about Mom and Dad. There's more to their story than we ever knew."

Before I could respond, the doorbell rang, slicing through the tension like a knife. Nathan's eyes widened, and my heart lurched. "Who could that be?"

"I don't know," he murmured, his expression darkening. "But we can't let them in."

I nodded, the weight of foreboding pressing down on me. But just as Nathan stood to move toward the door, the ringing intensified, echoing ominously in the stillness of the house. Something about that sound sent a chill down my spine.

"Lia, we need to—"

The door swung open before he could finish, revealing two figures silhouetted against the porch light, their faces obscured in shadow. My breath caught, a rush of adrenaline surging through me as I realized they were strangers, yet they felt eerily familiar.

"Nathan! Lia!" one of them called, and my heart dropped as I recognized the voice, a haunting echo from a past I thought was buried.

"What are you doing here?" I gasped, the words barely escaping my lips, just as the night descended around us, heavy with unspoken truths.